Noble's Quest

Noble's Quest

A Novel

Sequel to
Brotherhood Beyond the Yard

Sally Fernandez

Noble's Quest

Copyright © 2013 by Sally Fernandez

Dunham Books
63 Music Square East
Nashville, Tennessee 37203
www.dunhamgroupinc.com

Trade Paperback ISBN: 978-1-939447-05-0
Ebook ISBN: 978-1-939447-06-7

Printed in the United States of America

In loving memory of my maternal grandparents,
Orris Irving and Ruth Ellen Ames,
and my great-grandmother Ellen Agatha Jordan.

AUTHOR'S NOTE

This story is pure fiction, although the locations are authentic and play an integral part in the plot. The principal characters are fictitious as well. On the other hand, there are numerous facts for readers to sort out for themselves. The story may also seem to have a tinge of a conspiracy theory, which it is not. It gestated solely in my vivid imagination—a story concocted in my own mind that needed to be expressed.

Several people were intricately involved in helping to improve the structure of this story. Naturally, they will be recognized appropriately in the Acknowledgements. However, there is one person I must acknowledge from the start. Much love and gratitude goes to Joe Fernandez, my editor-in-residence, business manager, and loving husband, for his patience during my seemingly endless writing, the multitude of hours he devoted to repeated editing, and for other sacrifices of life's events, to help refine my story to make it the best it can be.

THE TURTLE AND THE SCORPION

A turtle was happily swimming along a river when a scorpion hailed it from the shore. A scorpion, being a very poor swimmer, asked a turtle to carry him on his back across a river.

"Are you mad?" exclaimed the turtle. "You'll sting me while I'm swimming and I'll drown."

"My dear turtle," laughed the scorpion, "if I were to sting you, you would drown, and I would go down with you, and drown as well. Now where is the logic in that?"

The turtle thought this over, and saw the logic of the scorpion's statement.

"You're right!" cried the turtle. "Hop on!"

The scorpion climbed aboard and halfway across the river the scorpion gave the turtle a mighty sting. As they both sank to the bottom, the turtle resignedly said, "Do you mind if I ask you something? You said there'd be no logic in your stinging me. Why did you do it?"

"It has nothing to do with logic," the drowning scorpion sadly replied.

"It's just my character."

Attributed to poet Nur ad-Din Abdar-Rahman Jami, known as Jami, the last great Persian poet from the 15th century. The Prophets of Islam influenced his writing. The translation is by William Braude, 1965.

1
USHERING IN A NEW YEAR

As the crowds huddled together trying to fight off December's frigid dampness, they waited eagerly for the French president's arrival. Thousands of Parisians, along with visitors from around the world, had gathered in the Place de la Concorde—Paris's largest public square—offering "*Bonne année*" to all they encountered. Within minutes, President Grimaud would be saying, "Bonne année," wishing the masses a Happy New Year, ushering in 2017.

At the south end of the square closest to the Seine River, was a simply constructed stage with a center podium. There was nothing simple, however, about the extraordinary view of the magnificent Eiffel Tower in the background, the site of the impending fireworks display, and the elaborately decorated fountains that dominated each end of the square. The setting provided a clear vantage point to eye one of the most famous fountains situated directly behind the modest stage.

The fountain, designed by Jacques-Ignace Hittorff—a German-born French architect and student of neoclassical design—represents the Atlantic Ocean and Mediterranean Sea. Surrounding this ornate structure are figures depicting daily life of harvesting coral, fish, and collecting pearls, along with statues of geniuses in astronomy, navigation and commerce. Hittorff's other fountain symbolizing the Rhone and

Rhine Rivers with baroque statues harvesting flowers, fruits, and grapes, adorns the north end of the square. Unlike the statues surrounding the south fountain, these are in river navigation, agriculture, and industry. Hittorff's themes of rivers and seas only enhanced the ambiance of the Place de la Concorde on this wintry night.

The hour was near and the partygoers in the crowd were becoming anxious, not only to hear their president speak, but also for the celebrations to begin. Preparations were also in play for the president's private celebration a few blocks away at the Elysée Palace.

Several hours earlier, there was a flurry of activity at the palace with vanloads of food from caterers and flowers from florists, all making their deliveries through the service entrance. Security was unusually tight that evening and it took hours to check all those who entered. Finally, everything was in place, and President Grimaud began to receive his guests. They would also have a spectacular view of the fireworks display from the palace gardens.

As scheduled, precisely at 11:50 p.m. central European time, the French president's motorcade pulled away from his residence at the palace and headed to the public square. President Grimaud, having had to leave his own fête, departed through the front gate. He planned to arrive only minutes before he was to speak at the opening ceremony. Then, after performing his presidential duty, he would discreetly return to his guests. The drive to Place de la Concorde would take only three minutes.

On cue, the limo swiftly pulled out of the palace gates and turned right onto Rue du Faubourg Saint Honoré. A few short blocks later, as the limo driver was about to turn right again—this time onto Rue Royale—he spotted a large white truck stalled at the intersection. Traffic was backing up. Nervously, he glanced down at his watch and noted it was 11:52. Midnight was only minutes away. After waiting a few more minutes, he caught a glimpse of the president in the rearview mirror and noticed that he was also becoming agitated. Refocusing on the cars ahead, the limo driver observed that, fortuitously, the man in the stalled truck had just started its engine and was speeding away. Without hesitation, the limo driver stepped on the gas pedal, much to the president's delight. Finally, he was able to make a right turn onto Rue Royale to continue straight onto Place de la Concorde. The limo pulled up to the staging area at exactly midnight—later than planned.

Suddenly, a loud explosion burst forth and blue and red sparkles filled the sky. Another explosion simultaneously erupted. The president's limo had just pulled up behind a ball of fire.

President Grimaud looked on in horror.

Earlier that day, the prime minister had urged the president to take extra precautions. All the president agreed to—was to send the first limo as a decoy.

Boom! Boom! Boom! The sounds of explosions were followed by crackling noises echoing through the air. At one minute past midnight, across the French border, the German citizens heard more explosions follow, one after the other, as they gazed at the smoked-filled sky. The onlookers watched excitedly as the red and gold lights streamed down from the black sky, mimicking their nation's flag, and ushering in the New Year. Over a million people witnessed the incredible display above the famed Brandenburg Gate, a gate erected in the 1730s. It is the only remaining gate in Berlin, which had been part of the fortified city. And it has become a national symbol for the Berliners and for the Germans as a whole.

Seconds earlier, the spectators had finished listening to Chancellor Mauer offer hope to the German people, and to the rest of the world for peace and prosperity in the coming year. The chancellor ended by saying, "*Einen guten Rutsch ins neue Jahr!*" And, on cue, those words—meaning "a good slide into the New Year"—set off a series of explosions. But the fireworks in the sky were not the only source of the sounds ringing out. Sounds of gunshots were also heard coming from somewhere in the midst of the crowd. And the festive noise muted the wailing sounds of the sirens speeding toward the viewing stand.

Unknowingly, the partygoers continued to revel in the lights that persisted to burst into the air. They paid no attention to the pictures on the large video screens flanking both sides of the stage. All at once, a volley of voices began to shout, "*Der Kanzler hat gedreht wurde.*" The words, "The chancellor has been shot" resonated over the bedlam in the square. It was unmistakable. The view on the large displays clearly showed the German chancellor lying on the platform, behind the podium, with security officers lying protectively over her. Moments later, the chancellor and her two bodyguards were ushered into the nearby ambulances, which hurriedly sped away from the crowd.

All the while, behind the famed Brandenburg Gate, a 1.2 mile-long party was about to begin as the multitude of stages, dance floors, and bars lined the boulevard at Straße des 17 Juni that stretched across the Tiergarten, Berlin's public park. The vendors, unaware of the tragic event, patiently waited for their party-loving clients.

Within minutes, however, rumors of the presumed assassination of Chancellor Mauer began to fill the air. And what was a scene of jubilance had become one of dread. Nonetheless, some partygoers with visibly dampened spirits, slowly left the scene and headed for Straße des 17 Juni.

In Florence, Italy, Enzo Borgini, the executive director of police services for Interpol—the International Criminal Police Organization—was attending the New Year's Eve festivities at the *Societá Canottieri*. The Canottieri is the prominent rowing club nestled on the right bank of the Arno River, next to the famed Uffizi Gallery. And while the night air was brisk, the gaiety kept everyone feeling warm. The onlookers gazed in awe as they watched the Italian array of national colors stream down from the Piazzale Michelangelo, high up on the hill on the other side of the Arno. The glorious fireworks continued to exhilarate the crowd as they illuminated the dark sky with a rain of green, white, and red lights. Nevertheless, Enzo had turned away from the fireworks as his mind drifted to another time.

Enzo could not help but stare in the opposite direction toward the renowned Ponte Vecchio. His eyes fixated on the bridge, famously lined with goldsmith shops, and the legendary Vasari Corridor stretched across its rooftops. He recalled the time so many years ago when he was a junior police officer at Interpol. It was a time when his supervisor had dispatched him to Florence, his hometown, to work with the American director of the SIA, the States Intelligence Agency. Director Hamilton Scott had requested that Interpol assist him in a sting operation he had organized to capture the notorious terrorist, Mohammed al-Fadl. Enzo remembered al-Fadl very well—but as Simon Hall, the man who got away.

It was a devastating turn of events as he and the director followed a messenger—suspected of carrying stolen funds—through the winding Vasari Corridor, hoping she would lead them to Simon. As he now stared at the corridor from a distance, he recollected all too well how he and Hamilton had to double-back through the Renaissance hallways, only to discover an empty satchel.

Simon and one hundred thousand euros had vanished!

Enzo's first assignment as a fledgling officer was not a career-building experience on its surface. But the lessons he had learned from the brusque intelligence expert from the U.S. served him well. Over the years, he gained valuable insight into the intelligence community's techniques, much of it from Hamilton. Officially, the knowledge he gained had spurred his career, promoting him up the chain of command at Interpol. Unofficially, the case spawned a friendship that endured until Hamilton's death five months earlier in August of 2016.

"*Cosa?*" Enzo snapped, startled by the abrupt intrusion. He spun around hastily and glared at the hand placed on his shoulder. "Cosa? What?" he shouted again over the sound of explosions in the sky. Having been lost in deep thought, Enzo had not seen nor heard his official driver yelling as he ran toward the wall where he was leaning.

The driver, not able to slow down his breathing, began to sputter rapidly. "You've been summoned to headquarters immediately! There have been bombings in Paris and Berlin! A plane is waiting at Peretola Airport to fly you to Lyon!" The driver finally took a deep breath and, more calmly, added, "I'll fill you in on the details in the car."

"*Oh mio dio*," was all Enzo could muster.

In London, British subjects had been partying for hours in the finest English tradition. The time was 11:00 p.m. Greenwich mean time. They had only one more hour before the fireworks display was to begin.

The 10 Downing Street party, a bit more refined than others, was also in full gear. Inside the gates, the entire length of Downing Street had been converted to an elaborate outdoor dining room. The round tables huddled under heat lamps, and the perfectly placed chairs stretched down the center of the road. The tables had been elegantly set with the finest china for a select group of guests who had been invited to share in the New Year's Eve celebration with the British Prime Minister.

From the street, the guests had an unobstructed view of the London Eye. This iconic landmark of modern Britain, the third largest Ferris wheel in the world, had a capacity of eight hundred passengers per revolution. More important was the view of the clock tower at the north end of the Palace of Westminster, home of the British Parliament. The clock, affectionately named Big Ben, would count down the minutes to a new year.

All agreed it had been a glorious meal, literally fit for the queen. Now the guests were in the midst of savoring their desserts in preparation for the fireworks display. Meanwhile, Prime Minister Teragram was engaged in conversation with the American ambassador seated next to him. All of a sudden, the prime minister caught a glimpse of his head butler walking out of 10 Downing, briskly heading his way.

Seconds later, the butler interrupted and, in his finest Liverpudlian accent, said, "Excuse me sir, this was just delivered from Scotland Yard."

With a nod of thanks, the prime minister opened the envelope. A slight chill, not related to the outdoor temperature, fell upon him as he unfolded the letter. It read:

> *At 12:00 a.m. central European time, there was an assassination attempt on President Grimaud at the Place de la Concorde. The president was out of harm's way. However, a bomb explosion killed the driver of the limo sent as a decoy. Simultaneously, shots rang out toward Chancellor Mauer while commencing the festivities at the Brandenburg Gate. The chancellor is unharmed, although one member of her security force was shot and later died in the hospital. Thus far, no one has claimed responsibility. Proceed with caution.*

It was signed by Chief Inspector Dary.

With only twenty minutes before Big Ben was to begin the countdown, the prime minister calmly moved through the crowd and requested, "Please move quickly into the residence. I will explain once we are all gathered inside."

Five minutes before 2017 was to arrive, forty guests, and a variety of house servants, clustered in the Pillared State Drawing Room, the largest of the three state drawing rooms at the residence.

"I have just received information that assassination attempts were made against President Grimaud and Chancellor Mauer." The guests gasped as Prime Minister Teragram continued, "Both are unharmed, but each head of government lost a member of the security team."

Without warning, a deafening noise shook 10 Downing and everyone fell to the floor. A short time later, which seemed like an eternity, silence prevailed.

2

THE REBIRTH

Celebrations were in high gear across the United States, especially in the nation's capital. It was Friday, January 20, Inauguration Day. People of all sizes, shapes, colors, and nationalities filled the streets and the restaurants. The bars were packed as well, especially those decked out with high definition screens plastered on a variety of walls. And although the party spirit reigned among those looking forward to this historic event, beneath the surface there was a slight wave of apprehension filling the air, coming on the heels of the devastating events in Europe.

The bombing in Paris took the life of a career police officer masquerading as President Grimaud's chauffer, and the gunfire pierced the heart of another brave officer as he protected Chancellor Mauer in Berlin. Fortunately, with the advance warning, Prime Minister Teragram was able to save the lives of all in attendance at his New Year's Eve celebration. The exploding tables and chairs outside the residence had blown out many windows of the Downing Street buildings, sending shards of splintered wood and glass in all directions. Miraculously, no one was injured. And with only five hours to go before dropping the storied glittering ball in Times Square, the United States was in lockdown mode, heeding the events a continent away.

Official celebrations were canceled.

No more attacks followed.

Although the reports of those abortive assaults were demoralizing and pervasive, all those participating in the day's activities set aside their feelings of those tragic events for a moment in history. They were in the midst of celebrating an entirely different sort of event—one the entire world would be watching. On this day, it was evident a ray of hope was sweeping through the swarms.

SIA Director Noble Bishop felt proud to be sitting only a few rows from President-elect Randall Post as he waited to witness the swearing-in of the forty-sixth president of the United States. From his chair on the platform, erected on the west side of the Capitol—officially referred to as the West Front—he had a perfect view of the National Mall.

However, something was definitely awry.

As Noble observed the crowds, he noticed they were set back farther from the stage than in past years. And the increase in security was evident. From reading the program schedule, he concluded that the entire event would be more streamlined and restrained than it typically was. Nonetheless, it was still a glorious sight. His heart swelled with patriotism.

Half listening to the Invocation, he couldn't help but reflect on the events that led up to this historic day. As he sat back, warmed only by the wool scarf wrapped around his neck, he vividly recalled that sweltering day on August 9, the day he held a press conference to expose the former president as a Libyan national. He had provided the press corps with evidence that the president illegally entered the U.S. and falsified not only his identity, but also most of his dossier. The fallout from the exposé forced President Abner Baari to step down and prepare for the legal action that was underway. Within days, he had mysteriously disappeared from public view.

The first lady had cleverly cloaked his exodus, stating that the president needed time alone to sort out his affairs. Out of respect for the First Family, Noble arranged for Baari to have a sufficient amount of time to put his affairs in order. However, it wasn't long until an investigative journalist discovered he had left the country alone—without the first lady and their nine-year-old daughter. How he arranged to leave the country remained a mystery.

Abruptly, a loud ear-splitting sound snapped Noble back to the events of the day, just as the Washington National Symphony Orchestra finished with a resounding crescendo. The U.S. Marine Corps Band then struck up "Hail to the Chief." Noble instinctively glanced to his left and noted the arrival of the outgoing president pro-tem, secretly referred to as the "president-in-leaving" by those inside the beltway. He smiled as he ruminated, *The Congress must be feeling a sense of relief. After spending months running around caught in their own underwear, compliments of the former V.P., he was now thankfully leaving.*

The most recent crisis that befell Congress began with the swearing-in of the vice president. In August, he stepped into the breach as the constitutional replacement for the president following Baari's untimely resignation. Congress collectively believed the unthinkable had occurred. Neither party ever considered the possibility that the vice president might one day hold the highest office in the land. Most were aware he became Baari's running mate only because of his alleged foreign policy experience, something the presidential candidate clearly lacked. Many considered him a "loose cannon," given to uttering off-the-cuff embarrassing remarks. Stifling his gaffes had become a weekly sporting event. And, with his newly anointed power, there was a tacit agreement among the insiders that it would be impossible to control his loose tongue. To protect their parochial interests from the intrusions of the *accidental president*, an unprecedented number of senators and representatives had cancelled their summer recess plans to remain in Washington. It truly turned into the silly season for politics, even sillier than usual.

Meandering between his thoughts and listening to the magnificent music filling the air, Noble sighed remembering with some pain, *they also remained in the Capitol to interrogate me.* He had been the focal point of a major congressional investigation coined *Saviorgate* by a bipartisan group of four senators and four congresspersons, referred to as the *Octocrats*. In the end, they exonerated him, but not before he had endured a series of biased questions, repetitive cross-examinations, and exhaustive interviews. Those painful months took a toll on him.

At age 47, Noble still possessed his somewhat boyish face and tall lean physique, but his dark brown hair was now predominantly gray. Moreover, after the death of the former SIA Director Hamilton Scott— his mentor and surrogate father—Noble began to contemplate his own mortality. While in the midst of reflection, the cymbals clashed without warning, emitting a powerful ring. The music came to an abrupt close, ending Noble's reverie. It was exactly noon. The current *appointed* president officially became part of Washington's checkered past. An amazing silence permeated the crowd. The moment had arrived. After two hours of prayers, readings, and music, it would be the next thirty-five spoken words that would change the course of history.

Randall Post stood tall with his right hand on the bible and his left hand held high, palm facing the audience. He repeated, "I do solemnly swear that I will faithfully execute the office of President of the United States, and will to the best of my ability, preserve, protect, and defend the Constitution of the United States."

Immediately, an enthusiastic applause erupted. One could almost hear the spontaneous ovations emanating from across the country. For many, the applause was a nervous release from years of anxiety. In the past decade, Americans were fixated on their country seemingly stuck in a state of constant volatility, albeit the nation was slowly recovering. At the same time, they felt the effects of Europe's sovereign debt crisis that threatened the soundness of the world economy. Behind the curtain of the world stage, the Middle East turmoil added to the volatility stew. The "Arab Spring" of 2011 appeared to be a permanent fixture with spring always in the air. U.S. attempts to find a winning formula for peace in the region failed repeatedly.

Absent a stable economy and a coherent foreign policy, it was no surprise that the electorate, by a vast majority, elected a former state governor in the recent election. Inexperience and glibness were no longer in vogue. Having been exposed to a decade of political infighting, with no recovery in sight, the voters were frustrated and exhausted. And, after seeing the downfall of their president, the electorate unhesitatingly pulled the lever differently when they went to the polls. Amazingly, almost overnight, calm befell the country and confidence slowly began to emerge—not only on Main Street—but also on Wall Street.

The subdued crowd was riveted by President Randall Post as he delivered his Inaugural Address, "The Rebirth of America." It was as powerful in words as it was in substance. From the reaction of the crowd it was clear that they agreed wholeheartedly, recapturing some of the traditional American spirit.

I now feel the decisions I've made have merit. The president's message has given me the resolve to continue to serve my country.

Noble reflected as the president's words continued to reverberate.

It was clearly a time for the rebirth of America, a message many considered long overdue. But the swearing-in was only a formality. Now, the electorate would stand by waiting for the words to evolve into actions—a missing link in the past.

3
THE DEAD ZONE

The swearing-in ceremony flowed seamlessly as it continued throughout an extraordinary day. Then, after making cameo appearances at five of the eight parties around town, Noble was finally able to maneuver himself out of the boisterous crowd and back to the comfort of his office.

Seconds after settling in, Max burst in shouting, "More missing persons reported in the *Dead Zone*!"

Having just returned from an inspiring day and after observing the inauguration, Noble wasn't quite ready for the abrupt shift, but he trusted Max's instincts. It had to be serious.

Maxine Ford accepted her position as SIA deputy director in 2010. Noble's selection was easy. Years before, they were colleagues at the CIA. They were also friendly rivals. Max was undoubtedly the best among the undercover agents and possessed the precise qualifications he was looking for. She was tall, slim, with straight blond hair and dark hazel eyes, and considered by many to be extremely attractive. Her beauty, however, was deceptive, disguising the tomboy within. Competing with four older brothers created a toughness that became her major asset, occasionally placing Noble on the defensive. But aside from their obvious physical differences, Noble and Max were very much alike intellectually. While Noble was brilliant, Max wasn't far behind. Most important, they were equally dedicated to their careers.

Max's outburst rattled Noble. Reflexively, he clasped his hands over his face as if he was screaming to himself. Then, unexpectedly, he stood up without saying a word and walked toward the conference room.

Max followed. Then she hurriedly sped past Noble at the entrance to the room and headed to the large multi-touch monitor. The screen mounted on the wall displayed a map of the *Dead Zone*.

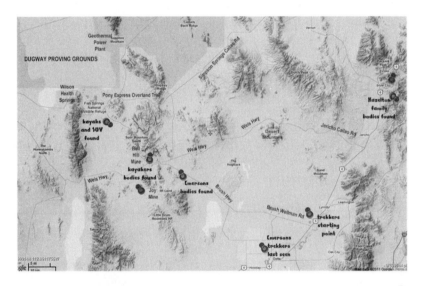

"Two male trekkers were last seen here." Max pointed to the area in the mid-western section of Utah. Then she tapped the screen several times to zoom onto the town of Delta, and then tapped again to focus in on the Quality Market on East Main Street. "They were reported missing on Tuesday by the father of one of the trekkers."

"It's Friday night. That's over three days ago and we are just hearing about it now!" Noble snapped, noticeably peeved.

"The local authorities evidently didn't feel the need to notify the FBI until yesterday," Max said. She was also angry, but responded marginally in a sympathetic tone. "They didn't know about the overall investigation and that the feds have taken over all missing person cases in the area you've dubbed the Dead Zone."

Since April of 2016, there had been three separate cases of missing persons in the same part of the state. Now there were four. The FBI had been unable to solve the first three cases and was unable to find any connections among them. For that reason, they enlisted the assistance of the SIA in September. At that time, Noble was enmeshed in the congressional hearings, so Max assumed responsibility.

"As you know, the feds are involved because the missing people disappeared on federal land," Max reminded him.

"I know. It seems as if all the land out there has mystically morphed into government land," Noble observed, in a mildly calmer manner, but no less sarcastic. He went on to note, "Reportedly, the government had claimed ninety percent of the land through eminent domain and the other ten percent by various methods. In fact, the federal government owns upwards of six hundred and fifty-three million acres of land, approximately thirty percent of the land in the United States. Those apparent land grabs are still hot topics in Washington today."

Max was aware the government land grabs were one of Noble's hot buttons and he would wax on the subject for hours. So she attempted to take back the floor, but not before he raised his right index finger in the air and said, "Hold that thought—you're also aware that the state of Nevada retained only fifteen percent of its land for private use. For all practical purposes, the state of Nevada is government owned. Records also show the federal government owns seventy percent of Alaska, and their third largest government land holding is—*voila*—Utah, possessing approximately fifty-eight percent of the state. How's that for real estate holdings?"

Not hesitating this time, Max jumped in fast and announced, "That brings us back to Utah. The one problem, however, may not be the feds but the Bureau of Land Management, which happens to be the caretaker of the area within the Dead Zone."

Noble glanced at his watch and noted the time, then sat back eyeing the map, urging Max to continue. "That could be an obstacle, but review what we know so far."

"In April of last year, the Emersons, an elderly couple in their mid-seventies, were reported missing. We found their bodies—here." Max pointed again to the map where she had previously added a pushpin and scribbled their names. The marker placed off the side of the Brush Highway was approximately six miles from Joy, an old mining settlement that had been deserted for years. "They had been traveling from their home in Sunrise Manor, a suburb of Las Vegas, to visit their daughter in Provo."

"That's what, a six hour drive?"

"Roughly, but I suspect they were probably driving more slowly than either you or I." Max grinned, and then continued. "We were able to trace their whereabouts from several credit card receipts their daughter had provided." Max confirmed that they made two stops after they left home. "Three and a half hours into their trip they stopped at a Dairy Queen in Beaver, just off Interstate 15. One and half hours later they purchased gas from the Chevron station in Delta."

"That explains why they turned off the interstate."

Max nodded in agreement. She then pointed to a location just north of the abandoned ghost town. "The bodies were discovered here, thirty miles northwest in the opposite direction from Interstate 15, which would have been a straight shot to Provo. A passing car found them the next morning."

"What was the cause of death?"

"The coroner determined the cause to be hypothermia. The night before they were found, the temperature had dropped below freezing."

"Why did they stop there, in the middle of this godforsaken country?" Noble asked, shaking his head.

"Evidently, they ran out of gas. Their fuel gauge registered empty." Max waited for Noble's reaction.

"But the tank had been filled thirty miles earlier."

"Exactly! That is the one piece of the puzzle still unresolved. But wait—the next case is stranger."

"In June, the Hazelton family of five was discovered here." Max then pointed to another pushpin she had placed on the map, indicating a dirt road about two and a half miles south of Eureka. "Their van apparently skidded into a steep ravine off the Silver Pass Road. The autopsy determined the parents were killed on impact, although there was only slight bruising to their foreheads. Three young children between the approximate ages of three and seven were in the rear seat, ostensibly unharmed by the crash—all still buckled into their seatbelts."

Noble recoiled with anguish. "Cause of death?"

"The children's deaths were attributed to a combination of heat exhaustion and suffocation. The temperature was in the mid-eighties, but all the windows were closed and only the windshield had been shattered in the crash, allowing a minimal flow of air. We know again from the receipts that the family had stopped for lunch at the Summit Restaurant in Eureka. According to the waiter, the family was headed to Salt Lake City, an hour and a half drive north in the opposite direction."

"So how did they end up going south?"

"Again, it's another puzzle to be solved."

Noble let out a deep breath. "Who found the bodies?"

"A group of hitchhikers between rides."

Noble noted the time again as he shifted in his chair. It was 6:30 p.m., but it was important to hear the rest. "What happened to the missing kayakers?"

Max tapped the screen and refocused the map on Utah's Fish Springs National Wildlife Refuge. "The wife of one of the kayaker's called the rangers at the National Park Service when her husband hadn't returned home the next day as planned. One of the rangers found their SUV here—just off the Pony Express Overland Stage Trail near Avocet Pool Road, approximately at this location. Another ranger found the four kayaks—here—on the banks of the Avocet Pool."

Using the highlighting function, Max moved her index finger across the map and drew a yellow line from the location of the SUV to the point where the ranger found the kayaks. Then she continued to draw the line moving south to her next pushpin. "Here is where the bodies were found off the Weis Highway just west of the Brush Highway."

"Max, slow down. The map is beginning to look like a football game as described by John Madden."

"Stay with me. What's curious is that the kayakers' bodies were recovered twenty miles south, away from where they left their kayaks, near a body of water."

"So what do you think happened?"

"They could have left their kayaks and decided first to walk out into the desert. I understand there are some awesome rock formations south near the Garnet Basin," Max conjectured.

"It's plausible, but why would they wander off into a desert and leave their supplies behind?"

"I'm not sure, but the feds checked the kayaks for any traces of evidence: fingerprints, hair, etcetera—any clues they could link to foul play."

"And?" Noble probed.

"They discovered the kayaks never entered the water. The spring-fed lakes are brackish and there was no trace of salt anywhere!"

Studying the map further, Noble grilled himself as well as Max. "What's going on? There's nothing out there except an old abandoned mine that looks to be about four miles north of where the bodies were found."

"I have no clue." There was clear frustration in Max's voice. The same frustration was reflected on Noble's face.

Heaving a sigh of displeasure he pressed, "And the cause of death?"

"This is another case of hypothermia. On that particular day in October, there was a wide range in the temperatures. During the day, the temperature hit ninety degrees, but that night it dropped below twenty-four degrees. It can't get more extreme than that!"

Noble was becoming visibly flustered. "Move on to the trekkers."

"A week ago today, two men in their mid-twenties began a seventy mile trek along Route 174, starting from Delta." Max pointed to the map. "They were to head north toward Fish Springs National Wildlife Refuge." She drew her patent yellow line with her finger along the route, highlighting their trail. "They were heading to the same location as our kayakers," she noted.

Noble acknowledged the coincidence, but remained skeptical. "What, are they crazy? That makes no sense. It's January! In that part of the country both the day and nighttime temperatures are brutal," he stated in a voice of disbelief.

"I agree." Equally amazed, she added, "Yesterday, they ranged from a maximum of thirty-eight degrees to a minimum of thirteen degrees."

Noble rolled his eyes. "What's their story?"

"The feds reported that the two men are recent graduates of Washington University in St. Louis, Missouri, with mechanical engineering degrees. In March, they're scheduled to leave for—of all places—Antarctica, to work for the IOAC, the Ocean, Atmosphere, and Climate scientific program. One would assume they'd be acquainted with local weather conditions."

Max paused. Noting that Noble was becoming antsy, she continued, but picked up the pace.

"According to plan, the father of one of the men went to pick them up today at the junction of Route 174 and the Pony Express Overland Stage Trail. He waited the entire day. They never arrived."

"Why did the father report them missing on Tuesday?" Noble questioned.

"Supposedly, the trekkers were scheduled to call in each night and report their location. The father received the last call on Sunday."

"So what was this adventure, an endurance test for their new occupation?"

"According to the father—yes!"

Noble simply nodded in amazement and then instructed, "Remove your artful yellow lines from the map and then zoom in so we have just a view of the Dead Zone."

Max complied.

"Okay, now start at the northwest corner near the south end of the Fish Springs National Wildlife Refuge. This time, use the red highlighter. Mark off where the ranger found the SUV and the kayaks." Noble waited briefly for Max to tap the appropriate icon and then mark the spots. "Now move south down Route 174 to where the kayakers' bodies were found."

"Got it. You want me to continue south down Route 174 to where the bodies of the elderly couple were found and also mark that location in red." Max spoke while simultaneously drawing the line with her finger, clearly getting the gist of Noble's little exercise.

Noble sat back and remained silent as Max continued to move her hand to Delta, leaving another red mark. She then moved her hand northeast up Highway 6 to Silver City to the location where the car and the bodies of the Hazelton family were discovered. After completing the trail, her red line appeared to resemble a half-circle.

"You didn't include the trekkers?"

"They're still missing, but this is the trail they were supposed to have followed." Max motioned her index finger up the Brush Highway.

Noble sat in silence for a moment of contemplation. Then, once again, he requested that Max remove all of the trail markings but leave all the pushpin markings in place. As Max followed orders, Noble sat back and gazed at the massive screen with a view of the Dead Zone—staring at the rugged terrain—searching for a pattern.

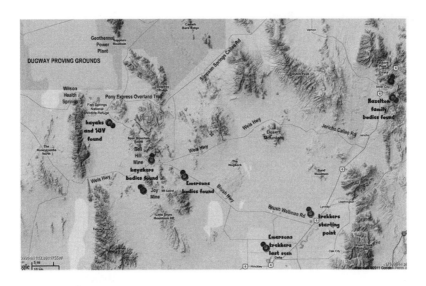

Without taking his eye off the screen, he asked, "What are the feds doing to find the trekkers?"

"They've been conducting ground searches daily since Wednesday, but each day they have to stop around five o'clock in the evening because the temperature begins to drop precipitously. Thus far, they've uncovered nothing." Max, openly frustrated, added, "I'll be receiving an updated report in the morning."

"I hope these are two smart guys who can hang in there," Noble said wistfully.

Max, trying to sound upbeat, informed Noble that the owner of the Quality Market in Delta reported that the two men had stocked up on provisions, and that they were carrying bags from the Delta Sports Center located on Highway 6. "So, if they know what they are doing, they'll be able to hold out for a few more days."

"Let's pray." Noble glanced at his watch for the third time. He stood up from the table and announced, "It's time to call it a night. Let's put our thinking caps back on tomorrow morning at eight o'clock sharp."

"Speaking of eight o'clock, isn't Amanda cooking for you tonight?"

It was seven-thirty.

"I can't be late. I cancelled our last date and was miserably late for the one before. I'm still trying to adjust to this relationship thing which, according to Amanda, is the next stage that follows dating." He admitted, "I'm petrified to think about what is in store."

"Buy her some flowers; it works wonders," Max suggested.

"Is that based on firsthand knowledge?"

"I'm out of here." Max retreated and headed for the door.

"Tomorrow." Noble waved Max on as she left the conference room. He returned to his office to grab his briefcase, which was never far from reach, and left for home.

4
PROOF OF LIFE

Noble inserted the key into his front door lock and couldn't help but notice that the minute hand on his watch pointed to the number six. As he entered his front foyer he immediately winced as he heard the words, "You're late," ring out from the kitchen.

Amanda soon approached with that all-knowing look and remonstrated, "Not again!" Then as her stern look morphed into a smile, she giggled, "Ah, they're beautiful."

Noble welcomed the passionate kiss and an endearing hug that followed, all the while grinning inside as he thought, *Thanks Max.* "I'm sorry to be late, but I had to return to the office after making a few cameo appearances at some boring inaugural events."

"A case?"

"Yes, Max is working it, but I needed her to bring me up-to-date."

"Is it a tough one?"

"Yeah, I mean yes," he sighed in a voice quiet and low, obviously tired from the day's events.

"Pour yourself a glass of wine and relax. I'll join you in a moment after I finish one more thing in the kitchen."

"Something smells wonderful," he called out as they headed in opposite directions.

Noble, not one to wear an overcoat—even in January—effortlessly unwrapped the scarf from his neck and pulled off his jacket and tie. Then he eased into the sofa with a glass of Capannelle Solare and began to unwind. As he felt the warmth of the wine trail down his throat, he couldn't help but reflect on the last six months. Admittedly, Hamilton's death had rattled him, causing him to rethink his tenure at the agency and to put into question his own mortality. Occasionally, he contemplated leaving the agency and returning to the solitude of the analyst role he once coveted. Then, the coup de grâce came when Hamilton charged him with the responsibility of exposing the former president. Shortly thereafter, president-elect Randall Post requested that Noble stay in his post through the transition of the new administration. Now embroiled in the Dead Zone case, he would postpone further thought on the subject once again. One thing he couldn't ignore, however, was a subtle personality shift that was changing his outlook. Those close to him also noticed that he was morphing out of *nerdom* and becoming more doctrinaire and assertive, something that gave him unease. Adding to his discomfort was the question of mortality, a catalyst for his entering the dating game. In the past, he had dated occasionally when he found the time, but always preferred his work to the "getting-to-know-you" scene. So, as a genuine veteran novice, he ventured ahead to give it another shot.

Amanda Kelley was an aide to Adam Ridge, one of the most prominent lobbyists for the natural gas industry. Noble's brother-in-law Paolo Salvatore made the introduction. Her appearance was strikingly dissimilar from his sister, Natalie. Other than being statuesque at five-foot nine, the similarities ended there. Her dark black hair brushed the top of her shoulders, unlike Natalie's shocking red hair. Her eyes were not green, but light blue, and her personality less strident. Paolo would often tease in jest that Noble never seriously dated because he was always looking for someone in his sister's image. In part, he was correct. But, thanks to Paolo, he now enjoyed the company of someone who only faintly resembled Natalie. And he relished her company from the start. She tolerated his erratic, non-stop work schedule, which endeared her to him even more.

Noble recalled, with a limp smile, the time when Amanda explained to him that, after four months of steady dating, she felt their relationship had moved to the next level. He finally owned up to himself that it had advanced, but he didn't fully grasp the progressive stages of romance that Amanda cited.

Stopping in mid-thought, he glanced up as he heard Amanda approach from out of the kitchen.

"You look a little more at ease than you did when you first arrived," she observed affectionately, as she refilled her wine glass.

"The mere sight of you, my dear, would put anyone at ease." He smiled as she sat down cozily beside him on the sofa.

"So, tell me about the inauguration. I watched it, of course, but not from your privileged vantage point."

Noble sketched in the details for Amanda on the music, the swearing-in, the departure of the president pro-tem, and the magnificent inaugural address. "It truly inspired me with some further resolve," he admitted, more to himself than to her.

Amanda cocked her head and offered a gentle smile. She was pleased that Noble finally found some assurance that the decisions he had made in the past were rational.

Their conversation continued over a delectable meal. At times, Noble stole periodic moments to admire Amanda from across the table. *Aside from her intelligence and beauty, she's a marvelous cook*, he thought. And, after taking his last bite, he mused, *how did I get to be so lucky?* After a delightful dinner and helping her remove the dishes from the table, they tidied-up the kitchen and then retired to the living room for a nightcap. The conversation ensued for a while longer until, finally, Noble had no choice but to break the mood.

"It's getting late, my dear, and I need to be back in the office early tomorrow morning," he said apologetically.

Amanda leaned over to kiss him and whispered, "I don't mind getting up early."

With smiles mirroring each other, they stood up, embraced, and then headed toward the bedroom.

The first sound was a vibration, followed by an annoying ringing noise. Noble reached for his phone, trying to catch it before it rang a second time. But no such luck.

Amanda rolled over in a semi-awakened state and groaned, "Not now. What time is it?"

"Four o' clock. Sorry, go back to sleep."

Max listened to the conversation on the other end of the line until she heard, "What?" he whispered with shrouded annoyance.

"They're all ghost towns! The bodies were all found near boarded up mine shafts in abandoned ghost towns!" Max blurted out loudly, knowing Noble was the only one in earshot. She had no one else to wake up that particular morning.

"Where are you?"

"I'm in the office. I couldn't sleep. I needed to study the map."

"Give me an hour. I'll see you there at five," he replied, while stifling a yawn.

The phone went dead.

5
A FAULTY PREMISE

"You look awful. Did you manage to get any sleep?"

Max's eyes were bloodshot, and she didn't look her meticulous self. Noble couldn't be sure, but it looked like she was wearing the same clothes she wore the day before.

"I got a few hours. How about you?"

"I slept like a baby." Noble grinned impishly.

"Can I assume the flowers did their magic?"

"They worked just fine." Noble blushed mildly, and then swiftly changed the subject, "What's with the ghost stories?"

Max raised her coffee cup. "There's a fresh pot in the kitchen—and they're towns—ghost towns."

"I'll be right back. I have a feeling I'm going to need some caffeine for this one."

When Noble returned to the conference room, Max was standing in front of the multi-touch screen staring at the map of the Dead Zone.

"Okay, what's your theory?" he challenged.

Before he had the opportunity to take the first sip of his coffee, Max asserted excitedly, "All the bodies were found near old abandoned mines. All of the mines are located in ghost towns! They all died of either hypothermia or heat exhaustion! It doesn't fit with the overall picture."

Noble cut her off. "Max, in that part of the country the land is harsh and the temperatures are horrendous. Sometimes people just get careless and they don't plan for the unexpected. Look at the Emerson couple. They were traveling in the desert; they didn't even have a bottle of water with them."

It was Max's turn to interrupt. Noble surrendered as he sat down, leaning comfortably back in his chair, listening intently.

Max continued. "However, the Hazelton family had several bottles of water in their car, but the children didn't unlatch their seatbelts to reach for the bottles. They had to have been thirsty. And the kayakers walked out into the desert and left their water with their kayaks and other supplies."

"You've made your point. Are you suggesting these are not simple cases of missing persons, but are cases of foul play?" He sensed Max was on to something.

"What if they were all murdered? And by the same person, or group of persons?"

Noble bolted upright in his chair. "Go back over each case and give me your scenario."

Max pointed to the red mark on the map representing the elderly couple. "We know the Emersons left the Chevron station and were heading to Provo. They should have turned right out of the station, then they should have taken the first right to Route 50 south, which would have put them back onto Interstate 15. What if they had mistakenly taken a left instead of a right and then took the first right after that?"

"I give."

"They would have been going north on west 1500 north," Max concluded.

Using the yellow highlighter, she ran her index finger up the map. "Thirty-six miles later they would have ended up here." Max pointed to Joy, an abandoned mine in the Drum Mountains.

"But the bodies were found on the side of the road on the Brush Highway at Route 174, which is some distance away." Noble pointed out.

"Obviously, they were lost, but assume for a moment they saw something they weren't supposed to see. Then they were killed and someone drove their car to the highway, six miles away from the mine, and left the bodies there."

"And the killer or killers siphoned off their gas to make it look like an elderly couple was lost. Whoever found the couple would assume they ran out of gas and then died of hypothermia from the freezing temperature during the night," Noble conjectured, buying into her argument.

"Precisely. It was exactly what we first theorized to be the case based on the information we were fed!" From the expression on her face, she was satisfied that she had successfully countered with her own theory.

"What do you think happened to the Hazeltons?"

"Same pattern. When they left the Summit Restaurant in Eureka they should have followed Main Street out to Highway 6, and then turned right. But, instead, they turned left. Let's assume they knew they had made a mistake and took the first left to make a U-turn, making a second deadly mistake. The road they turned onto is narrow, and it's difficult to find a place to turn around."

Noble barged in, confident he could predict Max's next sentence. "Three miles down that road is Silver City, another abandoned mine. Excuse me, the mine is actually a ghost town with some ruins. And you believe they also witnessed something they shouldn't have seen?"

"Yes, and we know their car was found another mile and a half past the mine, in a steep ravine on the Silver Pass Road," she added with assurance.

"Move on to the next case."

"The ranger found the bodies of the kayakers on the northern edge of the Bell Hill Mine—seventeen miles from their gear—a mine adjacent to another abandoned ghost town."

"It still doesn't explain why the kayakers would wander off into the desert and leave their gear behind," Noble posed, playing devil's advocate, after having arrived at some of his own conclusions.

"It's possible the kayakers were driving toward Fish Springs and decided to take a side trip to check out the Bell Hill Mine and, after seeing something they shouldn't have seen, they were killed. Then the killer or killers drove the SUV to the nearest body of water and left the kayaks on the bank of the Avocet Pool to make it look as if they had already been kayaking."

Observably proud of her own deductions, Max waited for a sign of approval.

Noble, saving the praise for the moment, stated matter-of-factly, "Interesting theory." Noting the look of displeasure on Max's face, he bowed to her ego, "You've convinced me. There's something more than meets the eye. It's more than just people making wrong turns, getting lost, or wandering aimlessly," he averred. "Our two missing trekkers would have also been passing by the Joy and Bell Hill mines as they worked their way up the Brush Highway."

Max walked over to the conference table to sit across from Noble. Just then, the phone rang.

"Director Bishop," Noble answered. It was 8:30 a.m., and his secretary had yet to arrive.

Immediately, the color drained from Noble's face.

"Agent, Max is here with me. Hold on while I put you on the speakerphone. Agent Darrow, please repeat what you just told me."

"Yes, Director. Four cyclists have been reported missing. A friend dropped them off on Thursday at the intersection of Highway 36 and the Pony Express Overland Stage Trail. The same friend was scheduled to pick them up yesterday in Ibapah, one hundred miles at the other end of the trail. They never showed." The agent then continued to express his personal views about the missing persons cases, which had little merit.

Max, wasting no time, interrupted to fill him on their revised theories. From the expression on Noble's face, Max could tell that he had a particular unvoiced expletive in mind for Darrow, one he would seldom mouth. It was a rare occasion for Noble, having one of the purest of lexicons in town. Not that he was so pristine, but in the workplace, he was always proper.

Of course, that didn't stop Agent Darrow from interjecting a few choice words of his own.

Noble, quick to bring the conversation back on point, declared, "We need to have the bodies exhumed."

Max recoiled and stammered, "All of them, even the children?"

"No, let them rest in peace for the time being, but we might have to later. To start, we'll assume that if their parents were murdered, the children met the same fate."

"It's federal land, and you'll need the attorney general's signoff," Agent Darrow reminded him, in his usual churlish manner.

Faintly irked at the agent for assuming he didn't know the necessary protocol, Noble retorted, "I'll handle it, but in the meantime you need to send in your agents to search the three mines in question. We are convinced our victims stumbled upon something forbidden. Find out what is was," he ordered in a tone typically intended for an underling. "I'll also get you some air search support. Your ground search is limited by the outside temperatures. We still have six people unaccounted for.

Find them."

With spurious politeness, Agent Darrow thanked Noble for the assistance, but then reminded him, "Your Dead Zone—as you call it—is located next to Dugway and, according to federal mandates, is restricted airspace. Of course, you are aware it's the largest continuous block of a no-fly zone in the U.S."

"I'll handle that as well, Agent. Max will get back to you by the end of the day."

"I'll await her call."

The conversation ended.

"You and Darrow don't seem to be on the friendliest terms. Something going on there?" Max inquired.

"The agent strongly opposes orders coming from the FBI director forcing him to cooperate with our agency. It's some sort of macho pride not to ask for help. I can understand his territorial pride, but he also tries to impose his authority. In the past, it has resulted in conflicts that have been detrimental to solving crimes." Noble huffed. "That's water over the dam, but he's tenacious, and never lets it go. Traditionally, there's been rivalry between our agencies. It's nothing new, but Darrow carries it to the extreme."

"What about Dugway?"

Max knew Dugway was the U.S. Army's Proving Ground facility for biological and chemical weapons testing. It was the size of Rhode Island, covering close to eight hundred thousand acres. Nestled within the acreage is a self-contained city, referred to as *English Village*, with a population of over two thousand, comprised of families and personnel. The entire complex rests under an invisible cover of protected airspace controlled by the U.S. Air Force and restricted to military flight operations only. It is also a major training facility for various armed forces.

"Call the defense secretary and tell her I need the assistance of an air search rescue team to locate six individuals missing in the area near Dugway," Noble requested.

"Shouldn't she know about the other cases and our suspicions?"

"Let's not complicate matters until we have more information. For now, it's just a preliminary investigation. Request an Apache helicopter with a thermographic camera, one with both cooled and uncooled infrared detectors. We don't know if we are looking for warm bodies or cold corpses."

"I'll call her immediately. Are you going to track down the attorney general?"

"Unfortunately," Noble mumbled dejectedly, "he's been impossible. But he knows, as part of the outgoing administration, his days are numbered, so he might be more amenable."

"I heard the president has a short list of names he is vetting for the AG slot. Noble, why not come out and say it. He's a son-of-a-bitch." Max laughed.

Noble smiled wanly at her comment, but more out of admiration for her directness.

"Good luck!" Max offered with a high-five to the air.

"Thanks, and after you get the approval for the air search, call Darrow and tell him to focus around the mines and the surrounding area."

"Will do."

Max left the conference room and Noble picked up the phone to place a call he hoped he wouldn't regret.

"The attorney general is in a conference with the president. Would you like to schedule an appointment with him for later in the day?" asked the voice on the other end of the line.

Noble thought, *perfect*, and said, "No thank you."

Even though it was Saturday, it was also a new administration and the White House was abuzz with activity. Noble hit the red button on his phone. "Is it possible for me to see the president? I know he's meeting with the attorney general, but it's of vital importance."

"Hold on, Noble, let me see what I can do," the president's secretary stated. Fortunately, she was extremely fond of Noble—a fact he knew, and one he would occasionally use to his advantage.

"Come on up; he'll see you now."

"Thanks, I owe you one."

"Mr. President, thank you for seeing me."

"Come in, Noble. Sit down." The president motioned to the chair across from him and the attorney general.

"Let me be one of the first to congratulate you, sir."

"Thank you, Noble. Thus far, it has been a constructive couple of days, with no crisis in sight—at least for the new guy on the block. In fact, I was just reviewing the General Accountability Office report with the attorney general and, according to their estimates, we are starting off with close to a five billion dollar surplus."

The attorney general flinched as the president continued to delight in the news.

"The Baari Administration had been out of control and had lost track of billions of unaccounted taxpayer dollars, which we have managed to recover."

Noble noticed that as the president spoke, the attorney general radiated discomfort. All the while he chuckled inwardly as he recalled hitting the enter key, personally transferring the money back to the treasury—the money Simon had stolen—and which Noble had placed in safekeeping until Baari was out of office. Noble's predecessor had ordered him to protect the money, fearing the former president would have squandered the taxpayer dollars on his off-the-books, social spending programs.

"You didn't come here to see me gloat. I understand you have something important to ask."

"Mr. President, at the request of the FBI, my agency is assisting on several major unsolved missing persons cases that have federal implications. We've located the bodies in the first three reported cases, but we are still searching for six other individuals recently reported missing"

"Is this going to be the first crisis of my presidency?"

"Sir, I hope not. However, the bodies we recovered were in three separate locations. Each location was near an abandoned mine located near the Great Basin, in the eastern region of Utah, just south of Dugway, on land owned by the Federal Government."

"Dugway!" the president exclaimed.

"We don't think it's related to Dugway, but we do suspect foul play in the first three cases, and that those cases are in some way connected." Noble inhaled deeply, then exhaled slowly, praying this was not a huge leap of faith.

"What is it you need from me?"

"Actually, I need the attorney general to approve the exhumation of eight of the bodies, excluding, for now, those of the three children who were also found." Noble sat back and waited for the AG to spout his usual legal blather. It didn't come, much to his relief.

"Bring me the petitions and I'll sign them," the attorney general replied, in an unexpected, positive tone.

So he's decided to use empathy in hopes of preserving his job. Nice try.
Noble stood up and faced the president. "Thank you Mr. President."
Looking the AG's way he remarked, "I'll have the papers on your desk
this afternoon, sir."

Bowing slightly, Noble left the room.

It had been a long and exhausting day, but much had been
accomplished. Noble had received eight signed petitions for
exhumation that would commence within the next few days. Max
was able to get approval for an Apache helicopter to search the area
beginning that evening. Before taking the next step to unearth the
bodies, she would also meet with each of the families personally. A
renowned medical coroner and a forensic pathologist were standing
by to analyze their remains.

In one hour, Noble was scheduled to meet Paolo at the Blackfinn
Saloon. He had made arrangements weeks earlier to meet with his
brother-in-law at their favorite watering hole. And, after a day with
a hell-of-a-start to a new presidency, he was ready for some light-
hearted conversation.

6
IL FRATELLO

C iao Paolo," Noble shouted, as he maneuvered across the crowded room and made his way toward the man seated in the last booth.

"You look exhausted." Paolo observed, genuinely worried about his brother-in-law.

"What I need is to sit down and enjoy a drink with my dear friend."

"*Perfetto*. I took the liberty of ordering a bottle of 1997 Capannelle 50&50, a highly sought after wine. *E molto buono*!" Paolo winked. "It's very good. You know the winemaker is a friend of mine?"

As he poured the wine into two glasses, Noble replied with a furrowed brow, "Yes and thanks—but what's the special occasion?"

Paolo, usually up to something devilish, flashed his charming Italian smile, raised his glass, and announced, "A toast to the end of the Baari Administration," adding, "Thanks to you!"

"And to you my friend—you share in the credit." Noble grinned.

Years before Noble and Paolo had become brothers-in-law, they came perilously close to becoming fraternity brothers at Harvard in a secret society known as *La Fratellanza*, or The Brotherhood. Fortunately, for Noble, he had resisted all invitations to join this clandestine group—a group that eventually was responsible for locating, educating, and grooming a man deemed the *Chosen One* for the United States presidency. What started as a seemingly innocent intellectual game ultimately morphed into a devious plot. Unknowingly, La Fratellanza also had a hand in unleashing a terrorist inside the government. In the final outcome, Paolo and his fraternity brothers were granted immunity for the valuable evidence they provided. It made it possible to bring down the deceitful president, and it almost led to the capture of the notorious Simon Hall—also known as Mohammed al-Fadl—a high-value worldwide target.

"I'm not sorry to see our forty-fifth president go, either, but that doesn't change the restrictions of your immunity," Noble declared in a hushed tone.

Ironically, it was Noble, then the assistant to the former SIA Director Hamilton Scott, who lobbied successfully for La Fratellanza's freedom. But, at a price that required the members to confess and to divulge the entire plot in detail. It was a no-holds-barred agreement. The outcome was generally regarded as a cheap price for vital information.

Noble looked directly at Paolo from across the table. As he leaned toward him, he whispered again, "If anyone were to disclose any of the facts of the case, I would have no choice but to start criminal proceedings. Not a threat, just a friendly reminder, dear brother-in-law."

Paolo discerned the sternness in Noble's voice, although he certainly didn't need the reminder. Keeping his voice low, Paolo countered, "You know you can trust me. I value my freedom. I gave up years of my life for La Fratellanza, and then for Baari as his speechwriter and then communications director. It almost destroyed my family and me." He hesitated briefly. Then, he implored, "Besides I would never put you in a precarious situation by violating our trust. I love you too much, *fratello*."

"Let's get off the subject." Noble raised his glass and said, "*Salute.*"

Paolo was more than happy to change the topic. Instantly, the playful smile returned to his face as he quizzed, "How are things working out with your *amore* Amanda?"

"Remarkably well," Noble responded, mirroring Paolo's expression.

"That's all you have to say—remarkably well? Tell me more."

"I enjoy her company. Surprisingly, I find it nice to have someone to share whatever little time I have. And she has been incredibly tolerant of my work schedule." Noble, unaccustomed to talking about his personal life, answered Paolo's question as honestly as he could—although he knew Paolo was probing for information that was a bit more salacious.

"And...?" Paolo pressed. This time, though, with an enormous grin and that devilish glint in his eye.

"That's great, too. Now let's get off this subject!" Noble exclaimed with a slight blush, and then quickly turned the tables on Paolo. "How have you been treating my sister these days? With kid gloves, I expect." Clearly, he was enjoying the role reversal.

"You know, we had a rough patch for several months after I confessed my role with La Fratellanza, but our relationship since then has been *fantastico*! Can you believe Mario will be eight-years-old next month? He misses his Uncle Noble and asks for you all the time," he scolded.

"Since Baari resigned, I have been inundated with committee hearings on Saviorgate, and now I am in the midst of another major case, unfortunately involving federal government activities again. Please apologize to Natalie and Mario and let them know we will get together soon." Noble smiled. "I'll even bring Amanda."

"*Benissimo*, they'll love that!"

Throughout the lovely family tête-à-tête, Noble continued to glance at his xPhad, hoping Max would call with an update on the air search.

"How do you like that exotic smartphone?" Paolo attempted to engage, noticing Noble's distraction.

"Thus far, it's been working great. The xPhad is somewhat thicker than an iPhone, but when you unfold the device, it becomes a tablet. It's the same thickness as the iPad, basically the same dimensions." He demoed his new toy for Paolo, showing him the full nine point, five inch, diagonal display. "Shockingly, the other devices on the market only offer a three point, five inch, diagonal screen."

"How are the search capabilities and the resolution?"

"Actually, the 10-G technology is much faster than the iPad, and the O-L-E-D screen is amazing."

"O-L-E-D?"

"The Organic Light Emitting Device screen technology uses a stretchable plastic between transparent plastic that is then infused with carbon nanotubes. It's much thinner, producing a brighter light than the liquid crystals that are used on other screen devices." As the metrics continued to flow off Noble's tongue, he could see Paolo's eyes glazing over and decided to end his techno-blitz. "It beats having to carry a phone and a tablet around. The xPhad with its combined features is the best of both worlds," He boasted.

"The technology sounds amazing, although I'm stuck in the dark ages with my less exotic smartphone. But it works for me," Paolo bragged. "So what's this major case you're working on that's keeping you so busy?"

Noble glared back.

"I know, you can't discuss SIA investigations." Paolo conceded.

"What I can tell you is that since I was appointed director in 2009, I have become incredibly isolated, relying too heavily on others to resolve our investigations," Noble complained, with self-criticism in his voice. "In fact, Max has been great as my deputy director. She frequently comes up with ideas that I should have concluded."

"What you do is of vital importance, and it's great that you have competent people working for you." Paolo offered supportively.

"Thanks, but I was much happier being the lone-wolf analyst that everyone relied on for solutions. In director-mode I'm forced to delegate much of the responsibility. I need to get back in the game."

Sensing that Noble was becoming a tad dispirited during what should have been a joyous occasion, Paolo interrupted, "By the way, congrats for surviving Saviorgate. I followed the hearings but, with all the political posturing, it was confusing at best. What was the entire hullabaloo about anyway?

"SAVIOR, as you know, is the SIA Vetting Information Organization Reporting system that I designed to vet all incoming senators and congresspersons. Hamilton alleged that without the requirement of having to be a natural born citizen to become a member of congress, there was the possibility that a terrorist faction could infiltrate our government. SAVIOR contains that vulnerability."

"Unfortunately, everyone knows that to be true with the spectacle that preceded Baari's resignation."

Noble nodded in agreement. "The problem is, I designed the system to download information from the FBI, CIA, IRS, and Interpol databases—without their permission."

"Is that legal?"

"Hamilton felt that the political ties between these agencies would impede them from operating efficiently. Hence, we circumvented them, contrary to inter-agency covenants."

"Wasn't it Rear Admiral Grace Hopper that said, 'it is often easier to ask for forgiveness than to ask for permission'?"

Noble grinned. "Yes, and that was exactly what Hamilton believed, and it worked. I was eventually forgiven and officially exonerated by the Congressional Investigative Committee. Finally, I can breathe a sigh of relief. However, Hamilton had to cut a deal to make SAVIOR available to the other agencies, including Interpol." Then, taking a rare opportunity to boast, he explained, "But not before I expanded SAVIOR's capabilities to go beyond just vetting. It's been developed far beyond its original purpose and is considered the go-to system for major international investigations." Noble's expression changed perceptibly as he grimaced, "Unfortunately, SAVIOR is now a matter of public record."

"So basically SAVIOR is a profiler on steroids," Paolo jested.

"Precisely. By utilizing information from the various databases, SAVIOR could objectively avoid any biases to an agency's particular mission, develop a profile of an unknown suspect, or validate a profile of a suspect who has been identified," Noble explained with atypical immodesty.

"So SAVIOR provided the information that led you to uncover Baari's deception in the first place?"

"In part, but your initial admissions exposing the plot, supplemented by the information derived during the interrogations of your La Fratellanza brothers, filled in the blanks. They provided the launching pad for a thorough exposure."

Paolo became predictably sullen. "Over time, we concluded that Simon was involved in something more vast and sinister than only the game we developed at Harvard, but we didn't understand his motives or his ultimate plan," he declared. "It's evident I was only a pawn. Hank took the lead and insisted that I convince you Simon was trying to gain access to the TAP funds from the Toxic Asset Program at the Treasury. Hank's motive was to enlist your support to capture Simon, so we could convince him to stop the financial meltdown," he recollected, even though he knew Noble recalled every vital detail of the investigation.

"It was an easy call on Hank's part. We know now that he manipulated Baari to hire the treasury secretary. That, of course, later created the opportunity for Simon to be retained as a consultant by the treasury secretary to design and program TSAR, the Treasury Sorting Accounting and Reporting system. It was the entrée he needed to carry out his plan to raid the Treasury. Simon then had access to billions of dollars as they flowed in and out of the Treasury during the financial crisis, including the TAP funds designed to sustain the too-big-to-fail banks," Noble recounted.

"And it worked beautifully. Simon was in the position to wield power, with billions of dollars at his disposal, creating havoc around the world. To this day, the members of La Fratellanza live in fear someone will spill the beans," Paolo underscored.

At Paolo's mention of the *billions of dollars*, Noble glanced down at his wine glass to avert eye contact. He reflected on the fact that, while the former director was unsuccessful in capturing Simon during his sting operation in Florence, Italy, Noble was able to recover the money and hold it in safekeeping. Seizing those funds was the game-changer that crippled Simon's operation. The rechanneling of Simon's diverted funds to a safely guarded location, of course, would remain Noble's secret. Meanwhile, the Treasury enjoyed an unexpected windfall from the recovered stolen funds, handing the new president a surplus.

"Do you ever hear from Hank? Noble quizzed, and then summarily injected, "Needless to say, I keep a safe distance from the former president's chief of staff."

"I ran into him a couple of weeks ago, and he looked awful. Evidently, he has been going through the *five stages of grief* ever since Baari disappeared. According to Hank, it was as though he had lost a son," Paolo related with little empathy.

"After all, he was the person who groomed and played the key role in educating Baari. And, it was clear from his testimony that his ego prompted him to believe he was solely responsible for creating the entire plot. Sorry, but my sympathies lie with the first lady and their daughter. It must have been devastating for them to have been abandoned by Baari." Noble asserted compassionately.

"The former first lady seems to have bounced back. Now, *Senator* Maryann Townsend, having dropped her married name, was just appointed to sit on the Senate Intelligence Committee. Unbelievable!" Paolo picked up his wine glass and made a toast to the air.

"So I understand. But how in the hell did she walk out of the White House and in one week get an interim appointment to the Illinois State Senate? And three months later, she's elected to the U.S. Senate? She must be following in her husband's path."

"According to Hank, the State Senate appointment was Baari's goodbye present to his wife."

"What a sweetheart," Noble said with more than a hint of sarcasm. "Hank has learned a few tricks from Simon."

"Actually, it was Baari. He simply called the State Senator and told him to step down, which coincidently, happened to be the same seat Baari occupied before he moved on to the U.S. Senate."

"Chicago politics lived up to its reputation. What did he have on him? Surely it must have been something!" Noble probed, muting his voice.

"Who's to know? He then called the Illinois governor—and *voila*—Maryann Townsend Baari was appointed to fill the vacancy in the State Senate. Rumor has it there was a plum appointment in the offing for the senator who resigned. The press did their usual commendable job of covering the whole affair with vagueness and distortions. Soon after, she was elected to the U.S. Senate post. Plainly, they were sympathy votes with some push by the Chicago machine."

"Or, Hank's still in the game hitting the right buttons. Otherwise, Baari must have promised both the senator and the governor that the vice president would use the Office of the President to continue to dispense favors after he was sworn in. What a joke." Noble chuckled. "You should have seen the face on our *accidental president* today while President Post was being sworn in. He looked like he was sitting on a bed of nails."

"It's unfortunate that President Post had to bide his time for four more years before moving into the Oval Office. I'm sure it was in part due to Hank's shenanigans." Paolo postured.

"Clearly, the releasing of a purported sex scandal two months before the voters went to the polls dashed Post's aspirations for another four years."

"I knew it didn't pass the smell test, but fortunately he was exonerated," Paolo admitted.

"But he wasn't absolved until after the election, when it was too late. Hank was always my prime suspect for that ploy, even then. But that was in the past."

Noble raised his glass.

Paolo followed.

"Cheers to the end of the Baari Administration and to the rebirth of America," Noble toasted.

"*Salute!*" They mouthed in unison.

Just as their glasses clinked, Noble heard his smartphone vibrate.

"Excuse me, Paolo, I have to take this call." Noble headed toward the hallway near the men's room away from the noise.

❦

Before leaving his office, Noble had set up call-forwarding from his private line to his smartphone, hoping to hear good news from the air search and rescue team scouring the Dead Zone. This was not the call.

"Director Bishop," he answered.

"This is Executive Director Borgini of Police Services for Interpol."

"Excuse me," Noble stated, not having a clue as to who was on the other end of the line.

"This is Enzo Borgini. I worked with Hamilton on the sting operation in Florence."

"Ah, yes, Director Borgini. I'm sorry I didn't recognize your voice at first. What can I do for you?"

"Director Bishop, I have been working on the New Year's Eve bombings that took place in Europe, and I just received a message claiming responsibility."

Noble was puzzled as to why the director would find it necessary to inform him. "And who's claiming responsibility?"

"I think you should see the message for yourself. Wait one moment, I'll forward it to you."

Noble promptly felt the vibration notifying him of the incoming message. As he glanced down at his smartphone, he was stunned to the point that he had to steady himself against the wall. He took a deep breath to calm his nerves before placing the phone back to his ear. Almost breathlessly, he asked, "What do you need from me?"

"I need your expertise and access to what we now know as SAVIOR." Enzo's voice echoed with the slight touch of irritation, having only recently learned of its existence. "Can you be at Interpol Headquarters in Lyon on Monday?"

The timing could not have been worse, but Noble couldn't resist the call to duty and an opportunity for a mea culpa. He trusted Max to continue with the investigation at hand while he broached a new angle. "I'll make the arrangements immediately," he submitted, knowing his hand had been caught in the proverbial cookie jar. Downloading data from the Interpol database—without their knowledge—was an act with potentially serious consequences.

"I'll look forward to meeting you, after hearing Hamilton sing your praises over the years." Enzo replied with a note of admiration. Then he hurriedly announced, "Goodbye," followed by a click.

✐

Paolo waited patiently in the booth enjoying his wine, until he glanced up from his wine glass and watched Noble, apparently deep in thought, return to the booth. "What's wrong? You look like you've received some bad news."

"I'm sorry I have to cut this short. I have to fly to Lyon tomorrow."

"It must be pretty serious from the look on your face."

"Interpol is asking for my help on a case they're investigating."

"Are you sure you're up to it?" Paolo wasn't probing that time. He was truly concerned.

"Yes, I was just caught by surprise. Give Natalie and Mario my love. I'll give you guys a call when I get back."

Paolo stood up and gave Noble an Italian hug with a cheek-to-cheek kiss.

Noble grabbed his scarf and briefcase and dashed out the front door. He could hear Paolo behind him calling out, "ciao."

Once outside he dared to look again at the message on his phone. It read, **HEADS UP!** ☾

7

THE FRENCH CONNECTION

I understand sweetheart," Amanda replied. "But how about getting together tomorrow tonight?"

Noble felt blessed that she understood the demands placed on him by his position. He was also starting to question those demands as they infringed on their time together. It was an odd feeling for him. "I can't. Right now, I'm sitting in the airport terminal at Dulles International waiting for my flight to Lyon," he answered dejectedly.

"Lyon, as in France?"

"I'm afraid so. Last night I received a call from Interpol asking me to assist them on a case. I should only be gone a few days, but I'll call you tomorrow." Noble paused, and then whispered, "I love you."

"I love you too," her soft voice cooed.

Just as Noble heard those words leave her sensual mouth, he heard a vibration causing him to glance hurriedly at his smartphone.

"I've got to go, Max is calling."

"Travel safely," was all he heard before taking the call.

"Max, I tried calling you last night, but your phone was turned off,"

Noble scolded.

"I had a hot date, and I didn't want to be disturbed. What's the problem?" Max snapped, signaling that she was equally annoyed.

"We are in the midst of a major investigation. I want you always to be available."

As he continued to sermonize, Max was recalling the many times Noble would say to her, *if the agency wanted you to have a personal life, it would issue you one.* She easily conceded. "Okay, boss. What's happening?"

Noble proceeded to tell her about his call from Enzo and instructed her to continue with the Dead Zone investigation.

"What makes you think Mohammed al-Fadl—your Simon Hall—is the one behind the bombings in Europe?" Max inquired in an even tone, having forgotten the tenor of their earlier repartee.

"The crescent moon and star are his calling card. No other member of al-Qaeda—or any offspring of that organization—has laid claim to using the Islamic symbol of faith, especially in that blasphemous fashion." Noble shuddered at the notion of Simon being out there somewhere. "In fact, my very last contact from him was back in August when Baari was forced to step down." He continued with an incredulous tone. "I remember vividly how Simon congratulated me for doing the *noble thing* and ending the message with that symbol."

"Bizarre. He must know the risk he's taking in offending the Islamic community." Noble sensed Max was talking to herself until she volunteered, "Let me know if I can assist you in any way from here."

"Thanks. I'll call you tomorrow for an update—and keep your phone turned on," Noble remonstrated, this time less belligerently.

"Bon voyage!" Max was the one to end the call.

෴

"Mr. Lord, you're free to board. Have a safe trip." The agent smiled as she handed Noble his boarding pass and passport.

He headed for the gangway.

Several years earlier, as part of his austerity measures, Noble grounded the agency's jet and opted for less expensive means of travel, much to his subordinates' chagrin. Since then, whenever Noble boarded a commercial plane he used a different identity. Today, he traveled as Air Marshall Nathan Lord. Mad Dog, the wizard in the CIA, was famous for producing all false documentations for agents working undercover. He unfailingly ensured its perfection.

Naturally, when airport security switched from using x-ray screening machines to retina scans, it was a simple task for Noble to transfer that information from the Noble Lord Bishop file to the Nathan Lord file in the appropriate databases. He was as much an expert as Simon, especially when it involved hacking into computer systems. The only difference was that Noble did it *legally*, as defined within the intelligence community—and never with ulterior motives.

After the death of Hamilton, Noble resolved that Simon was destined to become his nemesis—and that Simon would play a dramatically dissimilar role from the Harvard classmate who had helped him through a difficult time after the death of his parents. It was in 2009 when Noble faced the cruel reality that Simon had actually fabricated his presumed rapport with him. It was his attempt to co-opt Noble to join La Fratellanza—Simon needed his talents—not his friendship. And with Simon on the loose, Noble was on his guard, taking all precautions.

Once settled into his seat on the plane, he checked his e-mails. As he thumbed through them quickly, he also reflected on those *three little words* he had been using quite often, and with uncharacteristic ease. Noble rationalized he had successfully convinced Amanda that, while he loved her, he was not in love with her. She seemed to accept his distinction. Although, he suspected she was also confident their feelings would grow, bringing them closer to the next undefined phase of their relationship. What unnerved Noble was that he was getting dangerously close to that juncture. As visions of Amanda warmed his heart, he inadvertently hit the Text Messaging App. Instantly, his heart went cold as he stared again at the message Enzo had forwarded from Simon. Then the tedious announcements started to blare throughout the cabin.

Noble's only option had been to book an overnight flight, so he felt it best to lay back and get some shuteye during the seven-hour flight to Paris—despite thoughts of Simon on his mind. After a short layover, and within a couple of hours, he would be in Lyon.

"Will you be joining us for dinner Mr. Lord?"

"No, thank you. Just wake me for breakfast," Noble responded, as he was about to unfold his blanket. The night before, he had been restless and slept fitfully, thanks to Enzo's call. Now exhausted, he knew he would have no problem drifting off to sleep on the flight over, even if it was only five-thirty in the evening. The last thing he remembered, as his head rested on the pillow, was how he was already missing Amanda.

⌘

"Mr. Lord, we'll be landing in an hour. May I serve you breakfast?"

"Yes please," Noble grunted as he moved his seat in an upright position. Within the next hour, he sated his appetite, freshened up, and felt a renewed energy he had not experienced in recent days.

Noble was back in the game. Interpol needed him, presumably.

⌘

Upon landing, Noble found his way to Air France's first class lounge at the Charles de Gaulle Airport. He had a two-hour layover in Paris. The flight to Lyon would not depart until 7:30 a.m. He decided to spend the next hour reviewing the information he had about the New Year's Eve bombings. After unfolding his xPhad, he first examined the reports Enzo had forwarded to him. Then he began to search on the tablet for news articles describing each individual New Year's event. There appeared to be no new developments beyond what he already knew.

In Paris, the bomb intended for French President Grimaud's car, mistakenly exploded under the decoy limo. In Berlin, shots were fired at the stage set up at the Brandenburg Gate, missing German Chancellor Mauer, the intended target. In London, the bomb that exploded under the table on Downing Street failed to assassinate the British Prime Minister Teragram. All the news media reported the same facts, yet no group or person had claimed responsibility.

That was the one piece of information they didn't have. But I do, Noble believed, and then wondered whether in fact it was true. *Did Simon actually orchestrate those events?*

"Mr. Lord, your flight is ready to board," said the lounge attendant standing to his left.

Startled, Noble snapped his head upward. "Oh, yes, yes; thank you." Hurriedly, he folded his tablet and returned it to his pocket, collected his papers, grabbed his carry-on luggage, and dashed to his gate.

⌘

"Place your seat in an upright position, return your table trays, and fasten your seatbelts. We will be landing at Saint Exupery Airport in

Lyon, in twenty minutes. The local time is 8:40 a.m. if you'd like to set your watch," intoned the accented voice on the intercom.

Noble had no more time to contemplate the case. He folded his tablet and prepared to disembark.

For what, he was unsure.

8
THE VERIFICATION

Egad! Another Italian investigator. Noble chuckled quietly. He recalled Hamilton's description of his first encounter with Enzo Borgini in Florence, nearly a decade earlier. Now, as he viewed the man standing next to the black sedan, it was clear he was no longer a young rookie police officer, but the executive director of police services for Interpol. Few physical changes were apparent. He only seemed more mature than Noble recalled from the photos Hamilton had shared with him during his own visit to Florence. He appeared to be around five foot nine. His black hair was slicked straight back topping a pleasant face with dark brown eyes. Noble surmised they were similar in age.

"*Ciao,*" greeted the director, as he walked in Noble's direction. Evidently, Enzo had seen a photo of him as well. "*Benvenuto* to Lyon Director Bishop," he enthused, extending his hand.

"Thank you, Director Borgini. It's nice finally to meet you, especially after hearing Hamilton speak of you with such admiration."

"*Grazie,* we have much to discuss. Please step in." He motioned Noble to join him in the rear seat of the car.

Oddly, it seemed natural to have Enzo mix his Italian with English. Paolo often employed the same endearing technique. But when Enzo began to speak French with his driver, Noble realized he had arrived.

"I've taken the liberty to arrange a room for you at the Mercure Grand Hotel Lyon Perrache, only a ten-minute drive from headquarters. Would you like my driver to take you to the hotel first? It will give you an opportunity to rest and freshen up. We can meet in my office later this afternoon." Enzo suggested.

"That won't be necessary. I'd prefer to get started immediately. Actually, I'm quite rested, having been able to sleep on the plane."

"Very well. To the office, please," Enzo instructed his driver.

During the thirty-minute drive, they restrained themselves from delving into the investigation at any great length. They were both in agreement that it was best to wait until they had all the information at their disposal. Consequently, they spent the half-hour chatting informally, starting with addressing each other on a first name basis. Not surprisingly, they moved on to the topic of Hamilton.

"He told me you had maintained a friendship long after your collaboration in Florence." Noble, purposely vague, was not sure to what degree Hamilton had discussed their relationship or the details surrounding Simon.

Enzo, however, was forthcoming. "Simon's escape certainly left a stain on my early career." He confessed. "But at the same time, it forged a remarkable relationship with a man who had taught me so much."

Noble listened as Enzo waxed on and noticed that as he became more animated his tone became more melodic. The accent was familiar and reminded Noble of Hamilton's caretaker, Aldo, and the time he had spent in Florence with both of them on those last few precious days.

"You know my family is from Florence?"

"*Si*," Noble replied.

"*Bravo*, you know my language?"

"No, just a few words I picked up when I visited your enchanting city." Noble smiled at his failed attempt.

"Ah, well fortunately, each time I visited my family, I was always able to set aside a special time to spend with Hamilton." Enzo slowed his speech and sighed, "He was a great loss."

"For me, it was like losing a father."

Enzo felt it appropriate to change the subject to a less personal topic, and warmly stated, "Thank you for rearranging your schedule to come so quickly. I do believe you will be instrumental in helping us with this investigation. If Simon is behind this, you know him better than anyone." Enzo cut his statement short and announced, "We've arrived," as the car pulled up in front of a massive glass and concrete structure resting on the bank of the Rhône River.

Noticing the expression on Noble's face, Enzo explained, "Interpol headquarters house approximately six hundred staff members representing more than eighty-four countries."

"Impressive."

Enzo beamed proudly. "Perhaps you would prefer to leave your luggage in the car. The same car will return you to your hotel."

Noble agreed and stepped out of the car with only his briefcase in hand. He followed Enzo into the crystal palace, then through the metal detection system, and prepared for the physical search. After Noble received his visitor's badge, the two of them proceeded to Enzo's office.

"This is even more impressive!" Noble gaped, as he craned his neck to take in the stately room, focusing on the executive desk in front of a large window with a river view.

"Follow me; we're all set up in here." Enzo gestured toward another door.

Noble walked in to what looked like a war room. He was aghast.

There was a long conference table positioned in the center of the room. Noble scanned the number of chairs. He estimated that it could seat forty. Against the wall, parallel to the table, was a row of computer stations, each equipped with multiple flat screens and keyboards. On the wall at the far end of the conference table hung two massive multi-touch screens, similar to his, although twice the size and with triple the apps.

"Please be seated." Enzo pointed to the chair across from him at the end of the table closest to the touch screens. "I'll run through what our forensics team has concluded thus far."

Noble took his seat, prepared to focus.

"Let's begin with the attack on President Grimaud."

On the screen mounted on the left side of the wall was a photo of what appeared to be a limo in flames. In the background, one could see the Obelisk of Luxor decorated with hieroglyphics lauding the pharaoh Ramses II. The obelisk, a gift from the Egyptian government to the French, stood tall in the center of Place de la Concorde between the two famous Hittorff fountains. The screen mounted on the right side played a video taken by a partygoer, filming what he thought was the arrival of the president.

Noble studied the photo of the limo and simultaneously watched the video as he listened judiciously to Enzo's report. As usual, Noble was multi-tasking.

"We know that an explosive device was installed under the frame of the car in the center, just behind the front seats. We found traces of residue at that location from the initial blast. The explosive used was P-E-T-N, or Pentaerythritol Tetranitrate, and from the evidence it was detonated remotely." He paused for a moment as he watched Noble scrutinize the video with complete concentration.

Sensing the delay, Noble looked in Enzo's direction and urged, "I'm following; please continue."

Enzo took his cue. "From the size of the explosion, and the damage the car sustained—not to overlook the death of the driver—it was determined that less than one-sixteenth of an ounce of P-E-T-N had been used. We know that it would take only eight ounces of P-E-T-N to penetrate five inches of metal, easily blowing a sizeable hole in the side of a plane." Enzo paused again, expecting an assessment from Noble any time. He guessed correctly.

Noble spoke in a measured cadence as he deduced, "Based on the size of the detonation we can assume that it was not a terrorist attack per se, one that would do maximum damage. On the surface, however, it does appear to be an assassination attempt on the president."

"That was my conclusion as well. That leaves two remaining questions. Who had the ability to plant the bomb? And who knew what time the president planned to arrive at the Place de la Concorde?

"Actually, there is a third question. Didn't you say the explosion was detonated at exactly midnight, at the exact same time the fireworks began?" Noble questioned.

"Yes, but the president was late due to a stalled truck in the intersection. He was scheduled to arrive at 11:53, give his speech at 11:55, end with the words *bonne année*, and then the fireworks would begin."

Noble interjected, "The third question is—who was driving the truck? Play the video again."

Enzo, extremely curious, walked to the monitor, restarted the video, and watched along with Noble.

"Pause right there," Noble called out. "Look at the reflection on the rear door of the second limo—the one where the president is seated. It's the reflection of a white truck heading in the opposite direction. Let's have a technician from your forensic team zoom in on the driver. If he can enhance the image, you might be able to get a clearer picture."

"So, if you believe there was someone working on the inside, at the Elysée Palace, with access to the car, and that someone else drove the truck and another person detonated the bomb—then we are looking for three people," Enzo concluded, answering his own questions.

"Perhaps they are all one and the same." Noble gave Enzo time to consider his premise, and then continued, "There has been something gnawing at me ever since you forwarded Simon's message. Simon doesn't make mistakes, and if these assassination attempts were designed to fail, then what is his motive?"

"What are you driving at?" Enzo was openly mystified.

"Let's consider a new scenario as we review each case. Examine the events by focusing on the precision with which the attacks appeared to be intentionally foiled."

Enzo continued to be a trifle baffled, so Noble attempted to clarify his point. "First, Simon wouldn't run the risk of three individuals being involved—too much room for error. Let's assume someone works in the palace. That person was privy to information and knew the president had arranged for a decoy limo. Simon's accomplice attaches the explosive to the undercarriage of that car. The associate then drives a truck out of the palace gates and purposely stalls at the intersection, separating the two limos."

Noble stopped for a moment to study Enzo's perplexed expression.

"I see where you're heading. Please continue."

"According to protocol, Simon expected the driver of the limo to step out of the car and scan the crowd for any impending threats. He then should have walked around to the other side of the car and, in this case, make it appear as though he was opening the door for the president. The driver's one miscalculation was that he remained in the car."

"A deadly one at that," Enzo interposed.

"The accomplice driving the truck then pulled into the Place de la Concorde, several car lengths behind the first limo. When the second limo arrived shepherding the president, the accomplice detonated the bomb. He carefully used a miniscule amount of P-E-T-N to do minimal damage. Notice the photo."

Noble pointed to the photo on the left monitor, displaying a car that had imploded into a flaming mass of metal. "It did not *explode!*" he underscored, "spewing thousands of pieces of metal into the air, possibly killing others standing nearby. And had the limo driver followed protocol, he would not have died in the flames. He may have suffered some burns to the body, but there would have been no casualties." Noble ended his summation.

"Okay, then if Simon didn't want to kill the president, I'll ask your question: what was his motive?"

"It is important to hold that question until we delve further."

Enzo played along.

"Now, let's move on to Chancellor Mauer. Again, assuming the attack was intended to fail," Noble theorized calmly.

Enzo tapped the display on the right side, replacing the video with the photo of the stage at the Brandenburg Gate. The photo showed the chancellor lying on the ground behind the podium with her bodyguards positioned protectively over her. The backdrop for this tragic scene was the stage lighting illuminating the dark blue sky. The light also cast through the pillars of the gate and one could see the Unter den Linden, the renowned boulevard lined with linden trees.

Again, as Enzo proceeded, Noble studied the photo closely.

"The case of the German Chancellor was more straightforward. Shots rang out from the crowd at midnight, just as the fireworks display began. The cheering crowd and the blasts from the sky muted the sound of the shots."

"Didn't one of the partygoers testify that he heard the shots just as the chancellor wished the crowd 'a slide into the New Year', seconds before the fireworks began?"

"Yes, we searched the area which the local *polizei* suspected was the source of the shots and didn't find any shell casings. We scoured the rest of the plaza and came up empty."

"Shooting from within a crowd of people, all pushing and shoving one another in excitement, doesn't allow for exactitude," Noble pointed out. "The eyewitness was wrong. The shots had to have come from a precision rifle with a telescopic scope—a sniper rifle. Remember our premise—the goal was not to assassinate the chancellor."

"That would make sense. The bullet recovered from the officer's body, the hero and unintended victim, was a point-four-zero-eight *Chey Tac*. As you know, the Cheyenne Tactical cartridge is light, which translates into more cartridges per unit weight. This cartridge is designed specifically to be able to hit a target selectively, at a long range."

Noble jumped back in. "That would lead us to conclude that the shell casings could have been dislodged at a high point, in potentially any of the tall structures around the square. If time is spent trying to determine the trajectory in an effort to identify the location of the shooter, most likely it won't get us any closer to uncovering Simon's motive. But that's your call," Noble conceded, and then reminded Enzo, "I'm here only in an advisory capacity, but if you discover any evidence useful to my investigation, I ask that you pass it on to me. Simon Hall is still an open case."

"Deal, as long as we respect each other's turf," Enzo teased with a smile.

"Agreed, but right now we need to drive the investigation in a direction that will lead us closer to Simon's objective." Noble insisted.

"Did you retrieve any other bullets, other than the one from the body of the police officer?"

"We found two other bullets lodged in the podium, same caliber, fired from the same gun. On one of the bullets there's a partial fingerprint," Enzo replied, as he studied the expression on Noble's face. "What are you thinking?"

"The podium is lying on its side."

"It probably fell over when the police officer rushed to protect the chancellor," Enzo concluded, still curious as to where this was leading.

Noble took another moment to gaze at the view of the stage. "The podium was the intended target."

"What? Simon tried to assassinate a podium?" Enzo snickered.

Noble laughed. "The sniper knew the chancellor was scheduled to leave the stage immediately after her speech. He must have known that she also had received a warning threat earlier that day, just as President Grimaud had received. The sniper also knew the entire speech was radiocast. Therefore, when he heard the words *Einen guten Rutsch ins neue Jahr*, he shot at the podium—not once, but twice. The third time was also meant for the podium, except the police officer seeing the first bullet meet its target pushed the podium over unexpectedly when he rushed to the chancellor's side."

"Okay, so Simon's sniper fired shots toward the chancellor, purposely missing seconds before midnight, and before the fireworks began—his only window of opportunity," Enzo surmised.

"Exactly. He knew she would then be rushed off the stage. Someone also had to know exactly what words she would use to end her speech. She didn't just begin the aerial display. She unknowingly cued the beginning of the sniper fire!" Noble explained excitedly. "Again, as in France, someone's working from the inside."

Sensing the momentum building, Enzo asked, "Shall we move on to London?" He assumed the obvious. He tapped the monitor on the left and replaced the photo of the limo in flames. Promptly, the view of a street appeared. It was filled with debris, and a large Ferris wheel rotated off in the distance.

Enzo proceeded. "We found bomb fragments near where a table had been stationed before the blast, the exact table where the British Prime Minister and the American Ambassador were seated. We also found pieces of a detonator and a partial print on one shard. From the evidence, the bomb was a fairly simply designed explosive device made of ammonium nitrate with an electronic detonator used to set off the bomb—exactly at midnight."

"Exactly is the operative word!" Noble exclaimed. "It was the time when the bomber knew everyone would have been evacuated. The bomber had to assume that the attacks, which occurred an hour earlier in France and Germany, would have been broadcast to all heads of government throughout Europe and Great Britain, including the British Prime Minister."

Silence filled the room as they both paused and stared at the sight on the screen, thinking about what could have been a horrific outcome.

"You've gathered a lot of evidence from all three attacks," Noble acknowledged. "Now we need to make the link between our perpetrators and our prime suspect, Simon. We need to determine his ultimate motive—one I'm afraid may be even more complex than anyone could imagine." Noble shook his head, thinking, *here I go again.*

Enzo determined the time was more than appropriate to make the formal request. First, he granted, "From all the evidence, it appears you are correct. All attacks were enacted with such precision to ensure they would fail."

Noble sensed what was to follow.

"Now—you need to give me access to SAVIOR so we can make that link to Simon."

Noble looked toward him and flashed a smile. "I surrender."

Enzo continued with a slight jeer, "We all know your government negotiated hard on your behalf to keep you from being prosecuted for breaking into Interpol's database." Then, he softened his tone, flashed a wink, and allowed, "Personally, I'm thrilled to have another investigative tool to add to my arsenal, thanks to the generosity of your government."

Noble flushed. "I'm glad we could be of service, despite the unorthodox means to get there." Then, regaining his stride, he asked, "You are aware of the agreement between our two governments?"

Enzo cocked his head. "Yes."

"Then you know you'll be able to download information on a specific suspect, but only if that suspect has a valid record in the Interpol database. Otherwise, you'll be limited to the suspect's name and a photo. After all, the privacy of American citizens must be protected."

"I understand, but what if our perpetrators are linked to Simon and they only have a record in the FBI or CIA databases and not in Interpol? How can I make that link to Simon without complete access?"

Noble had anticipated the request. He was convinced Simon orchestrated the bombings in Europe and needed Enzo's help to prove it. "I want you to know that I'm putting my career on the line—and again for SAVIOR!" he bemoaned. "I'll program your password to give you complete access—temporarily."

Enzo smiled at his partial victory.

But before his smile had a chance to recede, Noble announced, "Hold on. Once the case at hand is solved, your password will be changed and restrictions will be placed on future access." Softening his tone, he added, "Naturally, you have the right to ask our government for additional information on forthcoming cases. I'm sure our agencies will cooperate within reason."

Enzo chose not to push his luck. He raised his hands and said, "Agreed." He was satisfied that, for at least the moment, his needs would be met.

After their mini détente, they mutually decided it was late, and that the lessons on the use of SAVIOR could wait until morning. Expecting an update from Max, Noble declined Enzo's dinner invitation and returned to the hotel.

9
THE POSTMORTEM

Noble entered his hotel room at Mercure Grand Hotel and, before he had the opportunity to notice the opulence, his eye caught the flashing red light on the desk phone. He quickly hit the lower, right-hand button to retrieve his messages. There was only one. It was from Max, asking him to call as soon as possible. He hurriedly pulled off his jacket and tie, ordered room service, and then prepared to place the call. Sitting at the desk, he unfolded his tablet and tapped on Max's photo, instantly dialing her phone number. While he waited for the call to connect, he tapped on the Notes App and primed himself for anything.

"I've been waiting for your call. I couldn't get through to you on your smartphone, and certainly you know how important it is to be in contact at all times," Max chided with chuckle.

"Sorry, I forgot to switch over to GlobalNet. What's up?"

"I received the results of the autopsy and you were right!" Max sounded anxious on the other end of the line.

"What was their cause of death?" The apprehension in his voice matched hers.

"They found traces of pancuronium bromide, or Pavulon, in the hair follicles of all victims, except for the Hazeltons."

Noble listened intently as she continued.

"As you know, this drug is a powerful muscle relaxant. If injected in large doses, the drug causes rapid and sustained paralysis to the skeletal muscles, including the diaphragm, eventually causing death by asphyxiation."

"I know." Noble sounded as though he was operating on forensic overload. "It's used as the second ingredient in a cocktail of three drugs used to administer the lethal injection for death row inmates. Apparently, it causes them to look like they are not suffering from the third shot of potassium chloride causing the heart to stop." He winced, and then took a deep breath. "Were you able to determine the injection sites?"

"We still have in evidence the clothing the victims were wearing when they were found. From the shirt and blouse of the Emerson couple, the forensic team found a miniscule puncture in the cloth that would have covered the back right shoulder. It appears they had been attacked from the rear," Max conveyed.

"What about the bodies?"

"Unfortunately, their families had entombed the bodies in relatively inexpensive caskets, and not hermetically sealed, so both bodies were terribly dehydrated. However, our crackerjack forensic team was able to rehydrate that part of the body and found the puncture wound from the petechial hemorrhage, the bruising around the site," Max explained.

"What about the kayakers?"

"They were more difficult to determine, but from the clothing and the bruising the forensic team was finally able to locate the injection sites."

"Were they all in similar locations on the bodies?"

"No. But they were all on the upper torso. It appeared as if they had fought back. Hair samples were collected from their clothing and skin tissue from under their fingernails. Maybe we'll get lucky and be able to trace the evidence to the perpetrators."

"There had to be more than one person to take these four guys down," Noble observed.

"I agree."

"Now, what about the Hazeltons—at least the parents? I shudder to think about the children." Noble tried to stave off any emotion. After a timely pause, he could only hear heavy breathing from Max's end of the line. "Max, are you there?"

"Noble, this is a tough one." She hesitated. "The Hazelton family died from ethyl amino sulfonyl phosphinate. It possesses some of the symptoms similar to Pavulon, but the drug the Hazeltons died from is dramatically different."

"What the hell is going on? Are you trying to tell me that this family of five died of a V-X nerve agent?"

"Yes. As crazy as it seems, that's our conclusion."

"Where the hell would they get V-X?" Noble was agog. "Just tell me what you know."

"To answer your last question first, in January of 2011, Dugway had a mysterious lockdown. The Army confirmed the next day that a vial of V-X nerve agent was missing, but insisted that it had been located after rechecking their inventory."

"How much are we talking about?"

"They reported the vial contained less than one milliliter or less than a quarter-teaspoon of V-X. We know that Dugway uses the chemical for testing, and has for decades. While most of what goes on at Dugway is top-secret, you may recall that, in 1986, during one of the testing phases, a jet aircraft sprayed the V-X nerve agent on a designated target area, which resulted in killing over three thousand sheep in the Skull Valley, approximately twenty-seven miles away."

"Max, back to my first question. How the hell did they get their hands on V-X?"

"I'm trying to tell you. After the Emersons were found dead, followed by the Hazeltons two months later, the feds were smart enough to confiscate the clothing and contents of the car, even though it was considered an accidental death."

"I'd like to meet the genius who made that decision," Noble commented.

Max ignored his remark and continued, slowly and methodically. She knew she was about to disgorge a flurry of conjecture, but Noble had to hear it all. "There were traces of the V-X agent on the right hand of the mother. V-X was also detected on the left pant leg of the male child and on a towel that had been left on the floor in the back seat of their car."

"What's the conclusion, Max?" Noble snapped.

Max knew Noble's frustration was not directed toward her personally. She chose to continue calmly. "The children must have been playing in the area near the Silver City ruins and discovered the vial. The boy either opened it, or dropped it, causing the oily liquid to spill on his pants. Presumably, the mother grabbed a towel from the car to clean off the pant leg and left the towel on the car floor, during which time she must have also come into contact with the substance."

Max wasn't finished with her findings, but she paused to give Noble a chance to respond.

"How could that much, assuming it was one vial, kill a family of five? It had to have happened within a short time because their car was sighted only a few miles down the road from the ruin." Noble concluded, "If any of them had suffered the initial symptoms of mild exposure, surely they would have headed back to town for assistance."

"You're right, but it only takes about thirty minutes for the V-X vapors to be released from a person's clothing. In this case, a pant leg and a towel were sufficient for them to feel the effects. It was also the month of June, and the temperatures where in the high eighties. Again, presumably, they had the air conditioning on and the windows closed. The vapors would have circulated more rapidly in a confined area."

Noble deciphered where Max was heading and insisted on summarizing. "So, the children, based on their size and weight, would have been affected first. If the air conditioning exacerbated the situation, the effects of a small dose would intensify. The children, within minutes, would have sustained paralysis of their diaphragm muscle causing death by asphyxiation. The parents most probably lost consciousness, causing the father to drive off the road, which caused the bruises to the parents' heads before they stopped breathing."

"The medical coroner concurs," Max confirmed.

"Aside from the coroner, who else knows about the findings?"

"Only you, me, several agents, the coroner, and the forensic pathologist."

"Great!" Noble grunted. "I want the records sealed. No one else is to know about this—no one." His order was clear.

"I understand, boss." Max recognized the full implications should the information leak to the public and, worse yet, to other government officials.

"Do we run a risk of an outbreak from any contamination?" Noble inquired substantially calmer, with a note of lingering concern.

"Between the times the bodies were discovered and now, nothing unusual has been reported. Someone may have suffered mild symptoms such as nausea, watery eyes, and a runny nose. Most likely, they assumed it was the flu. The agents also looked through the ruins for any unexplained vials, canisters, etcetera, to no avail."

"Why were they at the Silver City ruins anyway? I thought the waiter at some restaurant said they asked for directions to Salt Lake City. I know we presumed they made a wrong turn, but from our calculations the ruins are quite some distance?"

"Good point, which is why I ordered Agent Darrow to re-interview the waiter at the Summit Restaurant in Eureka. He discovered that the family had also inquired whether the ruins were a place for the children to visit before heading to their final destination."

"Shit, why didn't we know this before."

"Noble!" Max blurted out, shocked at his use of a crude expression.

"This case is getting to me," he confessed as he raised his eyes upward. "So the Hazelton family was not another case of homicide, only a horrible accident?"

"It looks that way. But let's not set aside the fact that it took place at another abandoned mine, and it may be somehow linked to Dugway."

"Trust me, I'm not." Noble hoped Max couldn't detect the desperation he was feeling.

"You okay, Noble?"

"Yes!" he half-whispered.

There was silence on both ends of the line. Max knew Noble was processing the results of the autopsies and planning the next step.

She waited.

"What's happening with the air search for the trekkers and cyclists?" Noble prodded, nudging Max out of the calm.

"Excuse me, what was the question?"

"The air search!" Noble repeated impatiently, as he was beginning to tire. And each time his stomach growled, he was reminded that room service hadn't yet arrived, adding to his irritation.

"Tonight is the last night. We agreed that by now the trekkers would have used up their provisions. The cyclists, who may have been staying at various inns along the way, also haven't surfaced. So, after tonight, they'll all be listed as unsolved missing persons cases." Max accepted reluctantly and with dismay.

"Let's hope they didn't meet the same fate as any of the victims and end up being reclassified as unsolved murders." Noble continued testily, "Let me know tomorrow if they find anything." Then, in a surprisingly subdued voice he asked, "Is everything else okay on your end?"

"Everything's fine. Go get some sleep; you sound exhausted." Max felt the same tension, but appreciated that Noble's was even greater, having to deal with both crises in the U.S. and in Europe. "I'll call you tomorrow as soon as I hear anything."

"Good night, Max." Just then, the doorbell rang.

"Finally," was the last word Max heard before the phone went dead.

Noble knew the next day would be long and tedious as he tried to explain the capabilities of SAVIOR to Enzo—his system, his baby. He'd now have to share it with others. But, it was no time to fret. He needed to eat his overdue dinner, and then prepare for a good night's sleep.

10
A PRIMER ON SAVIOR

I've been waiting for this moment." Enzo displayed a huge smile.

Noble also smiled in response. "It is best if you use the virtual keyboard to get started," he suggested.

Enzo flipped the switch on the top of the conference room table. Instantly, a black keyboard image with white numbers and letters projected on the surface of the table.

"Type in, z-z-z dot u-s-a-s-a-v-i-o-r dot g-o-v." Noble instructed.

Enzo proceeded to type, zzz.usasavior.gov, then hit the *Enter* key. Promptly, an official looking screen appeared on the multi-touch monitor, which was mounted on the right side of the wall closest to where Enzo sat.

In the center of the screen was a prompt for a security ID requesting a thumbprint.

Enzo looked up. "Now what?"

Noble, this time sporting a huge grin, replied, "I took the liberty of transferring your thumbprint from your record in the Interpol database and transferred it to SAVIOR. I trust that meets with your approval."

Enzo gave Noble a reproachful stare as he placed his thumbprint in the square box image projected on the table to the right of the keyboard.

Immediately, the massive screen displayed a series of boxes that looked more like a video game.

As Enzo studied the boxes diligently, Noble began giving instructions on how to use SAVIOR.

"The top four squares represent a window into each of the databases of the four agencies from which SAVIOR aggregates the information into a pool." Noble pointed to each of them, moving his index finger from left to right. "This contains access to the FBI database, next the CIA, followed by the IRS, and then, of course, your database, Interpol." Sounding thoroughly professorial, Noble continued. "The center box on the second row is referred to as the *Hot Spot*, the box to the left is the *Pending File*, and the one to the right is the *Interrogation File*."

"I trust this will start to make sense?" Enzo interrupted quizzically.

"Hang in there." Noble continued to elaborate. "The center box on the bottom row is where the data for a suspect, a possible suspect, a connection to a suspect, or a profile of a crime will be entered by SAVIOR, based on the answers to relevant questions. That accounts for the remaining two boxes on either side. The left-hand box contains the questions, the right-hand box or square contains the answers to those questions. Are you following me thus far?"

"So far. Now, do I get to play the game?" Enzo requested eagerly. He had learned about the capabilities of SAVIOR and had been champing at the bit ever since he discovered the U.S. government was giving Interpol access.

Noble gave him a nod.

"SAVIOR is designed to pose a series of control questions. Depending on your answer to one question, SAVIOR may generate a succession of other related but more penetrating questions. Various questions may solicit the same information, but from different perspectives, leaving no stone unturned. A single answer may trigger activity in various databases, providing multi-dimensional responses."

"What is the purpose of that form of questioning?"

"The design of questions is similar to a polygraph test, except the questions are directed to the investigator. They are not designed to identify deception, but for identifying correlations. Frequently, an investigator will unknowingly look for clues to fit his or her preconceived notions or subjectively target a specific suspect. SAVIOR's form of questioning reduces the human factor. It's a foolproof system, which clinically and logically will lead the agent inputting the data to a conclusion."

"Can you give me an example?"

"There have been several instances when the FBI and CIA worked on the same case, but the agents used competing methodologies and inadvertently ended up working at cross-purposes. SAVIOR eliminates the guess work," Noble beamed with pride.

"I understand. So the answers will provide the system with potential clues to pursue." Noting Noble's acceptance, Enzo asked with unabashed enthusiasm, "Now do we get to play the game?"

Noble thoroughly enjoyed the catbird seat. "Yes, but only a practice run." He explained that it would take hours, possibly days, to answer all of the questions—especially those relating to the evidence on the New Year's Eve bombing uncovered thus far. He described, however, the method of questioning and explained how SAVIOR would start out with simple closed questions, soliciting one-word answers, leading to other questions that would be more complex. "Try to keep those answers as concise as possible. Each question will ratchet up the level of detail, similar to the questioning you use when interrogating a suspect, but much more comprehensive." He offered to demonstrate. "Let's work a case, with which we're already familiar, as our example."

Noble turned on the switch on his side of the table and an identical keyboard appeared. He pressed the *Ctrl* and Q keys simultaneously.

The following question displayed in the lower left-hand box.

Are you looking for a:
(A) Suspect
(B) Possible Suspect
(C) Connections to a Suspect
(D) Case Profile

Noble hit the C key, followed by the *Enter* key.

Enter Name of Suspect appeared in the question box, replacing the previous question.

As Noble tapped on the keyboard, Enzo watched the name **Anwar al-Awlaki** appear in the lower right-hand *Answer* box.

Noble looked up at Enzo and noticed his smile.

"I know where this is leading," Enzo chuckled.

In the bottom center box, the photo of the Yemen-based cleric and American-born citizen, Adam Yahiye Gadahn, known worldwide as Anwar al-Awlaki, appeared. This self-appointed al-Qaeda spokesperson was a global terrorist who recruited other Americans to join his cause. In September of 2011, he was killed in Yemen in a drone attack orchestrated by the U.S. Two weeks later his sixteen year-old son, also of American descent, was killed in another drone strike.

"Wasn't Anwar al-Awlaki quickly replaced by Abu Yazeed al-Bastamy, another terrorist of American origin?"

"Yes, but let's stick with al-Awlaki. This trial run will be to determine whether he had any connections with the terrorist attacks on the U.S." Noble continued to respond to a series of other questions appearing in the lower left-hand *Question* box.

Enzo relented and sat back, patiently waiting for the results. A few minutes later, he observed the question in the left-hand box as Noble typed in a series of dates. Enzo continued to watch as they were unveiled, one-by-one, in the right-hand *Answer* box.

11-05-2009, 12-25-2009, 04-30-2010

"Notice, in all the boxes on the top row, the files for potential suspects have been stacking up as I enter the answers to the various questions. Now watch." Noble stood up and walked to the monitor on the right. He tapped the *Hot Spot* in the center. The suspects' profiles from the top boxes began to cascade downward into the center box as if a dealer were dealing from a deck of cards, except at warp speed.

As these actions took place, Noble explained, "SAVIOR is now cross-referencing all likely suspects in the databases, identifying those who meet at least ninety-five percent of the criteria, including any connection to the prime suspect in the bottom center square. The profile of anyone meeting the criteria is placed in the *Hot Spot* as it's being consolidated. If a person were to have multiple files—for example, a file in the FBI and CIA databases—the information is combined into one file."

"Awesome," Enzo responded, just as the monitor beeped, signaling the sorting process had finished. He eyed with delight the flashing words displayed across the *Hot Spot* box.

12 Records Match

SAVIOR had identified twelve profiles of suspects who had committed terrorist crimes on U.S. soil who had connections to Anwar al-Awlaki.

"SAVIOR can save thousands of hours of work, but it can't replace cognitive thinking. While SAVIOR is excellent at logical thinking, it can't replace reasoning. So now we investigate the old-fashioned way, manually." Noble, with his right hand, either dragged the displayed profiles to the left-to-center box into the *Pending File* or to the right-to-center box marked *Interrogation File*.

The profiles of three people whom Noble moved to the Interrogation File were U.S. Army Major Nidal Malik Hasan, who was responsible for the Fort Hood Massacre; Nigerian-born Umar Farouk Abdulmutallab, known as the Christmas Day Bomber; and the Pakistani-American Faisal Shahzad, who left a bomb in a car near Times Square in New York City. Each corresponded to the dates he had entered previously.

"Brilliant, Noble, truly brilliant." Enzo was in awe.

"Thanks." Noble smiled in appreciation as he took a slight bow. "Tomorrow, it will be your turn at the keyboard. And, when you start to respond to the questions, remember, the first question is crucial, and sets the stage that will lead you to follow-up questions." He reiterated, "SAVIOR will need to know who or what you are seeking, either a person or a profile."

"So I'll enter C for connection to a suspect and then enter the name Mohammed al-Fadl. I expect none other than Simon's photo will appear in the center box on the bottom row, reserved for SAVIOR's response," Enzo stated knowingly, showing he had mastered his lesson.

"Remember, SAVIOR will also consolidate all the information the four agencies have amassed on him in their databases," Noble reiterated.

Enzo was comfortable with the process and felt he had a good grasp, but felt it necessary to reaffirm. "I'll need to enter all forensic evidence. For example, in the case of the French assassination attempt, I'll assume I will have the opportunity to enter the type of bomb, the fingerprint on the fragment, and the information about the white truck?"

"Yes, and don't forget the embassy staff and the other people who may have had the opportunity to place the bomb on the decoy limo. We can't be a hundred percent sure that it was the person in the truck who detonated the bomb," Noble reminded him.

"Can I also enter the caliber of the bullets aimed toward the chancellor and the partial fingerprint found on one of those bullets?" Enzo added astutely, "I know, I must check out the staff as well."

"Yes. Then, of course, you'll have similar information to input regarding London, including the caterers and the waiters, etcetera." Noble continued, "Remember, I can't emphasize enough, SAVIOR searches precisely, using a variety of processes based on how you respond to the first question and all of the subsequent questions. As you are aware, SAVIOR had been upgraded to search beyond vetting senators and congresspersons, and it has become an all-encompassing investigative tool. It has the capacity beyond anything seen in the past."

"I'll enter all the pertinent data and hopefully we can not only identify the perpetrators, but also link them to Simon," Enzo affirmed.

"I have one more request." Noble paused briefly, and then proceeded with caution. "When you enter the names of the staff and other suspects who may have come in contact with the heads of government in question—even remotely—use SAVIOR to vet those people in line of succession. I would even suggest going down two levels."

Enzo, taken aback by the implications, blurted out, "So you think someone higher up in the chain of command is responsible? I thought Simon was our prime suspect, or at least the one orchestrating the assassination attempts. Isn't that our operating premise?"

Noble prepared himself to stick his neck out—but only a little. He assumed Hamilton had not divulged all aspects of the Simon case, so he chose his words carefully. "When you and Hamilton were chasing down Simon in Florence all those years ago, it was not just to recover stolen funds." Noble determined it was time to inform him of a fact known only to a few. It would be essential to concluding the case. "Enzo, what I am about to disclose is strictly confidential, and should be used only as part of your probing the motives behind the bombings." It was obvious he had Enzo's full attention. He took a deep breath and said, "Simon was also the one ultimately responsible for placing Abner Baari in the White House."

Enzo was dumbfounded. "You think Simon is actually planning to replace a head of government with someone of his own choosing? That these were dry runs and he already has someone ready and waiting in the wings? Is that his plan? Is that what you think is his motive?"

Noble took a deep breath and rejoined, matter-of-factly, "Yes to all questions. For now, you work on who, and I'll work on why." It was clear Noble had concluded his primer for the day.

Enzo, still aghast, took his cue. "I understand. Let's call it a night. We are going to have a long day tomorrow."

That night, Noble accepted Enzo's invitation to dinner, but with one caveat—they wouldn't speak about the case.

Enzo agreed.

Over their dinner conversation, though, it did predictably lead to Hamilton.

Noble opened the conversation. "I'm glad you and Hamilton became good friends."

Enzo reminisced sadly. "As I mentioned, we spent a lot of time together whenever I'd visit my family. Moreover, I continued to learn about intelligence gathering from Hamilton, right up until his death. He was an amazing man."

"Yes, he was. Do you remember anything about his life when he made Florence his home?"

"You mean before he moved into his villa on Viale della Torre del Gallo?"

"Yes, starting when he first arrived."

"Back then, he lived in a small, but charming, apartment in the Piazza Santo Spirito. Did you know he had a passion for art?"

"Yes, I saw his incredible collection when I visited his villa."

"No, I mean before he arrived in Florence."

Noble was shocked. Hamilton was like a father to him, but he never inquired about his art collection. Partially, because their conversations always seemed to be heavily entwined in a case, or, perhaps, it was simply out of respect for Hamilton's extreme privacy. Noble's apparent upset, however, was borne out by the fact that he had misconstrued Hamilton's ability to amass such a collection in Florence. He was clearly shaken by the revelation.

Enzo noticed. "Are you okay? You seem surprised."

"I just realized I never really knew Hamilton as well as I'd wished. To me, he was my mentor, my leader, whom I always placed on a pedestal. How sad that our personal relationship never developed fully, especially with the affection we had for each other."

Noble bowed his head and took a moment to compose himself. The realization that most of their relationship encompassed work struck him. While many dinners had taken place in his home, or his sister's home, most dinners of sorts took place in the office while discussing a case. It wasn't until Hamilton retired and moved to Florence that their conversations took on a more personal note. And still, they were long distance conversations and lost some of the intimacy of personal contact.

Having fully regained his poise, he looked directly at Enzo and introduced a rather lingering question. "How could he afford to amass such a collection over the years?"

Enzo, not finding the inquiry invasive, and happy to see Noble in his former state, answered, "He was incredibly lucky. Actually, I was fortunate to be with him when he ventured over to the Piazza dei Ciompi after he first settled in Florence. The piazza is primarily a market that sells antiques and paintings, and it was where Hamilton fell in love with a particular painting. It was quite a large canvas painted with several figures entering into what looked like Hell. He was captivated. I recall he paid two hundred and fifty euros for it. He was so proud of his purchase.

"Evidently, he started out small," Noble quipped. "I do recall him relating enthusiastically that he uncovered a painting in some flea market."

"Wait! There's more. Hamilton, always the investigator, was convinced he had discovered a real gem. Therefore, he started to do some research and learned he owned a fifteenth century masterpiece painted by a Venetian named Andrea Mantegna. Incredible, no?" Enzo continued to explain that Mantegna, known for his stony sculpture-like figures and metallic backgrounds, was what enthralled Hamilton the most. "Enough of my own art history. Are you ready for this? He sold the painting at a Sotheby's auction for close to twenty-nine million dollars. Nice profit, eh!"

Noble, at a loss for words, stated blandly, "So, that was it." He vaguely recalled, that in a later conversation, Hamilton mentioned he had scored an art coup, but provided no details, knowing art was not Noble's forte. Somewhat uncomfortable, he offered, "I guess Hamilton had a real eye for art."

"Not just an eye, a quest. Actually, it became an obsession. He continued to buy and sell until he amassed not only an impressive collection, but also made a bloody fortune in the process. That was how he was able to buy the villa and live a pleasant life to the end."

Noble felt he was on an emotional rollercoaster. Discernibly upset, he sat back as his face turned somewhat ashen.

"What's wrong? I thought you'd be pleased to hear how Hamilton thrived."

"I'm sorry. I'm ashamed, and at the same time relieved."

"Excuse me, but you're not making any sense," Enzo indicated in a worried tone.

"When I visited Hamilton in Florence, I saw how well he was living. I'm embarrassed to say, out of ignorance, I asked him a rather impertinent question—how was he able to provide for himself so lavishly.

"And what did he say in response?"

"Hamilton, as usual, answered a question with a question. So, when he inquired as to whether the U.S. Treasury was ever able to determine the total amount Simon had stolen before we managed to retrieve the funds, I was unresponsive." Noble paused and then spoke more slowly. "I knew he didn't expect me to answer his question, but by the look on his face and the angle of his mouth, I incorrectly assumed he had shared in the illicit pie. I agonized over it for years, but could not come up with a rational explanation."

"But, now you know he didn't. That should make you happy." Enzo tried to offer some solace.

"I'm mortified. Now I know his facial expression meant to convey, if you don't trust me, go back and count the money. Worse yet, I'll never be able to apologize."

Before Enzo could respond, Noble's smartphone vibrated on the table. Thankful for the interruption, he apologized, "I have to take this call. Excuse me." He stepped away from the table and headed to the corner in the room away from Enzo and the other patrons.

"Max, what's up?" Noble bellowed, still fixated on his emotional conversation with Enzo.

"Agent Darrow was murdered."

"Oh my God, what happened?" Putting Hamilton out of his mind, he gingerly refocused.

"Darrow was discovered in his vehicle parked off the side of the road, thirty-five miles east of the Brush and Weis highway junction, on the Jericho Callao Road. He was shot one time through the head."

"Irrefutably murder—perhaps a warning shot—literally for the rest of us." Noble cautioned. "What was he doing out there?"

"I don't know. But last night, during the air search, the pilot of the Apache helicopter picked up something strange on the screen from the infrared detectors. Four figures were pictured moving rapidly toward the Bell Hill Mine, and then they disappeared."

"Do the other federal agents think it was the cyclists?"

"They weren't sure. But this morning, Darrow personally went to the mine to check it out. At ten o'clock, he called in his location and reported something about an unknown tunnel leading away from the mine."

"Another tunnel?"

Max, anxious to update him on the rest of the pertinent activities, picked up her pace. "After walking approximately a mile into the mineshaft tunnel, Darrow said he entered a new modern tunnel that headed east. He followed the tunnel for miles and, finally, at the end of the tunnel, he found a standard 25-ton steel blast door. To the right of the door was a security fingerprint access pad."

"What?" Noble gasped. He could hear Max sigh from the other end of the line. "Continue."

This time, with measured speech, Max explained, "According to Darrow's report, everything about the tunnel and the door had military issue written all over them. He indicated he was going to head to Dugway and check out his findings with the base commander."

"What did he find out?" Noble waited edgily for the conclusion.

"Nothing," Max stated with dismay. "He never made it to Dugway. The Army conducted an aerial search this afternoon. That's when they discovered his body."

"If he was on his way to Dugway, how did he end up on the Jericho-Callao Road?"

"It doesn't make sense. The fastest way would have been to take the Simpson Springs-Callao Road on the Pony Express Route."

"What about the tunnel?"

"I spoke directly with the base commander, a Colonel Evans. He has no knowledge of the tunnel outside the Dugway base."

"If it's not part of the military complex, where does the tunnel lead?" Noble pondered, dreading an unsatisfactory conclusion.

For several seconds, silence prevailed.

"I'll leave on the next flight." Noble sounded drained. "I believe there is a 7:25 a.m. that will get me into Washington around 1:00 p.m. In the meantime, who stepped in for Darrow?"

"The Colonel said his name is Agent Burke."

"Have him post his agents at the three mine sites where we suspect foul play. I want them there around the clock. Also, in the morning, have the Colonel send in a few troops with Burke to check out the tunnel at the Bell Hill Mine, then check out the mineshafts at Joy and Silver City. Warn them to use extreme caution. I want a report when I arrive," he requested, asserting his authority.

"Noble, it's freezing out there."

"Get them a tent!" he yelled. "I want you also to make arrangements to fly to the site the day after tomorrow. You will be heading up this investigation until I arrive. If the killers are out there, I don't want them escaping," he demanded, and then, in a remarkably calmer tone, he added, "I have a few things to take care of first."

Max recoiled as Noble passed on to her a potentially career-ending responsibility, but quickly refocused on his agitation. He seemed more impatient than usual. "How's the case going there?" she asked, in an attempt to distract him from the Dead Zone.

"We'll talk when I return."

"Boss, what's happening?"

"Max, I'll see you tomorrow."

She conceded. "I'll send a car to pick you up at the airport. Until then, have a safe trip."

Noble walked back toward the table. Enzo, seeing him approach, sensed he was more distracted than he was before he took the call, but assumed it was nothing related to Hamilton. Unmistakably, their very personal conversation was preempted by another devastating event.

"I have to return to Washington immediately. I'll need to leave on the first flight in the morning. Can you work your way through SAVIOR on your own?" Noble tried to appear composed.

"Is everything all right?"

"A federal agent was killed while working on an investigation headed up by my agency. It may also have led us to our first lead on the missing persons cases." Noble spoke with surprising poise as he added, "Please keep me up-to-date with any links you trace back to the lists of suspects SAVIOR provides and, of course, any news on Simon. I'm almost certain he's the mastermind behind the bombings. Confirm that, and I'll continue to work on the motive."

Enzo flagged down the waiter and insisted they call it a night. "You'll need to be up early to catch your flight."

11
A DOUBLE SHOCK

Although it was an exciting and productive day, Noble returned to his hotel exhausted. Unfortunately, when he opened the door to his room, the predictable ominous red light was flashing on the phone. It was hard to ignore. He assumed Max was trying to call him at the hotel. For the moment, he would disregard the message. First, he needed to make another call.

"Aldo, this is Noble Bishop, Director Scott's friend."

"Yes, of course, Noble. How are you?" sounded the eloquent voice with a marked Italian accent. Aldo Tancredi was initially the valet and then became the dedicated caretaker of Director Hamilton Scott. He was also the executor of Hamilton's estate.

"I'm very well, thank you. I hope I'm not calling too late, but I have a rather personal question to pose." Noble hesitated with some trepidation. "I am in France working with Enzo Borgini on a case."

"How is dear Enzo?" Aldo interrupted. "I've missed his visits since the death of the *direttore*." Inadvertently, he had redirected the conversation.

Noble obliged.

"He's fine. Actually, this is my first acquaintance with him. But I discovered that he'd been a close friend to the director over the years."

"Yes, he and the direttore spent time together whenever he visited Florence. Did you know they shared a passion for renaissance art?"

"That's one of the reasons I'm calling," Noble confessed. Abruptly, his mood changed as he recalled his conversation with Enzo. "I recently learned about the director's obsession, something I had not known before."

Aldo, clearly bewildered by the conversation, replied, "Yes, he loved to buy and sell various art forms. Over time, he amassed an extensive collection." He also thought, *Odd that Noble wasn't aware.*

"Aldo," Noble addressed directly, "I know you were responsible for transferring the fifty-one million dollars to a bank account in Georgetown. The account number written on the note paper was in your handwriting."

Somewhat surprised by Noble's serious tone, he swore, "It was a gift from the direttore."

"I presumed as much—although a rather generous gift." Noble suddenly realized he had sounded more like an interrogator and not as a friend. He attempted to soften his voice. "Aldo, I've always been curious. Where did the money come from?" Noble was thankful Aldo could not see the expression on his face.

"When the direttore learned that he did not have much longer to live, he made arrangements to sell his villa to a gentleman, and his art collection to several parties. All agreed to pay in full and take possession after his death."

Noble detected the sadness in Aldo's voice. He remained silent, and allowed him to finish.

"The money I transferred to you was part of the proceeds from those sales at the request of the direttore." Aldo was thankful Noble could not see the tears welling in his eyes.

"I appreciate your sharing the information. It was a question that has plagued me for some time," Noble relented, with more warmth. Then, with genuine, heartfelt regret, he admitted, "There was so much I didn't know about the director. I should have visited more often after he moved to Florence."

"The direttore loved you like a son, and delighted in the phone conversations you had over the years."

"Thank you, Aldo, for all you did for the director and for me. We shall speak again soon."

"Stay well, Noble, and give my regards to Enzo. *A presto.*"

Noble hung up the phone and took a moment to reflect on the

conversation. Then, in a total about-face of emotion, he laughed aloud as he remembered doing—the *noble thing*. He had transferred all the money—unknowingly, his money—to the U.S. Treasury. "What irony," he wailed. He chuckled again, but this time in despair, as he thought, *If only Simon knew how noble I really was.* As he continued to muse over the irony, he caught the flashing red light out of the corner of his eye, having forgotten about the message waiting to be retrieved. He exhaled to prepare himself for another crisis as he reached for the phone.

The message was not from Max.

Pleasantly surprised, Noble found the voice of the messenger to be a welcome relief. He grabbed his xPhad, hit the appropriate speed dial button, and counted the rings.

"Darling, it's wonderful to hear your voice," she purred in a sleepy tone.

He viewed the clock on the nightstand, realizing he had not considered the time difference.

"Amanda, I'm sorry to have awakened you."

"I'm glad you called." She yawned.

"I'll let you go back to sleep. But can you meet me at my apartment tomorrow night at eight o'clock?"

"You're coming home?" she asked gleefully and seemingly more alert.

"Yes, I'll be back in Washington tomorrow afternoon, but I have to meet Max at the office as soon as I arrive."

Ignoring his comment, she inquired, "Is everything okay?"

"Just a break in the case," he murmured. While his heart truly ached for Amanda's company, he couldn't stop his mind from pondering a very different subject. *The fifty-one million dollars Hamilton gifted me—was not from the recaptured stolen funds—how could I have ever suspected any wrongdoing?*

She could tell he was distracted, and persisted out of concern. "Are you sure you're all right?"

"Everything's okay. See you tomorrow night. Love you."

"Love you, too. Goodnight."

12
OH MY GOD

"Air France flight 7-6-5-1 to Paris is now boarding. Please proceed to gate twenty-five," commanded a voice from the ceiling speakers.

Noble barely had time to sit down in the departure lounge before he had to gather his belongings and head for the plane. In roughly an hour and a half, the plane would touch down at the Charles de Gaulle Airport.

Instead of delving into the Dead Zone case, he decided to spend his time sorting through the countless e-mails he had ignored over the previous few days. He thumbed past those from Amanda and Max, which naturally he had read and already responded to, and several e-mails he had forwarded to Max for her to handle. The others he deleted.

Shortly after, the captain made the announcement, "Prepare for landing."

Noble downed the rest of his coffee, moved his seat into the required position, and mentally readied himself for the next leg of his trip.

ℒℴ

Comfortably settled into a chair in the Air France Lounge, Noble reached for his xPhad and attempted to focus on his own investigation. It was now officially recognized as the Dead Zone since the coroner had issued the autopsy reports, a fact he accepted with gloom. Slowly, the evidence uncovered in his case in the U.S. displaced the myriad of data that had been swirling in his mind about the New Year's Eve bombings.

He unfolded his tablet and retrieved the last e-mail he had received from Max, the one with the attachment of the updated map of the Dead Zone.

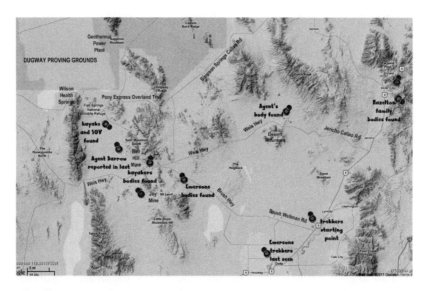

He noticed Max had added a notation next to the pushpin she had placed earlier near the Bell Hill Mine, close to where the rangers found the kayakers' bodies, and also the spot where Agent Darrow last made contact. She had also added a pushpin at the location where they found the agent's body. He continued to study the map with intensity as he began to look for something, anything that would explain the murders of so many innocent victims. He was convinced that each of them had seen something forbidden. And then, of course, there was the death of Agent Darrow.

Noble had focused on the map for over an hour when, all of a sudden, an announcement blared over the intercom. "Last call for Air France flight twenty-eight to Washington." Jolted out of deep concentration, he quickly grabbed his paraphernalia and rushed to the gate.

༄

After take-off, and settling into seat 5A, Noble retrieved his tray table and prepared for lunch. He was suffering from a combination of being famished and exhausted. He chose to eat first, followed immediately by a catnap. In just over seven hours, he would arrive at Dulles International Airport to begin—what he assumed would be—a long-harrowing day. And, after a restless night, he needed sleep desperately.

Following another fitful slumber, this time with visions of the map flashing in his mind, he decided once again to study the map of the Dead Zone to look for clues—clues that would lead him to the missing link. For over a half-hour, he racked his brain as he stared at the map. Then he began to doodle.

Using the highlighter tool with his right index finger, Noble attempted to connect the dots—literally. First, he made a mark at the Bell Hill Mine near the pushpin where Agent Darrow reported his last location. Then, he continued to make his mark down to where the kayakers' bodies were found. He ran his finger southeast connecting the line to the Joy Mine, near the pushpin that indicated the location of the Emersons' bodies. Using his finger once again to construct another line, he continued to move southeast toward the pushpin that pointed to the town of Delta, where the Emerson couple and the two trekkers were last seen. Continuing with the highlighter, he moved northeast to the junction where Highway 6 and the Brush Wellman Road intersected. It was the location the storeowner at the Quality Market in Delta reported the trekkers would begin their journey. According to the storeowner, the trekkers planned to follow along the Brush Highway on their way to the Fish Spring National Wildlife Refuge. Noble continued to move his finger north and connect the line with the pushpin at the Silver City Mine ruins, the location near where the hitchhikers happened upon the Hazelton family. It was also the location where he derived the vial of VX had been discovered. A slight physical response overcame him as he considered how the Hazelton family must have suffered in those final horrendous minutes in their car.

After a brief pause to reflect on the horror, Noble chose not to use the highlighter to connect the line to the next pushpin on the map. Instead, out of respect for a fellow officer, he used his finger to freehand the drawing of a star—the universal emblem adopted by law enforcement agencies—marking the spot where the helicopter pilot sighted Agent Darrow's body.

Noble sat back and stared at his artistry. Then he bolted upright in a state of shock.

"Oh, my God."

He felt his heart thumping a bit from the excitement. Then, after swallowing hard, he froze the image and slowly turned the tablet to a ninety-degree angle to the right.

He continued to stare at the screen with disbelief.

After taking minutes to absorb what could be a coincidence or, at worst, a sick joke, he hit the forward button, typed in Max, and hit send.

Noble was instantly drawn back to the text message Enzo had forwarded to him earlier—the message containing the same symbol—the message that read **HEADS UP!** ☾.

Still operating in high gear, he rapidly typed a message replying to the original SMS text sender of Enzo's message. His message simply said, SEE YOU SOON! Noble then swiftly used a special app tracking device to locate the longitude and latitude of the sender's smartphone. It was in the process of receiving the message. Literally, nanoseconds later, the following coordinates appeared on his screen: **40° 45′ N, 111° 53′ W.**

They were for Salt Lake City—the location of Simon's smartphone.

Noble had his confirmation.

13
THE STRATAGEM

M ax, what are you doing here? I thought you'd just send a government car."

"You forward an explosive e-mail like that to me and expect me to sit still? What the hell is going on?" she questioned excitedly.

"I honestly don't know." Noble shook his head, clearly without a rational explanation.

Max instinctively grabbed Noble's briefcase to free his hand, allowing him to manage his luggage.

They both headed out of the airport.

"Do you really think Simon has something to do with the Dead Zone?"

Noble put his left index finger over his lips and cautioned, "Wait until we're in the car."

They entered the rear seat of the sedan from opposite sides. Max hit the button straightaway, closing the soundproof window separating the front and rear seats, placing the driver out of earshot.

Noble was the first to speak. "Simon has to be involved in some way, but I'm also convinced he's involved in the bombings in Europe as well."

"Is there a connection?" Max gasped.

"That's the ultimate question."

"Do you really believe Simon dumped the bodies in specific locations—in our Dead Zone—knowing you would somehow connect the dots to reveal his calling card?" Max let out a deep breath, waiting impatiently for Noble's response.

"Simon's brilliant, but I still believe our victims spotted something or, in the case of the Hazelton Family, found something. I'm not sure it was a sheer coincidence that drawing a line from location to location would create a half circle, or crescent moon to be exact. I suspect it's Simon's handiwork."

"What about Agent Darrow's body?"

"Perhaps, leaving a law enforcement officer in that precise location was the perfect opportunity for Simon to continue his cat and mouse game."

"Cat and mouse? I don't get it."

Noble explained that Enzo had received a message from Simon, claiming responsibility for the New Year's Eve bombings, immediately following the nightly air-searches that began in the Dead Zone.

"And you don't think that was a coincidence?" Max questioned skeptically.

"No, I'm positive he was trying to lure me to Europe to distract me from our missing persons cases. He may have presumed we were on to something. Then, when Darrow exposed the tunnel, it gave Simon an opportunity to lure me back. Unfortunately, at the agent's peril."

"Why would he want to lure you back intentionally unless, of course, he was planning to trap you?"

"I think you just answered your own question."

"If Simon is involved in all of these events—we're in for big trouble."

Then, just as Noble was about to ask her what they had discovered in the tunnel and at the other mines, the car pulled through the White House gate.

❧

Max followed Noble into his conference room and they sat down across from each other at the table, which had become an essential part of their modus operandi. Plastered on the touch-screen display in front of Noble's view was a map of the Dead Zone, including his highlighted additions.

"Okay, tell me what's happening." He braced himself.

Max explained that Agent Burke, Darrow's replacement, and a few troops entered the Bell Hill Mine. They walked through the mineshaft tunnel for about a mile. Suddenly, the tunnel morphed into a new modern tunnel with lighting. Also, they discovered several Segway Personal Transporters.

"Was that in Darrow's report?"

"No, perhaps he never had the opportunity to finish it," Max remarked, as she envisioned the terrible fate the agent met.

Noble sensed the same disappointment, but forced her back on point. "Don't they use the Segways at Dugway for patrolling?"

"Yeah, and they were the same model. But wait until you hear the rest. There were only three transporters, so the agent and two of the soldiers rode them farther into the tunnel while the others waited behind." Max arduously continued to explain how they followed the tunnel for another nine miles, which took little time on the transporters. She clarified that a commercial Segway could travel at a speed of up to 12.5 mph. However, the Army had souped-up their Segways to operate at a speed of 25 mph. "Twenty-one minutes later they reached the end of the tunnel."

"What was at the end of the tunnel?" Noble urged with emphasis.

"A large steel door, just as Darrow had described when he called in his report." She detected the strain in his voice.

"Cut to the chase." Noble requested with more calm. He tried to stay focused, although jetlag began to overtake him.

"To the right of that door is an Intelli-Pass biometric fingerprint ID system, the same model used by the military." Finally, Max paused and waited for Noble's assessment.

"So, Darrow was correct; everything reeks of a military installation. And the base commander swears they knew nothing about the tunnel?"

"That's what he alleges."

"Then someone must have seen Darrow leave the Bell Hill Mine and concluded he'd discovered an entrance to something."

"Or *someone*—possibly Simon?" Max questioned with an arched brow.

"If it was someone, most likely it was one of Simon's accomplices." Disgusted, Noble quickly asked, "Whom did you say replaced Darrow?"

"Agent Burke. Thus far, he has joined the fray and appears to be on board, allowing us to steer the investigation."

"Great!" Apparently Noble was aroused coming out of his lull. "Did they find similar tunnels at the Joy and Silver City mines?"

"The troops trudged through each of the tunnels as far as they could but, within a few miles, in both tunnels, it became precariously dangerous and they were ordered to stop. Ostensibly, they are impassable and lead nowhere."

"In any case, I want them to continue to stake out all three mines. Also, instruct the base commander to carry on the night flights. If something is going on out there, we might get lucky and pick up some activity. In the meantime, update the map to show the location and direction of the tunnels."

"Let's hope they lead us to something of interest." As Max headed toward the door, she jibed, "Thanks for grounding the agency jet." Then, with less mockery, she informed Noble that she was scheduled to leave the next day at noon on a military transport out of Andrews Air Force Base. "I'll be arriving at Dugway's Michael Army Airfield around three."

"Suck up, Max. Times are tough. Stop in here in the morning before you take off. I'll have something for you to take with you."

"Later." Max waved her hand in the air and walked out of the room.

∽

"Mad Dog."

"Hey, Mr. B, how's it goin'?"

"I wish I could say splendid, but I need you to do something for me on the QT," Noble stated in a muffled tone, as if someone else were in the room.

"Director, as always, I'm here at your disposal. Use me and abuse me."

"Take down this number, 8-6-9 dash 5-7-4 dash 1 point 2. You will have two hours, starting from the moment I hang up this phone, to download whatever it is you need from this top-secret file. And then you'll be locked out."

"What gives?" Mad Dog's curiosity was piqued.

"I need you to make me a prosthetic thumbprint from a photo. Is that possible?"

"I've worked miracles for you in the past. But from a photo, that's a moon shot."

"Mad Dog, for you, nothing's impossible. That's why I rely on you. Oh, by the way, did I mention I needed it by nine o'clock tomorrow morning."

"No problem. That gives me fourteen hours, minus food and sleep, of course. You're a real sweetheart, boss."

"Night, Mad Dog. Thanks." Noble hung up, glanced at his watch, and realized he had barely enough time to meet Amanda without being late.

14
THE INTERMEDIARY

Noble carefully angled his key into the lock. Abruptly, the door swung open and before he was able to utter a word, he found himself wrapped in a passionate kiss. Several enjoyable minutes later, he pulled back from the embrace and whispered, "It's nice to be home."

"You look uptight—even after that kiss," Amanda inferred as she curled her lips slightly. Then, she insisted, "Give me your jacket and go relax while I pour you a glass of wine."

Noble succumbed without protest. He removed the scarf from his neck and handed it to her, along with his jacket. Then he retrieved his luggage and briefcase from the hallway and dropped them in the foyer. Soon after, he followed her footsteps into the living room.

"Here, this will help you unwind."

Amanda's smile began to soothe him even before she handed him the stem glass. She was the perfect cure. After a few sips of wine, Noble truly began to feel more at ease. Then, moments after he sat down on the sofa and relaxed against the cushion, he was forced to answer the inevitable questions: "Yes, the trip was fine. No, I can't discuss the details of the case. Yes, Max is doing well. No, I don't plan to return to France anytime soon." Eventually, he was able to fashion his own set of questions. "What's been happening at your office?" he asked, more as repartee than curiosity.

Not surprisingly, she seemed flattered at his inquiry. "Adam has been keeping me extremely busy. Actually, it's kept me from missing you too much," she cooed.

"Is it something you can talk about?"

"Sure!" She knew from the expression on his face that he was teasing, but she was more than happy to play along. "Things are starting to brew again with various states battling the government over land rights. Adam is trying to reopen Wyoming's suit that it lost years ago when it was overruled by the 10th U.S. Circuit Court of Appeals in 2011."

"Originally, didn't that have to do with the Clinton Administration cordoning off public lands and preventing Wyoming from building roads?"

"Yes, and Adam believes the White House overstepped its authority and that only Congress can designate wilderness lands. Currently, the federal rule bars Wyoming from developing nearly fifty million acres of roadless areas in the national forests. You may also recall that during the same time, the state of Utah filed a similar suit. But, in that case, the Baari administration had claimed the land as eminent domain. It prevented the state from building roads through the federally-owned land to get to state-owned parcels where they have drilling leases."

"Vaguely," Noble responded, while at the same time he thought, *I had forgotten about the suit totally.*

Now, she had his complete attention.

Noticing his interest beginning to peak, she continued. "Neither suit ever gained any traction. With the federal government, alleging sovereignty over all public lands, the natural gas industry is once again rallying support. They're hoping a new administration will back their cause. Adam Ridge is a combative lobbyist, but it's still going to be a tough battle."

"Is he fighting for other states with a common interest, as well?"

"Yes, Adam is also defending Colorado's right to drill. Those three states alone, with their shale oil and natural gas deposits, would end the U.S. energy dependence. It's crazy. Even for those states that have legitimate drilling rights, they can't get to the source because the government is preventing them from building roads on the federal lands necessary to access the sites," she declared.

Noble reached for his wine glass as he stated, "I remember one year—I believe it was 2009—the federal government wanted to set aside nine million acres of land to save wild horses. Rather extreme, I would say, even for the horsey set."

"Exactly! The government appears to be in a feeding frenzy, gobbling up all the land it can for whatever reason it can muster."

"It seems more like lame excuses."

"You're right, because when they don't find an acceptable reason, such as national parks, Indian land, military facilities, etcetera, etcetera, they resort to eminent domain. Anyway, you get my point!"

Noble enjoyed listening to Amanda speak passionately about her work. Being a workaholic himself, he found it an endearing quality, one that made them compatible. He also happened to be fanatical about the topic at hand. "These land grabs must come with a price. It's amazing there haven't been more legal challenges. At least I'm not aware of any. After all, everything the government owns is funded by the taxpayers."

"Including the pens used to sign the spending bills into law," she lamented.

Noble concurred. "Despite taxpayers' rights, I read that over the years and throughout many administrations, the Federal Government has managed to claim close to thirty percent of the land in the U.S. More importantly, by the same token, thirty percent of the natural energy resources as well!" Noble went on, "Didn't the Secretary of the Interior for the Baari administration also cancel seventy-seven drilling leases that had been approved by the previous administration?"

"You're correct. In 2010, those leases were part of Utah's canyon country, east of the Great Basin and south of Dugway," Amanda explained matter-of-factly.

"Dugway!" Noble blurted out, brusquely regaining an erect position.

Amanda, startled at his reaction, continued slowly, "In addition to the federal government owning close to eight hundred thousand acres of the Dugway Proving Ground, the Baari administration acquired most of the land south of Dugway. It is currently being managed by the Bureau of Land Management." She paused briefly. "May I ask what your apparent interest is in this land?" she searched, conceding her snooping would get her nowhere.

As anticipated, Noble gave her the "you-know-the-answer" look.

Amanda chuckled at his reaction as she continued to elaborate. "So, you can see Adam is fighting two issues. First, the legitimacy of the government's land grabs and, second, the reinstitution of drilling leases."

"It's going to be combat in the trenches," Noble opined.

"I know, but we're hoping President Post will be able to work with the battle-wise environmentalists. Our energy situation is becoming dire, especially with the turmoil continuing in the Middle East." Amanda stopped speaking briefly as she caught Noble trying to stifle a yawn. "I'm sorry. I've been rattling on, and you must be hungry and tired," she acknowledged.

"Just come over here and sit down next to me for a while," Noble gestured with an open arm.

Amanda stood up from the chair and walked over to sit next to Noble on the sofa. As she leaned back to relax in his arms, he asked, "What's Adam's wife like?"

What an odd question, she thought as she pulled back to look up at him. "Nancy's very pleasant. We've had lunch together a few times. Why do you ask?"

"Amanda, I need you to do something for me," Noble spoke softly and calmly.

"Of course, anything that's not 'illegal, immoral, or fattening,' as someone once said," she kidded as her curiosity was aroused.

"I need to speak with Adam off-the-record, and covertly. No one must learn of our meeting. We cannot be seen in public together."

"How can I help?" she volunteered enthusiastically. "Does it have to do with the case you're working on?"

Ignoring her prodding and enthusiasm, Noble requested that she invite Adam and Nancy to her townhouse, ostensibly as dinner guests. As part of the plan, Amanda would reveal to Adam the real purpose of the invitation and ask that he explain to his wife that it was important for him to stay behind for a confidential meeting—with an unidentified person. Amanda and Nancy would then depart for dinner at a restaurant nearby. Noble had questions for Adam, and believed he could provide the answers he desperately needed. For Adam's protection, it was imperative they meet in secret.

"Noble, please, what is this all about?"

"Shush, no more talk about work. Just lean back and let me feel you in my arms."

Within seconds, the chitchat had stopped and silence prevailed. Several minutes later, Amanda carefully extracted herself out from under Noble's arms and discovered him in a deep sleep.

⁓

Noble rubbed his eyes as he rolled over and found himself still on the sofa, but with a pillow under his head and a blanket tucked over his chest. Suddenly, he sat upright, having no idea what time it was, until he smelled the fresh brewed coffee wafting from the kitchen. He managed to amble his way groggily to the source of the aroma and to a vision of beauty that presented him with a cup.

"Good morning, sweetheart," she voiced softly, as she kissed him on the cheek.

"I'm a great date, am I not?" Noble teased.

"You were exhausted, and I didn't have the heart to awaken you."

Noble sipped his coffee while he half-listened to Amanda recap their clandestine plan from the night before. Sleepily, he looked down and glanced at his watch. "I have just enough time for a quick shower, then off to the White House." He kissed her hurriedly on the forehead, thanked her for the coffee, and dashed off to the bedroom.

15
GOING UNDERGROUND

Inside the White House at 7:30 a.m., the hallways were unusually quiet and absent the usual array of wandering souls. Noble enjoyed those rare occasions to meander silently through the hallowed halls, especially this morning, as it gave him renewed vigor. When he finally arrived in his office, he noticed immediately a small box sitting on his desk wrapped with a large red bow. He smiled as he untied the ribbon. Mad Dog had worked miracles many times before. Noble was confident he had done it again. He opened the box. "Perfect!" he exclaimed, then set the precious gift off to the side.

He continued to enjoy a few more moments of precious solitude as he slowly digested the bran muffin Amanda slipped into his briefcase. Then, after sipping another cup of strong coffee he had just brewed, he began to delve into the jumble of evidence he needed to decipher. While the breakfast went down easy, he was having difficulty digesting the connections between the state of Utah's suit, the Dead Zone, the European bombings—and Simon.

Only a week earlier, President Post had delivered his inaugural address on "The Rebirth of America." And, over the past seven days, Noble's feeling of renewal was turning to dread. Some of the same old problems appeared to be looming ahead. He sat back in his chair and spent the next hour assembling and disassembling in his mind all he and Max had discovered relating to the Dead Zone. Then, angrily, he thought, *there's one person who may be able to add some clarification.*

Just then, Max burst into his office without warning. But before she had an opportunity to speak, Noble held up his left hand and said, "Hold that thought." With his other hand, he reached for his phone and punched in a series of numbers.

"Noble, how nice to hear from you," replied the voice on the other end.

"Hank, this is not a social call. I want you in my office tomorrow."

"Not a good time, Noble."

"This is not a request. Call my secretary and schedule the appointment." The line went dead.

Noble then hit the lower left-hand button. "Doris, Hank Kramer will be calling to schedule an appointment for Friday. Rearrange my calendar as necessary. It is imperative I meet with him."

"What was that all about?" Max inquired.

"I'm not sure, but I have a feeling the former president's chief of staff might have some useful information regarding our investigation. I'll let you know if I uncover anything important."

"You don't want me to sit in on the meeting?" Max whined, sounding dejected.

"No, I'll deal with him. I know this guy. And I know how he behaves when being questioned. I'll get more out of him if I handle it one-on-one. Besides, you'll be in Utah."

Max was not aware of Hank's connection to La Fratellanza and, more important, to Simon. All evidence against Hank for his part in perpetrating the plot was on a flash drive and on the memory sticks retaining the video recordings from the interrogation. Noble had securely tucked them away in a safe-deposit box where they would remain unless, of course, one of the members of the group was to break the confidentiality agreement.

Noble knew he had to manage this interview on his own.

"Now, what was so important that you had to burst into my office?"

"You summoned me to your office before I leave for Utah," Max responded unflapped.

"Next time, try to enter more leisurely. Now close the door behind you and sit down. There is something I need to tell you before you take off."

Max obeyed.

Noble began guardedly. "What I am about to divulge must never leave this room."

The seriousness in Noble's voice sent momentary chills up Max's spine. "Are you okay?"

Without deviating from his tone of voice, he began to explain, "Almost seven months ago, when I spoke to the media, ultimately forcing Baari to resign from the presidency, I gave them only part of the story. That goes for the congressional committee investigations as well."

Max reacted visibly to the idea that Noble would be less than truthful, especially with the presidency at stake.

Acknowledging her uneasiness, he specified, "I did not lie or distort, but in answering the questions I also did not embellish. It's what I didn't say."

"Noble, I don't understand!"

Ignoring her reaction, he continued. "In the mid-nineties, a group of students, while attending Harvard Graduate School, created a secret society called La Fratellanza. Simon was the group leader. Their mission was to groom, educate, and elevate an illegal immigrant to the Oval Office. Simon tried to recruit me to be a member of the group, which I resisted. I did embrace them as classmates and socialized with them at times." Noble waited for Max's response, but none was forthcoming.

She was visibly taken aback.

Increasing the seriousness in his voice and focusing on her expression, he emphasized, "At all times, I was unaware of their mission." Noble hesitated and then admitted, "I honestly believe Simon never forgave me for shunning his invitations to join the group and, most certainly, for being the one to expose their incredible plot." Proceeding slowly, he described how Hamilton hired him to design SAVIOR. How he used SAVIOR to unleash the identity of Abner Baari, which then led him to the individual members of the group. He spoke of the interrogation in broad strokes and of the ultimate sting operation that failed in Florence. "According to the immunity agreement signed by the individuals in the group, their identities are not to be divulged. But, circumstances have changed. For now, all you need to know is that Hank Kramer was a member of La Fratellanza and was the only link between Simon and the president. Even Baari didn't know about the group. He was told that a few wealthy executives were his benefactors and wished to remain anonymous."

Max broke her silence. "Kramer. So that is why you don't want me in the meeting?"

"I know Hank, and he won't open up with you in the room."

"You think Hank is still connected to Simon?"

"I suggested to Hank on several occasions that it would be in his best interest to distance himself from Baari—a suggestion he chose not to heed entirely. However, as part of the immunity agreement, he was never to have contact with Simon. But, if Simon were to contact him, he was obliged to report it to me immediately."

It was clear by Max's demeanor that she grasped the enormity of the situation.

He continued. "Simon disappeared in 2008, but for the last eight years some of the policies established by the Baari administration seem to be linked to the situation in Utah today. By all accounts, Baari was taking directions from other sources. I believe Simon was still manipulating Baari like a puppet through Hank for unknown purposes." Noble wavered and then added, "But I think we are getting close."

"You're still convinced that Simon is involved with the tunnel that Darrow uncovered?" Max stopped abruptly and then shook her head from side to side. "My God, Darrow's murder too?"

Ignoring her questions, he hastily requested, "Show me the direction of the tunnels."

Noble stood up and walked into the conference room.

Max followed, closing the door behind as though they had entered the inner sanctum.

Standing next to the map on the large monitor, Max pointed to the arrows she had inserted.

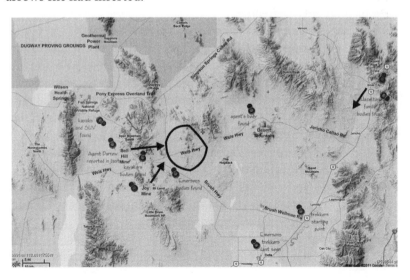

"The tunnel leading from the Bell Hill Mine heads in this direction. The tunnels at the Joy Mine and the Silver City Mine head in these directions. This is our best guess, based on the information from the troops that dug through the tunnels until they had to retreat."

She waited a moment for Noble to study her additions. Then, she noted, "The area I circled is our approximation as to the location of a subterranean facility—if it does exist. The steel door has to lead somewhere."

Noble agreed. "Max, I'm convinced we're dealing with what appears to be some sort of terrorist camp. It may seem far out, but possibly a grooming center for a future head of government." He knew he was making a great leap in deduction but, as he juggled with reality, he also knew to follow his instincts. "We have to find their escape route. Logic tells me Simon is directly involved and has to be on the scene. I can feel it."

Max detected the grim, yet confident tone in his voice.

Without further deliberation, Noble reached into his pocket for the box the Secret Service guard had left on his desk earlier that morning. "Here, take this with you to Utah. If I'm correct, you'll have the answer to your earlier questions."

Max took the box from Noble, opened it cautiously, and peered inside. She impulsively recoiled and exclaimed, "What the hell is this?"

"A thumb, Max. And if Mad Dog pulled off another miracle, it will give you access to whatever is behind that steel door."

"Simon's thumbprint!" She gasped.

Noble nodded in agreement.

"Brilliant, but where did you get it?"

"Years ago, Simon vacated an apartment in Menlo Park, California. Based on a hunch, Hamilton had the apartment searched. On the light switch near the front door, the forensic team discovered a lonely thumbprint. That's what led us to learn that Simon Hall and Mohammed al-Fadl were the same person. That thumbprint has been resting in a top-secret file I have been preserving all this time."

"Didn't Agent Burke report that the security pad was an Intelli-Pass biometric fingerprint ID system?"

"Yes, Max, I know it was designed as a two-factor authentication system that requires not only a thumb scan but also a PIN for access. Write this down—one-one-two-zero-zero-eight."

"Now where'd you get that from?"

"It's the month and year of Baari's first presidential election—and it was always Simon's password."

"You think he's still using it?" Max asked, doubtfully.

"Simon is a creature of habit, and his greatest weakness is his arrogance—believing he's always one step ahead."

"Ahead of what?"

"Not what—who. First, it was Hamilton. Now, it's yours truly."

"So, that is what you meant by his cat and mouse game?"

"Precisely." Noble paused.

Max could tell from the look on his face that he had more to say. She remained silent.

"There is something else you need to know." Then couching his words carefully, he continued, "With Simon on the loose, and knowing his capabilities, Hamilton took certain precautions. I've taken the same precautions. Should any harm come to me, should I meet a premature death, I want you to obtain a court order permitting access to a safe-deposit box at the National Depositors Trust Bank in Georgetown. The box number is six-nine-eight."

Max wanted to jump in, but resisted, and held her tongue.

"The box contains a letter to a news organization, a flash drive, and several memory sticks. They contain all the evidence and testimonies from La Fratellanza. Deliver the information according to the instructions in the letter. Hamilton also arranged with a third party to reveal the evidence in the event we both met an untimely demise. That person has since died, but I made the same provision. It's not necessary to know with whom at this time."

Up until that moment, Max had not completely understood the extent of Simon's deviousness. And, the possibility that Noble's life might be in jeopardy was not beyond the pale. She could no longer remain mute. "You think Simon is still using Hank to get to you? And Simon ultimately wants to destroy you in retaliation?" she questioned in utter disbelief.

"You have a plane to catch."

Max inhaled deeply. It was apparent Noble had ended the discussion on the subject.

"Will you be joining me after you speak with Hank?"

"I'll join you as soon as I can, but first I need to speak with a few more people here in Washington. By the way, I spoke with the base commander, and he will cooperate with you anyway he can. To start, you need to find out what is on the other side of that door."

"I'm one step ahead of you." Max returned a relaxed smile. "I've already made arrangements for Burke and several troops to enter the tunnel with me at ten o'clock tomorrow morning. In the meantime, they are still standing guard at the mine entrances. The night flights are continuing as well."

"Good work. And Max—please be careful."

"Don't worry, boss. I'll call you when I get things squared away." Max stood up and headed for the door.

"Don't forget your IMAC, and dress warmly," Noble shouted.

Max shivered at the thought, but without turning around she offered her typical backhanded wave and broadcasted, "It's already packed. I'll patch you in at noon, your time."

16
THE COVENANT

Punching in the four-digit code promptly opened the gate, giving Noble access to the interior courtyard of the housing complex. As he strolled through the garden, filled with Italian sculptures and fountains, he viewed the barren trees and longed for the lush greenery and flowers that would return in the spring. Surrounding the perimeter of the courtyard was a series of colorful townhouses in harvest hues, fashioned after mini Italian villas. This time, using his key, he entered through the back patio door and walked into the kitchen of unit number nineteen.

"Anyone home," he called out.

Silence greeted him.

They had agreed to meet that evening at seven o'clock. Noble quickly looked down at his watch and noticed for the first time in months that he was early. He grabbed a bottle of water from the fridge, sat down on the living room sofa, and thumbed through a magazine as he waited for Amanda. Moments later, he heard the sound of a key turning in the front door knob.

"Noble, are you here?"

"In the living room."

"You're early. Shocking! Think of your reputation," she teased as she walked over to give him a quick peck on the cheek.

"What did Adam say? Is he coming?"

"They'll be here at seven-thirty as agreed."

"He understands the need for absolute secrecy?"

"Yes, of course. You know his record proves he is a person of the highest integrity."

"I've only had the occasion to meet him a few times, but I am well aware of his reputation."

"Then you know you can trust him. He's looking forward to meeting with you. He'll mention to Nancy before they arrive that he'll be staying behind to meet with someone on a confidential matter of some urgency. And that I've offered up my home to assure them privacy. In fact, at dinner, I'll explain to Nancy that I acted as the intermediary to avoid possible public exposure."

"Isn't Nancy going to want to know who he is meeting with?" Noble inquired with some skepticism.

"Trust me, as a lobbyist, Adam has many clandestine meetings. She just thinks it goes with the territory. Besides, she'll look at a night out for girl talk as a real treat."

"And for you too!" Noble smiled.

"No!" Amanda punctuated. "You know I have very little interest in small talk, especially small girl talk."

"I thank you for your sacrifice." Noble averred, as he offered a slight bow.

Ignoring his jest, she continued, "When they arrive, I will escort Adam to the living room, and then Nancy and I will depart."

"Bear in mind, you are not to return before nine-thirty! I expect our conversation will take about two hours."

"Yes, Director!" She saluted derisively. "Does this make me an honorary secret agent?"

"For one night only," Noble allowed, as he leaned over to solicit a kiss, hoping for one more ardent than the one he received on her arrival.

"Now, go freshen up, they'll be here shortly," he instructed with a sheepish glance.

Amanda, with her sensual pout, challenged, "I need freshening up?"

"You look ravishing, my dear—as always—but you might want to repair your lipstick."

Amanda retreated after one more kiss.

Noble resumed flipping through the magazine.

⁓

When the doorbell rang, they assumed their posts. Amanda headed for the front door to greet her guests, while Noble made himself scarce in the bedroom.

"Please come in." Amanda waved her hand, ushering the couple into the foyer. "Nancy, it's lovely to see you again. It's been far too long."

"I'm looking forward to dinner and an opportunity to catch up." Nancy flashed Adam a curious look.

Noble, standing behind the bedroom door thought, *Enough Amanda; move it along.*

Just then, he heard her say, "Let's get going to maximize our time together." Then, she hastily informed Adam that the person he was scheduled to meet would arrive shortly. "He'll knock instead of using the doorbell. You shouldn't hesitate to answer the door."

"Thank you, Amanda, for arranging everything. Now, you two ladies get going. I'm sure you have lots to discuss." He kissed each of them on the cheek and bade them a good evening.

Finally, Noble heard the front door close. The time had arrived for his covert meeting to begin. He left the bedroom, walked into the living room, and greeted Adam with an outstretched hand.

Adam returned the handshake, but with a faintly perplexed expression. "Where did you come from?"

"I was in the bedroom waiting for the gals to leave."

"You and Amanda?" Adam inquired coyly. "I had no idea."

Noble ignored the inquisitiveness and proceeded to thank him for agreeing to meet. "Please, have a seat," he offered. Settled into chairs opposite one another, Noble stipulated, "Before we get started, you understand that this meeting is strictly off-the-record. In fact, this meeting never happened. That's why I didn't risk meeting in a public venue. It's unprecedented, but essential."

"You'll have no problem with me," Adam replied. "If my clients knew I was consorting with the enemy, it would make my job impossible. I also have some skin in the game. As you know, I began my career in Washington in the Department of Energy as Assistant Secretary for Fossil Energy. Now, I'm sitting on the other side of the fence. Besides, Amanda gave me the impression that I may have information that is mutually beneficial."

"That's true. Although I'm not at liberty to divulge the specifics of a case I'm investigating, I do have a series of questions that may potentially prove to be invaluable. Shall we proceed?"

"Fire away," Adam volunteered, as he settled more comfortably into his chair.

"I'm aware you are working with several state governments to resurrect some prior suits they had filed against the federal government." Noble asserted.

"That's correct, specifically Wyoming, Utah, and Colorado. Each case is, to some extent, different on its face. In essence, the issue is the seizure of public land by the federal government."

"Why aren't you representing the oil and gas industries directly?"

"Our strategy has changed since the Baari Administration escalated its apparent land grab."

"In what way, specifically?"

"When Baari's Omnibus Public Land Management Act of 2009 passed in the Congress, the government set out to claim a laundry list of additional land. Some of which included two hundred and fifty thousand acres of new wilderness around the Rocky Mountain National Park in Colorado and another two hundred and fifty thousand acres of wilderness near Zion National Park in Utah. And, then there's a whopping one-point-two-million acres in the Wyoming Range—get this, to protect future oil and gas leasing. Coincidently, those three states alone comprise the largest deposits of shale oil in the U.S." Adam, clearly disconcerted, elaborated. "So, because of the escalation in the change of ownership, with the euphemism *management of the land*—from the state government to the federal government—all drilling and exploration permits must be processed through the Department of the Interior. This, as you must know, is a veritable nightmare. It has become a black hole, with thousands of permits waiting for review. It's our belief that the Interior's objective is to stifle the process."

"So the frackers are waiting in a line going nowhere?"

"Precisely, even though hydraulic factoring—as you correctly referred to as fracking—has been scientifically proven to be environmentally safe. And, might I add, these delays have also been a real job killer."

"So, you believe you have a better chance working in conjunction with the affected states to recover the seized land?"

"Yes, exactly. It's a backdoor approach, but we feel it's our best chance for success."

"Are your oil and gas clients on board with this strategy?"

"We believe the odds of prevailing in the courts will increase with this strategy, and the oil and gas guys agree."

"I assume you've already reached a deal with each state that will ultimately benefit your clients?"

"Naturally. Wyoming is sitting on nearly thirty-five hundred federally approved drilling leases, Utah has over seven hundred, and Colorado has nearly five hundred. Yet, through various shenanigans, the federal government has quarantined land in many areas, which prevents the construction of roads and bridges to provide the necessary access to the drilling sites. It renders the land useless until the federal government returns the public lands to the states. At that time, the holders of the permits can then proceed, although Utah's case will be more difficult."

"Why Utah?"

"Because, a few years ago, the Secretary of the Interior arbitrarily cancelled seventy-seven drilling leases that the prior Administration had approved. In Utah's case, we will have to overcome major obstacles to have them reinstituted. But, before that can happen, we have to win our challenge to the right of eminent domain, and reclaim land that has been seized by the feds."

"It's my understanding that the federal government has claimed approximately fifty-seven percent of the land in Utah outright, and controls another fifteen percent."

"Right on. But, do you know that in Tooele and Juab counties combined, the government controls over five-point-two-million acres, more than seventy-six percent?"

"Interesting. Why do you mention those two counties specifically?" Noble asked.

"Have you heard of beryllium?"

"Isn't it some kind of rare mineral they use in metals?"

"Actually, it is an atomic element derived from the mineral bertrandite. It would be overly simplistic to say it's a metal. Beryllium is also a hardening agent that, when mixed with other metals, produces a byproduct low in density, but with high thermal conductivity. As you can see, it doesn't produce just a metal, but a valuable metal with the right characteristics for use in computers, communications satellites, aerospace, and defense—and also for the outer layers of the plutonium pits in nuclear weapons designs."

"Incredible! I had no idea." Noble was obviously amazed.

Adam continued slowly. "Recently, certain renegade countries are using beryllium as the material to clad nuclear fuel rods."

"This is all quite interesting, but where is this leading?" Noble questioned, not making the connection to Utah's Dead Zone.

"Beryllium is extremely rare and extracted only at industrial levels in the United States, Kazakhstan, and China. Take note that eighty-five percent of the beryllium ores are mined in the U.S. in the Spor Mountain area of Juab County."

"Juab!" Noble reacted uncharacteristically. Catching himself, he quickly regained his composure and stated knowingly, "Just south of Dugway." Still bewildered as to the connection, he delved further. "How does that fall in your bailiwick? I thought you represented only the oil and gas industries."

"One of my clients was the largest and only producer of beryllium in the U.S. It's vital to his company's interest that the state of Utah regains ownership of the public land, allowing free access to the drilling sites. Once access is available, the federal government's position will have no legal merit to deny the leases." Adam paused to give Noble time to grasp the issue.

"I'm following." Noble signaled him to continue.

Picking up his cue, Adam explained, "In 2009 a temporary two-year ban on new mining claims was put in place, more specifically those of my client. The administration then extended that protection until 2011 while they reportedly contemplated implementing a twenty-year ban—a clear act of pandering to the environmentalists."

"Why do you say pandering?"

"Because the language the Secretary of the Interior placed in the budget bill supposedly would remove the ban."

"Isn't that a favorable move?"

"Yes, if it had happened, but it was just an illusion. They never intended to lift the ban. We skeptics believed it was political window dressing. So, here we find ourselves in 2017 with my client still prevented from accessing some areas. As a result, the beryllium production for the U.S. has been reduced dramatically."

"So where is the beryllium coming from?" Noble inquired.

"The U.S." Adam specified.

"Now you've confused me." Noble allowed; an expression he seldom uttered.

"Here lies the crux of the problem. The administration's temporary ban I referred to earlier, was actually to give them more time to amend the 1872 Mining Act signed into law by Ulysses S. Grant. The act was created to protect mining claims on public land and the major caveat was that the claimant had to be a U.S. entity. Since then, foreign companies have established U.S. shell corporations, opening up a legal loophole, abusing the process as they mine beryllium.

"Wouldn't that incite government action?"

"Yes, and it did." Adam explained that a Canadian-owned corporation, Denison Mines, with multiple mining leases in Arizona, extracted uranium used to fuel nuclear power plants and was selling some of their uranium to South Korea's primary electric utility company, Korea Electric Power Corporation, or KEPCO. When the *Arizona Republic* reported in 2009 that KEPCO purchased seventeen percent of company shares in Denison Mines and that KEPCO also had two employees on Denison's board of directors, the federal government finally took notice of the deception.

Noble protested, "That loophole clearly creates an unfair advantage to U.S.-based corporations. It would appear that the government has no control of the resources being taken out of the country—including the profits—as the mining act is currently written."

"Exactly! During the alleged moratorium, several other Canadian-owned companies entered the picture and were awarded drilling leases—leases my client was denied. Both the IBC Advanced Alloys and Neo Material Technologies have moved my client to third place as a producer of beryllium. It's projected that the spot market for this rare mineral will promote a multi-trillion dollar commodity with an annual growth rate of ten percent per year."

"Why do you think the U.S. government gave a free pass to foreign companies?" Noble questioned.

"My personal belief, and one shared by many, is that our government is operating a two prong plan. They can exact a higher price from the foreign companies for their licenses, along with a portion of their profits. And, at the same time, use some of the revenues as subsidies to pacify U.S. companies, easing their pain."

"So, it takes on the appearance of a win-win situation all around," Noble perceived.

"Yes, for the participants and for the administration. It's more like having your cake and eating it too," Adam noted caustically. He paused for a moment, as though he had ended his summation. But, before Noble had an opportunity to respond, he asked, "Is this of any help to your case? Any possibility you can help mine?"

Noble spoke slowly, selecting his words carefully. "It's been most enlightening, and I appreciate your taking time to meet with me.

Again, it's imperative you not discuss this matter with anyone. What may seem innocuous may not be, and could do great harm to U.S. interests. The best I can do to help is to discuss the issue with the president, in the hope he can resolve any injustices. It will be up to him to reach out to your cause. We'll talk again soon."

"Thank you, Noble. It's more than I had expected."

Noble nodded in agreement and then looked at the clock on the mantle, hoping all the while that he wouldn't have to utilize the balance of his time with small talk. *Beautiful timing*, he thought, as he heard a key turning in the front door knob. Hurriedly, he stood and shook Adams hand, thanked him in haste, and dashed into the bedroom.

Adam greeted the ladies and complimented, "Your timing was perfect, my meeting ended just a few moments ago."

"I hope it was a productive meeting?" Amanda queried.

"Extremely! I assume you gals had a productive time as well?"

"Immensely! If you include the delicious food and the fine wine," Nancy teased knowing full well Adam had not yet had dinner.

"Let's not take up anymore of Amanda's evening. I'm sure she has other things that require her attention," Adam commented with a devilish grin, which Nancy didn't spot.

"I'll see you in the office bright and early." Amanda smiled as she walked them to the door. After a polite good night hug, she closed the door behind them and headed for the bedroom.

17
FEIGNED IGNORANCE

After a restless night with Simon uppermost in his thoughts, Noble was once again in his office. He sat back in his chair sipping his usual eye-opening morning coffee and mentally prepared for Hank Kramer. Once a classmate and friend at Harvard, Hank was now a former co-conspirator in a plot to defraud the American people. It was almost a decade earlier when Noble interrogated Hank and the other members of La Fratellanza. Memories of the interrogation were still as fresh as if it had occurred yesterday. Especially Hank's testimony when he pontificated brazenly. He boasted, with no sign of modesty, that he was the one personally responsible for educating and grooming the former president of United States. Even more enlightening, he claimed to have paved the way for the treasury secretary's appointment. As it developed, that was the decision that ultimately created the opportunity for Simon to infiltrate the Treasury Department to steal U.S. funds.

Noble knew he'd have to keep Hank's trademark bluster on point. In addition, he didn't trust Hank, and he couldn't be sure that he'd severed all ties to Simon—a crucial part of his immunity agreement with the SIA.

"Damn," Noble blurted out. Startled by the intercom buzzer, he knocked over his cup. A rush of coffee splattered over the file folder lying on his desk in front of him—the folder containing the map of the Dead Zone. In a hasty manner, he readjusted himself in his chair as he reached over to hit the lower left-hand button.

"Director, Mr. Kramer has arrived," Doris announced, noticeably perturbed at the visitor's tardiness.

Unlike the former administration, when Hank sailed through security, the guards now required him to turn over his smartphone and pager. Hank's chronic paranoia caused him to suspect that a guard intentionally caused him to be several minutes late. In his mind, the guard needlessly heckled him about the pager being a relic as he worked his way through security. Hank simply retorted that it was a memento.

"Give me a moment, and then send him in." Noble had no compunctions about having Hank wait for a few more minutes as he finished dabbing at the folder with stacks of napkins. Then, he heard the door handle click. He dropped the coffee-soaked papers in the waste bin and stood up to greet the former chief of staff, but remained behind the desk and simply shook his hand.

"It's been a while, Noble," Hank commented, as he perused the room. Then, with a touch of resentment, he acknowledged, "You've done well."

"Please, be seated," Noble gestured, and then remarked, "I'm sorry you've had a difficult time since Baari stepped down."

Hank was not the only one touched by the scandal. Various committees repeatedly grilled Noble. In the end, it was determined that his role, unlike Hank's, had not put the country at risk, although the congressional committees admonished him harshly for creating SAVIOR. Nonetheless, someone had to be held accountable for deceiving the American public. And, with the disappearance of Abner Baari to parts unknown, Hank had become the natural fall guy. Undoubtedly, his prominent status in the administration made him vulnerable. Now, even Hank had misgivings about all the occasions he shared in the limelight next to the president, a position he once coveted.

"Noble, I'm sure you didn't order this tête-à-tête because you're interested in my career," he complained, obviously annoyed at having been summoned.

So, he wants to play offense, Noble reasoned. Although he felt only marginally sympathetic toward Hank's self-imposed predicament, he was superficially acquiescent at times. Wasting no time, he opened the conversation directly and succinctly. "During the Baari administration, the government procured land east of the Great Basin in Utah. What was the basis for that acquisition?"

"I don't remember the details specifically, but yes, a lot of land was being appropriated in that section of the country to protect the parkland and wildlife. May I ask what this is about?" Hank inquired casually.

Noble, ignoring his question, posed another, "Whose idea was it?"

"It was part of an overall strategy to preserve national monuments." Sounding slightly exasperated this time, he stated, "Presidents have used executive orders hundreds of times since 1906, when Theodore Roosevelt signed the Antiquities Act into law."

"Thank you for the history lesson, but it doesn't answer the question. Whose idea was it to set aside the land in Utah?" Noble pressed, appearing unruffled.

"I suppose that particular land was Simon's idea," he answered impassively as he diverted eye contact.

"Simon?" Noble, apparently taken aback, quickly reminded Hank of the immunity agreement.

"I have not spoken to Simon since he vanished during the financial meltdown." Now, looking straight at Noble, he alleged, "It was an idea that gelled during the campaign when Simon laid out the plan to appease the environmentalists to curry their votes."

"Go on."

"He earmarked several acres of land for various reasons. The parcel you referred to was simply one of them."

"So Baari was only following Simon's campaign strategy, relayed by you?"

"Yes."

"Then why such an escalation of land grabs after Baari took office?"

"That's what presidents do!"

Perfect, I now have him on the defensive. Noble let him continue.

"Carter was the father of the land grabs. Under his administration, he kicked off the trend by grabbing more than fifty thousand acres in Alaska as federal land. Following suit, Clinton used his executive order—twenty-two times—claiming five-point-nine-million acres to create nineteen new monuments. Having the same insatiable appetite, Baari only continued in the same vein."

Noble knew he was making a false argument because other presidents had taken the opposite approach. He recalled that, in 1980, on the eve of Ronald Reagan's presidential nomination, he announced support for the Sagebrush Rebellion, a group of six western states fighting to take back public lands to promote urban growth through recreational, agricultural, and industrial uses. And, he vividly remembered that in 2006, the Bush Administration attempted to sell some of the national forests back to the states to raise money for the Treasury. The Democratic Congress railed against it, and the House Appropriations Committee refused to grant authority to the administration.

"Whatever the motives, there is a history of states' rights over public land. The selective pillaging of the land, placing it in the federal trove, was the issue."

Hank had missed the point.

"The heart of the Great Basin in Nevada was purportedly for scientific research to study climate change. Nine million acres of land were set aside to save the wild horses, and fifty-eight thousand acres in New Mexico were needed to protect the dune lizard and the lesser prairie chicken." Noble stared at Hank in anticipation.

"Noble, when did you become so cynical? The intent in using the 1906 Antiquities Act is to preserve our priceless legacy, our wildlife, our national monuments, and our parklands. They imposed the act for scientific, cultural, educational, and ecological studies. Who in his right mind is against that?"

"Hank, when did you become so altruistic? For that matter, when did Baari?

Hank didn't take the bait, and sat back trying to decipher what Noble was really pursuing.

"Let's switch subjects for a moment," suggested Noble, acknowledging Hank's evasiveness. "Aside from purely philanthropic reasons, what can you tell me about beryllium?"

Hank cocked his head and, with a furrowed brow, retorted, "Berry what?"

"Never mind. Did the Baari administration target specific energy-rich land to preserve as natural resources?"

Hank flinched. His poker face was beginning to fade. "Some of the acres in Utah you mentioned earlier were targeted, among others," he admitted, meekly.

"The land Simon targeted—the acreage you convinced Baari to set aside as federal property?" Noble, knowing the answer, summarily fired off another question before Hank had a chance to respond. "Why was Baari so intent on stirring up the Middle-East, further putting at risk our energy dependency on the Arab states?" He wasn't exactly sure of the relevance of the second question, but he was interested in Hank's body language, as well as his responses.

He was sclerotic, without a trace of reaction. Avoiding all of Noble's questions, Hank asserted without expression, "I don't understand. The land is now federally owned, Baari is no longer in office, and Simon has vanished." But, privately, he thought *Simon's past requests on the surface seemed unrelated, until now. Why would Noble bring up the Middle East? He is just fishing.* Hank continued to play innocent. "Where are you going with this?"

Without further adieu, Noble ended the meeting. "Hank, I'm sorry to have taken up so much of your time. Thanks for coming in."

"That's it? Thanks!"

"Okay, how have you been?"

"Miserable."

"I'm truly sorry the press has been so harsh on you, and that the political sharks haven't let up, if that's any consolation."

Noble stood up.

Hank took the cue.

As they headed for the door, Hank turned and offered Noble his hand, along with a parting shot. "It appears Simon is still messing with your mind." His half-grin immediately deflected Noble's probing mind.

Just then, the phone rang and Noble turned to pick up the receiver. When he looked back at Hank, he had already walked out the door.

18
TRIPWIRE ACT

Noble hit the flashing button on his phone and answered his private line. "Max, trust you had a good trip?" he joshed, then waited for the onslaught.

"Have you ever flown on a military transport? They're uncomfortable as hell." Her irritation dripped with each word.

"You made it there safely," he pointed out. "Now, are you ready to enter the mine?"

"Yes, I'm outside the Bell Hill Mine with Agent Burke and four army privates. They managed to get more Segways into the new tunnel using a pulley system, but the old part of the mineshaft can only be managed on foot, so we'll have to walk the first mile."

"Have you patched me in?" he asked eagerly.

"Turn on the touch-screen monitor and see for yourself."

"Hold on a minute. I'm in my office." Noble put the call on hold and walked into his conference room. He hit the speakerphone button on the other phone and at the same time, turned on the large display. "Wow!" he exclaimed, astounded by the view. "Beautiful country out there."

"It's gorgeous, but there's some bad stuff happening out here," she countered with concern.

"Just be careful, Max." Noble also sensed some uneasiness but refocused on the screen. "You're coming through loud and clear and the IMAC is working fine. Move your head around so I can see how the panning works." The agency was currently testing the latest version of the IMAC, an Internet Microphone and Camcorder device that looks similar to a Bluetooth earpiece. It comes with a built-in webcam, and connects to the Internet wirelessly. "This state-of-the-art technology is amazing." Even the unflappable Noble was impressed.

"I know. It operates with an ultra-wide angle optical lens that produces amazing 3-D clarity, and the innovative anti-shaking technology surpasses all other webcam devices."

"Now, who's the techie?"

"Me! How's the panning so far?" Max asked, tiring from moving her head about.

"The panning works fine. It's so clear, I feel as though I'm standing next to you." Noble reached for the button on the speakerphone. "I'm letting the IMAC take over now."

Max heard the line go dead on her smartphone. She hung up as well.

The IMAC had successfully synced wirelessly, providing visual streaming on the display monitor. They would communicate orally through the speaker system. "We are good to go!" he called out. All was functioning, so Noble sat back and watched the operation commence on the large screen in front of him. "Do you have that little gift I gave you?"

"Tucked right here in my pocket. Are you ready to rock and roll?"

Noble took a deep breath and then cautioned Max again. "We don't know what we are dealing with. Be careful, and let the soldiers lead the way. You and Burke keep a safe distance behind."

"Roger that. Let's go," Max ordered, gesturing to the soldiers to enter the mine.

လၥာ

Noble sat with a touch of apprehension while he watched the entire passage from his conference room. He could see the four soldiers in the lead and could hear Max telling Burke, "Stay close behind."

"Noble, is everything okay on your side? We're descending into the mineshaft rapidly at a sharp angle. I just pray you don't lose the signal."

"Just keep talking." Noble could see them head down into the mine.

Each of them was wearing a hardhat with a headlight. From his view, he could tell they were beginning to level off. The tunnel appeared to be about six feet by six feet. Max, taller than the rest, had to stoop after they entered the mineshaft to maintain a clear vision, sparing Noble a screen featuring only her feet for the remaining miles.

Thirty minutes into the trek, the view changed dramatically.

"Noble, are you seeing this?" Max was awestruck.

"Incredible!" On the large display in front of him was a concrete tunnel, approximately ten feet wide by nine feet high, and fully lighted. He also could see six Segways off to the side. "Are you sure the Colonel claimed this wasn't part of a military facility?"

"I spoke to him directly. They have no knowledge of anything like this."

"Max, have you ever ridden a Segway?"

She could hear Noble chuckle and rejoined fearlessly, "No, but it looks like fun."

"You're not there to have fun."

"I know—be careful!" she mocked.

"You should be there in about twenty minutes. Take it slow as you approach the last quarter mile," Noble cautioned. He continued to fixate on the screen as they sped through what looked to be, basically, a straight tunnel.

Abruptly, chatter on the other end ceased—all eyes were focused ahead.

Noble checked his watch and noted that they should be approaching the end of the tunnel within minutes. "Max, are you still there?"

"What! You can't hear my heart pounding?"

"Just take it slow and hope Mad Dog worked another miracle. Remember—let the soldiers enter first. We have no idea what is behind the door."

"What do you mean *hope* Mad Dog..."

Noble cut her off short and responded encouragingly, "You'll be fine." Just then, he could see them approach the large steel blast door Agent Darrow had described. To the right was the security pad.

"It's show time," Max whispered, as she dismounted her Segway.

Noble heard Max in a hushed voice instruct the soldiers to enter first. Then he saw her approach the steel door. As Max looked down, Noble could see her pull the box from her pocket and place the prosthesis over her right thumb.

"This better work," Max mumbled, then she looked over toward

Burke and the soldiers and said, "Don't ask." She took a deep breath and proceeded to place her thumb on the fingerprint pad. Suddenly, a green light flashed. Max inhaled deeply again, took a few quick gulps, and then punched in the numbers 112008. Instantly, a second green light flashed.

Noble felt as though he was watching the entire operation in slow motion, but it had all taken place with precise timing.

Quickly, Max reached for the door handle. At that moment, more than just one heart was beating at a fast pace. She stood behind the door, with the agent to her side. The four soldiers positioned themselves on the opposite side, ready to enter. Slowly, Max dragged the handle downward and promptly pulled the steel door in her direction.

The troops moved in.

Seconds later, Max and Agent Burke heaved a sigh of relief as they heard someone shout, "All clear!"

Even Noble eased slightly back off the edge of his chair.

"Noble, are you still there?" Max spoke softly.

"I'm watching it all with bated breath. Go easy."

Noble stared at the screen and eyed the massive room filled with cubicles and office equipment. It looked to be the size of a typical big box store without the massive shelving. He continued to watch as the soldiers moved guardedly from desk to desk, looking for signs of activity.

Max and Agent Burke stood back and surveyed the room. Then, as the serial *all clears* were shouted, Max and the agent moved in and scoured the individual office areas for clues as to their former inhabitants. They counted over a dozen computer monitors and keyboards, stacks of unused paper and pens galore, but no hard drives, and no telephones.

"Over here!" Max heard one of the soldiers call out.

Agent Burke was the first to dash toward the shout. Max immediately followed behind.

"We discovered these two guys shouting from a locked room over there." The soldier pointed.

"The minute we broke the lock and opened the door, they started spewing about how they had been kidnapped," the other soldier reported dubiously.

Standing next to the soldiers were two clearly frightened young men who looked to be in their mid-twenties, although seeing them handcuffed made them appear less terrified and more menacing.

Both soldiers stood on guard with hands on pistols.

Max entered the area and briefly interrogated the two men with a series of questions.

While Noble listened intently, he heard them explain that they had been camping near the Joy Mineshaft when captured.

Simultaneously, Max and Noble concluded they had found their trekkers.

The captives claimed that one night someone invaded their campsite and knocked them unconscious. When they were awakened, they found themselves locked in a room. Allegedly, it was the same room where the soldiers found them.

"What did they want from you?" Noble heard Max ask.

The brawniest of the pair spoke first. "Over the past two weeks, several attempts were made to recruit us—to join what they called *the cause*—but we resisted," he claimed with brio.

The other, seemingly more cognizant of the situation, stated, "The prime goal of the camp was to recruit us to join them to help purge the world of non-Islamic influences—in essence, destroy the western culture." He continued to describe how their captors tried various techniques, short of outright torture, to convince them to sign up. "It was abundantly clear that a positive answer was our only salvation, and time was short. We were about ready to relent to save our skins and to buy time."

Noble shook his head in disbelief. He sensed Max was thinking the same.

"Fortuitously, their captors stumbled upon two virile young men testing their endurance in that unforgiving part of the country— obviously, prime candidates for a terrorist mission." Max heard Noble articulate through her earpiece. "Did they hear or see anything that would lead us to the terrorist members of the camp?"

Max repeated Noble's question, directing it to the more responsive trekker.

"A few days before, it sounded like everyone was packing up in preparation to leave in haste. During that time, four men arrived. I remember overhearing one of them say that they cycled to the camp. I thought it odd, given the temperatures outside. From their conversation, I got the impression they were new recruits," he speculated.

Max then showed each of them the photo of Mohammed al-Fadl. They both nodded, acknowledging they did not recognize him.

Max sighed.

Noble remained stalwart. Nevertheless, he sounded a tad disappointed. "If they turn out to be our missing cyclists, then four more young men willing to commit terrorist acts against their own country have slipped through our fingers." Reverting swiftly to form, he ordered, "For your own safety, keep the trekkers handcuffed and under military control until we can conduct a more thorough investigation back at the base."

Max relayed the command.

The soldiers nodded in agreement.

While Noble had focused on Max's activities, he was unaware that Agent Burke and the two other soldiers had been surveying the rest of the facility until Max looked over in Burke's direction. Now viewing a different scene from the IMAC, Noble grilled her with his storied impatience. "Did they find any documentation, computers, any evidence as to who was there?"

Max shouted out the question to Agent Burke.

"It looks as though they had time to destroy everything that would leave any clues," he replied.

Behind the agent, in the far corner on the opposite end of the room from where they had entered, appeared another series of doors.

Max walked over to where one soldier had just opened one of those doors.

Noble immediately eyed a large shredder. From the debris on the floor, someone ostensibly had been working overtime. "Max, I want all of the shredding brought back."

"Okay," she responded.

Noble could hear her issue the order.

As Agent Burke continued to peruse the rest of the office cubicle, Max continued to follow behind two of the soldiers. Every time they opened a door, Max was ordered to step back while they investigated the room. Each room proved to be primarily private office spaces, containing only a desk and a few chairs.

"Are you thinking what I'm thinking?" she muttered.

One of the soldiers looked over to Max, ready to respond. He then realized she was talking to the director on the other end of her IMAC.

"The cyclists reached their goal. It looks like we found their recruiting center," Noble answered.

"Or, perhaps, an indoctrination center," she added.

"But, for what? Purge the world of non-Islamic influences? I'm not so sure. It sounds a bit farfetched."

As Max listened to Noble, she spotted something on the floor near one of the doors they had not yet opened. She headed in that direction.

"Stand back!" a soldier called out. "Ma'am, let us enter first."

"I'm just looking at something on the floor." As Max leaned over, Noble felt a jolt, as though he had grabbed a live wire. He glared at the screen and watched Max's hand reach for a flash drive near the bottom rail of the door—a flash drive etched with the initials *LF*.

"Boom!" echoed a loud blast through Noble's speaker system that seemed to shake the room. The scene on the monitor began spinning rapidly out of control. Abruptly, a cloud of smoke rushed toward Noble as though it would pierce the touch-screen display and envelop him.

Then, a silence shrouded the room.

The spinning stopped—and everything reverted to slow motion.

Those last few moments seemed surreal. Even Noble found himself brushing off his jacket as if he was covered in debris.

"Max! Max!"

Without missing a beat, Noble grabbed his phone and hit the speed dial button for Dugway. "Get me the Colonel. This is Director Bishop."

"He's standing right here, sir. One moment, please," the sergeant replied.

"Director, I know about the explosion."

"What the hell happened?"

"All I know is that one of my men guarding the Bell Hill Mine reported the blast. I've dispatched emergency vehicles to the area. They should be arriving momentarily."

"Agent Burke is on line two," the sergeant interrupted.

"Director, I have Agent Burke on the other line."

"Can you conference me in?"

"Yes, hold on. Agent Burke, this is Colonel Evans. I have Director Bishop on the line as well."

Moments later Noble heard a voice say, "Director."

Oh my God, he thought. "Where's Max?" he yelled, while at the same time feeling guilty. *That should have been me.*

"Director Bishop, Max will be okay. She had the wind knocked out of her and has a nasty cut on her head, but her pulse is good."

"What the hell happened?" Noble demanded in a feigned, calmer tone.

The agent, noticeably shaken, described the events in rapid-fire succession. "Evidently, one of the soldiers turned the knob on the door near where Max was standing. The door appeared to have been booby-trapped to set off a grenade when it was opened. The blast knocked all of us to the ground! Rocks and debris were flying everywhere!"

The Colonel cut in. "Calm down, Burke. The other soldiers; how are they?"

"Two are dead, sir. They took the brunt of the blast and were killed instantly." His speech pattern slowed, and he sounded dazed. "The other soldiers and the two men we are detaining are okay. They were on the other side of the room at the time of the explosion."

"Burke, are you all right?" The concern in Noble's voice was intense.

"Just a few scrapes and bruises. Nothing of any consequence, sir."

"Can you tell what is on the other side of the door?" Noble inquired in a steadier voice.

"Sir, right now the entrance is completely blocked. I can't see how far it extends. Wait a minute! Can you see it on your screen, Director? I'm holding Max's IMAC."

"No, it's completely blank. The blast must have knocked out the webcam. Thank god your smartphone works and we didn't lose communication." Although relieved, Noble was surprised.

The agent noted the tone of the director's voice and responded, "I'm amazed it works. Whoever operates this place must have found a way to boost the satellite signal. That would explain the absence of any telephones."

Without warning, Noble heard a moaning sound in the background.

Agent Burke must have also. He looked down. "Hold on sir, she's coming around." He handed Max his smartphone, and Noble heard a welcomed voice.

"Noble, we lost two soldiers in the blast," she reported, understandably stunned.

"Burke filled me in on what happened. Thank God you're not injured seriously."

"My dates might not think so. I think I took some shrapnel to the head," Max lamented as she reached for her temple, only to encounter blood streaming down her face. Fortunately, the wound was superficial. She held the smartphone to her ear and waited for an encouraging retort, something to erase the horror of what just occurred. There was no response. "Noble, are you there?"

The Colonel, still listening on the other line, remained silent and allowed the conversation to ensue between the director and his deputy without interruption. *It's their show*, he thought.

"Yes, I'm trying to absorb the enormity of the blast that killed two soldiers and could have killed you." Noble paused. "Max, I don't mean to be insensitive, but do you still have the flash drive?"

"What drive?"

"Max, are you sure you're all right?"

"Oh, yeah, hold on." Max slowly reached into her pocket. "Noble, it's gone," she gasped. "I must have dropped it in the explosion."

Noble could hear the pain resonate in her voice, but she persisted. "I recall there were initials etched on the drive. What do you think they mean?" As she envisioned the two letters, she suddenly blurted out, "L-F—La Fratellanza—you think it's his?"

"Max, now listen to me. Forget all this for now and get to the base."

"But, Noble."

Noble was cognizant that others were listening. He ignored her plea. "Tomorrow, I want the base forensic team to scour the place for prints, hair, anything, everything, and the flash drive. Have them look through all the shredded paper to see if they can match anything that will give us a clue as to what kind of operation was really being run down there. Also, bring in some troops to start digging through the debris, but as soon as they find an opening they are not—I repeat—*not* to enter the tunnel. Stand down until I get back to you."

"You think there are more facilities like this? You think that's where the occupants are hiding out, somewhere in the complex?"

"Yes, to both questions and, if we are lucky, the elusive leader will be among them."

Noble was careful not to mention Simon by name. He knew Max would follow his cue.

"Where do you think the tunnel leads?" Max inquired, knowing she might regret the answer.

"My best guess—to an underground terrorist camp." Noble, aghast at his own words, was glad Max was not in the room to see his expression.

"If that's so, what about escape routes?" Max probed further.

Noble swiftly reviewed the situation with Max. The Colonel listened. "Continue to have all three mines guarded and have the soldiers and the feds look for any suspicious movement in the surrounding areas," he instructed. He knew he didn't need to remind her to be circumspect and trusted she'd heed caution when dealing with everyone she encountered.

Then, not wanting to delay their departure any further and to provide the medical attention they needed, the Colonel finally interrupted and announced. "Excuse me Director, but the ambulances have arrived and are standing by at the mineshaft. They won't be able to bring the stretchers into the tunnel. Max, can all of you return through the tunnel using the Segways?"

"Hold on, sir."

Noble and the Colonel could hear Max ask the soldiers if they could carry their fallen comrades on their shoulders. Their response was affirmative. She could also be heard instructing the soldiers to arrange for the two trekkers to ride the two Segways that unfortunately, became available with the demise of the two troops.

Noble broke up the conversation. "Max, I want them handcuffed to the transporters. They are to ride behind the soldiers and in front of you and Burke. You are in no shape, but instruct Burke to shoot if necessary. Let's not assume they are innocent. Now, get back to base and have the medic check you out. I need you to be in top shape."

"Noble, can you send me my other IMAC?"

"I'll have it to you in the morning. Later, Max." The sound from the speaker system ceased.

While Max was speaking with Noble, Agent Burke had removed his jacket and had managed to tear off the left sleeve of his shirt. He wrapped the sleeve securely around the wound on Max's head, a lesson he had learned in his first-aid training.

Max passed on Noble's orders.

"Are you sure you can you handle the trip back? We can both try to go on one Segway," Burke suggested.

Max, clearly touched, replied stoically, "I can make it on my own, thanks."

To be on the safe side, the agent trailed closely behind, keeping a close eye on Max, as well as the two trekkers.

Max, wobbly at times, managed the ride, a ride she would never forget.

The return trip through the tunnel was slower and more solemn. The only sound she sensed was the pounding in her head. She watched as they followed behind the two trekkers. In front of them were the two soldiers on Segways, each carrying one of his mates draped around their shoulders.

19
WAASP FOR SAVIOR

Hours earlier, the sun had lowered in the sky, casting an orange and pink hue over the Rhône River. The sunset should have signaled the end of day for Director Enzo Borgini. But, it was another day at Interpol working with SAVIOR—guaranteeing several more hours of work. Enzo was convinced that his wife suspected he was harboring a mistress. Unlike his Italian counterparts, however, he had spent most evenings with a cold computer program on steroids. It was nine o'clock in the evening when he finally decided to call it a night.

Just as he began to assemble his papers and place them in his briefcase, his smartphone rang. He placed his phone securely between his left ear and shoulder and continued to shuffle his papers as he broadcasted, "I'm leaving right now." As he held his breath and waited for the maternal blitz, he heard, "Ciao Enzo, it's Noble." Startled, he realized it wasn't his wife calling. "Hold on a second." He switched the phone to his right hand, sat back down in chair, and hoped it wouldn't be a long conversation. "What a coincidence. I had planned to call you tomorrow and update you on the case."

"I can't wait to hear—but first I need a gigantic favor." The tentativeness in Noble's voice came through loud and clear.

Enzo picked-up on the tenor, which only added to his trepidation.

"Should I be glad I'm already sitting down for this one?"

"I need the WAASP," Noble asked reticently, knowing he wasn't supposed to be aware of the top secret testing of a new aerial surveillance system—but it would be crucial to his investigation—and time was of the essence.

It was a known fact that, in 1985, the Swedish National Defense Research Agency for their Ministry of Defense, conducted a theoretical study to test the first prototype of the Coherent All Radio BAnd Sensing program, known as Carabas, manufactured by the Swedish company Saab. Carabas uses SAR, synthetic-aperture radar technology, but its capacity exceeds the 20-90 megahertz frequency interval in the VHF band, utilized by typical SAR imaging.

"Your government is already using the Carabas II!" Enzo underscored, believing Noble was fully aware.

"I know, Enzo, but let me enlighten you," he needled, and then switched to an increasingly professorial tone. "Since 1996, my government has installed the Carabas II on our UAVs. In fact, in 2003, our government spent over one billion dollars for Unmanned Aerial Vehicles for the first time. But, you know, I'm not talking about the Carabas II—I need the WAASP!" he emphasized.

"Noble, how do you..." Enzo stopped in mid-sentence, and then quickly relented, "Oh never mind. Hamilton always remarked that you were the best," he sighed, knowing full well that Noble knew Interpol was working on their own secret version of the Carabas II.

The Wide-Area Aerial Surveillance Penetration system, called WAASP, went beyond the capabilities of Carabas II. The Carabas II ignored vegetation and reflected off manmade objects, but could detect only those objects under foliage and below the surface, limited to a depth of twenty feet of penetration. The technology had been indispensable as a military and law enforcement tactical defense weapon used to thwart illegal activity, such as drugs and arms smuggling. And, although it was vital in terrorist surveillance, it didn't have the capabilities of the WAASP.

"You know the Carabas II's limitations. That's why I need the WAASP!" Noble reiterated firmly, and with equal animation. "I know you're aware the technology has been further advanced, and its SAR capability can detect underground structures at greater depths through solid objects, including mountains."

"*Mama mia*, What are you looking for—Atlantis?" Enzo jested.

"You might say that," Noble replied in a more serious demeanor.

"So, can you help me out? I just need it for a day. Oh, I also need it retrofitted for an Apache helicopter."

"And, I assume there will be a limited number of people who will know about this?" Enzo inquired in a dubious tone.

Noble sensed he had won Enzo over and assured him, "Only a highly select group with top security clearance credentials will be engaged. Please arrange to have it sent to the base commander at the Dugway Proving Ground in Utah. I'll give him a heads up."

"Noble, it's Friday night. The best I can do is to get it there on Monday." Then, with no hint of capitulation, he ordered, "I want it back in my possession no later than next Wednesday. *Capito?*"

"I understand. I owe you one," he stated, clearly relieved.

"You're right. You owe me big time! By the way, does this request come with the president's authorization?" Enzo quizzed with a degree of skepticism.

"Umm, not yet. I'm scheduled to give him an update in a few hours." He impulsively added, "Don't worry, he'll concur. Besides, I'm putting my career on the line for this case."

"You and me both, my friend. Mind telling me what's happening, Noble?" Enzo had been in the business long enough to know everything functioned on a need-to-know basis. Trying to snoop on a pro got you nowhere. Absent a response from Noble, he added apologetically, "I thought I'd try."

"Would you like to tell me what's happening with your case, Enzo? Noble was itching to know the results of his findings, especially whether there were any definitive links to Simon.

"I had planned to review the case with you tomorrow, but I guess now is as good a time as any. First, I have to call my wife to let her know I'll be late, again. I'll most likely end up with cold pasta and warm wine thanks to you." He chuckled. "I also need to set up the video conference. Give me about ten minutes."

"Fine, I'll get set up on this end. Ciao for now." Noble hung up the phone.

Noble collected his file folders, walked into his conference room, turned on his monitor, and waited for Enzo's call. Meanwhile, he scribbled a few notes to prepare for his meeting with the president. After all, he had already taken it upon himself to authorize valuable resources, followed by the request to bring in top secret technology from another country under the radar—all based on logic, but nonetheless conjecture. Even the dumping of Agent Darrow's body in the middle of the Dead Zone could simply be an unbelievable coincidence. And, based to a large degree on inconclusive evidence, his sensors still told him that Simon was behind the events in Utah and in Europe. The thumbprint was the giveaway making the link. He also needed to speak with Paolo, his brother-in-law, the former president's communications director and speechwriter—and he needed his hands on the flash drive Max was hopefully able to recover. *Things are moving too fast*, he admitted to himself.

Without warning, a beeping sound emitted from the phone system built into the video monitor.

Noble walked over and hit the button.

Enzo appeared on the screen.

"That was quick," Noble responded as he sat back down in his chair. His computer was poised to record the facts.

"I'm anxious to go home. The wife was none too happy."

Noble could see the sparkle in Enzo's eyes, suggesting he was just as anxious to fill him in on the results of his findings. Directly behind him, Noble could see the two massive touch-screens, already displaying some of the evidence from the New Year's Eve bombings. He loved the state-of-the-art technology and, with his video monitor, he felt as though he was in the same room as Enzo. For a moment, it caused him to recall fondly the exhilaration he felt the first time he reviewed the evidence of the European investigations during his visit to Lyon.

"Where do you want to start?" Enzo asked.

Noble could see vividly the still shot of the limo in flames on the left-hand screen. On the right-hand screen was the photo of Chancellor Mauer lying on the ground behind the podium. "Let's start with Paris."

Enzo walked over and stood next to the screen on the left. "We rechecked the forensic evidence from the bomb fragments and everything stands as before. P-E-T-N was used as the explosive and it was meant to implode—not explode as you previously observed."

"What about the truck?" Noble asked eagerly.

"I was just getting to that. I took your advice, and we were able to focus in on the face peering out the driver's side of the unmarked white van." Enzo explained how they were able to take a digital photo and capture about three quarters of his face, but the resolution was extremely low. "However, using face hallucination technology to produce a super–resolution of the image, we were able to run the photo through our Facial Recognition System. And we produced a match."

"Okay, so who is he?" Noble's impatience was coming to the fore.

"His name is Said Ahmed and he is a French citizen of Moroccan descent. He was one of the profiles SAVIOR placed in the *Hot Spot*. We have not been able to locate him yet, but we were able to ascertain that he has made at least three trips to Pakistan in the last four years. Currently, we have him on our watch list."

"But what is his connection to the explosion?"

"We showed the photo to the guards at the Elysée Palace, and one of them remembered him being at the palace on New Year's Eve."

"What caused them to remember him on an evening when hundreds of people must have been coming and going through the palace gates?"

"According to the guard, Ahmed pulled up to the palace entrance in a florist truck to deliver a large flower arrangement. The guard remembered telling him that he had to make his delivery through the rear gate. Evidently, Ahmed explained that he had only one arrangement to deliver and he was running late for his next delivery."

"So the guard allowed him to leave the flowers at the front entrance." Noble leaped to an obvious conclusion.

"Yes, but when Ahmed returned to his truck it wouldn't start. After several attempts, he explained to the guard that he would have to call the florist shop and arrange to have the truck towed away. He then told the guard that he would wait at the entrance for his colleague to arrive."

"That still doesn't explain the unmarked van and how he knew about the decoy limo," Noble insisted.

"Wait a minute. It gets better. First, we tracked down Ahmed's brother-in-law who works in a garage—at none-other-than the Elysée Palace. We have him in custody, and I suspect he is about to give up the whereabouts of Ahmed."

"So, he knew about the decoy limo and informed Ahmed? He must have also told him which florists were on the approved list."

"Exactly! We also have surveillance tapes showing Ahmed entering an unmarked, white van outside the palace gates. In addition, we contacted the owner of the florist shop and discovered there is no record of a Said Ahmed working for his company. The owner insists that their truck had been stolen on the afternoon of New Year's Eve, which he had reported."

"Good job. So, we now know the bomb was attached to the car, most probably by the brother-in-law, and Ahmed was able to separate

the president's limo from the decoy limo. It allowed sufficient time for
the implosion, creating the impression it was an assassination attempt
without actually killing the president. But is there any connection to
Simon?"

"The only connection SAVIOR made was that Ahmed and Simon
had both traveled to Pakistan in the same time period."

Noble then glanced at the horrific sight on the screen to the right.
The German Chancellor was lying on the ground with two police
officers over her body to shield her from the rapid fire of bullets. "Let's
go over the Berlin shootings," he urged.

"In this case, I ignored your advice." Enzo's broad smile was clearly
visible to Noble on the monitor. "We placed the podium in the upright
position and we were able to determine that the trajectory of bullets
had originated from the Ritz Carlton Hotel at Potsdamer Platz 3."

"Wasn't it reported that there were unusually high winds that
evening? I recall there was even concern for the fireworks display."

"The reports were slightly exaggerated. But using calculations for
windage, the bullets appeared to come from either the fifteenth or
sixteenth floor. We searched all the rooms on both floors that faced the
Tiergarten, located west of the Brandenburg Gate."

"Did you find any shell casings?"

"Not only shell casings, but a fingerprint on one of the casings,"
Enzo bragged. "I have to give credit to SAVIOR, though, for first
identifying the suspect."

"The suspense is killing me." Noble raised his hands to let Enzo
know he was impatiently waiting for that link to Simon.

"The print belongs to a Syrian national named Badi al-Diri, who
spent time at the same training camp as Simon, or rather Mohammed
al-Fadl, near Kursu in Srinagar. We picked him up at the Berlin
Brandenburg Airport as he was boarding a 12:55 flight on Qatar
Airways heading for Karachi."

"I knew it!" Noble exclaimed, barely audible, but loud enough for
Enzo to hear. "Good work, but how did he know precisely when the
chancellor would end her speech?"

"We interviewed her entire staff, except for one person who worked
in the copy room. The clerk never returned to work after New Year's
Eve. Thus far, we have been unable to track him down. He lives alone,
and with no apparent family that we were able to contact. Basically,
he's a loner. I'm dubious as to whether he has ties to Simon or our
sharpshooter. Chances are he was paid off simply to deliver an advance

copy of the speech to the plotters. We still plan on bringing him in for questioning, as soon as we locate him."

"That leaves us with the London bombing." Noble urged him on.

"You're aware that we identified the bomb fragments, and it was a simple design using ammonium nitrate and an electronic detonator, but we discovered two additional clues." Observing Noble's eagerness, Enzo spoke more rapidly. "The bomb in Paris had a magnetic casing, and attached easily under the carriage of the limo, but the bomb in London was attached with half-inch screws to the table where the Prime Minister would have been sitting."

"So, that means the bomb was brought in with the table and not placed there afterwards."

"You're quite right. That's why we interviewed the supervisor from the Event Hire Company, who delivered the tables and chairs. His name is Karim Yakob, an American-born Saudi, and his print matches the partial print we found on one shard of the detonator." He paused and, then with disappointment, stated, "Sorry, in this case there is no obvious link to Simon, according to SAVIOR." Enzo could see Noble's discouraged face looking out from the video monitor and, in an attempt to lift his spirits, proceeded. "There were some additional findings the forensic team happened upon."

"Continue," Noble responded, not in the mood for delay.

"We retraced our steps and compared both of the bombs from Paris and London to see if we could find any similarities. None were found, but the dissimilarities are what caught our attention."

Enzo caught the look on Noble's face. It was evident he had his attention. "As you know, a typical bomb, for this purpose, is made with three basic components: the detonator, a high explosive charge, and a metal casing."

"Right, so we know the detonators were different. The explosives were different. One bomb was in a magnetic casing and the other was a metal casing attached to the table with screws. So how does the fact that they are different lead you to a conclusion?" Noble was obviously perplexed.

"Not a conclusion—necessarily—but a puzzling clue."

"That's helpful."

Enzo ignored his snide remark and continued. "The bomb in Paris was made out of simple materials, easily obtainable. However, the London bomb was encased in a metal that is not only rare, but extremely expensive—not a material your average terrorist would stockpile!" he emphasized. "The detonator used a metal wire, point-eight-five millimeters in diameter and point-zero-five meters in length. One reel costs over five hundred dollars." Enzo caught sight of Noble's gaze. "Wait, it gets even crazier. The bomb casing was lined with a metal foil, point-two-five millimeters in thickness and twenty-nine millimeters in diameter. One disc costs over fourteen hundred dollars. Using that metal to build a bomb doesn't make any sense!"

Before Noble had the opportunity to interrupt, Enzo added, "Allegedly, the properties of this metal are designed to increase the force of the explosion. It is also used as one of the components in nuclear weapons."

Noble, an ocean away, sat in disbelief.

For Enzo, it seemed as though he were sitting directly across from him. "Are you all right?" His concern was noticeable.

"We have our connection to Simon—it's beryllium!" Noble blurted out, then quickly regained his composure.

"How did you know?" Enzo asked, also visibly stunned.

"I'll call you when the WAASP arrives. Now, Enzo, go home to your wife."

The video monitor went blank.

20
THE FORGOTTEN LAIR

Any chance I can get in to see him now?" Noble requested.

"He should be finished with his meeting momentarily, but then he's expected in the Press Briefing Room in fifteen minutes," explained the officious voice on the other end of the line.

"I only need ten," he pleaded.

"Why do you always do this to me, Noble? Get down here now, and I'll see what I can do."

"You're a doll, thanks! Am I allowed to say doll?"

"Only to me, sweetie."

He smiled as he heard the click on the phone.

After the inauguration, and at the request of the newly elected President Randall Post, Noble's office moved from the ground floor of the West Wing up to the second floor. The move also elevated his stature among his colleagues. However, his staff was still scattered among the undisclosed buildings around Washington, where covert greets you at the front door. Luckily for him, he was still just a stairway from the president and could scoot down the stairs to the Oval Office.

"He's waiting for you." She winked.

As Noble entered the Oval Office, the president stood up from behind his desk chair, walked over to Noble, and motioned him toward the sofa.

"Mr. President, thank you for agreeing to see me."

"Make it quick, Noble. I've only a few minutes, but I gather this is urgent," he surmised, as he sat down across from him on an identical sofa.

"Sir, you are aware that the mysterious deaths in Utah have been declared homicides."

"Yes."

Noble proceeded cautiously. He filled him in on the death of Agent Darrow, the discovery of the tunnel, the underground facility, and the explosion causing the death of two soldiers. He provided an overview of the evidence Enzo had uncovered as it related to the bombings in Europe. He informed the president that it was highly probable Mohammed al-Fadl was involved in each of the events. Moreover, he admitted to borrowing the top-secret WAASP from Interpol.

The president listened patiently, showing no emotion. Then he unleashed. "So you believe there is an underground training camp organized for the purpose of recruiting and training terrorists? That in some way it is connected to the New Year's Eve bombings. And, a head of state may have been an actual target to be replaced by a mole waiting in the wings? And you believe al-Fadl is orchestrating all of this?" the president challenged.

"Yes, sir," Noble responded. "We now know that the election of Abner Baari was merely a dry run for an even broader plot coordinated by al-Fadl, masquerading as Simon Hall. It provided him the opportunity to test his ability to infiltrate the top levels of our government and its most confidential components."

"How can we be sure he is connected to both events in Utah and in Europe? Do you have actionable intelligence?"

Noble, self-assuredly, explained, "Before the explosion, Max Ford, my deputy director, came upon a flash drive. I am positive it's Simon's, or as you referred to him, al-Fadl. Max is combing through the debris trying to locate the drive that was lost during the blast. We're hoping to be able to analyze it shortly. I'm confident it will provide us with vital information. And, of course, there was the London bomb, made with beryllium components, which I described earlier." Noble stopped suddenly, and on impulse changed his tone to an even more serious demeanor. "Sir, with all due respect, we need to move swiftly. If Simon is operating from an underground facility, we need to find him before he can execute any part of his plan."

"A plan you're not even sure exists?"

"Yes, sir," Noble allowed.

The president, in a more conciliatory tone, prompted, "You have faith that with the capabilities of the WAASP you can identify the underground camp, the one you suspect is located somewhere under a mountain in Utah?"

"Mr. President, the WAASP will narrow down the amount of ground we'd have to cover. We need to know what we are dealing with before we proceed further and, most important, we need to seal off any possible exits." Noble was beginning to feel a sense of support.

The president glanced at the clock resting on the fireplace mantel on the north side of the room. He realized he had only a few minutes more. "Show me exactly the territory you are talking about." He reached over and picked up the remote control device on the coffee table. Instantly, a large touch-screen monitor lowered from the ceiling, stopping in front of the fireplace.

Noble, on cue, stood up, walked over to the monitor, and selected the electronic map app. After he tapped the screen several times, he zoomed in on the state of Utah. Then, as the president watched, he typed in the coordinates. On the top of the screen, the president viewed the following numbers and letters: **39°40'12.71775" N-112° 35'43.5973" W.**

Within seconds, the screen zoomed in on the Dead Zone.

Noble turned around and was surprised to see the president reach for the phone receiver and hit the intercom button.

"Tell them I'll be about twenty minutes late." He returned the receiver to its cradle.

Noble strode back toward the sofa, but before he had an opportunity to sit down, he heard the president speak again. This time he was looking directly at him with deadly seriousness.

"What I am about to tell you is highly classified and totally confidential."

Noble slid back into his seat uneasily and waited for the president to proceed.

"I trust you are aware of the Continuity of Government Plan or the C-O-G-P?"

"Yes, sir." Noble, careful to get his facts straight, outlined slowly.

"It's a contingency plan to ensure all branches of government continue to function in the event of a disaster. My understanding is that The National Security Act of 1947 became the primary foundation for the C-O-G-P, and then in 1950 President Eisenhower signed Executive Order 10186 establishing the Federal Civil Defense Administration." Noble sat back apprehensively, waiting for words of wisdom, preferably with approbation.

"Correct. In essence, it requires all federal agencies to develop a C-O-G-P to ensure their essential operations continue to function and to develop overlapping capability in the case of a national emergency or catastrophe. But, the C-O-G-P goes beyond functionality. It also includes provisions for the protection of the president and those individuals in the line of succession."

"Sir, I realize in accordance with the Presidential Succession Act of 1947, it would have also included the vice president, the speaker of the House of Representatives, the president *pro tempore* of the Senate, and the cabinet secretaries in a sequence specified by Congress," Noble noted.

President Post hesitated. Then, with exceptional caution, he proceeded to explain, "In order to protect those individuals, as stipulated by the Succession Act, the C-O-G-P had to incorporate plans for civil defense, communications, and transportation, among a whole host of life-sustaining needs, including underground shelters."

Slightly confused as to where the president was leading, Noble thought it best just to confirm his understanding thus far. Once again, he chose his words pragmatically. "It's widely known that there are underground facilities at both the White House and at the Capitol buildings. As well as six underground bunkers that are part of the C-O-G-P's original design. They're still in operation today in some capacity." Not wanting to appear overtly quizzical, he casually tossed out, "And, of course, there are rumors that have been swirling for years about hundreds of other hidden underground bunkers that exist throughout the country."

"The rumors are grossly exaggerated!" The president, clearly dismayed, persisted, "Granted, over the years more and more information—that should have remained classified—has surfaced."

"Are you speaking about The Mount Weather Emergency Operations Center?"

"One example," the president responded impassively.

President Post had hoped to avoid the subject of Mount Weather, also referred to by some as the Doomsday Hideaway. He assumed Noble, as many others, understood the underground facility was more than just a place to house key government officials in the case of nuclear war. And, while the land located near Bluemont, Virginia, is the training ground for FEMA—the Federal Emergency Management Agency—the underground facility beneath remains a secure undisclosed location.

Noble, attempting to find a connection between Bluemont and the Dead Zone explored, "One of the rumors being tossed about is that Mount Weather is literally an extensive underground city with its own power plant and water purification system, including streets with sidewalks and a mass transit system. Maybe even a Starbucks." From his last comment, it was obvious he was looking for a reaction from the president as much as an answer.

After a brief pause, and absent any reaction, the president responded, emphasizing each word slowly and deliberately. "There is a similar facility known only to me and all former U.S. presidents." The president glanced over to the electronic map on the monitor hanging above the fireplace.

Noble's eyes followed. He studied the map.

The president studied Noble. The expression on his face appeared nonchalant. *Understandably, a trained response*, he suspected.

Yet, no longer able to resist further, Noble blurted out, "In Utah, sir?"

With some reservations, the president revealed, "There are several such underground facilities throughout the United States today, which are currently managed and maintained by FEMA. It allows them to play out their role in the event of a national disaster. But, in 1953, one facility was decommissioned by executive order and its location was removed from the roster." President Post gave Noble a moment to grasp the situation and then specified, "Out of forty-six United States presidents, there are only seven of us living today who know the location of that facility, tagged as the *Presidential Lair*."

Still stunned by the president's admission, Noble hesitantly pointed out, "Sir, if I may be so bold—I believe there are at least eight people who know." Totally immersed, he took a deep breath, and then spoke what seemed to be the impossible. "I believe al-Fadl discovered the existence and location of the Lair."

For the first time, President Post expressed a modicum of emotion. "How is that possible? The information is only transmitted from president to president during the handover of the office."

"Excuse me sir, but may I ask exactly how the information is communicated?" Noble delved, in a calm and cautious manner. But then, without warning, and without giving the president an opportunity to respond, the words slipped through his lips, "*The President's Book of Secrets!*"

Noble had stepped out of character, but the president remained controlled outwardly. Both sensed the same dread. The enemy had uncovered one of the country's most precious secrets. Noble felt as though he had trod on a landmine and was reluctant to make the next move.

Stepping into the breach, the president broke the momentary silence.

"You have the reputation of being extremely patriotic, and your integrity is beyond reproach. I'm going to trust that you remain in good standing." It was apparent to the president that Noble understood the gravity of the situation but felt he needed further clarification as to its significance. Without acknowledging or denying the existence of the *Book of Secrets*, the president determined it was best to let Noble expound on his findings. So he eased back into his cushion and asked, "How do you think al-Fadl was able to locate the Presidential Lair?"

Noble's mind was already churning to construct a credible scenario. He knew the next steps would ultimately rest with him. Speaking in a measured tone, he stated, "Logically, the location of the Lair must have been communicated to you by the former-vice president, who served as the forty-fifth president for six months before the election. He would have received the information from Abner Baari before he resigned. We know Baari was planted in the White House through the brilliant machinations of our nemesis, Mohammed al-Fadl."

The president interrupted. "To this point, it is my understanding that Baari was unaware of his core supporters. He was basically convinced they were anonymous wealthy businessmen."

Feeling it was time to be forthright, Noble finally succumbed. "Sir, I have some additional treasured secrets to share with you." He proceeded to reiterate to the president about Simon's initial plot, starting at Harvard with La Fratellanza, the Banking crisis, and TSAR. He explained the sting operation that led Hamilton to travel to Florence in an attempt to capture Simon, and how, on Hamilton's deathbed, his mentor passed the mantle to him. It then became his responsibility to force Abner Baari to resign from office.

As Noble discussed Hamilton's role in more detail, he couldn't help but recall the one request Hamilton made him promise—a promise he had broken for a second time earlier that morning—*never use SAVIOR to vet the president.* Although Noble had great respect for Randall Post when he was governor, and then as president, he felt he couldn't run the risk of divulging any of his suspicions about the case, unless he was completely certain he wasn't dealing with another one of Simon's pawns. SAVIOR gave him the assurance that he could trust the president without hesitation or qualification.

At that juncture, the president became intensely concerned with the situation. "If President Baari never had any contact with *your* Simon, then you must have surmised that one of the members of La Fratellanza may have had a hand in this affair?"

"I'm quite confident that three of them have not broken the terms of their immunity agreement. Although, I am quite troubled at the possibility that Hank Kramer, Baari's chief of staff, still might be in contact with Simon to some unknown degree." Noble explained his reasoning and the president appeared to concur.

Just as Noble concluded his comments, the president reached over to the phone on the coffee table. He picked up the receiver and hit the intercom button once again. Noble knew his time had run out and astutely stood up.

"Please come in for a moment," the president requested.

The president's secretary entered on cue. "Yes, sir."

"I need another ten minutes with Noble, and I want you to erase any record of this meeting from your appointment book," the president instructed.

She glanced over toward Noble with the hint of a smile as she responded, "Yes, sir." Then she walked back to her office, closing the door behind her.

"Sit down, Noble. We're not finished. I won't be the first president late for a briefing."

"I'm sorry, sir. I thought you were about to leave." Slightly embarrassed, Noble sat back down.

The president, still sitting across from Noble, made direct eye contact and, with profound seriousness, revealed, "After a president takes the oath of office, there's always a brief, but private, conversation with the outgoing president. During that time, political ideologies are set aside. And, being a skeptic at times, I believed it was the one event where two powerful leaders actually set aside politics to put the world first. Many things are shared, but it is always the responsibility of the outgoing president to put into perspective the importance to study the notes of past presidents, so we are not doomed to repeat the same mistakes. The most serious of those notes are recorded in—the *President's Book of Secrets"*

President Post reverted to silence.

Noble used the time to digest the fact that he had received highly privileged information, known only to a few people on earth. He felt his pulse accelerate as the next obvious question came to the fore. "Does the book describe the location of the Presidential Lair?"

"It did."

"It *did!*" Noble exclaimed. He couldn't believe the president had used the past tense, but before he had the opportunity to offer a follow-up question, the president broke his silence.

"I can't explain what it's like to read the book, starting with the fact that we are dealing with the handwritten words from our first president, George Washington. It's an awesome feeling to move from reading about his vision, to Lincoln's aspirations, to Roosevelt's predictions, to Kennedy's conflictions, to Nixon's fears, to Reagan's hopes—each former president providing a trove of useful insights. I'm exhilarated as I describe it to you now." He then halted a moment. "Perhaps it is vanity, but I felt as though they were all writing to me personally, helping me to guide the country." The president stopped speaking, clearly moved.

In an attempt to fill the void, Noble said with admiration, "I can't begin to imagine the enormous weight it must have placed on your shoulders."

The president emitted genuine gratitude as he continued with some of the highlights that impressed him. He began to describe the notes from Eisenhower that included descriptions of the Presidential Lair. He detailed how Eisenhower purposely decommissioned the underground facility and removed it from the roster in the hope it would be forgotten. He wanted to preserve the Lair as a failsafe, believing the end of WWII didn't end the threat to world peace. During his presidency alone, he saw the end of a devastating war and the beginning of the Cold War. The Presidential Lair would be a place of last resort should the other facilities be discovered and endangered by our enemies. "So you understand why the total secrecy of the Lair is so essential?"

"Yes, sir, but now I fear Simon not only knows the location but is utilizing it for his own malicious purposes," Noble cautioned, then quickly added, "The good news is that we now know where the facility is located and can zero in on him."

"Not so fast, Noble. You wanted to know if the notes described the location of the Lair and I stated it did. However, much to my horror, when I turned the page to review the handwritten blueprint referred to in the notes, it was missing." The president was clearly concerned.

"Missing!" Noble snapped incredulously.

The president, a bit startled by his reaction, explained, "Yes! It was clear someone had removed a page from probably our most sacred book, next to the Bible. Naturally, I immediately contacted the former president and invited him to the Oval Office to show him what I had uncovered. Much to my chagrin, he revealed he had only perused the book casually and never noticed the page missing from the Eisenhower Notes."

"Excuse me, sir, for interrupting, but that is a blessing in disguise reducing the possibility of further blunders. Also, it's a perfect example why a failsafe location is essential."

Sensing the same relief, the president smiled, even chuckled faintly, when he recalled vividly the time the former vice president attended the annual Gridiron Club dinner in 2009, filling in for the president. Allegedly, according to the media, he revealed to his dinner mates the existence of a secret bunker, which the White House later denied. Fortunately, most considered it another one of his frequent gaffes.

"I pray I was able to silence him on this matter," the president sighed. "Being of no help, I called the forty-third president who remembered the blueprint being intact."

"So it had to have been removed during the Baari administration," Noble concluded.

"Okay, what does your inner spy tell you?" the president quipped.

"Do you remember Paolo Salvatore? You know, he's my brother-in-law?"

"Yes, go on."

"Oftentimes, Paolo described Baari's first days in office as being the *babe in the woods* time. To Kramer's credit, he trained him well, and Baari's gifted oratory carried him a long way as he seduced the electorate. But, evidently, he was naive when it came to managing the day-to-day duties of the Oval Office, outside of politics."

"And your point?" The president looked down at his watch.

Noble picked up his cue accurately that time and answered briskly, "The person most likely to have access to the book and the blueprint would be his chief of staff, Hank Kramer—but it's Simon who would've had to persuade him to steal the page."

Both the president and Noble appeared in a state of shock, contemplating the consequences if Hank had actually stolen the book and not just a page.

Regaining composure, the president posed, "The problem with your logic is that Simon would first have to know such a place existed."

"This is that only conjecture," Noble countered, "but it could have simply been word of mouth from Baari to Hank, passed on to Simon, presenting him with a ready-made path to carry out his goal. If his plan was to build an undetectable terrorist camp, the Presidential Lair would have been the perfect location."

"Amazing!" the president exclaimed. "The place is perfect. It's never been utilized, but it was designed to be easily provisioned. In addition, the facility is equipped with several escape routes and is sheltered by Dugway's protected air space. I take that back. It's brilliant!"

Noble probed further, eager for an explanation. "Excuse me, sir, will you elaborate on your remarks about provisioning and escape routes?"

"Eisenhower's notations mentioned the use of a secret passageway in the Desert Mountain that would lead to the underground facility. But without the blueprint, there's no way to locate the entrance."

"What about the escape routes?"

"All I know from the notes, is that the facility's ventilation system is comprised of intake and outflow ducts that are installed throughout the tunnels. Sections of the ducts have escape hatches and, when powered down from the inside, they can be used as exits to the nearby roads. Sorry Noble, but that's all the information I have. I guess *Old Ike* was relying on the blueprint for the specifics and not his handwritten notes."

"Would it be possible for me to study the notes more closely?" Noble knew it was a long shot at best, but he thought he would ask anyway.

"Sorry, that's not possible. Besides, the *Book of Secrets* doesn't exist." He flashed a cautious smile.

Not wasting a moment, the president glanced at his watch for the second time and Noble discerned this time he would be shown the door. "Mr. President, I thank you for your candor. I'll be leaving for Utah on Monday and will report back as soon as I have any information."

"Are you getting full support from the base commander?"

"Yes, sir, and the feds are cooperating as well. Trust me to use discretion—the Presidential Lair will be reported as an abandoned bunker that was decommissioned during the Cold War. However, should I encounter difficulty—may I invoke your authority?"

"Yes, but go easy."

Both Noble and the president stood and shook hands with shared concern.

"Leave through my secretary's office. It will look like your trying to get in and not out." The president grinned.

21
REMAINS OF THE DAY

The clock struck seven as Noble returned to his office. Fortunately, Doris had left for the day. The last thing he needed was the twenty questions that usually followed his visit to the Oval Office. The conversation with the president, still casting about in his mind, was all the intrusion he could tolerate. For the next hour, he leaned back in his chair disinterested in his surroundings. He focused entirely on the Dead Zone—and the Presidential Lair.

Finally, with a clearer head, Noble sat upright. The pivotal moment had arrived. He had no choice; he had to protect the Lair. He had to immerse himself fully in hunting down Simon. He had to stop Simon from executing his plot. *What plot?* He grimaced. *The president was correct. I have no firm idea,* he confessed to himself. Shaking his head in utter frustration, he began to sort through the stack of notes his secretary had left for him. He then checked the messages on his voicemail. And, after ignoring most of the messages, he proceeded to place a few crucial calls.

"Colonel Evans, please. This is SIA Director Bishop."

"One moment, Director," answered an unfamiliar voice.

"Ah, Director Bishop, to what do I owe the pleasure?"

"Colonel, I will be instructing Deputy Director Ford to send the entire squad of feds home except for Agent Burke. In the meantime, I want you to pull all troops back and assign the 1st Special Forces B Team to work on the case exclusively!" Noble was aware that the B Team, made up of thirteen outstanding men, was in training at Dugway preparing for a special overseas mission.

Colonel Evans agreed, believing it would provide the perfect training opportunity. "As you are aware, they are not only experts in reconnaissance, nocturnal operations, and combat, but also in demolition and forensics." Without a pause, his voice shifted, sounding a tad crustier. "Excuse me, Director, you're asking me to assign some of our finest to the mission. Do you even know what or who we are supposed to be looking for?"

Noble ignored the Colonel's insinuation and stated directly, "This mission is top-secret, sanctioned by the president."

"Yes, Director, I understand," the Colonel responded, quickly changing his tune. "You can count on us."

Noble informed the base commander of the pertinent events, limited only to his suspicions. He felt it served no purpose for the moment to delve into the connection to Simon. He chose only to focus on the death of a federal agent on federal land. "We are looking for an underground bunker that is being used as a terrorist recruitment and training facility. We believe the building your soldiers discovered is an indoctrination center and is connected to a larger portion of the encampment by a tunnel system. We believe those responsible for killing Agent Darrow are hiding out somewhere in another part of the complex, planning their escape."

Noble then reported to the Colonel that a special surveillance camera would arrive at the base on Monday, at which point Deputy Director Ford would provide him with further instructions. " I will also need the use of an Apache helicopter and your best pilot," he requested, and then again reminded the Colonel of the importance of maintaining the utmost secrecy. Noble paused briefly to let the Colonel absorb the details of the mission. Then, in an effort to change the thrust of the conversation, he offered his personal condolences for the loss of the two soldiers.

The Colonel continued to maintain a cordial manner. "I appreciate that, sir. I'm just thankful that Max, I mean Deputy Director Ford, and

Agent Burke were spared."

"You can call her Max, if she lets you get away with it," Noble quipped. Then relapsing into his more serious tone, he requested, "Please follow Deputy Director Ford's directives regarding the investigation, unofficially known as Operation NOMIS." Noble knew he had to protect the Lair at all costs and affirmed, "The location of the bunker must not be disclosed. Please destroy any documentation you may have compiled making reference to the facility. Those orders come from the president."

"I understand, sir."

"Thank you again, Colonel. I'll be in touch." Noble ended the call.

ℰℱ⌀

"Ciao fratello. Where have you been hiding out?" Paolo prodded with curiosity.

"On the second floor of the West Wing," Noble joked.

"Well, I am honored that you finally took the time to return my call. Although, I presume you're only calling to check in on Natalie and Mario."

"Paolo, I'm sorry, but this is not a social call. I need to see you in my office tomorrow morning at nine." Noble tried not to make it sound like a command.

"Come on, it's Saturday. Can't we talk over a few beers at the Blackfinn Saloon? Besides, Kansas State is playing against Baylor tomorrow."

"Seriously, Paolo, this is important. Nine o'clock." Softening his tone, he remarked, "And, of course, I want to know how you're all doing. We'll catch up tomorrow. Give them a kiss for me."

"*A domani.*" Paolo signed off, sounding irritated.

That went well, Noble thought. *Now let's see how Amanda handles it.*

ℰℱ⌀

"Hi Sweetheart."

"Noble, I've been texting you for the last hour. If you're calling from the White House, you have less than thirty minutes to get home, freshen up, and pick me up at my place before we have to leave for the concert," Amanda chided. She didn't intend to, but she confessed to herself that she sounded like a wife.

Concert, dammit. Noble had forgotten completely.

"Are you okay? I didn't mean to sound like a-you-know-what," she admitted apologetically.

"Amanda, I'm sorry. It has been a horrendous day and, quite honestly, I forgot about the concert. In fact, I was calling to tell you that I have to work this weekend and then I'm leaving on Monday. I will be out of town for a few days." He knew it was best to lay it out in its entirety and accept the consequences.

Silence was Amanda's response.

"Now it's my turn. Are you okay?" he asked caringly.

"I know your work will always take priority. It's just difficult sometimes to accept the demands it places on you." She paused, and then changed the subject, not wanting to prolong the inevitable. "Adam seemed extremely pleased with the outcome of your meeting."

Noble was somewhat dubious. "What did he say exactly?"

"He said nothing specific about what you discussed, only that you would present his case to the president."

Relieved, Noble reminded her, "There is no guarantee the president will act. All I can do is lay out the facts."

"Adam understands, and is thoroughly grateful."

Noble was pleased to hear Amanda sounding more like herself until he heard, "Won't you have any time at all this weekend?"

"Let's play it by ear. I have a meeting tomorrow morning, and then I will be pouring over forensic evidence on a case. I need to be fully prepared before I leave on Monday. Perhaps I'll have some time Sunday evening. I'll give you a call."

"I miss you, Noble, but I recognize it goes with the territory."

"Thank you for understanding. I love you, Amanda."

"I love you, too. Goodnight."

Noble truly felt horrible. He could have made the concert had he not been emotionally spent. And he still had one more call to make. Then, he would head home and attempt to get a restful night's sleep.

"Noble, where have you been? I've been trying to reach you for the last hour." Max prodded irritably.

"I was in with the president."

"The president! What's up?" Forgetting her ire, she was eager to know.

"In a minute. First, how are you feeling?"

"Lucky. The head wound wasn't that serious. It just bled a lot. Aside from a gigantic headache, I'll be just fine."

"Thank God. Max, where are you now?"

"I am in my quarters on the base. Why?"

"Are you alone?"

"Yes. And remember, you also called me on my secure line. What's with all the cloak and dagger speak?"

"We just need to be extremely cautious while we try to figure out this case. Max, we can't take any chances. There are so many complex dynamics to this puzzle. I honestly don't know how it all fits together," he confessed.

Max detected from the other end of the line that the investigation was irking Noble. She suspected that he was becoming obsessed with capturing Simon. She also recognized it wasn't an ordinary case for the legendary Director Bishop.

"Max, what about the flash drive?"

"I just found it about an hour ago. You can't believe the number of boxes of debris we had to sort through to locate it."

"What was on the disk?"

"Hold on, boss. Right now I'm waiting for a converter to be delivered. Every piece of equipment on this base is state-of-the-art and there's not a USB connector to be had anywhere."

Years earlier, data storage had migrated to online data centers, known as Clouds. There was no longer a need for hard drives, DVD drives, or USB's, the universal serial bus connectors, to transmit and store data.

"You can thank the North Koreans for creating the impetus to further our technology," Noble mocked.

Max was aware that the transformation to Cloud computing had escalated after 2009 when a North Korean went on a three-day hacking spree and broke into, not only the White House computer system, but also the Pentagon and the New York Stock Exchange. The State Department and Homeland Security Web sites had disappeared temporarily. While there was no attempt to steal or damage the data, clearly it was a trial balloon. By 2015, all U.S. computers connected wirelessly to storage networks, with all data stored on a cloud.

"Thankfully, the U.S. Government systems had their data tightly secured on a government owned satellite," Max noted.

Noble didn't respond.

"Noble, are you still there?"

"I was just marveling at Simon's penchant for using such an outdated device."

"He's the ultimate techie. Why wouldn't he want to store his data on a secure cloud?" she questioned.

"Even though cloud storage is mandatory, it really wouldn't make any difference to Simon. I doubt he cares one way or the other about the Data Protection Act of 2014."

Naturally, both Noble and Max were up-to-date on the act that required all information, both public and private, to be stored on an online data storage facility of the owner's choice. Citing public safety, the Data Protection Act was similar to the federally mandated Digital Transition and Public Safety Act of 2005. Even though it did not go into full effect until February of 2009, the act forced households to switch from analog to digital television for the sole purpose of receiving emergency broadcasts. Because of this shift in data storage, by 2015, manufacturers were no longer producing in-home storage devices of any kind.

Noble recalled a time when there were desktops with hard drives. Now there were only tablets with touch-screens, synched, when necessary, to a Bluetooth keyboard. Moreover, the only internal storage maintained by these devices was the absolute minimum, enough to manage the operating system and basic application software.

Max had an uncanny ability to sense when Noble's mind was churning, even when they were miles apart. It was time for her to draw him back to the question at hand. "Noble, do you think Simon intentionally left the flash drive in the indoctrination center in an effort to string you along?"

Noble readjusted in his chair and responded, "Simon doesn't make mistakes, which is why we can't fully trust whatever information is on the drive. Keep that in mind when you review the data. Now, did you uncover any evidence from within the facility?"

"Recovering any fingerprints may be impossible. There is at least an inch of dust from the explosion covering everything. The forensic team is still trying to piece together paper from the shredder, but we did discover various training manuals." Max's voice became quiet and low for the first time. "Noble, you were right. It was an indoctrination center. What's strange is that all of the furnishings and equipment are military issue. I haven't had an opportunity to talk to the operations officer in charge of inventory to see if anything is missing." Max explained that many of the boxes contained mostly manuals primarily geared toward basic tactical maneuvers, rifle marksmanship, engagement skills, situational training exercises, etcetera. "I should have more for you by tomorrow,"

"What's happening with the tunnel?"

"They are still digging. They managed to plod through a quarter mile of debris, but there's no light at the end so far. By the way, did you send me my other IMAC?"

"No, I'll bring it to you on Monday."

Somewhat surprised, she questioned, "You're finally coming out to Utah?"

Ignoring her question he continued, "I just had a conversation with Colonel Evans. He's prepared to take orders directly from you, offering his full support."

"Thanks, Noble, but what aren't you telling me?"

"I'm tightening up the mission, which we will now refer to as Operation NOMIS. I ordered the Colonel to pull back all soldiers and replace them with a team of Special Forces. I want you to send the feds home except for Agent Burke. Tell them the orders come from the president."

"Do they?"

"Sort of." Noble then skirted further discussion on the subject and tried to seem nonchalant. Without telling Max the specific details regarding his conversation with the president, he told her that he received confirmation that an underground facility did exist somewhere in the Dead Zone. "Once we locate the encampment and retrieve all the evidence, it will then be permanently sealed, and its whereabouts will be expunged from any records." With a more jocular air, he said, "After all, we wouldn't want another terrorist cell to come up with the same idea."

Max, obviously curious as to Noble's change in strategy, chose to leave any further inquiry on the matter for a more appropriate time. Serenely, she requested, "What other steps do you want me to take?"

Maintaining his stride, Noble stated affirmatively, "Just hold the fort until Monday. Tomorrow morning, I'm meeting with Paolo. You remember he was Baari's communications director. I have a strange feeling that without him actually being aware, he may be able to provide some of the pieces of the puzzle. In the meantime, start analyzing the data on the flash drive."

"It's not a problem. Just tell me what I can do."

Noble proceeded to inform her about his video conference with

Enzo and that the evidence did point to Simon, including the London bomb's beryllium components. He told her about the WAASP and that he believed it would be able to determine the exact location of the bunker. "I will be arriving at the base on Monday afternoon around one thirty. If the WAASP arrives before I do, have it installed on the Apache helicopter that the Colonel will have standing by."

"Will they know what to do with it?"

"They are familiar with the Carabas, and its functionality is similar, but improved. In my conversation with the Colonel, he also assured me that he would have his best pilot handle the surveillance. As soon as they set it up on the helicopter, I want you to program the WAASP to transmit all photos directly to the SIA Cloud. I already set up a folder on our server named NOMIS, requiring a separate password. I'll text you the password as soon as I hang up."

Naturally, Max had access to the SIA database. Now, only she and Noble would have access to the data in the NOMIS folder. Noble wanted to ensure that they had the only photos of what he knew to be—the Presidential Lair.

"I assume the WAASP has a touch-screen that will allow me to connect with our satellite?" Max inquired.

"Yes, Enzo confirmed it is quite straightforward," he assured her. "Max, remember the WAASP is a top-secret prototype that we're not supposed to know about. Limit any discussion as to its source. And, as soon as we get the surveillance tapes, you need to return the WAASP to Enzo immediately, but not before you erase the WEP connection and password linking it to our Cloud." Noble cautioned. "It is only on loan briefly, and under strict conditions."

"I understand. Anything else, boss?"

"I kept my conversation with the Colonel brief, but I want you to speak with him and ask if he's ever noticed any activity around Desert Mountain."

"Isn't that near where Agent Darrow's body was discovered? In the middle of the Dead Zone?"

"Precisely. It's possible he saw something or followed someone there and he wasn't cleverly placed in that location by Simon after all," he admitted.

"Then it could have just been a brutal quirk of fate on the agent's part."

"Max, back to Desert Mountain. We are looking for any possible entrance into or under the mountain. There should be a substantive opening allowing for the delivery of equipment and provisions."

"Got it."

"Also, have the newly assigned team of Special Forces survey along the Brush and Weis Highways and the Jericho Callao Road, in the area surrounding the Dead Zone. They need to look for anything that resembles a ventilation system, something that would project out of the ground."

"You think that's how they are getting their air supply?"

"Yes, and it can also be rigged to serve as an escape route as well"

"I'm impressed, Noble. You've been doing your homework," she kidded.

If only Max knew where I get my information, Noble mused as he grinned.

"Max, if they find anything that looks like an escape hatch, post a guard around the clock. Make sure no one goes in, and they are to detain anyone coming out." Noble gave Max a moment to make mental notes. Then, he vowed, "If Simon is down there, he will not get away this time." He swore to himself as much as to Max. Then, feeling a wave of exhaustion, he surrendered. "Goodnight, Max."

"Night." As Max was about to complete her sentence, the line went dead. "Noble, get some sleep, was all I was going to say."

22
THE SCORNED

It was an overcast day and Hank was thankful to be sitting inside at his favorite table in the Solar Café. As he sipped away at his steaming cup of black coffee, he watched a woman walk through Franklin Park and cross I Street. She was clenching her coat collar tightly around her neck. A scarf covered her head. What appeared to be a final attempt at camouflage was a pair of dark sunglasses, but it was fruitless. It was no disguise for an experienced operator like Hank. He knew from her stature and the cadence of her walk that it was the former first lady, Maryann Townsend Baari. Besides, the Secret Service agents posted behind the various trees were a dead giveaway—maybe not to the public's eye—but to Hank's trained eye it was routine, having witnessed the scene many times.

The day before, shortly after leaving his meeting with Noble, Hank had received a text message from Maryann asking him to meet her. At the time, he considered it an odd request but, being extremely curious, he texted her back—8:00 a.m. Solar Café.

During their days together in the White House and on the campaign trail, they were usually at odds with each other, both believing they knew what was best for Abner. But, for the sake of the presidency, they managed to coexist, despite their strained relationship. Nevertheless, their communications ended the day Abner Baari resigned from the Office of the President.

Hank eagerly waited, wanting to know the compelling reason Senator Townsend called the meeting.

∽

"You look like hell," Maryann commented as she walked toward his table.

"I could probably say the same for you if it weren't for the masquerade," Hank razzed.

She knew he was right. Abner's disappearance had devastated both of them. It showed particularly on her face. As she sat down across the table from Hank, without removing her scarf or sunglasses, she unbuttoned her coat and let it flow to her side.

They chatted for a few minutes about trivial subjects while waving off the server as she attempted to pour a cup of coffee, unknowingly for the former first lady.

"How's the foundation?"

"Fine. How's the Senate?"

"Out of control," she retorted. Then warily, with a subtle movement of her facial expression, she glanced suspiciously toward the left side of his chest. "Hank, you seemed to have put on some weight," she observed.

Hank instinctively reached to his side as she chastised him furtively, "Have you lost your senses?"

"I," was all he was able to utter before he found himself following her instructions.

"Drop your napkin on the floor, and as you reach down to pick it up, calmly hand the gun over to me."

"Are you crazy?" Hank whispered, and then cowered like a scolded child.

The senator carefully slipped the gun into her handbag and then ordered, "Let's take a walk in the park."

"It's freezing out there," he protested.

Ignoring his whining, Maryann stood up and walked toward the entrance of the café.

Hank relented. He left a five-dollar bill on the table and followed her out the door.

"Aren't you taking a huge risk?" He discreetly glimpsed over at her shoulder bag.

Maryann placed her right index finger across her lips to silence him. Then, with the same finger, she pushed a tiny button on the side of her watch that was strapped around her left wrist.

They slowly crossed the street and strolled through Franklin Park.

"Now, what were you saying?"

"What was that all about?" he queried as he glanced at her watch, forgetting his last question.

"The Secret Service loves to listen in on my conversations. This handy device," she indicated, while shaking her wrist in the air, "blocks the frequency on their ear pieces."

"Don't they know what you're doing?"

"Of course, but I have forbidden them to intrude on personal conversations. They keep changing the frequency and I keep jamming it," she replied, all the while looking straight ahead.

"Where did you get such a device?" Hank asked with great interest.

"It's not important. Now, what's with the gun? You, of all people, Mr. Anti-Second-Amendment. In fact, I recall you were instrumental in helping Abner push through legislation making it more burdensome to purchase guns and ammunition."

Hank shook his head and sputtered, "Times have changed." As they continued to stroll through the park, he explained, "Ever since Abner left the country, I've been receiving death threats. Many people wrongly concluded I knew Abner Baari was an illegal immigrant and that I had aided and abetted in the deception."

"Did you know Abner was Hussein Tarishi?" she demanded pointedly.

"No!" He quickly diverted the discussion. "I believe we were talking about my life," he sniveled. "As much as I disagree with the arbitrary right to own a gun, I care more about my own personal safety at the moment. Be dammed with the critics. I don't know where the threats are coming from, and I'm not taking any chances." *Simon's playing with me, trying to keep me on my toes for some future purpose.* A repeatedly passing thought he did not share with the senator.

"Let's sit over there." She pointed to a park bench positioned away from the passers-by.

As Hank sat down next to her, he could eye several of the agents shuffling between the trees looking annoyed but on full alert.

Maryann stared out into the park. "Have you heard from Abner?"

From the tone of her voice, Hank could tell she was clearly

distraught. "Not since he left the U.S."

They were both aware of the rumors that had been swirling about the beltway. Purportedly, the former U.S. President, Abner Baari, had fled to Libya to work on the National Transitional Council. After the ousting of Qaddafi, the council had failed miserably in their attempts to restore the government. In fact, several dictatorial leaders who stepped in following Qaddafi met the same fate. Apparently, with Abner's arrival in 2016, the council was able to institute a quasi-democratic regime. Recent reports confirmed that Abner reverted to his birth name, Hussein Tarishi, and was appointed President of the Senate in the Libyan parliament.

"I never understood why he was so hell-bent on throwing money at the Libyan rebels to help oust Qaddafi. Now it all makes sense. All along he was planning for his own homecoming," she carped.

Playing the perfect insider, Hank passed along information he felt Maryann should know. "You may not be aware, but Abner knew his days were numbered and that he would eventually have to step down from the presidency. He told me before he resigned how Qaddafi destroyed his father's business and forced his family into poverty. In hindsight, Abner believed it was a directive orchestrated by Qaddafi that forced him to go to the university and ultimately to work for his government. Obviously, the set of circumstances provided the perfect opportunity to get back at Qaddafi," Hank opined.

It was plain to Maryann that Hank was sympathetic to Abner's plight. Attempting to feign indifference she replied, "I guess he finally received his hero's welcome. His revenge must have been sweet."

Hank glanced toward Maryann. Even though he was only able to observe a sliver of her profile behind the headscarf and the left temple of her sunglasses, he couldn't help but stare.

In a surprise move, Maryann began a personal confession. "I'm not sure whether I feel betrayed because Abner left me and his precious little girl Tasha, or because he never trusted me enough to tell me the truth about his identity. Whatever the motive, it's devastating."

Surprisingly, and highly unusual for Hank, he felt a need to console her, and admitted, "I believe, over time, Abner forgot he was Hussein Tarishi. I know, because I tried repeatedly to trick him as a way of testing him. One thing I am sure of is that he truly loved you."

Maryann turned sharply and looked squarely at Hank. "You lied! You did know Abner was Hussein—you were part of the plot."

Hank sensed that behind the pair of dark sunglasses were piercing, steely eyes boring down on him. He had seen them many times before. He attempted to dodge the answer to the question. "That's no longer important. His behavior underlies my belief that he has forgotten he was Abner Baari and, once again, he has become Hussein Tarishi."

In her heart, she knew that was true, but was still unable to bring herself to file for divorce. But, for the moment, she directed her anger solely toward Hank. Maryann continued to stare imperiously.

Hank stared back and she didn't retreat.

Glowering through her glasses, she announced, "Simon wants you to keep your pager turned on—at all times."

Hank's jaw dropped as he remembered he had turned it off the day before when he went to see Noble. Years before, Simon had reconfigured the antiquated pager to receive text messages directly and solely from him. Hank was only able to respond yes or no. For reasons he couldn't explain, he had been reluctant to turn the pager back on.

"So, how do you know Simon?" he tested with unexpected composure, hiding his shock.

"I met him while he was attending Harvard. We maintained our friendship throughout the years." Maryann confessed as though it were common knowledge. "In fact, he encouraged me to attend DePaul. After I graduated from law school, he contacted me again and referred me to a friend who was looking for a civil rights attorney. Evidently, you were that friend."

"Certainly, you must know Simon's true identity?" Hank was incredulous.

"Sadly, I only learned that Simon was a notorious terrorist when Abner told me about the stolen TSAR funds. When Mohammed al-Fadl, the suspected perpetrator, and Simon disappeared at the same time, I drew my own conclusions."

Hank wasn't buying into what he considered her act.

Although it happened in 2003, during Baari's run for the U.S. Senate, Hank vividly recalled the circumstances as if it were yesterday. He could envision the expression on Simon's face when he announced to the members of La Fratellanza that Abner Baari needed a wife. Hank always mistrusted Simon's selection for a first lady. It was much too easy and there had to be more behind his choice. Harboring some suspicions Hank, on his own time, vetted Maryann Townsend and discovered she had attended Radcliff at the same time the members of La Fratellanza attended Harvard, including Simon. But, at the time, he never made the connection. Now, he was having flashbacks of Simon's apartment and remembered the bedroom that was off limits. He smiled inwardly. *Simon knew all of our schedules and could have easily arranged for her to meet him at his apartment without us knowing,* he thought. *Oftentimes, Simon left Jake's Pub early using numerous, seemingly legitimate, reasons to leave.* Not knowing how much Maryann actually knew, he decided to play it safe and avoid further questioning.

Evidently, Maryann noticed his reverie and observed, "Is there anything else you want to ask me?"

Hank had learned a few tricks from Simon, borne of his psych classes—you show your weaknesses, they'll show you theirs.

"I was just reminiscing about the power I once had and then lost. I didn't realize how much it had affected me until now. Working in the White House, side-by-side with Abner, was my greatest achievement. And, when he stepped down, it destroyed me and some of my most treasured friendships," Hank related, with tongue in cheek.

Then, he paused, hoping she'd take the bait and relay her feelings as openly.

It worked.

"I understand how you feel. Abner is an incredible man. He's mesmerizing, and I truly love him. At first, he was like a hypnotic drug, but later it became deadly. I watched it destroy the Abner I knew. The more power he amassed, the more his soul shrank until it shriveled to nothing, leaving only the shell of the man I once knew. Perhaps it's best my daughter will never fully grasp what he had become."

"Be careful of Simon as well," Hank cautioned.

Maryann sat erect. Straightaway, her demeanor changed and she spoke as though she were speaking to a servant. "He's just a friend who asked me to pass along a message. I don't know what is going on between the two of you, and I don't want to know."

Much to his disappointment, she hadn't taken the bait. But Hank knew there was something more profound going on between them than she revealed.

Maryann caught him glancing at her watch, the one she used to jam the agents' hearing devices and, in an effort to avert the subject, she apologized, "I forgot to thank you again for manipulating the state senate seat for me. It was the kick start I needed to launch my political career."

Her sudden uneasiness did not escape Hank, but he felt it best to leave the inquiries for another day. He simply responded, "That gift was from Abner."

The State Senate seat may have been a gift from Abner, she couldn't help but ponder, *but perhaps Simon manipulated the U.S. Senate race. After all, at the last minute, the fraud accusations hurled at my opponent dramatically changed the outcome. Has Simon been manipulating me the same way he was Hank?*

Hank assumed she was lost in thought until the senator stood up abruptly and started to walk away, startling not only Hank but the Secret Service agents as well. They prepared to move into action.

Without turning around, Maryann could hear Hank say, "Can I have my package?" Ignoring his plea, she continued to walk out of the park.

Hank stood frozen in his stance. *What was that all about?*

Coincidently, only a few blocks away, Noble was about to meet with Paolo at the White House to share a very similar discussion.

23
NEW REVELATIONS

For a Saturday morning, it was eerily quiet at the White House. The dark, stormy January skies added to the dissonant atmosphere. It was evident that many staffers had chosen to escape the frenzy of the prior week as the new administration settled into their unfamiliar roles. The president also joined in and spent the weekend with the first lady and his sons at Camp David, their first visit together as the First Family. Unfortunately for Noble, he was in his office as usual, scouring through the evidence from the Dead Zone victims. And, within minutes, he would disrupt someone else's weekend, having no choice.

Engrossed in the autopsy reports, he ignored the sound of the phone ringing until it was too late. It stopped. Seconds later, it rang again, finally grabbing his attention. He glanced at his watch. It was exactly nine o'clock. Without hesitating, he snatched the receiver out of its cradle. "Yes."

"Director Bishop, Mr. Salvatore is here to see you," the Secret Service duty guard announced.

"Please bring him to my office."

Moments later, he heard a knock at the door and shouted, "Come in."

The guard swiftly opened the door and ushered Paolo into the office.

Noble stood up to greet him as the guard respectfully turned and left, closing the door behind him.

"Ciao, fratello." Paolo called out, then quipped, "Remember the good-old days when I'd walk through the White House *un*escorted," exaggerating the prefix *un*. Pleasantly surprised, Paolo walked over to greet Noble with the traditional Italian style cheek-to-cheek peck and a warm hug.

Noble was delighted. Evidently, Paolo had recovered from his earlier annoyance.

Then, intentionally ragging, Paolo needled, "Now, what's with the damn summons?"

"Why don't we sit over there where we can talk more easily?" Noble invited him to be seated in the overstuffed chairs on the opposite side of the room.

Paolo trailed behind and plunked himself down into the comfortable seat.

Noble had determined it was vital to have a serious discussion with Paolo before leaving for Utah. Paolo was the key informant in the investigation leading to President Baari's downfall. Noble wanted to know for certain what he knew or didn't know during his tenure in the administration—and after Simon vanished. The primary focus during the interrogation of the other members of La Fratellanza in 2009 was to capture Simon and to return the stolen funds from the Treasury. Now, Noble needed to expand the scope of questioning, leaving no stone unturned. However, he thought it best to ease into the conversation and start with the family.

"Tell me how Natalie and Mario are doing? I miss them terribly, but lately I've had no time to call my own." He spoke dolefully.

"They're both fine, and miss you as well. Did you know that Natalie has decided to go back to teaching at the University? She feels the time is right, now that Mario is doing so well." Paolo beamed, and then added proudly, "He's only in the third grade, but he's amazingly self-sufficient."

"Obviously, he takes after his mama," Noble teased. "I knew Natalie had been contemplating going back to work for some time. She has a great legal mind and should keep it sharp."

"I agree. It's a perfect arrangement. She'll be able to coordinate her schedule around Mario's."

"Speaking of Mario, isn't his birthday in a few weeks?"

"Noble, I'm shocked you remember. In fact, Natalie will be throwing him a party. It's more a party for adults, but it's a good excuse. Will you and Amanda be able to attend?" Paolo already knew in advance that the answer would be tentative.

"You know I'll be there if I can," Noble responded a bit forlornly.

Ignoring Noble's lament, Paolo cocked his head and elicited impatiently, "I know you're not prone to chitchat, so why did you really ask me to come here?" Then he scolded, "Fratello, I'd like to return home before the weekend is over."

Noble was equally anxious to move the conversation forward and, having thoroughly exhausted the family discussion, he knew the time had approached. On impulse, he changed the focus.

"Have you heard from any of your brethren?"

"La Fratellanza? Why?" He was unmistakably surprised by the question. The prior week when they met at the Blackfinn, they had already discussed extensively those painful past events and the dramatic mass trauma that ensued. "We already went over that," Paolo protested, then pondered, *why does he want to rehash it?*

"Last time we spoke you mentioned that you ran into Hank, but what about the others?"

Paolo conceded with a slight huff. "I haven't spoken with Chase but, according to Hank, he's having a really difficult time."

"In what way?" Noble's tone was laced with concern.

"Purportedly, he'd suffered a mild emotional breakdown a few years ago, and he's currently in therapy. Based on Hank's account, Chase blames himself for the financial meltdown and for trusting that Simon would stop the crisis from spiraling out of control. His wife reported that when he reads the headlines about the economy, he suffers from recurring guilt pangs. Chase has had a tough row to hoe but, apparently, he's on the upswing."

"Any chance he'd had contact with Simon?"

"Absolutely not! There's no evidence that he's violated his immunity agreement," Paolo snapped, seemingly overprotective of his fraternal brother. "After Simon disappeared, the Securities and Exchange Commission was suddenly all over Chase, accusing him of accounting errors. He weathered that storm, but he always believed the high pressure investigation could be attributed to Simon's revenge for the part he played in divulging the plot during the interrogation," he elaborated.

"I must admit, I always had a weak spot for Chase. He seemed like a lost soul, and it was evident Simon could manipulate him easily," Noble theorized.

"That's probably why Simon chose him for our study group at Harvard," Paolo suggested. *Why he chose me is my nagging question.*

"Speaking of Harvard, I've always been curious as to how all of you ended up there at the same time?"

Paolo keenly took notice that the conversation was turning into an inquiry.

"I'm sure you'll recall that, during the interrogation, we all learned that Simon had established a relationship with Chase, long before we attended Harvard."

"I remember. Let's move on. What about Seymour?"

"Well, it's public knowledge that Seymour became *persona non grata* for a time, especially in Washington D.C. Mysterious leaks about his negative campaign ads and the fabrication of the campaign sound bites for Baari sealed his fate in and around the Capitol. He went back to L.A., dabbled with some political documentaries, and then finally was welcomed back into the inner circle when his film *The Framework* was nominated by the Academy for best picture." Paolo hesitated. "As in the case of Chase, Seymour was convinced Simon was behind his demise, and also responsible for the leaks."

"What about attending Harvard?" Noble seemed to be a bit overeager.

Paolo heaved a shallow breath, signaling his annoyance. "I recall him telling me, once, that one of his father's friends had suggested Harvard because of their excellent program in film and visual studies." Paolo's demeanor shifted, and he became more pleasant. "Seymour liked to mimic his father and, when he did, it was hilarious. I remember him quoting his father exactly, 'My pal Hal says, if it's good enough for him, it should be good enough for you. You're going to Harvard.' His facial expressions were priceless."

"What did you say the guy's name was?"

"What, the father's friend? Hal—I think Hal Simmons, something like that. Why?"

"It's not important," Noble scoffed, feigning a lack of interest but thinking *it's vitally important. Paolo had no way of knowing that was one of Simon's aliases.* He relaxed slightly into his chair, displaying his presumed indifference. "I never asked you for any details, but how did you end up at Harvard?"

Paolo, feeling marginally more comfortable, clarified, "That's simple. One summer, I interned in my uncle's law firm in Florence. It was an easy gig. I spent three months editing briefs by day and entertaining the ladies by night."

"Okay, Romeo, but what about Harvard?' Noble prompted, attempting to redirect Paolo, who had a tendency toward braggadocio.

"My aunt was a professor of art and believed strongly in the importance of a good education. She and my uncle agreed to subsidize my tuition if I'd apply to Harvard. I was considering graduate school at the time, but Harvard was nowhere in my budget—until they made the offer, of course. Naturally, I accepted." Paolo frowned. "What difference does this make?"

"May I ask the name of your aunt?"

"Obviously, you've been working too hard and you need a vacation, fratello," Paolo advised. Then, he watched the edgy expression slowly cloak Noble's face and responded, "Simona Ducale. What does this have to do with La Fratellanza or Simon?" Seconds after Paolo mouthed the words, he had answered his own question, much to his own shock. "You think Simon somehow manipulated all of us to converge at Harvard long before he molded us together in the study group?" Giving Noble no time to answer, he elaborated, "Are you suggesting Simon became acquainted with my aunt when he was in Florence during the early nineties? It never occurred to me to link my family and Simon in any way. It's so farfetched."

Noble didn't respond immediately. He easily recalled that Professoressa Ducale was instrumental in helping Simon escape years later in Florence with one hundred thousand euros, foiling Hamilton's sting operation. Focused once again on the conversation, he admonished Paolo. "You've posed way too many questions. For now, fratello, I'm the one looking for answers. What about Hank?"

Paolo settled down after his outburst. For the moment, he acquiesced. "One night, I had drinks with Hank when he finally came clean about meeting Simon a few years before he had entered graduate school. The details were sketchy, but it had something to do with an organizing drive that was giving Hank problems. Simon intervened and, within weeks, the situation sorted itself out. Simon and Hank became fast friends."

"Now, do you have the answers to your own questions?" Noble inquired jocularly.

Paolo, with a deadpan expression, admitted, "After Simon disappeared, Seymour voiced to the rest of us that he always suspected it wasn't a coincidence we all landed together at Harvard." He paused, and then looked directly at Noble. "Seymour was also convinced you were the linchpin—the one designated to play a major role in Simon's plot."

Noble was shaken by the thought that Seymour had deciphered one key element of Simon's insidious plan. The entire plot had hinged on his admittance to Harvard. In fact, he recalled his own experience entering the university at the eleventh hour. His financial resources were limited, and he had applied for a scholarship but had not received a timely response. Amazingly, the day before the Harvard acceptance deadline, he was awarded a partial scholarship, accompanied by a letter of apology attributing the delay to a computer error.

"Simon," he muttered under his breath.

"What?" Paolo asked, not sure he had heard him correctly.

In the blink of an eye, Noble changed the direction of the questioning. "I want to talk about the time when all of you, except Chase, worked in the White House, particularly during the time after Simon disappeared."

"Noble, please tell me what this is about," Paolo appealed.

"Bear with me. Who directed Baari's policies in the early days of his administration?"

"I guess the impetus for some of his policies started back at Harvard when we first began our *intellectual game*." Paolo winced. "During our study group, Simon had suggested we predetermine various policies— social, economic, foreign, energy, etcetera, that might become useful. Especially, as course material for the person we ultimately deemed the Chosen One." Paolo quickly added, "Of course, at the time, it was only a game, an intellectual challenge. Little did we know that years later in Chicago we would actually utilize the course materials."

Paolo gauged Noble's demeanor carefully before he continued. "As part of my assignment, Simon encouraged me to write speeches to sell each of those policies for the Chosen One's presidential campaign. Of course, we all now know they were meant for Baari," he submitted with embarrassment. "As part of the game, he even had me project out to 2008, so the speeches would be timely and could be easily adjusted to be in tune with current events." He stopped and looked across the room, diverting eye contact with Noble, then confessed, "Naturally, after the election, we expected Baari to appoint Hank as his chief of staff. Hank was expected to bring the rest of us into the fold."

Noble showed little emotion and moved the questioning forward. "Earlier, you mentioned energy as one of the policies you tackled."

"Yes, someone pointed out during one of our sessions—I think it might have been Hank—that the Middle East would always be in turmoil and we would be forced to sleep with the devil as long as we were energy-dependent." Paolo paused, trying to recollect the exact conversation. "Oh, yes, it was Simon who contended, 'the more turmoil the better.'"

"What did he mean by that?"

"Simon lectured us about how our country was replete with resources, but that we couldn't drill to full capacity because the government was beholden to the environmentalists. The same environmentalists were a voting bloc that was key to electing the Chosen One."

"So how did Simon reconcile the issue?"

"He suggested we stir things up in the Middle East through a foreign policy strategy, ultimately forcing the tyrant leadership in various countries to step down. Simon predicted that it would precipitate their replacement by other tyrants who would step into the breach, creating more turmoil, with the goal of creating a dire energy shortage for our country. The president would then be forced to approve drilling for oil domestically. Oh mio dio." Paolo paused as his expression contorted with understandable concern. "The fog has lifted. It's all coming to me now. The environmentalists would've had to capitulate under the circumstances." He spoke as if entranced.

Noble was troubled. "Are you all right?"

Paolo, rapidly regaining his composure, fired off, "Noble, there were so many balls in the air. In those first few years of Baari's presidency, we were trying to manage the financial crisis, containing his spending frenzy, and his furtive attempts to control as much of the private sector as possible. It was mayhem in the White House. Baari's inexperience was coming to light. We did all we could do to try to keep him under control."

Then, in a breathless manner, Paolo owned up to the fact that Baari's energy and foreign policies seemed eerily in parallel. In his own defense, he avowed, "Noble, I had to focus on the day-to-day issues and may have missed the bigger picture. Baari is an egocentric who didn't confide in us totally. I honestly didn't recognize that aspects of our Harvard game were playing out before our very eyes. As reckless as it may seem, we focused obsessively on electing Baari. That was the game—not what would happen after he was elected president."

Noble knew Paolo was sincere, even though he found it difficult to believe he was obtusely unaware of some of the broader issues. Certainly, he was in the midst of key events. At a minimum, he was the kingpin of communications for the White House. Noble remembered many of Paolo's clever speeches as he defended the actions of the Oval Office against critics, both public and private.

Changing the course of the conversation once again, Noble insisted, "Why the drastic increase in federal land claims during Baari's first four years?"

"Odd you would bring that up. I questioned the same thing," Paolo admitted.

"Questioned whom?"

"I asked Hank, repeatedly, why such an escalation was taking place. He ascribed it to the acquisition of energy resources. Quoting him directly, he would arrogantly say, *that is where the energy resources are located*. He stated, on more than one occasion, that the goal of the administration was to control the U.S. energy supply, eventually insuring energy independence from rogue nations."

"Rather altruistic, I would say."

"In hindsight, rather risky, I would say."

"Why do you say risky?"

"The government's claim on public lands was killing jobs and impeding private enterprise. The same private enterprises that could have helped solve the energy crisis."

"I don't understand. Give me an example."

"Noble, there are many examples, but one in particular has to do with the state of Utah."

Paolo thought he detected what might have been a slight reaction from Noble at the mention of Utah but chose to let it go unchallenged. He continued, "Over the past several years, the federal government has succeeded in either owning or managing most of the land in that state. It has become impossible for many of the private companies with legitimate mining claims to build roads or other means of passage on the federally claimed land, necessary to access their drill sites. Utah, along with land in Colorado, Montana, and Wyoming have some of the richest energy resources, all lying in wait below ground. And, for some unknown reason, there was an overreaction on the federal government's part to protect specific land in Utah from being excavated or reshaped in any way."

"I'm confused. Who directed those policy decisions? Was Baari really that astute?"

"He had a host of advisors in the form of business roundtables, self-appointed Tsars and a select group of congresspersons, all invited to his doorstep. The exercise was only a sham. It was the old rope-a-dope Ali used when he was heavyweight champ. After they had played their public relations role, he ignored them and, ultimately, adopted Hank's strategy."

"Hank?" Noble barked.

"Speaking from personal experience, Hank constantly tried to reshape my speeches and control the communications leaving my office on this issue," Paolo attested, as he shook his head in despair.

Noble sat back into his chair, staring at his clasped hands.

Paolo remained silent as Noble pondered.

Then, in a flash, Noble stood up and walked toward his desk as he went on the attack. "Other than his skill in directing social policy, Hank is not that versatile! He had to have been taking his direction from Simon the entire time he was ostensibly working for Baari. That son-of-a-bitch has been lying to me all along, just as I suspected."

Paolo was astounded. "Noble, your dialogue has become perceptively more colorful the more time you occupy this office," he snickered.

"It's this goddamn case—it's Simon," Noble remarked in a raised voice. As he turned around to face Paolo, he realized his slip of the tongue.

"Simon!" Paolo exclaimed. "You're tracking down Simon. That's your case?"

Noble glared at Paolo.

"I know, can't discuss." Paolo backed off, stood up, and walked toward Noble.

"You are to forget we had this conversation. And, I'm sorry, but you'll have to be escorted out of the building. Hold on while I call the guard."

"I miss the days when I could roam at leisure," Paolo moaned.

"Mr. Salvatore is ready to leave."

A few seconds later there was a knock. Noble gave Paolo a warm embrace and, in silence, they headed together toward the door.

Noble thanked Paolo for giving up his Saturday morning. "We'll get together soon," he proposed with a pat on the back.

Paolo looked at Noble with some apprehension and said, "Ciao, fratello." Then he turned and departed with the Secret Service guard.

24
A FLASH FROM THE PAST

After Paolo's departure, the picture of the flash drive insidiously crept back into Noble's mind. He could still picture Max reaching for the device just before the explosion. He could still picture the initials **LF**. Noble had a similar flash drive with the same engraved initials, the one he had received from Paolo on that cold day in Franklin Park. A day he recalled vividly. It was the day Paolo broke down and divulged the plot, the role the members of La Fratellanza had played, and the disappearance of Simon. The other members of La Fratellanza had also turned over their identical flash drives during the interrogation that followed Paolo's exposure. Noble was certain the USB device Max picked up was Simon's flash drive. On the other hand, he was suspicious as to what degree he could trust the data stored on the drive, knowing Simon's devious mind. Noble harbored doubts as to whether it would provide the missing clues to the ultimate plot.

As he continued to recollect the details of that painful conversation in the park with Paolo, he heard his smartphone vibrate, bringing him back to the present. He grabbed his phone and blurted out, "Max, what's happening?"

"You'll never believe it!"

"I'll believe anything these days. Shoot."

"I spoke with Colonel Evan about Desert Mountain."

"What did he say?"

"He appeared curious as to how I knew, but then he acknowledged the U.S. military actually has a storage facility inside the mountain. Imagine him being Ali Baba saying *open sesame* when he finally opens his sealed cave for us. It's wild. Anyway, they use the facility to house emergency vehicles and construction equipment, having it readily available when conducting training and testing exercises outside the Dugway Proving Ground."

"Max, slow down!"

"Slow down! I'm just warming up. Noble, we found another opening!" She went on with consternation. "We entered the mountain from the north face, unbelievably only a mile from where Agent Darrow's body was found. We discovered another opening leading out of the mountain heading south. The Colonel swears it was not installed by the military, and he was unaware of its existence."

"What's on the other side?"

"It opens to a tunnel that looks exactly like the one that led us to the indoctrination center. The only difference is it's three times wider."

"That would explain how they were able to provision the facility."

"Exactly, and right now the Colonel has a couple of troops staking out the area. They also found two air ducts with escape hatches protruding out of the ground, just as you described. Each one was about thirty-eight inches in diameter. One was located off the Weis Highway, almost exactly where Darrow's body was recovered." Max paused, and then delved more slowly. "Why would Simon or the killer be so careless as to discard the body near two potential clues?"

"Good question, for which I don't have an answer. Where was the second escape hatch found?" Noble inquired.

"Off Route 6, near Silver City, where the Hazelton Family met their deaths. It was located in an old chimney that still stands. A possible connection?" Max contemplated more than questioned. "Soldiers are guarding that area as well."

"Now, do you believe there is an underground facility somewhere out in the desert?"

Max could almost see Noble smirking. She picked up with a hint of sarcasm, "You know me. I wait until I have all the data. Besides, I don't have your historical perspective."

"Hold on, Max. I have to take this call."

Max, accustomed to being cut-off, sat back and tolerated the silence on the other end of the line.

✑

Noticing the caller's name on the display, Noble attempted to keep his anger at bay. He answered steadily, "Hank, what can I do for you?"

"I have a message," he responded hesitantly.

"What is it? I'm on another call." Noble's impatience was evident.

Hank took a deep breath, then sputtered, "Simon paged me and left a text message for you. His exact words were *back off or the world will be sorry.*"

Astonished by the threat, Noble became infuriated. "Why the hell didn't he contact me directly?

Sounding faintly downcast, Hank claimed, "It's one of Simon's attempts to keep me in the game."

"A game you've been participating in all along. As I recall, that violates your immunity agreement," Noble reminded sharply.

"I've never violated the spirit of our agreement."

Noble knew the truth and ignored the semantics. "How does he communicate?"

"On the rare occasion he tries to reach me, it's by pager. I know it's obsolete. But while we were in the White House, Simon would always update all of our pagers with the latest technology. And, before he disappeared, he set mine up to receive only alphanumeric messages from him. The only way I can communicate a response is to page either *yes* or *no* to his request." Hank vacillated. "Noble, I'm deathly afraid of responding *no.*" The fear in his voice was apparent.

"You should have gotten out of the game entirely when I gave you the choice," Noble scolded. Then, he pulled back his anger ever so slightly. Even though he believed Hank was quite unprincipled, he did have an ounce of empathy. *After all, Simon had also manipulated me, to a certain degree,* he confessed to himself.

But, Hank being Hank, ignored Noble's ire and rambled defensively. "I had no choice. Simon does not tolerate betrayal. I'm sure you know what happened to the others. I told you. He scares the hell out of me."

At the mention of the others, Noble immediately insisted, "Why hasn't Simon targeted Paolo?"

Within seconds, Hank's demeanor changed dramatically. This time he boldly came back with, "Trust me, he'll eventually use Paolo to get to you. He is only holding him in abeyance in his arsenal of manipulation."

Noble, while unnerved, restrained himself and continued to maintain his composure. He reproached Hank for aiding and abetting Simon during the Baari administration. Then, without missing a beat, he did a U-turn and reversed his direction. "However—I want you to continue to maintain contact with Simon."

"What? Am I hearing correctly?"

"I'm not finished. You are to report to me all messages you receive without fail—before you respond." Then, for the first time—in a chilling voice—he commanded, "I will find out if you defy my orders and, should that happen, I will put you away for a very long time. You will go down alone and secretly. Your brothers are individually insulated. Do you understand?"

"I hear you, Noble."

Noble hit the swap button switching back to Max's call.

Max heard the click on the line, sat upright, and prepared to continue the conversation.

"Good work. Is the Colonel cooperating?" Noble acted as if there had been no interruption at all.

Max, however, detected his voice seemed more strained. She assumed his change in demeanor had something to do with his phone call. She chose not to meddle. So, in a more lively tone, she responded, "He's been great, along with the Special Forces and, believe it or not, Agent Burke. They've all been cooperative."

"They must enjoy taking orders from a woman," he teased, instantly feeling more at ease with the sound of her voice.

"Unlike you, Noble," she retorted. "Now, I assume you'd like to talk about the flash drive?"

"What have you been waiting for—an invitation?"

"So, you really think the flash drive is Simon's, and he left it intentionally?"

"Simon has some foibles but doesn't make mistakes," Noble reminded.

"What about his fingerprint that was found in the Menlo Park apartment, and his using the same password for all his bank accounts," she emphasized, adding, "even intelligent people have vulnerabilities, and people with vulnerabilities can make mistakes."

"Now you're a shrink?" he joshed, and then admitted, "I don't have all the answers, but perhaps the flash drive will shed some light. Hold on. I'm transferring your call to my secure line, and then I'll put you on the speakerphone." After a brief pause, he said, "Can you hear me?"

"Loud and clear, sir," she replied, and then instructed, "log onto to the SIA Cloud and access the NOMIS folder. You'll find a subfolder named FDrive."

It took Noble a few minutes to access the system. Using his virtual keyboard he typed in his password, which was then encrypted. He then entered a series of security PIN numbers followed by a separate password for NOMIS. The complex, security login procedure was something Noble himself had successfully lobbied for with Congress. The procedure was not only for access to the SIA Cloud, but also for access to all federal government databases.

While Noble was busy entering the appropriate passwords, Max explained that the flash drive contained many files with various file extensions, which she had sorted and separated into different folders she had created.

"I'm in," he announced. "I'll take over the keyboard."

From each of their respective monitors, they could view the files on the cloud.

Max began to describe the individual folders and their contents. "Okay, you'll notice I placed all the documents in the DOC folder and photos in the PHOTO folder. There were several diagrams and blueprints, so I moved them to the DIAGRAMS folder." She paused. "Noble, most troubling is that there were several filenames with file extensions that I couldn't identify. So, I put them into the MISCELLANEOUS folder. Let's start there," she suggested.

Noble adjusted his chair, faced his monitor, and prepared himself for what he was about to uncover. Using his mouse pad, he tapped on the MISCELLANEOUS folder. Predictably, he was uneasy as Hank's words rang in his ears, *Simon's exact words were back off, or the world will be sorry*. "Back off from what, from where?" he wondered.

"What did you say?"

"I'm just talking to myself." He didn't know exactly what he was looking for—evidence linking Simon to the European bombings, or to an underground facility in the middle of nowhere. The words *back off* continued to occupy his mind.

Max couldn't tell what Noble was thinking, but she could watch on her monitor as he moved his mouse through the list of files in the

MISCELLANEOUS folder. To her surprise, she noticed that he had highlighted twenty specific files. Overtaken by curiosity, she continued to watch her screen for Noble's next move. From nowhere, another subfolder appeared, and he swiftly cut and pasted the files to the new folder.

"What's going on?" She was no longer content to be an onlooker.

"Study the file names. What common link do they have?"

Max sensed Noble already had the answer, but was now putting her to the challenge.

"Give me a minute." Max perused the first eight file names, examining them with laser-like focus. "They all start with letters that look like stock ticker symbols for companies." She contemplated for a moment, and then blurted out, "For banks! Yes, of course, for banks!"

"Exactly!" he exclaimed. "Look at the first one, **STI7890321Z6** is for SunTrust Bank. It's followed by **FITB958219X9** for Fifth Third Bank, BAC222934Y3 for Bank of America, **STT236492W3** for State Street Corp, **WFC889233V2** for…"

"Slow down. I get it. It's Wells Fargo," she interrupted, quickly adding, "Noble, you named the folder ROB. You think these files are a connection to Simon's slush fund, the one he affectionately named Uncle Rob when he was working with La Fratellanza? Could he still be siphoning off money from the banks?" she asked with amazement.

"It will take me some time, but I think these files contain the backdoor code to each of their databases. Unbelievably, after all these years, and all the added security, he is still able to tap in and transfer funds."

"To quote Yogi Berra," Max cited, "'It's like déjà vu all over again.'"

"If only I could travel back in time. I'm sure, knowing what we know today, Hamilton and I could have prevented Simon from escaping in Florence, and all of this would have ended years ago." Noble's voice was dripping with distress.

Max hesitated before making the next profound statement. "Ostensibly, Simon did lose his flash drive. What if it wasn't an attempt to mislead us?"

There was no response from Noble.

Max watched as he switched to the DOCUMENT folder and hurriedly scrolled through the files, seemingly examining only the filenames. Many of them referred to training exercises one would expect: *Cyber-terrorism, Unconventional Warfare, Propaganda, Insurgency, Intimidation,* and *Suicide Attack.*

"When I scanned the documents briefly, something didn't seem right. The info seemed like it was downloaded from Wikipedia, not up to Simon's standard, but there were a lot of handwritten notes that we'll need time to study." Max assumed Noble had heard her, but she could see on the monitor that he was still spinning past the multitude of files.

Suddenly, he stopped at a document titled *Civilian Casualty Ratio*. Max heard him grunt the word, "Disturbing." Next, he opened one titled *SERE Instructor Training*.

Max heard him say, "very interesting," as he skimmed the pages. She knew that SERE was an intense military training program, an acronym for **S**urvive **E**vade **R**isk Escape. She continued to watch carefully as Noble proceeded to scan the other titles, passing by *Tactical Maneuvers*, *Explosives*, and *Special Forces*.

"Stop!" Max called out impulsively. "Check out the one titled *Explosives*."

Noble obliged, opened the document, and briskly flipped through the pages, stopping occasionally to speed read certain paragraphs. He had the habit of reading the screen by first highlighting the sentences as he read them. Max found it annoying while in his presence, but as she watched her monitor, she actually found it easier to follow along. When Noble opened the chapter listing bomb components, she noticed that a line was drawn through the words *raw steel casing* and *p. 28* was written in the margin. Noble skipped to that page.

"We've got him." He let out a deep breath, and then rapidly announced, "The documents describe the same dimensions and materials that were used in the Paris and London bombings. The components are Pentaerythritol Tetranitrate and beryllium." Noble had deciphered that the Pentaerythritol Tetranitrate, or PETN, alone was not significant because it was widely used in bomb making. But, the use of beryllium was extremely rare. The metal referred to on page 28 was a vital clue.

Before Max realized, Noble had highlighted another paragraph in the document titled *Special Forces* under the chapter dealing with ammunition, specifically a list of preferred cartridges for sniper rifles. Halfway through the list was typed *Cheyenne Tactical*, and someone had drawn a thick black circle around the words.

"Finally!" he exulted. "I have my connection to the New Year's Eve bombings."

Max, not meaning to dampen his spirits, questioned, "Do you still think it was just a test, a sort of trial run?"

"Yes," he stated with slight annoyance. Noble's mind was in overdrive, speedily switching gears. "Did you spot anything in the photos?"

"Mostly they were shots from what I assume now to be a training camp. A few of them looked more like movie sets with different props."

Noble promptly switched over to the PHOTO folder and tapped the slideshow tab. Both Max and he sat back and began to look for clues. As the pictures scrolled by slowly, Noble first viewed the scenes Max had assumed were from the training camp, but the others she mistakenly thought were movie sets were actually locations.

Noble paused at the first location. "Max, what do you see?"

"Two ornate fountains, and what appears to be the bottom half of the Eiffel Tower in the background."

"It's the Place de la Concorde, the location of the presumed assassination attempt of the French President." Noble moved to the next photo. "Now what do you see?"

"I see a series of pillars with a long boulevard running behind them." Max sighed, "I know, it's the Brandenburg Gate, and the boulevard is the Unter den Linden."

Noble remained silent and simply displayed the next photo. It was a view of Downing Street with the London Eye in the background.

"So, this is further evidence that Simon was responsible for the New Year's Eve attacks," Max conceded. "Sorry, Noble, I didn't catch it. They looked like movie sets, especially without people in the photos."

"They must have been taken early in the morning, before the locals hit the streets," Noble conjectured, cutting her some slack. There were several more photos of the same locations but from different vantage points. Noble quickly passed by those and then continued the slideshow. Shortly thereafter, he paused and backed up to a previous photo.

"Now, that is a stage with props setup for a speaker," Max surmised, sensing a need for redemption.

Noble shook his head. "What do you see next to the podium?"

Max viewed the podium and then the stack of flags resting in the left-hand corner of the room. Next, she refocused on the podium. "Oh, my god!" she gasped. She gazed to the left of the podium, which would be to the right of the speaker, and eyed the European Community flag—standing next to the German flag. "Supposedly, he was using the props as a training exercise. Do you honestly believe Simon was training another one of his pawns to replace the German Chancellor?" she asked in utter disbelief.

"It would appear as a real possibility. The chancellor is certainly on the list, but we can't discount the French President or the British Prime Minister."

Max heard Noble let out a deep breath as he observed, "This is Abner Baari—all over again. This time, the consequences could be even more deadly."

"Frighteningly, he's upping the stakes."

"Possibly, but one thing I still find difficult to grasp is that Simon is capable of killing and bombing indiscriminately." There was obvious despair in Noble's voice as he brought to mind his personal relationship with the Simon he once enjoyed.

"What do you think is Simon's ultimate motive?"

"I honestly don't know. It's the primary question that continues to haunt me." Noble knew he had to augment his thinking. "In order to unearth his plot, I have to test my own doubts about Simon."

"What we do know is that Simon is a notorious terrorist, also known as Mohammed al-Fadl, and that he originally operated under the direction of Osama bin-Laden," Max recalled.

"Yes, I know all that. And, I know that shortly after the bombings of the U.S. Embassies in Nairobi and Tanzania, in 1988—for which al-Qaeda took credit—al-Fadl reportedly had spun off from the group and parted ways with bin-Laden."

"But, does he still maintain loose ties with the terrorist organization, even though he purportedly operates independently? He can't be a one man band."

Noble didn't answer Max. He still found it problematic that al-Fadl had committed such atrocities. He knew that Simon was al-Fadl, but he couldn't dispel the notion that Simon was also his college classmate and friend. And, by a quirk of fate, he ended up investigating Simon for federal crimes. Now that Noble was on the verge of finally capturing his nemesis, he was also mindful that there might be other threats embodied in his global plan.

"There has to be a clue somewhere in these documents," he concluded in a whisper, forgetting Max was on the other end of the line.

"We'll find it. Don't worry. Check out the DIAGRAM folder. There are some bizarre blueprints."

Noble obliged, as she watched him scroll through the files until, apparently, one caught his eye. It appeared to Max that he had surreptitiously changed the filename, but it was with such speed, she questioned herself as to whether it really happened. Evidently, he was in the process of opening a file named Camp.

"What are we looking at?" Max avoided commenting on his wizardry.

At the same time, Noble hoped that she hadn't taken note of the previous file name that read, *The Presidential Lair*. True to his word, he kept his promise to the president—never to reveal the true purpose of the underground bunker. "It appears to be a blueprint of a large facility with several connecting buildings. I feel confident that it is our encampment and the large X drawn across one of the buildings is the building you identified as the indoctrination center," he pointed out, maintaining composure.

"Why the X?"

"Because Simon blew it up and it's no longer functional," Noble concluded.

While Noble may have appeared calm, Max was shocked. "Simon knew all along that we were close to discovering the building. It was part of his plan to detonate the explosives that killed the two soldiers."

No longer composed, and noticeably concerned, Noble exclaimed, "And almost killed you and Agent Burke!"

"If this really is the encampment shouldn't we enter without delay?" Max prompted.

"Let's not lose sight of the prospect that this may still be a trap, and that Simon dropped the flash drive intentionally."

"You really don't believe it was a mistake?"

"At this point I'm playing it both ways. We'll wait for the WAASP and see if the photos corroborate the information we have thus far."

"Okay, I'll go through each of the files and see what other surprises he has in store for us," she volunteered.

"I'll need time to decipher the bank files and, if he is siphoning money, I need to shut him down immediately—again."

"You're sure they are backdoor codes?"

"I'm never sure when it comes to Simon, but if the codes provide access to the bank databases it will prove, once and for all, that he lost the flash drive—and committed what could be a crucial error." Noble took a moment to revel at the possibility. Then, abruptly, he caved in to voice his nagging concerns. "The terrorist camp, the federal land grabs, our energy dependency on foreign oil and, believe it or not, the New Year's Eve bombings, all lead us to Simon. But, there are still some pieces missing. I'm not yet able to connect the dots!"

Max, surprised by the sound of his frustration and his outburst, answered reticently, "So, you truly think it's more than Simon recruiting and training terrorists? And that it's simply not a plan to place one of his pawns waiting in the wings, to eventually step into the role of one of the European leaders? Is there a larger underlying plan that is driving his behavior?"

"On the surface, that should be enough, but we are dealing with Simon. There has to be more. He's like the Rubik's Cube, a three dimensional puzzle. He's vexatious."

Suddenly, Max felt as though she was holding the pin of a grenade. They had to find Simon and destroy his entire scheme—a scheme they believed he had not yet fully carried out.

Noble refocused summarily. "Where is the flash drive now?"

"I have it in an evidence bag, along with Simon's fingerprint that I lifted off of the drive before uploading the data."

"Don't let it out of your possession. I know a few European countries that would love to get their hands on the infamous flash drive."

"Are you going to hand it over to Enzo?" Max asked, a little surprised.

"Only if I deem it vital to aid in the conviction of Simon's accomplices. In that case, we'll be forced to share some of the details." Switching gears, Noble added, "I'll try to change my flight and arrive tomorrow so we can work through the rest of the files together."

"Good luck," Max cautioned. "There's a storm front about to hit the Midwest. It might be best to wait until Monday. After all, you were the one who said, 'we need to stand down until after we get the photos from the WAASP.' Nothing will happen until then, anyway. Besides, boss, I've got everything covered on this end."

Max was always confident, one trait Noble most admired.

"You win. I have some loose ends to tie up anyway, including a call to Enzo to alert him to what we've uncovered. See you on Monday. Stay warm."

A click was the next sound she heard.

Noble glanced at his watch and noticed it was half past one, later than he thought. He decided to take a break to stretch his legs and walk down to the ground floor to the kitchen next to the Navy mess. There, he was able to scrounge up a few sandwiches, a bag of chips, and a strong cup of black coffee—somewhat past its prime. He carried the tray of goodies back up the stairs to his office on the second floor and prepared to settle in for the next several hours. After noshing half of one sandwich and gulping a few swigs of coffee, he sat back in his chair. Using his virtual keyboard, he opened the MISCELLANEOUS folder and began to unravel Simon's codes.

25
NO REST FOR THE FIXATED

Sundays are sacred to many in the western world. A day set aside for many to worship and for many more to kick back and relax. Even Noble enjoyed an occasional day to unwind, work on the *New York Times* crossword puzzle, and sip on a cappuccino—a habit he picked up from Paolo. But it was not in the cards on this Sunday. Noble had worked throughout most of the night, returning to his home only a few hours before the church bells began to ring. After grabbing a couple hours of sleep, a hot shower, and a quick breakfast, he was once again on his way back to his post at the White House.

As might be expected, Noble finally managed to break and disable the codes in all twenty files that housed the backdoor programs to the various banks, preventing Simon access to his fraudulent accounts. For the time being, the money would remain in those deactivated accounts until he had sufficient time to notify the banks, so the stolen funds could be recovered.

Fortunately, Noble's acumen in COBOL-60 was still sharp, and he awarded himself with a pat on the back for recollecting. Nevertheless, he found it curious that Simon had never progressed beyond that virgin programming language developed in 1959. There had been a number of modifications and improvements to the language over the years, but Simon stayed with a language that had become antiquated and unfamiliar to the vast majority of programmers today. *Perhaps that was his intent,* Noble mused.

COBOL, an acronym for **CO**mmon **B**usiness-**O**riented **L**anguage, was widely used as the programming code for back office administrative systems, primarily in the financial and government sectors. However, it had severe limitations. Noble was acutely aware of its shortcomings.

One failing was the code stored only a fixed two-digit entry for the month, the day, and the year. The years 1900 and 2000 would be represented as 00 in the system. Also, for the first time ever, the date September 9, 1999 occurred. It was entered as 9999. The system stores that number as the standard entry for any unknown date. By the end of the twentieth century, many of the business operating systems became heavily reliant on the use of dates as the basis for calculations, for age determination, pension programs, actuarial tables, and numerous other uses. The two-digit entry limitation would have resulted in massive miscalculations in systems throughout the world.

However, leading up to the new millennium, this half-century-old programming inadequacy became evident. Programmers from around the globe, including Noble, worked diligently to correct the problem. Long before the New Year arrived, a worldwide panic had set in— referred to as Y2K, or the Year 2000 problem—adding to the drama.

Although the programmers were able to deflect most of the problems, Noble could recollect that the global scare proved to be valid in some respects. He remembered, vividly, the radiation-monitoring equipment that failed in one country and ticket-validation machines that wouldn't operate in another. Then there were reports of patients receiving erroneous medical tests, Web sites that reflected inaccurate dates, and the master clock that keeps the U.S's official time had lost its way.

Y2K presented a sizable problem, but it was also a gift for a man named Hal Simmons. It was in 2008, when Noble and Hamilton revealed Simon's other alias, so they began to track the doings of Hal Simmons, past and present. To his surprise, Noble discovered Simmons was also one of the leading international programmers retained to fix the errant codes in the operating systems at the major banks across the U.S. It handed him the perfect opportunity to program the backdoor access code to their databases, creating his personal piggy bank and placing him in the driver's seat.

I guess we've come full circle, Simon. And now, once again, I've taken away your slush fund. He rejoiced at the thought. "Enough reminiscing," he chided himself aloud.

Noble reached for his phone and placed the first of several important calls he would need to make before departing for Utah.

∽

"Don't tell me you're working on a Sunday, my friend?" Enzo questioned.

"I'm afraid so, and I apologize for interrupting your day with your family. I've uncovered more information about your case that I'm sure you'll want to know."

"We're taking about Simon, I presume."

"Who else? We finally have solid evidence that proves he was responsible for the New Year's Eve attacks."

"I'm all ears!" Enzo stated enthusiastically.

"Has the German Chancellor's successor been vetted through SAVIOR?"

"No. I just finished with President Grimaud's cabinet and those in line for succession. They're all clean. Why do you ask?"

"It may be possible Simon has someone waiting in the wings to take the helm. The chancellor could be a real target. Next time—not a ploy. From what we've deciphered thus far, Germany could still be vulnerable." With pronounced concern in his voice, Noble continued. "I don't know, but I have this troubling feeling that the case I'm working on here may have a direct link to your case. As you check, please go down two levels of succession. Let me know what you find."

"I'll have SAVIOR start to vet them first thing tomorrow."

Noble described in detail what he discovered in the documents and photos, suggesting that Chancellor Mauer may be a genuine target for elimination. He also cautioned, "We should not discount President Grimaud or Prime Minister Teragram as probable targets as well. There's something afoot that leads us to deduce mere assassinations of leaders are not the end game. He chose not to tell him about Simon's new slush fund. That was a U.S. embarrassment he preferred not to highlight.

Enzo had listened with great interest, but then he interrupted and proceeded to ask a series of questions. Noble was forthcoming and did not withhold pertinent information. Enzo then posed a follow up. "You honestly believe that Simon is trying to pull off another Abner Baari? This time in Europe?"

"All the evidence leads me to that conclusion. We can't dismiss the possibility that one of the leaders will be assassinated and replaced, in a Three-card Monte maneuver, by one of Simon's pawns waiting to take the helm. Meanwhile his pawn may already be functioning within the government under our noses," Noble surmised, confirming a fear they had contemplated earlier.

"You've convinced me the attempts on the leaders' lives were trial runs, preparing for some unknown future event. However, we still don't when, where, or how."

Noble could hear the uncertainty in Enzo's voice, and attempted to alleviate his concern. "I'm closing in on Simon, and when I take him down, it should thwart any plans he may have in the works."

"Luckily, we have some of his trained assassins in hand. I'm happy to report that, after raids in several countries, we now have many of his known acolytes in custody," Enzo boasted, feeling more confident.

"Were you able to uncover any additional information—any solid links to Simon?"

"You're aware we turned Badi al-Diri, the Syrian, over to the German authorities. Naturally, he claimed he was operating alone, but we had already established his connection to Simon.

"What about Ahmed?"

"His brother-in-law finally gave us the location of Said Ahmed's hide-out after only a few hours of interrogation," Enzo passed on proudly. "He was staying in an old hotel in the Goutte-d'Or, a section of Paris, referred to as *Little Africa*. We arrested him on Friday, a few hours after I spoke with you. He's pleaded guilty to placing the bomb under President Grimaud's limo.

"Fortunately, it was a decoy, although it did kill the driver." Noble recounted.

"Now, he is in the custody of the French government, and they are trying him for the murder of the limo driver and the attempted murder of President Grimaud."

"Unfortunately, France abolished the death penalty."

Enzo did not comment.

"Did Ahmed admit to being on Simon's payroll?"

"No, like al-Diri, he professes he was operating alone, but we've already confirmed the connection. For instance, we know that he and Simon were in Pakistan at the same time on three separate occasions."

"Tell me something I don't know about Karim Yakob, our American-born Saudi." Noble wasn't anticipating anything enlightening.

"What you don't know about him is that his real name is Hal Simmons."

"What? That's huge!"

Enzo took note of Noble's excitement, but continued to explain, "From the fingerprint we lifted from a section of the detonator, SAVIOR produced a complete dossier. Karim Yakob was born in Oakland, California. His mother, born in Saudi, met his father while working for Halliburton at their headquarters in Al-Khobar. After they married, Simmons and his new bride relocated to the U.S. and reared one son. In 1995 their son converted to Islam and Hal Simmons changed his name to Karim Yakob."

"In-cred-i-ble," Noble scoffed. "Simon recruited Karim and then assumed his identity."

"I'm confused," Enzo admitted.

"Hal Simmons was one of the aliases Simon used in the early nineties." Noble explained that Hamilton's first case, as a fledging agent, was to track an elusive hacker who was siphoning accounts for various bank computers. Then, when the hacking stopped and the trail went cold, his superior officially closed the case. However, for many years after, Hamilton continued to work doggedly on the case on his own time. "Finally, it led him to an apartment in Cambridge rented by a Hal Simmons. Further evidence eventually led us to Simon."

"*In-cre-di-bi-le*," Enzo mimicked, enunciating his accent. "There's more. Karim was off the radar for a while, but in the past few years he popped up again and we were able to trace several trips he made between London and Salt Lake City."

"The beryllium connection—of course! Gotta go, Enzo. We'll talk soon. Thanks."

"Wait a minute. Every time you mention beryllium, you hang up."

"Enjoy the rest of your weekend."

"Noble, keep me posted." Enzo let out a deep breath before ending the call.

Noble placed his next call to the base commander at Dugway, hoping that his office phone was set-up to transfer the call to his smartphone, not expecting to find him at the base headquarters. He was beginning to feel as though he was the only one working on a Sunday. After several rings, he finally heard a click making the connection, and then a familiar voice answered on the other end.

"Director, what a surprise. I trust all is well."

"Hopefully, all will be well very soon." He proceeded to fill the base commander in on the events, but only those limited to his suspicions that the terrorists in the camp have the means to escape through the mineshafts. He felt it best not to delve into the connection with Simon but narrowed the conversation to the death of a federal agent on federal land.

I have additional evidence that leads me to conclude that we may be closing in on the leader of the terrorist cell. His name is Mohammed al-Fadl, and I have every reason to believe that, at the moment, he is trapped in the underground facility."

"What do you want me to do?"

"Continue to maintain ground surveillance. As you know, I will be arriving tomorrow and, if we are successful in capturing al-Fadl, I need him placed in maximum security as quickly as possible."

"Of course, we have a military prison on base, but it's not designed for high-value prisoners."

"I understand. Actually, I prefer a state prison. For now, I'll play the liberal game and keep him out of the federal jurisdiction. Technically, he is an American citizen."

"In that case, I would recommend the Utah State Penitentiary in Draper. It's the only prison in Utah with a super-maximum security unit. Their Supermax houses over thirty-seven hundred prisoners and has some of the most violent populations in the U.S. It's just the place for your fella."

"Will you make the transfer?"

"We can transport him by helicopter. Would you like me to call the warden to make the arrangements?" the Colonel offered, adding, "He's a good guy. His name is John Lowell."

"I'd appreciate your giving him a heads-up. Please let him know I will be calling him within the hour."

"No problem. I'll take care of it as soon as we hang up. Hold on, Director. Let me get the number where he can be reached on the weekend."

Noble waited as he listened to a few clicks on a keyboard.

"Here it is."

Noble jotted down the number as dictated by the Colonel.

What else can I do to help?"

"Just give Warden Lowell a call, and then prepare your brig for an indeterminable number of prisoners. I don't know what we'll discover, but we need to be prepared. Also, have the Special Forces stand ready."

"Yes, sir."

"Enjoy the rest of your weekend, Colonel, but get ready for some intense times ahead. I'll see you tomorrow."

Noble hung up and readied himself for the last two calls he needed to make before calling it quits for the day. First, he decided to handle the more difficult of the two.

⌐∽

"You sound exhausted."

At the sound of her voice, the tension began to melt away. Surprisingly, until that moment, he hadn't even realized how tense he had become. "Hi sweetheart, it's been a long, tiring few days."

"Will I see you before you leave for your trip?"

"I wish I could come over, but it's late. I must admit I'm drained physically and emotionally. I need to go home, pack, and try to get some sleep before my flight tomorrow."

Amanda had reminded herself as she reached to answer the phone not to place any pressure or guilt on Noble. She swore that she would be supportive and help him through this case, but during their respite, they needed to have a very long, serious conversation about their relationship. "Can I drive you to the airport?" she offered.

"Thanks, but I have to be at Dulles International at six a.m., and I've already arranged for a car."

"I can't even..." She bit her lip in mid-sentence and, after a slight hesitation, she responded, "I'll miss you. Travel safely, and give me a call when you have the opportunity."

Noble wasn't as obtuse as he seemed at times, and he was aware that his career was putting a strain on their relationship. To temper her concerns for the time being, he promised, as he attempted to stifle his yawn, "Things will be different when this case is over. I love you, Amanda."

"I love you, too. Now, go home and get some sleep."

Noble could hear her soft voice trail off as she hung up the phone.

After a moment of reflection, he realized that the receiver was still in his hand. He reached over to establish a dial tone and placed his last call.

⁐

"Hello."

"Warden Lowell?"

"Yes, who am I speaking with?" he asked brusquely.

"I am SIA Director Bishop, and I'm in need of your assistance."

"Yes, Director. I just spoke with Colonel Evans. How can I help?" His tone softened a tad.

"We're about to move in on a high-impact suspect. If all goes according to plan, he will be in our custody within the week. With the assistance of the base commander at Dugway, the detainee will be transferred to your prison by helicopter. I want him held in Supermax."

"I'll make the necessary arrangements."

Noble sensed his ambivalence. Evidently, the warden was not a man accustomed to taking orders, but that was not his concern. "My instructions are no visitors other than me, and he is not to speak to the other inmates. I want him placed in twenty-four hour solitary confinement. Soon after, I will arrive and conduct the interrogation."

"What crime has been committed?"

"Warden, I'm sorry, but for reasons of national security I can't share anything more at the moment. Please just make sure he's confined to his cell."

"Yes, sir, I understand."

"I'll be arriving in Salt Lake City tomorrow morning, and I'll want to inspect the facilities before I drive to Dugway. Please arrange for my admittance to the prison at eleven thirty."

"I'll see you then, Director."

"Thank you, Warden. I'll see you tomorrow." Noble placed the receiver back in its cradle. He sat in his chair for a moment longer and for the first time that day his body told him he was totally spent. He collected his papers, grabbed his xPhad, and headed out the door.

26
THE ACCOMMODATION

A s the plane was about to make its approach, Noble could see the Great Salt Lake and the Bonneville Salt Flats set off to the west. *Strange, one of my boyhood ambitions was to become a geologist,* a passing thought that crossed his mind as he observed the unusual landscape. "Look at me now," he mumbled, before noticing the awkward gaze from the woman in the next seat. Fortunately, the speaker system began to blare as the voice on the other end prepared the passengers for landing.

It was exactly 10:30 a.m. when Delta flight 1681 touched down at the Salt Lake City International Airport and promptly pulled up to the jetway. As Noble grabbed his carryon and shuffled through the aisle, he noticed he had plenty of time to get to his appointment. The base commander had offered to send a driver to escort him to the prison and then to Dugway, but Noble declined. He enjoyed driving and looked forward to the solitude, giving him the time to contemplate and prepare for his next move. Besides, a helicopter was available at the base if time were of the essence. So, all that was necessary was to pick up the leased car and arrive at the Utah State Penitentiary in Draper by 11:30.

Entering I-15 South from I-80 was a little tricky with its veins of highways twisting and turning, but once he veered onto I-15, known as the Veterans Memorial Highway, it was a straight shot to the prison. The drive itself was quite unimpressive, with tractors, trailers, and containers dotting each side of the highway. It didn't resemble anything as beautiful as he had viewed from the air, but gradually the landscape improved. Approximately two-thirds of the way toward his destination, the droning voice from the GPS directed him to stay in the right-hand lane. Following the instruction, he saw a Ramada Inn out of the corner of his eye. From his estimate, he was about ten minutes away from the prison. He would keep the hotel in mind should the interrogation extend past one day.

Noble glanced again at his watch as he was about to swing onto Prison Road. "Perfect. Eleven thirty on the dot." Moments later, he pulled into the prison parking lot and headed toward the guard tower next to the entrance gate. Standing directly outside the gate, he spotted a stocky man in an ill-fitting business suit, obviously waiting for someone. "That has to be the warden," he presumed. Of course, not sporting a uniform was a telltale sign.

As Noble walked toward the man, he was astonished by the gorgeous backdrop behind the six hundred and eighty acre prison that lay in the shadow of the Wasatch Mountains. The scenery improved even more dramatically from his earlier sightings. From this vantage point, he could view the vast Point of the Mountain in the eastern section of the Traverse Range with its peaks and crevices overflowing with glistening white snow. Immediately, he felt more invigorated. When he greeted the warden, it was with a hardy, but officious handshake, effortlessly assuming his director mode.

Warden Lowell, to Noble's surprise, seemed rather congenial compared to his unctuous tone on the phone the day before—a stark contrast from his earlier demeanor. However, his personality was of little consequence. He had complied with all of Noble's demands, which were of greater significance.

After receiving his visitor's pass, Noble hopped into a jeep with the warden and they headed to one of the outer buildings. Led by the warden, Noble entered Uinta 1, a building named after the Uintah Indian tribe. It was one of two buildings that housed the Supermax prisoners. Each building, divided into four units, contained twelve cells per section. The two buildings combined contained ninety-six of the most dangerous offenders.

Continuing to follow the warden, Noble walked down a wide

corridor and, after passing through several gates, each closing behind them, they entered one large rectangular room. Off to the right, was a row of six steel doors. At the end of the row was a metal staircase that led up one flight to another identical row of doors. Each door had a panel that could be opened from the outside, allowing the guards to look through the heavy glass and view the occupants. Another smaller door, referred to as the cuff port, was large enough for a prisoner's hands to slide through to be handcuffed. The cuff port had other graphic names such as bean slot or chuck hole because it was also used to pass the meal tray. Across from what looked like a cheap motel was a two-story glass wall. On the upper level was the guard station with a clear view of all of the cells.

Standing in the bleak rectangular room between the guard station and the cells, Noble found the dank, musty air to be offensive, unlike the air-conditioned corridors. His fine-tuned senses also made him conscious of an eerie din that echoed from within the small chambers. He assumed the prisoners were talking to themselves, considering they were in solitary confinement and separated from the others by an impregnable cement wall.

Noble was surprised at how unsettling it was to experience such a toxic environment, despite the fact that throughout his career he had visited various prisons—including a few tours at Gitmo—which seemed luxurious by comparison. Even more disturbing was an odd sense of apprehension that began to overtake him—maybe because he knew Supermax was occupied by the meanest and the vilest, or perhaps it was that one of those cells had been prepared for Simon.

"Where will my prisoner be housed?"

The warden pointed to the cell on the far-right end of the row on the bottom tier. "As you requested," he acknowledged. Then he explained that the guards use a computer system to open and close the cell doors. "Of course, there is a failsafe," he mentioned. "When essential, a guard can use a master key." Using a talking device on his wristband, the warden communicated to the guard in the upper-level station and ordered him to open cell number six.

Walking over to inspect the cell, Noble found it only necessary to peer in to view the six by twelve foot chamber with a stainless steel sink and toilet opposite a hard bed topped with a thin mattress. Without commenting on the accommodation, he turned back to the warden and asked, "Where is the interrogation room?"

"Follow me, Director."

Noble shadowed the warden, retracing their footsteps down the long corridor. At the end, they passed another guard station, also behind a glass wall. Several feet ahead, the warden opened a steel door and gestured for Noble to enter first.

The room was barren, except for the steel table in the center of the room and a chair on either side. Interestingly, the chair on the far side was bolted to the floor. The only illumination in the room came from a single row of lights that hung over the table. Satisfied, Noble turned to exit the room and eyed a video camera in the upper left corner close to the ceiling, which appeared to operate on a motion sensor.

"Is a guard always posted at the station?" Noble questioned, pointing to the desk about ten feet from where they stood.

"At all times. Anyone visiting a prisoner must first sign in and then be escorted by a guard." The warden then pointed in the opposite direction and noted, "There are three other rooms down that corridor that we also use to interrogate prisoners, but I thought you would prefer this one." He beamed, seeming more amused for anticipating Noble's preference.

Noble, noting the warden's self-approval, concurred. "It appears to provide the shortest distance between the prisoner's cell and the interrogation room. There's less of a chance for a mistake to occur."

The warden grimaced faintly at Noble's use of the word *mistake*. He then began slowly to wind down the visit. "I trust the accommodation is satisfactory?"

Noble concluded that Supermax was more than adequate, and that the warden understood the importance of twenty-four hour confinement. It was also apparent that the warden had a clear understanding that the prisoner, under no circumstance, was to be processed in Uinta 5. That specific facility is used to receive, orient, and classify all new prisoners. Simon was no ordinary prisoner and the warden grasped the distinction.

"All appears to be in order," Noble confirmed. "Thank you for your time. I'll be in touch as soon as we have our man in custody."

They shook hands and Noble left to begin his hour and a half drive to Dugway.

27
OPERATION NOMIS

During the drive to the Proving Ground, Noble passed by terrain that resembled the Utah he had envisioned. Aside from the few towns he drove through, most of the stretch of roads was barren, surrounded by mountains—some craggy, some majestic. The sparsely vegetated area was dotted with juniper brush and pickle weed interspersed with salt flats. In spite of the breathtaking scenery, he began to feel a bit logy. About forty minutes into his drive, and sensing the effects of traveling, he rolled down his windows to invite in a refreshing breeze. Notwithstanding the radiating sun, the outdoor temperature was in the low twenties. But within a short time, the frigid air had revived him and raised him from the doldrums.

Finally, feeling revitalized, he began to think about what lay ahead. *Every mile is a mile closer to Simon*, he ruminated. To his surprise, the rest of his trip passed by quickly, and before he realized, he had turned onto Stark Road and was approaching the security entrance to the Dugway Proving Ground.

"I'm Director Bishop here to see Colonel Evans," Noble announced as he passed the soldier his credentials through the open window.

"Yes, sir. The Colonel is expecting you." The soldier returned the I.D. card and directed Noble to the Colonel's headquarters. The route was straightforward, and he arrived in short order. As he pulled up to the building, he was pleased to see a familiar figure standing outside, notwithstanding the slight bruises.

"Hey, boss," Max shouted as she waved, wearing a huge smile.

Now standing next to her, he gently touched her forehead and, in a rare moment of intimacy, he said, "You look like hell."

"It's great to see you, too," she teased. Then, turning sharply, she instructed, "This way, sir," accentuating the word *sir* as she entered the building.

"Spending too much time on the base?" he needled as he followed her down the wide corridor. Then the jiving stopped, and his tenor changed. "Did the WAASP arrive?"

"Early this morning. In fact, it's now on a plane heading back to France. I called Director Borgini to let him know the arrival time."

"Did you speak with anyone else?"

"No, I spoke with Enzo," she reacted speedily, and then challenged, "Why are you so uptight?"

"Sorry, I'm eager for this to all come to an end," he admitted, as he thought, *where is Simon now*? He instantly refocused. "Did the WAASP give us what we need to know?"

"Yes, it confirmed that the underground bunker exists—which I suspected you already knew."

Noble didn't respond to her assumption. "Are we ready to enter the encampment?"

"We're set to go, but first I need to bring you up to date on some additional information we've uncovered." She spoke rapidly, matching his tempo.

"Max, are you nervous?"

"Yes," she affirmed, throwing a beady-eyed look in his direction. Then, she turned left sharply to enter the Colonel's reception area.

The sergeant seated behind the desk directed, "Max, go in. The Colonel is waiting." Then, he promptly stood up to stand at attention and clasped his hands behind his back. "Director," he greeted, followed by a respectful nod.

Noble followed behind Max as they walked past the Colonel's office and headed straight to his conference room.

"I have the command post set up in here."

Noble gestured for her to walk in first.

When he entered the room, he observed a long conference table. Around the table stood three men, all wearing various attire, but it was obvious to Noble who was who.

"Gentlemen, I'd like to introduce SIA Director Bishop. He will take charge of the mission," Max announced and then proceeded to introduce each member of the group. First, she presented Colonel Evans. He was wearing his fatigues, having just returned from the testing grounds, but the fabric nametag attached to the right side of his chest was a give-away.

Then, she coolly presented Major Stanton, the leader of the B Team, who was standing to the left of the Colonel. He was also wearing fatigue pants, but he was topped with a black tee shirt. Protruding from his shirt were bulging biceps and a neck almost equal in diameter to his head. Despite his formidable physique, his cropped blond hair and blue eyes softened his hard-edged features. He was the perfect poster boy for the U.S. Army Special Forces.

Agent Burke, standing on the opposite side of the table next to Noble, interrupted Max and formally introduced himself.

In spite of the fact they had spoken on the phone earlier, Noble spotted him the moment he first entered the room. Seemingly, the agent enjoyed working solo and traded in his *Mad Men* suit for jeans and a shirt with an open collar.

Having made the cordial rounds, Noble headed back to the front of the room and the others sat down in their chairs. All eyes were now focused on him as he announced, "We are about to commence Operation NOMIS, a top-secret mission sanctioned by the president. Everything you hear in this room—including any assumptions you make—are classified." As Noble was about to take his seat and turn the session over to Max, the Colonel interjected.

"By the way, Director, what does NOMIS stand for?"

"**N**etting **O**peration with **M**ilitary **I**ntelligence and **S**urveillance," Noble answered, without hesitation. He scanned the faces of the men in front of him, noting each seemed pleased with his answer. From their smiles, they must have concluded that it was in recognition of the roles they would play in the mission. Noble also smiled inwardly because he knew that NOMIS was not an acronym, but a personal reminder of the reversal of fortune Simon was about to encounter. Satisfied with his retort, he walked back to the table and took his seat.

Max picked up the cue and swiftly moved to the front of the room. Standing at the podium, using the virtual keyboard, she began to type. As she pecked away, the Colonel once again interrupted.

Focusing his attention directly on Noble, the Colonel announced,

"Director, before Max begins, I have information that may be pertinent."

"Go ahead, Colonel."

He proceeded to tell Noble that when Max reported that the furnishings and equipment in the underground facility appeared to be military issue, it brought to mind an investigation he initiated in 2012 when he assumed the command at Dugway. He explained that his first order of business was to meet with each of his officers individually. "When I met with my supply officer, we reviewed the current inventory, along with prior monthly reports and all outstanding requisitions. It became evident to me from the reports that there were an unacceptable number of variances."

"How were they explained?" Noble asked, as others listened with interest.

"Each discrepancy, on the surface, had a plausible explanation, but in the totality, something seemed out of balance. I conducted an investigation which revealed that a vast amount of office furniture and equipment inventoried was, in fact, missing."

"What happened to the supply officer?"

"He was suspended from duty and confined to the base, pending further investigation. I needed more time to evaluate the case to determine how to proceed." The Colonel paused, let out a shallow breath, and then continued in a tone seemingly out of character. "It's never an easy decision for a commander to initiate Article 15 under the Uniform Code of Military Justice. However..."

Max, ignoring the Colonel's moment of earnestness—and impatient to move the conversation—chimed in, "As I recall, the article permits the commander to file for non-judicial punishment, according to the UCMJ. What was the outcome?"

The Colonel, slightly irked by her interruption, was also impressed with Max's acumen. He calmly reverted to his earlier demeanor and announced, "As I was about to say, the decision was no longer mine to make. Two days after the officer was suspended, he went AWOL."

Noble followed the conversation closely. It seemed evident that the supply officer was the one responsible for provisioning the underground facility. *There has to be a connection to Simon*, he pondered. Without a pause, it was his turn to interrupt the Colonel—but with an unrelated question. "Do you inventory rare metals at the base?"

The Colonel raised an eyebrow. "Odd that you should ask." After surveying the others' reactions, the Colonel elaborated, "Actually, there was one item that first caught my attention. We stockpiled a particular metal for testing purposes. I discovered in one of the monthly inventory reports that a sizeable shortage was evident." Frowning, he continued to explain that the variance identified that particular metal being requisitioned by a testing supply officer. But, there was no record of the transaction because of a reported malfunction in updating the computer system. "I personally was aware that the metal wasn't scheduled to be tested until 2013. So I interviewed the same testing supply officer and he reported that no requisition had actually been issued by him or his staff."

"What rare metal are you referring to?" Noble fished, positive he already knew the answer.

"I'm sorry. Director, but since the V-X debacle in 2011, all testing materials are classified."

"That's okay, Colonel. I'm sure you're referring to beryllium."

The Colonel was unmistakably shocked by the statement, as were Agent Burke and Major Stanton. The only one impressed by Noble's deduction was Max.

"Now that we know the metal, what tests were scheduled to be conducted?" Not relenting, Noble pressured, "If you prefer, I could ask the president to make the inquiry."

The Colonel felt trapped, but he recalled in Noble's opening statement, *everything mentioned in the meeting is classified.* Cautiously, he capitulated. "The Defense Department's National Defense Stockpile supplied the beryllium metal to be tested for various uses—including worse case scenarios."

"Is that a euphemism for nuclear weapons?" Noble queried.

The Major seemed somewhat uneasy in his chair, but remained silent.

"I'm sure you're aware that the metal is already a component in valuable products being used in the aerospace and defense industries," the Colonel explained, wanting to cooperate within reasonable bounds.

"Including nuclear weapons and reactors," Noble persisted.

The Colonel ignored the intrusion and explained that beryllium also possesses a disadvantage. "The metal is brittle and highly toxic. However, during the processing of the metal, it can break easily, releasing poisonous dust particles into the air. We have been challenged to find ways to manufacture the metal safely, without the volatile effects," the Colonel stressed, hoping to put an end to the discussion.

Noble believed the Colonel's explanation was a trifle simplistic. Of prime importance was the changed expression on the Colonel's face when he mentioned the word *nuclear*. However, Noble chose not to pursue the subject further in the current venue. They needed to refocus on the mission at hand—the entry strategy—the capture of Simon.

Naturally, the others in the room were entranced by the conversation, but now that it had been tabled, they were eager to move on to the mission as well.

First, Noble had one simple request. "Colonel, can you please e-mail me the fingerprints you have on file for your missing supply officer?"

Pleasantly surprised at the shift in conversation, the Colonel was more than happy to oblige. "Surely, what is your e-mail address?"

While Noble called out nlb@sia.gov, the Colonel reached for his tablet and retrieved the file.

Within seconds, Noble's smartphone vibrated and he opened the e-mail. "One moment." He excused himself as he tapped the envelope icon and then selected the *Forward* option. He then entered Enzo's e-mail address and in the text box typed: **another favor run print thx.**

"Okay Max, what have we got?" Noble requested as he placed his xPhad back down on the table.

Max had been standing ready at the podium during the distraction. Now, she was more than ready to shift into gear. First, she addressed Noble. "Before you arrived, Agent Burke and I briefed the Colonel and the Major on the cases that lead us to the Dead Zone. Certainly, they are aware of the tunnel that led us to the indoctrination center. I've informed them that it is our belief an underground terrorist camp is operative." Turning to face the others, she added, "Now, our goal is to determine how to enter the facility safely and without a shootout, while at the same time preventing anyone from exiting." Satisfied that everyone was now on the same page, she reached over and tapped a few more keys on the keyboard.

Instantly, on the large display screen, a map of the Dead Zone appeared, but with some alterations.

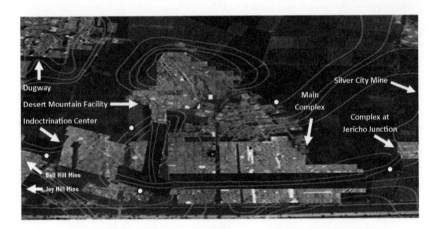

"What you're looking at is an aerial photo of the underground facility in the Dead Zone that was retrieved by an infra-red surveillance camera."

Max observed their expressions.

Unquestionably, the Colonel and the agent were astonished.

The Major's excitement matched Noble's intense satisfaction. Finally, Noble's suspicions had been confirmed.

Max was also careful not to mention the WAASP in any specific detail. The Colonel obviously was aware that some newfangled camera arrived at the base. He was also told its use was classified, requiring security clearance from the White House.

Now, focused entirely on the monitor, the men watched Max point to the upper left-hand corner, just below the Dugway Proving Ground.

"Here, you can see the tunnel leading into the indoctrination center from the Bell Hill Mine. From there, you can view a series of tunnels converging in what seems to be the major complex. The tunnel entrance at the Desert Mountain facility looks to be about sixteen miles from the main facility. We estimate that the complex covers approximately three hundred and fifty acres, or point five square miles. Another tunnel that appears to run through the center of the complex is roughly one mile, or twenty north-south New York City blocks."

Max paused for a moment, and glanced back quickly to check the group's demeanor to assess their level of attentiveness. She then pointed to the upper right-hand corner, near the town of Jericho. "As you can see, the tunnel from the main facility continues and connects to a smaller complex. I've also indicated on the map, with a sun shaped symbol, each of the ventilation escape hatches we've located thus far.

Note, they are positioned symmetrically around the perimeter of the encampment." Focusing in on the Major, she informed, "The members of the B Team are staking out each of those locations."

"What is the status at the mineshafts?" Noble questioned.

"The Special Forces are also guarding the entrance to the Fish Springs mineshaft, along with the mineshafts at the Joy and Bell Hill Mines."

"Didn't the feds report that the Joy Mine entrance was in such ruins that it was impossible to either enter or exit?" Noble asked.

"Yes, but presumably our elderly couple must have stumbled upon something in that area that led them to their horrible fate," Max surmised. Turning back to the monitor, she tapped a few more times to retrieve an earlier map of the Dead Zone. Then, she circled the area around Silver City.

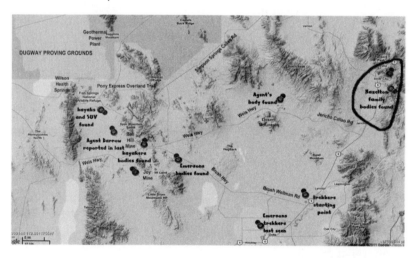

"In addition to the Silver City Mine, we recently identified three other abandoned mines in the vicinity, all with possible exit points."

Noble leaned back in his chair. "Explain."

"If you head up Route 6 from Delta to Silver City, you first pass the Diamond Mine. Nothing is there except an old nineteenth century cemetery and mine tailings. Then, a few miles further northeast is the Irontown Mine. That mine is quite interesting with its foundry remains, along with a charcoal kiln and the chimney from a blast furnace."

"Which could make for a nice escape area," Noble added.

"Except for the fact that there are a few homes surrounding the ghost town. Supposedly, it has some appeal, but I think it's unlikely to be an exit point," she pointed out. "However, I agree it should be staked out. There is also one more mine before we get to Silver City, and that is the Mammoth Mine. Moreover, while it appears to be a real ghost town with several old dilapidated buildings, there are a few inhabitants; another unlikely prospect."

Noble attempted to ask but, before he was able to get the words out, Max spouted, "I know. Assume nothing, I'll have it staked out immediately."

She grinned at Noble, and then glanced over toward the Colonel, who was, evidently, listening with undivided interest. However, at the same time, he was taking down copious notes, as he had been throughout the discussion. Agent Burke appeared bored, having heard it all before, but the Major sat back, eager to enter the encampment. Noble was restless as well, but he wanted to ensure that no one could escape before they went in.

Max picked up the pace and pointed to the Silver City Mine. "We know the Hazelton family's car was discovered near an open-air shaft, which looked to be very deep. The shaft was next to a pile of old mine tailings, and all that remains are a few old foundations and some mining equipment left behind. I believe that's the most viable exit point."

Noble looked toward the Colonel and Major, who were sitting next to each other, and asked, "Colonel, when the Major and his team enter the encampment, who will replace them at the mineshafts and ventilation escape hatches?"

"There is a Special Forces Army National Guard unit stationed in Draper. With your authority I can have them deployed within the next few hours."

"Excellent," Noble responded, pleased that the Colonel seemed to be on top of things.

Major Stanton turned toward the Colonel and chimed in, uttering his first contribution to the meeting. "I'll leave the camps intact with all of the equipment available for their use, but they'll need to bring their night vision gear. We don't know exactly what to expect when we go in, and we'll need our own goggles."

"Thank you, Major. I'll inform them."

Max faced the Major squarely and added with a hint of sarcasm, "The new guys might want to draw straws for their assignments. The weather has been brutal, and I hear the Silver Mine is the best location because the soldiers are able to use much of the ruins for shelter." She eyed the Major suspiciously; she knew he had selected that mine for his own stakeout. Then, in a more serious frame of mind, she heeded caution. "Also, I'm sure I don't need to remind any of you that booby-traps could be set up all over this place, inside and outside."

"Piece of cake," the Major boasted, still stinging from Max's earlier dig.

Max recoiled at his self-assurance, recalling the death of the two soldiers, and replied, "If you're lucky, you'll be able to eat it, too."

Turning away from the Major, she resumed her position at the monitor and redirected their attention to the mission at hand. "As confident as we may be that no one will escape, we must still consider that possibility." She then selected another app from the top right corner of the screen. And, dramatically, a different map appeared.

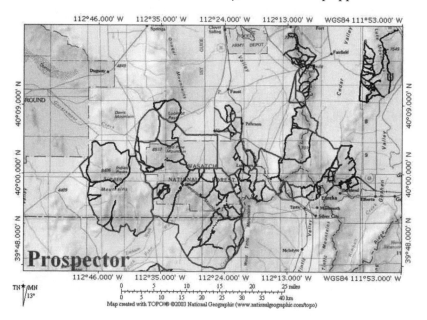

"What's that?" Noble seemed agape.

The Colonel looked up from his notes and beamed at the group. Then, he adjusted his position to face Noble and emphasized, "That's a map of your Dead Zone, sir, along with all of the other possible trails that can be used as escape routes. Director, this is God's country. There are roads out there that have never felt a footprint."

Noble shook his head while he pursed his lips. Then, he redirected his questioning to Max. "Make your point!"

She drew another circle around Silver City on the new map and called attention to the lines in the outer boundaries that resembled continents on a globe. "These represent the trails that are relatively flat and wide, mostly dirt or gravel surfaces. We've already presumed they are using a special vehicle to maneuver within the tunnels and the encampment, and those vehicles could also be used to help them escape."

"Discount the trails in the interior," the Colonel remarked confidently. "Most of which are loose gravel with rocky surfaces. It's highly unlikely they would rely on these trails as functional routes."

"So, it would narrow down our search area to here." Noble stood up and used his finger to circle the area from Eureka, just north of Silver City, over to the Wasatch National Forest and back. "We're talking about fifty-square miles of very unfriendly territory," he observed, with a trace of tension in his voice.

Max moved in and replaced the map, going back to the one that displayed the aerial view of the underground encampment.

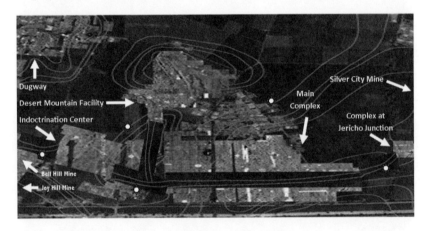

"Remember, the Emersons were killed near the Joy mineshaft and the trekkers were knocked unconscious at the same location. The Hazelton family lost their lives near the Silver City mineshaft, over here." She again pointed to the map. "We can't assume anything."

Noble got the point. "It's apparent we capture the terrorists on their own turf while they are still inside the encampment. It's clear should they escape. It would be extremely difficult to apprehend them." He was aware that the landscape was not only their friend but also their enemy. It had the potential to foil all their plans. "We can't discard the fact that they may have also built their own escape chimneys along the horizontal tunnels that run away from the encampment. You're correct, they could escape from anywhere," he conceded.

"Sir, if I may." The Colonel stood and walked to the monitor. "The possible exit points we've identified have been under twenty-four hour surveillance. I assure you that if any terrorists attempt to escape, we will capture them. Now, our best point of entry is through Desert Mountain." He pointed to the location on the map and reiterated the purpose it served for Dugway and the strategic value it now provided to access the recently discovered tunnel inside the mountain. "It would place the B Team approximately—here," he pointed, "at the end of the facility, allowing them more options once they enter. In addition, the width of tunnel will allow the Special Forces to be transported in the Humvees."

"Major, do you having anything to contribute?" Max needled.

Still smarting from her earlier rebuke, he walked over to the monitor. In a husky voice, he directed his comments to Noble. "I agree with the Colonel. Our best entry point is through Desert Mountain. Using Humvee's to transport my team and our equipment will get us to the target within twenty minutes." The Major described with military precision how he would deploy his men once inside the facility and confirmed his mission was to capture everyone. "We should go in at zero six hundred hours tomorrow, giving our terrorist friends a wake-up call. While it's highly unlikely, if they should attempt to escape, the sun will be rising, providing plenty of visibility and no place to hide. We've handled this type of operation many times." Turning his head slightly toward Max, he added, "Meaning no disrespect, ma'am, but it's a walk in the park." The Major returned to his seat.

"So we're all in accord. Operation NOMIS goes into effect at zero six hundred hours!" Noble commanded.

Noble barely finished his wrap-up when his smartphone vibrated. He excused himself to check the message, hoping it was from Enzo. Sensing all eyes were focused on him, he was careful not to display any emotion as he read the words that appeared on his screen. **Where did you get Karim Yakob's prints?** In a steady voice, Noble informed the Colonel that his supply officer's real name was Karim Yakob. He quickly glanced at Max to minimize her reaction, and then continued to explain that Yakob is a member of a terrorist cell that had been on Interpol's watch list for years.

The Colonel, while trying to hold back the obvious embarrassment he personally felt for the military, admitted, "That confirms he was the one supplying the underground facility with provisions." He paused, then added, "And the beryllium."

Noble felt the group was more than ready to swing into action. "Have all the soldiers in position—we go in just before sunrise."

As everyone stood to leave, Max faced the Colonel. "Sir, I need to speak with the Director in private. May we continue to use the conference room for a few minutes?"

"Take all the time you need."

Max and Noble remained in the room.

Everyone else departed.

⌁

"What's with you and the Major?

"Oh, he's got this macho thing going on and resents taking orders from a woman."

"I don't know. I saw the way he was watching you throughout your presentation."

"Knock it off, boss. There's something you need to see," Max prodded. Then, she went on to explain, "We were able to recover a surveillance camera that was installed in the indoctrination center. The camera was badly damaged from the explosion, but a technician was able to restore a portion of the video. It's quite grainy, but you'll be able to decipher the scenes."

Max took a deep breath, hit the *Enter* key, and then the *Play* button.

Promptly, an office appeared on the large flat screen. At one of the desks in front of a computer, they viewed the backside of a man dressed in fatigues, typing on the keyboard.

"Watch this," she urged.

A few seconds later, the man grabbed a device from the USB port. Something metallic appeared to be dangling from the device, but he hurriedly placed it in his right pants pocket.

"Keep watching."

Noble's eyes were riveted on the screen when, suddenly, the person stood up, spun around, and dashed for the door at the back of the room. Everything happened so fast Noble wasn't able to catch a glimpse of the man's face, but what he did see was shocking. "What's hanging out of his pocket?"

Max paused the video and walked over to point to the lower right edge of the monitor. "Watch right there." She returned to the keyboard and hit the *Play* button again.

As the man hastily disappeared behind the door, the doorframe lightly brushed against his pant leg and knocked the metallic object to the floor. Attached to the heavy metal object was a flash drive.

Then, the door closed shut.

Max hit the *Pause* button.

"Was that Simon?" Noble called out, not believing his own eyes.

"Yes, and he accidentally dropped the flash drive—it was not a ruse after all!" Max exclaimed.

"Evidently, he must have rigged the door to explode the next time it was opened—when the solider opened it for you." Noble looked toward Max, painfully remembering her narrow escape. Then, still stunned by the chain of events, he concluded, "Simon must have discovered that he had lost the drive and knew he wouldn't be able to return and retrieve the device. Trapped by his own trap."

28
THE CAPTURE

It was 0500 hours. Noble, Max, and the Colonel had arrived early at the command center eager to begin the mission. Shortly thereafter, Agent Burke appeared, followed moments later by Major Stanton.

"Director, my men are standing by and ready to enter the tunnel," the Major announced.

"What about the National Guard troops?"

"They are already stationed at each of the assumed exits around the perimeter of the encampment," he assured. "Sir, when you are ready, I will drive you and Agent Burke to the Desert Mountain storage facility."

The day before, all had agreed that Colonel Evans and Max would remain at the command center to oversee the operation on the large flat-screen monitor, as it was streaming from the Major's video device attached to his helmet. Noble and Max had also arranged to use their secure IMAC's to communicate directly with one another, on the off-chance they needed to convey classified information. Also, the IMAC's video technology provided a sharper close-up shot on his tablet than on the large central monitor in the command center.

Max, however, had another plan.

"Sir, I should be the one going in with the Major," she stated hesitatingly, prepared for Noble's consternation.

"Max, it's already been decided. You're staying behind this time. We need you to operate from the command center. I'm going in with the troops."

"Boss, I'm dispensable. You're not," she replied, more emphatically. Then, as though she was issuing an order, she remonstrated, "We need you here to direct the operation."

"Max!" Noble pushed back.

The others in the room shifted their attention to the Director and his deputy, and then swiftly refocused on the map displayed on the monitor to review the operation.

With an unusual display of affection, Max reached over and lightly brushed Noble's hand. While her back was faced toward the other men, she made direct eye contact with him and whispered in a less officious tone, "I know this is an especially important time for you. There's no question you are more valuable to the operation at the command center. You'll have plenty of time with him later. If he's down there, we'll capture him—you'll have your *personal* day in court."

Noble stepped aside with annoyance, which startled Max.

Then, with obvious reluctance, he reached into his pocket and handed her the other IMAC. Grudgingly, he acknowledged to himself that Max was right. His place was in the command center. "Be careful," he cautioned, and then turned to face the Major and ordered sternly, "Get everybody in position. Deputy Director Ford will be going in my place."

Without a hint of having won the battle, Max collected her gear and departed without missing a step to join Major Stanton and Agent Burke.

The Colonel then turned on the speaker system, sat back, and waited for the Major to make radio and visual contact once he reached Desert Mountain.

Meanwhile, Noble placed his IMAC around his right ear and synchronized it to his tablet. Then, he waited for Max.

Twenty minutes later, the Colonel and Noble, clearly on edge, finally viewed the B Team, along with Max and Agent Burke on the large flat-screen monitor. They were now in two-way contact with the Special Forces team leader, Major Stanton.

"B Team in position," sounded the Major's voice through the speakers.

"You are coming through loud and clear," the Colonel responded.

Noble looked down at his tablet and was able to view the scene transmitted from Max's IMAC. "Max, watch your step," he spoke softly.

"As the Major said, 'Piece of cake boss,'" was the muffled retort that echoed through his earpiece, followed by, "Can you hear me, Director," dismissing her personal comment.

"Loud and clear," Noble reacted affirmatively, and then said in a softer tone, "I can also see you checking out the Major." As he looked up from the device, he eyed the Colonel's grin.

Max could feel her face flush as she quickly jerked her head to face the entrance to the tunnel.

Noble now faced the large screen monitor and focused all his attention on the mission underway.

For the next ten minutes, Noble and the Colonel watched as the Humvees transported the members of Operation NOMIS through the shadowy tunnel. After a few twists and turns, they finally approached a large steel door, similar to the one that secured the indoctrination center.

Max, always prepared, had the prosthesis thumb ready to go again. *Perhaps I will now have Simon under his own thumb*, she mused. Following the established procedure, Max placed the thumb on the fingerprint pad and then entered the PIN number she had used before.

Noble prayed that Simon had not changed the security access.

Instantly, the door unlocked.

Two of the Special Forces thrust open the door and entered the encampment, followed by the others. As the B Team proceeded with caution, neither Noble nor the Colonel could believe what they were seeing on the big screen—nor could the soldiers on the ground.

"Unbelievable!" Max gasped.

They had just entered an extensive underground city without a soul in sight. As Max looked straight ahead, Noble could view on his tablet a wide boulevard with buildings lined up and down both sides. Actually, they looked more like shops in a mall, absent windows filled with manikins and merchandise. The buildings appeared to be older, and better constructed—unlike the indoctrination center—which appeared to be an afterthought. In place of sidewalks were moveable walkways, and in the center of the boulevard were two sets of railway tracks.

Noble continued to eye the scene from his tablet while the Colonel viewed the same scene on the large screen monitor. Seconds later, the Major, using his special issue infrared binoculars, reported that approximately five city blocks ahead on the tracks were two small train-like vehicles stationed side by side. From the monitor in the command center, they were barely visible.

Noble suddenly became acutely aware of the eerie silence that permeated the airwaves from both his IMAC and the speaker system. Only whispers were detected as the Major passed out his orders.

The Major, leading the Alpha group, ordered, "Beta, take your men and clear all buildings on the left side of the street. Kappa, take the buildings on the right. Consider anyone you may come into contact with armed and dangerous—capture anything that moves."

Totally absorbed, Noble and the Colonel watched the soldiers as they began to spread out on each side of the boulevard. The Alpha group was also in clear sight. The four soldiers, along with Max and Agent Burke, were standing behind the Major, holding their position as they waited for the *all clears*. Their mission was to move toward the trains and render them inoperable. Each time, the Major heard "Beta all clear" or "Kappa all clear" he would lead his group and proceed past the next set of buildings, moving closer and closer toward the train cars.

"Stand back," the Major ordered sharply, startling both Max and Agent Burke, bringing them to a sudden halt. Up ahead, they could see the Beta group escort several men and women toward the center of the boulevard, each with their hands cuffed behind their backs.

Previously, the Major had noticed an open courtyard between two structures. It was akin to a typical food court that one would find in a mall. He brusquely ordered Beta and Kappa to place all prisoners in the open space. He then ordered one soldier from each group to remain behind and stand guard.

Back at the command center, Noble and the Colonel continued to focus on the screen, unable to anticipate what would happen next. Periodically, Noble glanced at his tablet to obtain a birds-eye view, which made him feel as though he were actually at the scene, offering himself some consolation.

"Alpha, this is Kappa," the group leader said in a voice quiet and low. "We just found four young guys in one building that appears to be a dormitory. They claimed to have been kidnapped. What do you want me to do with them?"

"Cuff them. We'll deal with them later."

"Major, this is Director Bishop. Ask Kappa their names?"

Without wavering, the Major complied and responded.

As Noble had suspected, they were the missing cyclists. But, from the testimony of the two trekkers discovered in the indoctrination center, he knew they were also the latest terrorist recruits. "Isolate them from the other prisoners. We'll interrogate them separately."

"Yes, sir!" the Major replied.

Max listened to the conversation with great interest. She believed the cyclists would provide invaluable information that may not be volunteered by Simon—should he be captured.

From the command center, Noble and the Colonel continued to hear the all-clears from the group leaders as they reported in and, on occasion, they could view more prisoners being escorted into the courtyard.

The Alpha group continued to inch closer and closer toward the trains.

"Major, what's that?" Max called out, as she pointed to an object moving toward one of the cars.

The Major, with the use of his field glasses, eyed a man jumping onto the car on the left track as it began to move away from them in the opposite direction.

Max observed the same movement and, before the Major had the opportunity to respond, she blurted out, "He's getting away. We have to get to the other car and go after him."

"The other buildings haven't been cleared. We'll have to wait," the Major insisted.

"By then, it may be too late," Agent Burke argued, in Max's defense.

Having obtained the unexpected support, Max became more assertive than usual. "Agent Burke and I can move carefully, edging our way along the buildings until we reach the other car. Certainly, the two of us are qualified to take down one bad guy."

"Stand down," the Major barked, annoyed at having his directive questioned.

"Major." Noble's voice resonated in his earpiece and the Major sensed what was to follow. "Let them go. They know what they are doing."

"But, sir, with due respect..." the Major replied, stopping in mid-sentence, knowing it would be fruitless. After a moment's pause, he conceded. "Yes, Director, but for their own safety, Alpha group will escort them."

"Roger that, Major." Noble heard the Major's voice issue the orders immediately.

"Beta, Kappa, continue to clear the buildings. Alpha group

will proceed directly to the car. Continue to report in as additional prisoners are captured."

"Beta to Alpha, roger."

"Kappa to Alpha, roger."

The Major looked at Max with a furrowed brow and then nodded to Agent Burke, as if to say, "Keep her in line." One order was clear, "Stay close behind."

Following in lockstep with the Major and his soldiers, they managed to pass by several buildings without harm. And, within minutes, they had approached what they thought was a train. Actually, it was a single open-topped car on the opposite track and was positioned in the direction they had just traveled.

"Major, can we reverse the direction?" Max asked urgently.

Not waiting for an answer, they swiftly hopped into the six-passenger car. The Major had already begun to make the necessary adjustment and put the car into reverse gear. Instantly, they began to move toward the fleeing car. After rapidly passing several buildings, they entered another tunnel.

Max, envisioning the complex from the WAASP photo, recollected they were heading toward the other facility identified earlier near the Jericho intersection. She felt exhilarated and sensed Noble was as well. They both determined that the person who had escaped on the earlier car must have been Simon. Otherwise, the other terrorists in the encampment would have most likely attempted the same escape. It appeared they were following Simon's orders to stay out of sight, knowing a mass exodus would be impossible.

Within minutes, Max spotted the car they had been pursuing just a few yards ahead in front of a building. The car appeared to be empty. "That's the car we've been chasing," she yelled.

The Major noticed it as well, and had already slowed down their car to a crawling pace.

He cautioned them to stand ready.

"Go easy, and stay behind the soldiers," whispered a voice, emanating from Max's earpiece.

"Yes, boss," she mumbled.

Agent Burke glanced at Max, having forgotten for the moment that Noble was in complete communication with her as he watched the events unfold.

All of a sudden, the car jolted, and then came to a complete stop in front of a large cinderblock building with no windows. The only entry point was another large steel door. This time, however, there was no security pad, only a special keyed lock above the handle.

Each of them slipped quietly out of the car.

Max watched as the Major spoke to one of his soldiers, but she couldn't hear his words. However, from the actions that followed, the soldier's orders were clear.

"Stand back," the Major hollered. This time loud enough for everyone to hear.

Max obliged, as she prepared herself for an ear-piercing blast.

The soldier deftly wrapped the C4, a putty-like plastic explosive, around the lock, and then inserted a pencil detonator to ignite it. Much to her surprise, there was only a hissing sound, followed by a pop. Hastily, the soldier swung open the heavy door, allowing the Major to enter first. The rest of Alpha group, along with Max and Agent Burke, trailed closely behind. As they entered the long, dark corridor, the only illumination came from a white light streaming under a door at the far end of the hallway.

Back at command headquarters, the large screen monitor and Noble's tablet were completely black.

"Max, what's happening?" Noble shouted.

Afraid to break the silence, Max murmured, "Shush."

Before Noble had the opportunity to counter, the scene on the monitor unexpectedly changed. The pitch-black screen transformed into a dimly lit room. While Noble and the Colonel scanned the room, spotting various pieces of computer equipment, Max quickly turned and looked straight ahead.

The Major was facing the same direction.

Everyone now viewed the same scene.

Noble had an even clearer view from his device.

The shadowy chamber was actually a control center for the complex. It was unoccupied, except for one man sitting at the far end of the room. His back was faced toward them, and he appeared to be typing frantically on a keyboard. To his right, was another monitor with a view of the door they had just blasted open. He had seen them coming.

"Quick, stop him!" Max screamed.

The Major snapped a look at her before swiftly passing the order to his soldiers. Instantly, they whipped into action and wrestled the figure to the floor.

Max moved forward. Standing only a few feet behind the soldiers, she looked down at the man lying helplessly on the ground.

Noble looked up from the scene on his tablet as his heart raced. On the large monitor was a face that appeared to be staring directly at him. It was the face of the notorious terrorist—it was the face of Simon Hall.

"Noble, what is this?" Max blared into her IMAC.

Noble, still fixated on the vision on the large screen, missed the fact that the view from Max's IMAC was different. It faced the computer screen where Simon had been typing desperately. He refocused and peered down at the tablet. "Max, do not touch the *Enter* key. I repeat, do not touch the *Enter* key," he called out in a steady voice.

She froze, and then panic began to set in. As she attempted to slow down her pace, she pleaded, "What is this code? I've never seen it before."

"It's COBOL. Deliberately, he is still using the antiquated language— the same programming language he used on the flash drive." Noble was positive Simon was relying on the fact that most people would not be able to decipher the language, let alone write the code.

"What is he trying to do?" Max tried to contain her nervousness.

"Tap the *Page Up* key—only once." Noble waited, and then skimmed the code in a hurry. "Okay, again."

"Noble, please tell me what's going on," she pleaded.

"Go ahead, Noble. Tell her what's going on," bellowed their newly captured prisoner.

"Ignore him, Max. Now slowly scroll down."

"Noble, you're really unnerving me."

"Okay, now hit the *Enter* key," he said, evenly, attempting to calm her.

Max took a deep breath and, although she trusted Noble with her life, she was a bit frightened.

"Max, hit the key," he repeated, maintaining his composure.

She reached down and pressed the key marked *Enter*. Clearly exasperated, she cried, "There! Now will you tell me what that was all about?" Before Noble could respond, Max had taken off her IMAC and positioned it so she could stare him squarely in the eye.

From his tablet, Noble could plainly see she was fuming. In a repentant tone, he stated, "al-Fadl was programming the security system to lock down the facility, attempting to trap everyone inside. Fortunately, he hadn't yet compiled the program, so it could not be executed."

It was evident from the look on Max's face that she had heard him through the earpiece. Then, as she slowly placed the IMAC back over her ear, Noble could hear her exclaim, "You son-of-a-bitch! I thought he was going to blow us all to smithereens."

Ignoring her momentary flare-up, he immediately refocused on the monitor. The Special Forces were in the process of pulling Simon to his feet, with his hands cuffed securely behind him. It sickened Noble as he watched Simon on the large monitor leer at Max with amusement.

Noble took a deep breath. It was time to issue orders.

"Major, I want you to transport the prisoner personally to the Utah State Penitentiary in Draper. I've arranged with the warden to have him placed in Supermax. He is to speak with no one."

"Director, may I ask who the prisoner is, and why he requires special handling?"

"Major, you have your orders."

Facing the Colonel, with Max and the Major listening in, Noble directed, "Please detain all prisoners in the brig on the base." Then, he asked, "Major, what was the total count?"

"We captured thirty-five prisoners plus the four men who insist they'd been kidnapped."

"We have the capacity to detain all prisoners," the Colonel responded, without hesitation.

"Hold them without questioning until you hear from me."

"Yes, Director." The Colonel obliged.

Max chimed in, "What do you want us to do with the encampment?"

Noble was grateful that Max's anger had subsided and that she had refocused on the mission. "Major, have your men work with Max to sweep the facility and collect all forensic evidence. I want fingerprints, hair—anything and everything you can lift or swab." Looking over toward the Colonel, Noble requested, "Do you have a secure location to store whatever evidence they gather?"

"Director, there is a storage facility next to building number twenty. I'll give Max the combination to the lock."

"Thank you, Colonel."

"Max, start combing through all the evidence as soon as possible."

"Yes, sir."

"Major." Noble wavered slightly before issuing his next command.

"Yes, Director." The Major noticed the hint of hesitation.

"Once your men have gathered the evidence, all other perishables and any personal belongings not in evidence are to be taken out to the desert and destroyed. Leave each of the ventilation escape hatches intact. While they are somewhat camouflaged, cover them with any vegetation you find in the area. Make all entrances to the facilities impassable, permanently, with the exception of the Desert Mountain entrance. Secure the entrance discovered inside the Desert Mountain facilities. It must be concealed and undetectable. Major, do you understand your orders?"

"Roger that, sir."

As a matter of course, Noble would inform the president privately as to the location of the only accessible entrance to the Presidential Lair—a new notation waiting for the President's *Book of Secrets*. But, now, Noble would issue his final and most vital directive. "The underground encampment will officially cease to exist once the evidence is collected and the entrances are sealed." He paused, giving each of them time to absorb his words. "If the location of the underground facility is ever disclosed by any person, it will be considered an act of treason. This directive comes from the president. Do each of you understand?"

The Colonel was the first to respond, recalling the president's earlier edict delivered by Noble. "Yes, Director. You have my assurance."

Max looked at the Major, urging his response.

"Director, you have my word and the word of my men." The Major glared back at Max and mouthed, "Your turn."

"Max," Noble voiced, waiting for her pledge.

"Yes, sir. I understand completely," she replied, while visually rebuffing the Major.

Noble was thankful military orders were accepted without question. He anticipated, however, that in a private venue Max would grill him on the details. Most important, he was confident each of them understood the seriousness of the presidential mandate. Satisfied, he cautioned, "Major, do not let the prisoner out of your sight. I want him in Supermax within the hour. I suggest you take one of your men to assist in the transport. That's all. Proceed." Before removing his IMAC, Noble half-whispered to Max, "I'm heading to Draper to interrogate our prisoner as soon as I alert the president."

"Good luck—and we need to talk."

"Later, Max."

☙

Noble informed President Post that they had captured Mohammed al-Fadl, and that the Special Forces were transporting him by military helicopter to the maximum security prison in Draper. Noble then requested that the president make the necessary arrangements to transport him to GITMO, since it required presidential authority.

The military base in Guantanamo Bay had remained open against the wishes of the liberal left, and continued to house "enemy combatants," or, more properly, identified as terrorists of the worse kind. In fact, in 2012, the former president changed his position and signed the National Defense Authorization Act that codified the indefinite detention of terrorist suspects. In addition, it sanctified the military commissions' role to preside over the trials for these prisoners.

President Post was acutely aware of the human rights activists who continued to wage their protest against the incarcerations. To appease the outspoken critics, he personally arranged for three senators from the intelligence committee to travel to Utah as special envoys. Their primary role was to be present during interrogations and to ensure the protection of the prisoner's rights that were often in dispute. Then, they would personally escort the prisoner to the military prison in Cuba.

Noble needed to reach the Utah State Penitentiary first.

29
THE FACEOFF

Noble stood in the doorway of the poorly lit interrogation room, illuminated only by a single row of lights. Dangling precariously from the ceiling, the lights cast an ominous yellow glow over the sparse furnishings situated below. Centered in the room were the two chairs and the table he had inspected on his earlier visit. Seated comfortably in the chair, bolted to the floor, was Simon Hall, flashing his famous, unnerving Cheshire grin.

Noble chose to linger in the doorway for a few seconds as his mind flashed rapidly through the surreal events that led him to this reunion. And, while he resisted staring at the grin on the face of his former Harvard classmate, he did notice the subtle telltale signs of aging. Then, he glanced downward to inspect Simon's hands—shackled to the arms of the chair.

Hunting down Simon burned through years of Noble's life. First, he sought him to repay the tuition money Simon had loaned him in his time of need. Then, he set out tenaciously to capture the notorious terrorist and to seal his fate—most probably to face a death sentence.

"Hey, Noble," said a voice from the past, instantly ending his reverie. "You're a little gray around the temples." Simon chuckled. "But, you're still the epitome of a computer geek."

Hearing his name mouthed by Simon surprisingly irked him. He quipped, "You, however, never appeared the nerdy sort. Perhaps, that should have been my first clue." Noble forced a constricted smile. Then, he walked to the empty chair and sat down across from his nemesis. While seated, he continued to study intensely the face of someone he once considered a friend.

"What's the matter, Noble. You look like you've seen the devil."

"I have. The devil is you."

Taken aback, Simon stiffened in his chair. "What do you mean?" he rebuffed in a flaccid attempt at innocence. His broad smile relaxed as his lips tightened. He appeared aggrieved as he leaned down to cross his heart with his shackled right hand and implored, "I'm just a highly competent computer hacker and a profitable cyber-thief." Then, he sat upright and, in a harsher voice, he parried, "What do you really know about anything, Noble?"

Noble had learned ages ago that Simon was a master of psychological manipulation, so he maintained his guard. He was on alert, and proceeded with caution. Fortunately, over the years, the CIA's resident shrink had coached him on probative techniques, usually before entering into a serious interrogation. Over time, he became quite adept at understanding social behavior. But, Noble continued to remind himself to be wary of Simon. Thus far, he wasn't buying Simon's antics.

Oddly, this was the first time they had been together, where Noble found himself in a one-on-one situation on neutral ground. Of course, there were social events, when they tossed down their share of beers at Jake's Pub and shared several casual dinners, but always with the other members of the group. The only real time clocked alone with Simon was when Noble was his most vulnerable. He remembered the time when Simon recovered his computer program that mysteriously disappeared into cyberspace. Then, of course, there was the time the campus hooker approached him, and Simon swooped in to vouch for Noble's character to the campus security officer. With sadness, he recalled Simon's kindness when he learned of his parents' death. Simon had provided him with an airline ticket to return to Kansas to attend the funeral and loaned him the full tuition for his final semester at Harvard. Apparently, Simon did not anticipate repayment. However, it was a debt Noble tried fervently to repay.

But that was then.

Now, as he observed him sitting impatiently in the interrogation room, he could easily conceive how Simon had seduced the other members of La Fratellanza. He, too, had fallen into his web. Without question, Simon had successfully manipulated the group to carry out his clandestine plot.

Using the skills he honed at the CIA, Noble became an accomplished interrogator. He understood the importance of maintaining control of the debriefing, especially when facing someone who was accustomed to being in control. For the moment, he chose to avert the main topic until he had the suspect talking freely.

With Simon noticeably agitated so early in the session, Noble sensed an advantage and redirected the conversation to La Fratellanza. There would be plenty of time later to edge his way into the more explosive aspects of the plot—a plot he believed was a work in progress and had not yet come to fruition. Besides, he had waited over a decade to hear the answers to specific questions with a more personal dimension.

"Let's discuss a topic with which we are both familiar, your study group at Harvard. I was quite amazed at how you were able to convince the others to go along with the game and shape it into a reality."

Simon eased back into his chair and began to drum his fingertips on the armrest, an attempt to forestall answering. *He thinks by using innocuous statements instead of questions that he will somehow induce me to confess.* Suddenly, he shifted closer to the edge of his chair.

To Noble's surprise, Simon's mood had also shifted, and he seemed rather entertained and prepared to respond.

"Honestly, it took me years to assemble our illustrious group. It was no easy task. First, I had to locate the talent. Then, I screened each of them—including you—through what you might call an *assessment phase*. I identified each of your personal vulnerabilities. We all have them, you know—even you Noble." His smug look reverted. Clearly, he was delighted with his personal affront.

Noble noted Simon's emphasis on the words *assessment phase*. And, while they are innocuous words to most, Simon—a master of psychology—knew it was a clinical term to describe the basic manipulative strategy of a psychopath. Simon wasn't technically a psychopath, but Noble had already discerned that his conduct paralleled psychopathic behavior. *He's toying with me,* he mused. *Now, let's see if he follows up the assessment phase with the standard manipulation phase.* But, first, Noble decided to try some manipulation techniques of his own. Ignoring the provoking comments, he expertly redirected the conversation back to Simon. "It's evident that you've discovered their weaknesses, but you must admit that these extremely intelligent men also have strong wills of their own. Naturally, they would be more resistant to manipulation than the average person."

He took the bait.

"Noble, I pride myself on being an ardent student of human behavior." He bragged, and then expounded on, how he tested each of their inner strengths and desires to determine what tactics were likely to be most effective. "Over the course of time, I was able to build a personal relationship with each of them. It wasn't difficult to entice them to become part of an exclusive group—so I created one. It was a simple matter to appeal to their considerable egos." Simon watched Noble's expressionless face and, with slight annoyance, he boasted, "I'm proud to say it took just over a year for us to bond as brothers. Our campus classmates used to refer to us as the *Brainy Rat Pack*. But, you know all this—you were on the periphery."

There was still no reaction from Noble, despite the fact he was repulsed each time Simon invoked his name.

Simon continued to pontificate as he amplified his eye contact. "I preyed on the one thing all great men have in common—the desire to accomplish the impossible." Appearing as though he had just given a victorious summation, he beamed with a look of self-satisfaction.

Noble thought it was a gesture akin to taking a bow, but he continued to ignore Simon's theatrics and moved the conversation along. "These intellectuals had to have known they would end up flirting with the law and would put themselves and their families in jeopardy," he countered.

"No, they didn't." Simon denied. "I assured them I'd take all the risks. In the final analysis, avoidance of risk is a common human behavior trait and, when offered, it's irresistible bait for most people. Actually, I carved out the riskiest assignments for you, specifically. You, however, were a no-show. So, having no choice, I was forced to assume that role."

Noble smiled wanly. "You missed the mark, being unable to identify my presumed vulnerability."

"But, I did, Noble. It was that your rock solid integrity. The problem at the time was that I couldn't quite figure out how to exploit it—until recently." Simon's grin returned.

Noble recognized that he had inadvertently opened the door to personal counter plays, but he chose to allow Simon to indulge in his own power game. However, this time he posed a question. "Once you convinced the others to play the game, how did you retain their loyalty for all of those years?"

Simon, enjoying the stage, gleefully carried on with his dogmatic statements. "Each year, as the technology changed, I'd update La Fratellanza's pagers. We had a system for sending and receiving messages, and they each knew they had to respond. It was like keeping them on a tether. However, during one of the upgrades, unbeknownst to them, I included a GPS and listening device to monitor their activities," he admitted with egotistic pride. "I always knew where they were—and what they were saying. I found it great sport to listen in on their conversations. They could never figure out the connection, but it created a touch of paranoia among the group that became a very powerful and extremely useful instrument." Simon paused as he furrowed his brow. Then, with another complete turnabout in behavior, he said sternly, "It was a terrible blow to discover they were testifying before you at CIA headquarters—and before the game had finished."

For the first time, Simon appeared perturbed.

Or, was he simply feigning anger, trying to lure me to admit to something? Noble rolled around in his mind.

Steering away from the direct response, Noble inquired calmly, "Simon, you've already taken your revenge on our government. Baari did a superb job of damaging the fabric of our society through your maneuverings. Why did you still find it necessary to seek revenge on your brothers, the same people who helped you carry out your plot?"

Simon maintained his cold expression as he shouted, "Betrayal!"

Noble was incorrect in his assessment. He learned immediately that Simon was genuinely angry. But, he continued to sit back in his chair with crossed arms and remained complacent.

"I demanded loyalty!" Then, in a remarkably calmer tone, Simon avowed, "I was loyal to my brothers, and they betrayed me. It's that simple."

Up to that point, Noble's objectivity had remained in check. But, then, it became a bit more personal, enticing him to open up another line of questioning. "So, you found it fitting to destroy Chase, removing him from his dream job, and to slander Seymour, banishing him from the Washington scene. You only toyed with Hank's career but, interestingly, you left Paolo's life intact."

Simon confessed freely. "Hank had been a good soldier and still provided utility, but it appears that has changed. As for Paolo," he paused, "I'm saving him in case I decide to destroy you." He gloated menacingly.

As anticipated, Simon had moved to the predictable third and final phase of manipulation, that of *abandonment*. He no longer found La

Fratellanza useful in his discourse and, most likely, moved on to find someone else to join him in the master plot. The *who* would have to wait—for now Noble wanted to know *why*.

As Noble glowered, a peculiar stillness set in. Each was trying to gain the advantage, as in a fencing duel. Noble reasoned, however, that it was vital that he be the one to break the eerie silence and maintain control. "The assassination attempts against the French President, the German Chancellor, and the British Prime Minister were intentionally designed by you to fail. We've concluded that they were a preliminary test, a veritable dry run."

"Perhaps, one could say that."

"Is the German Chancellor your next target?"

"A wild guess, old boy?"

"Why are you targeting the European leaders?"

Simon slouched back into his chair. "Noble, you're boring me with your questions. I expected a more innovative approach coming from you. Please, do tell, what are the rules of engagement?"

Simon's attempt to provoke failed.

"Why did Yakob use beryllium to make the casing for the bomb used in London? Its rarity made it fairly easy to trace."

Simon continued to appear blasé but, actually, he was quite impressed with how much Noble had already deciphered. "Well done. You've done your homework. Now, to answer your question. First, beryllium was readily available." That annoying half-smile returned. "Second, at the time Yakob made the bomb, it was inconceivable that you'd be snooping around a desert in the middle of Utah."

Noble summarily relaunched. "Is that why you purposely lured me to Lyon?"

"Wasn't it obvious?" Simon shook his head. "You were getting too close for comfort and were about to expose the encampment. And, might I add, you cost me dearly in time and money." He waved his right hand as best he could. "Enough with the inquisition."

"Sorry, Simon, I have many more questions. And you *will* answer them," Noble warned.

He proceeded with his questioning as he tried hard to feign indifference to the responses. Finally, Simon stopped his sparring and began to speak more freely again. Noble seized the opportunity to delve deeper into the evidence that Enzo, Max, and he had uncovered, starting with the specific attacks on New Year's Eve. After several hours, Simon only substantiated what they had already deciphered—

the attempts were predetermined to fail.

Then, Noble moved on to the activities in Juab County, Utah. He was able to confirm that the camp was indeed a recruitment and training center used to build a militia. The purpose was still unclear, and the number of recruits still unknown. He ascertained that the four cyclists were Americans who had joined the camp. Then, Simon claimed that the murders of the Emerson couple and the four kayakers had been unfortunate collateral damage. He allowed that the victims had witnessed crucial events taking place around the mineshafts. He ascertained that the recruits at the camp felt threatened, and determined they had no recourse but to silence them. Simon swore that neither he nor his soldiers were responsible for the deaths of the Hazelton family.

"It is not our mission or our style," he insisted.

Noble was suspicious of his repudiation but, strangely enough, Simon appeared to be sincere. However, there were other possibilities Noble had yet to pursue. The questioning proceeded for another hour, with periodic bouts of boasting, elucidations, and very few denials. But, when Noble attempted to wind down the discussion, Simon threw a parting shot.

"Unfortunately, I wasn't able to persuade the two trekkers to join my cause. It was a real setback. It reminded me of you, Noble. They also appeared to be nerdy," he baited.

Clearly, Simon was in a comfort zone. He continued to reveal an unforeseen flurry of information, much beyond Noble's expectations. As for the information specific to Utah, there was nothing illuminating divulged.

Simon again appeared to return into his protective shell. He was no longer forthcoming.

At that juncture, Noble believed he had gathered all the information he could evoke from their first encounter. He was well aware that it would take hours, possibly days or weeks, to analyze the events of the day. He was also confident that Simon was tantalizing him, forcing him to dig deep into the content to find the elusive nuances. Noble maintained his resolve, and he continually reminded himself, *I'm better at this than he is.*

Noble miscalculated. Simon had not finished provoking, arousing Noble's suspicion.

He abruptly edged to the front of his seat and peered directly at Noble. "Do you ever examine your own theories? Allow your thinking process to evolve beyond your initial premise?"

Noble was stone-faced. "Appeal to motive—of course."

Frequently, as a matter of routine during investigations, Noble would use this pattern of argument and call into question his own theory of a case by challenging his premises to determine if he had missed any fallacies. It was akin to playing both offense and defense.

Though Noble was tiring and ready to wrap things up for the day, he decided to appeal to Simon's elephantine ego. "I understand your method of argumentation is one of many of your strong suits, Simon— one you've successfully used among the members of La Fratellanza to your advantage. As each formulated his thesis at Harvard, you were effective as the devil's advocate. By weaving your convictions into what they subliminally regarded to be their own, by questioning their motives, you used the method brilliantly—and they obliged unknowingly."

"Thank you, Noble, for the praise, but I was speaking about you when you cleverly attempted to turn the tables. Have you ever questioned your own theory about my ulterior motives, applying the techniques you espouse?"

Noble was irked at how often Simon tried to gain control of the interview. Nevertheless, he was curious about his line of questioning and played along, at least for the moment. He sat back and waited, urging him to continue.

Simon took his cue.

"You discovered a bank statement with an address, a fingerprint on the light switch in the apartment in Menlo Park, and a flash drive with photographs. But, you doggedly pursued the clues that fit your own presumptions. I observed this flaw from a distance."

Disregarding Simon's attempt to bait him, he turned the tables once again. "I presumed the trail of evidence was intentionally left behind by you—including the flash drive." Purposely being dismissive, he indicated, "The reasons behind your decisions are not important to me at this time. I'm not here to engage in psycho-jousting."

Simon tried hard to look unaffected as he unwittingly took the bait. He craned his head to the right, in a slightly contorted fashion, and glared at Noble. "You're correct. I dropped the flash drive deliberately to lure you into the encampment. Too bad you had to send that pretty agent in your stead."

Noble knew full well that dropping the flash drive was unintentional. It was plausible that Simon would assume that he'd found the drive by chance, after the explosion. Most important, Noble had his *tell*, another interrogation technique he had mastered. Simon's response provided him with a telltale sign, which he would use to determine the veracity of future statements—it was the first time Simon had moved his head in such a manner during the lengthy interrogation—it was a recognized physical gesture indicating he had lied.

Not revealing the existence of the video that proved Simon had accidentally dropped the flash drive, Noble began to use his own reverse psychology. "At last, all the pieces of the puzzle are falling into place." *It's not true, but it's important that Simon believes I've exposed his plot.*

Not missing an opportunity for one more jab, Simon responded, "You disappoint me, brother. I thought you'd consider the reasons behind my actions to be just as relevant as the actions themselves."

Acting exasperated, Noble blurted out, "Okay, I give up. Why?" His question, however, proved to be mistimed and risky.

"Did you ever question why or how your parents died?"

Noble felt sucker-punched by the lowest of personal blows, but maintained a stoic expression. He refused to delve into that emotionally charged subject. He would not succumb to Simon's baiting the trap. While he had long suspected Simon was in some way responsible for their deaths, he avoided Simon's ploy, and resolved to stay on point. Staring directly into his nemesis' eyes, he intoned, "You asked me earlier what I knew." He then paused briefly to garner Simon's full attention. "Let me put things in perspective for you. Your name is Mohammed al-Fadl, and you are responsible for horrendous terrorist acts killing many innocent people. You placed an illegal immigrant at the helm of the U.S. government and stole from our treasury. You are responsible for several deaths in Juab County, in Paris, and in Berlin. All of these actions are dry runs to prepare for your next major act of terror."

"It's amazing what a little intellect and money can accomplish."

His glibness was unsettling. Noble was clearly annoyed. He had allowed Simon to outflank him. *What's done is done,* he admonished himself.

In the meantime, Simon's grin had returned to its full glory as he flapped his hands with restricted motion, mimicking a grand applause. "Well done, Noble, but you are forgetting two things. First, when using syllogistic logic, your operating premise must hold true, otherwise your theory will not be valid. Second, let's not forget your role in all of this!" he decried in a raised voice, twisting the proverbial knife a bit further.

Noble remained mute—a clear signal for Simon to continue.

Reflecting on his past actions, Simon moved to recap. "Obviously, hacking into the banks was the source of my war chest. It was a matter of necessity for me to accomplish my lofty goals. The robberies intrigued Hamilton, so he took it upon himself to pursue me, poor fellow."

The mention of Hamilton disturbed Noble, but he replied evenly, "You're not telling me anything I haven't already proved."

"Noble, your insolence will not help you get any closer to the truth," he reprimanded, as if he were scolding a child.

"You're being evasive. None of what you have divulged explains your mission in Utah, and it doesn't fully explain Europe either," Noble answered matter-of-factly, ignoring his rebuke.

"Perhaps, but I'm not finished."

"Finished with what?"

"Noble, I don't intend to make it easy for you. It's been a lot of fun, stringing you along all of these years. At first, the game was between Hamilton and me, but that became boring. I was thrilled at the irony and my luck when you joined the SIA." Unabashedly, he continued with his superficial charm. "By the way, I never congratulated you on finding the backdoor code to access my bank accounts. Although, I wasn't happy with your siphoning most of the money out of those accounts. I have to admit that was my one great failing—underestimating your abilities."

"You changed the author's name on your thesis from your name to mine, exposing me to possible future legal vulnerability. You purposely lured me to read your thesis. You had to assume I'd uncover your programming code designed to hack into various databases, including banks. But why did you lead me to find the backdoor code to your computer program in the first place?" Noble asked with observable curiosity.

"I was hoping you'd come after me. But then Hamilton came up with that lame sting operation in Florence and ruined all my fun," Simon conceded with the same annoying grin.

"That's not why." Suddenly, the appeal to motive struck Noble like a lightning bolt. *He never thought I would get this far. Now he's trying to convince me that his purported cat and mouse game was intentional. He is trying to mislead me into believing that he was going to assassinate one or several heads of state, who were only decoys—but that's not his plan—or is it?* Noble resolved to analyze his assumptions more thoroughly, away from the interrogation room, away from Simon. But, for now, he would play along. "Your plot spanned decades. Initially, Baari becoming president was only one of several dry runs. He was also your strongest means to an end and provided you access into the government, and ultimately to the government coffers. Do you already have puppets in place in various roles in European governments?"

"Perhaps," Simon insinuated coyly.

There was no craning of his head this time, but Noble sensed Simon was lying by omission, recognizing the blatant evasiveness.

"Noble, aren't you curious as to why I've been stringing you along?"

Unmistakably, he was attempting to divert the conversation once again, but Noble decided to extend one final opportunity and shouted, "WHY?" in a clearly exasperated tone.

"Finally, I have your attention!" Simon trumpeted, and then the rant began. He had been savoring the moment. "It's RETRIBUTION. You rejected me, my brother. You were the one and only person capable of performing a key role in my game. When you refused, the responsibility fell to me, and it forced an insurmountable delay in the operation. And, at a crucial moment you restricted my brothers—my invaluable assets—from participating further. The mission, scheduled for completion before Baari left office, was delayed. His premature departure, again thanks to you, forced me to adjust accordingly." Simon stopped unexpectedly, seemingly spent by his outburst.

Noble seized the opportunity to jump in. "I've missed something," he admitted. "Why drop your clues like breadcrumbs? You could have taken your revenge on me at any time."

"The clues were supposed to be a hint of my original intent, starting with placing your name on my thesis. They were the same clues I would have planted had you joined La Fratellanza. But the game is not over and, at some point in the future, when I no longer need you— whenever that might be—I will plant evidence implicating you in the ultimate plot. And, I will seal your fate. My bag of tricks is far from empty." Simon basked in the glow of his admission.

Noble was finding Simon more disturbing and out of character as he openly revealed his own cunning. He also found it odd that Simon even felt it necessary to take credit for being so ruthless. Apparently, he had no qualms about causing harm to those he befriended and had relied upon. Nothing stood in his path. *A true character trait of a psychopath,* he pondered with unease. Noble detected Simon was using another psychological technique, generally recognized as definitive *covert intimidation*—posing thinly veiled threats in an effort to put him on the defensive. He also took into account another frightening possibility—*perhaps Simon actually is a psychopath. He certainly is exhibiting the classic traits.*

One thing was certain. In those last few moments, Noble had expertly coaxed Simon to reveal his vulnerability—*control freakery*— an obsessive need to be in control, documented in psychiatric research. *I played him all wrong. I gave him the control he craved, thinking it was the best way to expose the plot. Now it was time to take that control away and hit him hard.*

"Are you still working with al-Qaeda, or are you on your own?"

Simon flinched. "What makes you think I'm connected to al-Qaeda?

"We have surveillance tapes of you with Osama bin-Laden at the training camp in Kursu, in Srinagar, and again in Abbottabad at his compound in Pakistan."

Noble had caught Simon off guard with the abrupt change in direction and demeanor.

"Kursu, ah, Kursu. Years ago, I conducted training exercises for al-Qaeda. I've been in that camp many times. As for the compound in Pakistan, I was never there, nor was bin-Laden," he stated emphatically.

"Our intelligence shows that bin-Laden was last seen in Pakistan in 2011 when he was killed."

"Your intelligence is weak at best. The assassination was an illusion." Simon revealed.

"Why do you say an illusion?"

"Neither I nor bin-Laden were ever in a compound in Abbottabad. The last time I saw Osama was in October of 2001, a month after your precious towers imploded. Two months later, he died. I remember the day explicitly; it was the fourteenth of December."

"How is that possible? He was killed on May 2, 2011, by our U.S. Navy Seals in a raid on the compound," Noble objected.

"Perhaps you should ask your government for the truth. I'm telling you Osama bin-Laden has been dead for over a decade. He died ultimately from Marfan syndrome, a genetic disorder of the connective tissue. The disease affected his kidneys for years, and then it moved to his lungs."

"I'm familiar with the disease. Go on," Noble insisted, hiding his skepticism.

"He's buried in the mountains in southeastern Afghanistan, outside of Kandahar. Over the years, as Osama's health deteriorated, he had relinquished most of his power to others, and his role became more symbolic. When he died, the al-Qaeda elders thought it best to preserve the image that he was still alive, which they did successfully with rigged videos. His name alone continued to evoke rabid support for the cause. Your government's plot to assassinate bin-Laden in 2011 was simply a production orchestrated by the Baari administration. You're foolish to believe otherwise. Has anyone produced a body?"

Noble had contemplated the same question, but ducked the debate. "What purpose would it serve the U.S.?"

Simon appeared self-assured as he offered an explanation. "Actually, it served several purposes. First, it distracted the public from the growing question of Baari's legitimacy as a natural born U.S. citizen. Second, it was a way to deflect Pakistan from retaliating for the predator drone strikes that killed hundreds of Pakistanis." Then, his tone changed, suddenly sounding more calculating and less conciliatory. "It also created another salutary effect. By escalating the war throughout the Middle East, it provided many opportunities for my brethren to swoop into positions of power in the various failed governments. Whether that was an intended consequence on Baari's part, I'm not sure. Evidently, he reaped the benefit in Libya."

Simon's last statement unnerved Noble. He held there was some truth to his conjecture. But, he vowed to stay on point. "You were still actively pulling Baari's strings through Hank during that time. What was your involvement in this alleged cover-up surrounding bin-Laden's death?" Noble remained detached.

"Absolutely none!"

Noble's lack of emotion seemed to irritate Simon. *Perfect*, he thought.

Simon, wasting no time, continued. "By that time, Baari had become a cunning lone wolf, abandoning those of us who created his role. He was acting out mostly on his own accord. Remember what I said earlier about intelligent men and their lust for power—prime example."

"Let's go back to your mission. Are you working in conjunction with al-Qaeda?"

"Noble, what I have planned goes far beyond their parochial jihads. They suffer from tunnel vision, thinking they can blanket the world with Sharia Law in an attempt to replace all professed godless regimes with Islamic regimes."

As Noble continued to maintain eye contact, he noticed that Simon's eyes were becoming beadier by the moment. He maintained silence and let him continue.

Simon fumed about how the western values had corrupted much of the world. He elaborated about the positive aspects of Sharia Law, the original law of Islam, laid down by the Prophet Mohammed. Several minutes passed, and then, surprisingly, he relaxed his sermon and mildly commented, "There is a better way to accomplish this lofty goal without indiscriminate killing. Certainly, by destroying the U.S. one building at a time, like a game of dominos, won't further the cause any closer to the objective. In fact, a simple flip of a switch is all it would take to bring America to her knees. Osama agreed, and sanctioned my plan, a plan that is much broader in scope and goes far beyond religion."

Noble sensed he had just opened another door, one perhaps he should have left closed—at least for the time being. He knew he was unprepared for that line of questioning. Of the moment, his head was spinning. In part, he was still reeling from Simon's prior outburst.

"Who the hell is Simon Hall?" He was completely frustrated. *"I need more time to review the situation in the Middle East. I need to find the connection,"* he concluded to himself, not revealing the inadequacy he was sensing.

It was late. Once again, Noble began to wind down the grilling, although, as he shuffled through his notes, he looked over in Simon's direction and hurled one more question. "How did you learn about the underground bunker in Utah?"

Simon's mood took a complete turnabout yet again.

Noble found it perplexing to witness those instant transformations.

This time, Simon reverted from an adversary to a docile witness. Aside from the fact that the interrogation had spanned more than five hours, he appeared astonishingly energetic and quite happy to continue their discussion.

"Pure luck!" He grinned, and then continued to enlighten. "During Baari's first days in the Oval Office, while he was in the midst of learning protocol—and before he learned to keep his mouth shut—he blathered to Hank about some President's *Book of Secrets*. He described a hush-hush underground hideout known only to the U.S. presidents. Hank, of course, told me. It was the perfect solution to one of my dilemmas. Consequently, I instructed him to get a copy of the blueprint with the location."

"So how did Hank manage to get the blueprint?"

"Easy. A week later, Baari was reading the book when Hank entered the Oval Office. A few moments later, the First Lady called to speak with Baari. He excused himself and took the call in his study. While he was out of the room, Hank simply ripped the page out of the book," Simon explained passively, without giving any recognition as to the enormity of the violation.

On the other hand, Noble was aghast at the thought of Hank desecrating a national treasure. Not giving Simon time to comment, he asked, "How did you secure the location?"

"Land grabs. And, of course, the cancellation of drilling leases in that area. Hank took care of the details."

"So, Hank knows the whereabouts of the underground bunker?"

"Only in general terms. He never made a copy of the map; that's not his M-O. And, I never told him about my plans—and he knew not to ask."

"So Hank and the other members of La Fratellanza were simply puppets being manipulated?"

"Bingo!" Simon leaned back in his chair and shrugged his shoulders. Then, abruptly, he returned to an upright position.

For a split second, Noble feared that Simon would leap over the table and grab his throat, forgetting that his wrists were shackled to the bolted-down chair.

"You got me! And, in the fullness of time you'll know everything," he trumpeted.

However, knowing Simon, Noble correctly discerned it wasn't quite that simple—there had to be more.

The hour was now late, and Simon had finally worn him to a frazzle. Noble finally decided to end the questioning and continue in the morning. He needed to be sharp throughout the rest of the interrogation. "I'm finished with you now, but I will be back early tomorrow. And, you will answer the remaining questions," Noble cautioned, then quickly called for the guard.

During the next few moments, Simon tried to engage Noble in small talk, but he resisted any attempt, as he feigned taking notes, disregarding him in the process. Fortunately, the guard arrived promptly, and personally escorted Simon back to his cell.

As Simon walked out the door, he couldn't resist looking back at Noble to flash his Cheshire grin.

Noble ignored him and ruminated, *it's imperative I uncover Simon's overall plan. Especially before the President's special envoys arrive.*

He left the interrogation room and stopped at the guard's desk.

"I'd like the digital feed from the video, please," Noble requested.
"Director, I'd first have to get permission from the warden."
Noble gave him an icy look. "It won't be a problem."
The guard complied.

30
THE SCORPION

Noble checked into the Ramada Inn and proceeded to his room. After removing his jacket and tie, he poured himself a glass of mediocre wine from the mini-bar and prepared for a late night. He needed to update Max. He prayed that she had some invaluable evidence, something he could use during his second round with Simon. But, first, he felt compelled to review the interrogation.

Noble opened his xPhad and retrieved the video to revisit his last six and half hours. At first, he fast-forwarded, periodically pausing at random scenes. Ironically, he seemed to stop at points where Simon had assumed control. The agitation resurfaced instantaneously.

Who is Simon Hall? A question he could not escape.

Noble hit the *Pause* button again.

"What do you really know about anything," rang out from his speaker system.

He couldn't help but stare at the man he had called the devil. Shaking his head, he hit the *Fast Forward* button, and then instinctively paused at the part where they discussed the killings in the Dead Zone. *Simon claimed the murders had been unfortunate collateral damage. Eerily, he seemed sincere. Why is it so hard for me to believe he's a killer?* He tried to envision the possibility.

He froze the scene again, just after he heard Simon's voice ask, "Did you ever question why or how your parents died?" The monster on the screen was staring back. Strangely, that statement caused Noble to think back to the time when Hamilton had answered his question with a question, as if to say, *how could you think I'm culpable? Could Simon possibly be challenging the question—one he knew I must have asked myself time and time again? Is it possible he was not responsible for their deaths? Stay focused*, Noble reminded himself.

Moving the video along, he hit the *Play* button.

Simon was in the midst of asking, "Do you ever examine your own theories? Allow your thinking to evolve beyond your initial premise?"

Noble hit *Fast Forward* again, then *Play*.

"First, when using syllogistic logic, your operating premise must hold true, otherwise your theory will not be valid."

He hit *Fast Forward*, then *Play*.

"Osama, on the other hand, sanctioned my plan, a plan that is much broader in scope and goes far beyond religion."

Punching the *Stop* button on the tablet, Noble shouted in frustration, "Who the hell is Simon Hall?"

He marched over to the mini bar and, reluctantly, traded in his wine glass for a pot of black coffee. It was going to be a long night. It was eight o'clock, and he anticipated Max was impatiently sitting by the phone, waiting for his update. But, before he made the call, there was one more source which might provide the answer to that nagging question.

Seated back at the desk, he synchronized his keyboard to his tablet and logged into SAVIOR.

In 2009, the only connection made between Simon Hall and Mohammed al-Fadl was from a fingerprint retrieved from the apartment in Menlo Park. Noble first ran the print through IAFIS, the Integrated Automated Fingerprint Identification System, but it returned a *No Match*. Then fortunately, Interpol was able to match that fingerprint with a fingerprint taken from a bomb fragment used in the bombing of the embassy in Nairobi in 1988. After making the connection, Noble ran Mohammed al-Fadl's name through SAVIOR, retrieving a complete profile. In 2009, it seemed immaterial to run Simon Hall through the system, because the fingerprint match identified them as the same person. This time, however, he sensed it was vital to run Simon through SAVIOR.

Now logged into the system, Noble pressed the *Ctrl* and Q keys simultaneously and entered option D for *Case Profile*. Then, he entered "Simon Hall" for the *Name of Suspect*, followed by B for *Profile without an Alias*. The next question prompted *Additional Identification*, producing a list of options. Noble selected F for *Fingerprint* and quickly cut and pasted Simon's fingerprint from the NOMIS file to SAVIOR's Answer box. Rapidly, the system produced a dossier for Simon Hall. He saved the file and then duplicated the steps, except for the answer to *Name of Suspect*. This time, he entered Mohammed al-Fadl. Then, he displayed each profile side by side on the split screen and began to scrutinize the data.

Noble was dumbfounded.

⌘

"Max."

"I've been waiting hours for your call. How did it go?" Her eagerness was apparent.

"Open your xPhad and let's conference."

Max obliged, and hit the webcam. "You look as if you've had a hair-raising day!"

Noble eyed the concern on her face and teased, "Speaking of hair, nice," in an effort to deflect her angst. Even with her hair mussed and without makeup, she was still extremely attractive. Certainly, she was a pleasant diversion from the face he had been studying for the past six hours—a face clearly etched in his mind.

"Give me a break, boss. I've been in this damn room all day combing through documents and pouring through boxes of evidence, looking for something—anything—we might have missed," she protested. Gradually, her pout converted to a pleasant smile. "How did it feel after all those years of tracking down Simon to finally be able to question him face-to-face? It must have been exhilarating. Tell me what happened?"

"First, there is something I have to share with you."

Noble explained how he ran Simon's name and al-Fadl's name separately through SAVIOR and discovered some discrepancies along with additional background information on Simon. He let it drop that SAVIOR was originally designed to consolidate profiles from the various agencies. Evidently, it was not programmed to highlight any inconsistencies within each of the files.

"So, SAVIOR isn't perfect." She winced, afraid Noble would take her words personally.

"No, I'm not perfect. And, if Simon had designed the system, he most likely would not have made that programming error."

She ignored his momentary wallowing and moved the discussion back on point. "What did you uncover that is so shocking?"

"Simon and al-Fadl were both born on November 16, 1966."

"Of course, they are the same person." She agreed, and then mocked, "How appropriate, Simon was born under the sign of Scorpio."

"Hold on. The records show Simon was reared in Irvine, California, and homeschooled until the age of sixteen. In 1982, he entered the University of California at Irvine and majored in computer science."

"That, we already know." Max was becoming increasingly impatient.

"Max, please, hear me out. What we didn't know is that, the following year, he began to attend a study group at the Islamic Society of Orange County. There are reports that he obtained a 'certificate of Islam', an informal means to become a Muslim. And, he took the name Mohammed al-Fadl when he converted to Islam. But, there is no official record of a legal name change to al-Fadl." He continued to elaborate on Simon's dossier and explained that he dropped out of school in 1984 and, on September 1 of the same year, he flew from Los Angeles to Paris. From there, he seemed to have vanished for the time being. "What's most interesting, is that on September 2, 1984, Mohammed al-Fadl arrived in Karachi, Pakistan and began to support jihadi causes."

"So, Simon was working with al-Qaeda. We assume that to be true." Max shrugged her shoulders. She was no longer edgy, but seemingly a bit confused.

"Officially, al-Qaeda had not formally established until 1988. But, although it was in its infancy, al-Fadl became embroiled in Osama bin-Laden's organization, and he moved up the ranks at a rapid pace. He was personally responsible for developing the wire-transfer system to move funds undetected between Hawalas in the U.S. During the interrogation, Simon admitted he had trained with al-Qaeda, but he denies being part of their organization today."

"And you believe him?" Max asked, somewhat doubtful.

"He ranted at length about the greatness of Sharia Law and supports al-Qaeda's attempt to create a new world-wide Islamic nation. But, he decries their characteristic technique of using suicide attacks and finds it difficult to accept the fact that the killings are religiously sanctioned."

"I repeat…. And you believe him?

Noble saw the doubt continue to wash across Max's face. "Honestly,

I'm not convinced that Simon is a killer, but I keep wrestling with the notion." He then carried on and explained that, in 1986, Mohammed al-Fadl reportedly disengaged from bin-Laden and disappeared. The same month, Simon resurfaced and began to attend classes at the University of California, this time at Berkeley. In 1987, he received his BS in computer science and, in 1989, he received his master's degree in psychology."

"Wait a minute. In 1988, he was responsible for bombing the U.S. embassies in Nairobi and Tanzania. He couldn't have been in both places," Max concluded.

"The fingerprint in the Interpol file came from a bomb fragment found in the debris at the Nairobi embassy." Noble determined that the bomb was either used by al-Fadl or was simply assembled by him earlier and used later by another person. "From the bank and credit card statements, Simon was actually leading a busy life in Berkeley. And, there is no record of his leaving the U.S."

"How do you know he didn't fabricate the data? We know he has the capability."

Max had not yet bought into Noble's presumptions.

He noticed her skepticism, and attempted to convince her. "His spending patterns mirror those I uncovered from his statements while living in Menlo Park, and before he disappeared during the banking crisis. I don't believe he was in Africa in 1988."

Max raised her eyebrows.

Not wanting to regret any assumptions he was about to make, he proceeded, choosing his words with care. "The way Simon spoke about his time with bin-Laden, I came away with a sense that when he traveled to Pakistan in 1984, he had converted to Islam. Conceivably, it started out as a social experiment."

"What, akin to joining a cult in the sixties?

"Yes. But, all the while, Simon continued to utilize both identities interchangeably to suit his own needs. I believe he was being truthful when he said no longer worked in tandem with al-Qaeda."

"Isn't that a huge leap in conjecture, especially for you?"

"Max, let's get back to 1989. We know Simon was still attending classes at Berkeley but, after graduation, he disappeared again. According to the testimonies of the members of La Fratellanza, he spent the majority of his time in Florence, Italy. However, in 1993 he returned to the states and established a free-lance consultancy. It was in 1994 when Simon befriended Hal Simmons. We already knew

Simmons had converted to Islam and changed his name to Karim Yakob, and shortly thereafter he joined al-Qaeda. That must have been when Simon stole Hal Simmons' identity, but in name only."

"Why would he need another identity?" Max asked, perplexed.

"He needed a scapegoat should his illegal activities be exposed. Remember, it wasn't until 2009 when Hamilton and I made the connection between Simon, Simmons, and al-Fadl, that Hamilton placed all names on the Terrorist Watch List, sealing Simon's fate, and forcing him—literally and figuratively—underground. Up until that point, Simon Hall's record was clean."

"So, he used Hal Simmons' identity to establish bank accounts, obtain credit cards, and to rent the apartment in Cambridge?"

"Precisely, and all the while Simon Hall was attending Harvard. Can you guess who paid the bills?"

"Uncle Rob—the affectionate name he gave his ill-gotten gains. Okay, so he siphoned funds from various banks and transferred the money to bank accounts registered under the name of Hal Simmons."

"Yes, and while Hamilton was tracking the elusive hacker Hal Simmons, he unknowingly was tracking Simon. And, a further strange twist is that, sometime between 2009 and 2016, Simon located and recruited his friend from the past, Karim Yakob, to work for his cause. Yes, the one, and the real, Hal Simmons."

Max interrupted, "He's quite brazen. But, Noble, what does this have to do with Simon's plot? A plot that to this day is still gauzy." She was thoroughly uncertain as to where he was leading.

"Max, when I went back and traced Simon's trail and the various roles he occupied over the years, it gives validity to what he admitted in the interrogation. What you don't know is that, in October of 2001, Simon traveled to Kursu as al-Fadl, and secretly met with Osama bin-Laden. He said that he implored bin-Laden to stop al-Qaeda from bombing the U.S. He claims to have told bin-Laden that his autonomous mission was well under way and would have a greater effect without al-Qaeda's intrusion. According to Simon, bin-Laden died a month later. Presumably, he didn't pass along Simon's message and the terrorist strategy continued."

"What? bin-Laden was killed in 2011."

"Not according to Simon. He claims it was an illusion perpetrated by the Baari Administration."

"Unbelievable. So in what way does his grand plan depart from that of bin-Laden or al-Qaeda?"

"That's the question we keep asking, and it's still unanswered. But, I'm convinced Simon has his own agenda and is working alone, separate from al-Qaeda."

"That could make him even more dangerous. Did you discover anything during the interrogation, anything that would lead us to understand what he's really up to?"

"No. Frankly, it was maddening. I couldn't break him. He hasn't forgotten any of the lessons on interrogation techniques and the related psychology he'd learned over the years. In fact, he's wilier than ever. To start, I had exacting control over the interview, and then I intentionally let him think he was in control. I'm embarrassed to say that, at times, he actually wrested control briefly. It was parry and thrust all day."

Max saw the unease on Noble's face, but chose to ignore his sense of disappointment. She let him continue without interruption.

"I tried to bait him with abject impartiality, but then he'd revert to a reverse *irk mode* trying to agitate me. After a while, I switched tactics again and played strictly to his ego, which provided a large target. Nothing worked." Noble's frustration was brewing. "I tried every interview technique I could muster and Simon reacted tangentially. When that guy was created, they threw away the mold."

Max continued to eye Noble's facial expressions on her tablet as he briefed her on the outcome of the interrogation. It was obvious Simon's storied mendacity had a negative effect on his mood. She reminded, "And, now, you have him locked in a six by twelve foot cell." She then attempted to accentuate the positive in an attempt to redirect Noble's lament. "We may never know his ultimate mission—but the game is over!"

Noble recognized Max's effort to placate him. He decisively moved back on point. "Did you uncover anything from the flash drive or the other material relevant to the encampment?"

Max rightly discerned that he wasn't up for any lengthy discussion. *Just the facts ma'am*, she mused, but now it was her turn to unload. "My further analysis of the files on the flash drive presented some disturbing possibilities."

Her words, *disturbing possibilities*, caught Noble's attention. His facial muscles immediately began to tighten. "Go on," he urged.

"I reviewed all of the documents and photos we obtained from the flash drive repeatedly. Remember, there were also certain documents on the flash drive we couldn't identify at the time?"

"Yes, and?"

"Simon had used military grade encryption for those files, but I was finally able to unencrypt them. The files contain the file extension *sdr*. They're from proprietary software called SmartDraw that is used for compiling and creating maps, organization charts, and a myriad of other applications. Those files included organizational charts and schematic drawings of electrical grids. I still need time to sort out the grids. I haven't been able to identify their location. I don't even know if they're in the U.S."

"That could be the vital link. Stay on it Max."

"Noble, there's something else on the organization charts." She paused briefly. "The charts are for government organizations—ours, and Europe's western countries, including the U.K."

Noble interrupted. "You're forgetting that, from the photos and other documents on the flash drive, we already deciphered that he is going after an unknown head of state. With the possibility that we're dealing with a mole, Enzo is already vetting those people in the line of succession for each of the threatened leaders on the premise that their head of state is a potential target. And, I've already vetted the vice president and the majority leader of the house. They're solid—nothing's hiding in their closets."

Max's instincts were usually spot-on, and Noble detected she had damning evidence. "So, what's so peculiar about these charts that we didn't already conclude?"

"The only marking on the chart for the executive branch of the U.S. Government was a red circle around the box indicating President Post. Around each box for the heads of state on the charts of France, Germany, and Great Britain were identical circles. This naturally fits snugly into your theory that Simon is going to target one of them."

"So, what are the disturbing possibilities?" Noble prodded, sensing things were about to metabolize.

"There are additional charts displaying the hierarchy of each government, stemming from the head of state!" she said excitedly. "Noble, attached to the chart for the U.S. Government, deep in the stack of pages, is the chart for the Department of Energy." She halted, to collect her thoughts. And just before Noble was about to urge her to move it along, she took a deep breath and called out, "The box for the Office of the Secretary of Energy is also circled in red!"

"What? That doesn't compute."

"Wait. There's more." She was dismayed. "Additionally, there was a chart for the Department of Homeland Security, but the box for the secretary was not circled. However, there was a connecting line drawn in red from the Homeland Security organization box to the Federal Emergency Management Agency box."

"FEMA—is that box circled?" Noble was thoroughly confused.

Noting his reaction, she responded uneasily, "Not on that particular chart, but on the chart specific to FEMA. The box for the administrator of the agency is also circled in red."

"Did you find anything similar on the subsequent pages for each of the European countries?" Noble questioned with anticipation.

"No, only the heads of state for the three countries where the bogus assassinations occurred were circled."

"I'm afraid to ask," Noble grunted, "anything else?"

Still reeling from all of the horrible possibilities that could explain the findings, Max wasn't sure whether she had saved the worst for last. She proceeded to describe that, an hour before she discovered the charts, the forensic team delivered yet another suspicious package they had unearthed from the indoctrination center.

Max watched Noble's face carefully as she expounded, "It contained twenty-five various guides on preparedness."

"Preparedness?"

"You know, those used for natural disasters. Many of those guides were published by FEMA."

"I want you to start working on something else."

"What's up?" Max was more baffled than curious at the abrupt shift.

"Send me the files for the charts and grids when we hang up. Then, I want you to conduct an argumentation exercise, as we've done with past cases, to ensure we haven't strayed off course along the way. We must take into account every possible theory."

Max again interrupted, "I don't understand. The charts and grids are disturbing, but all the evidence still points to Simon's plan to assassinate a world leader. What we don't know is which leader or—God forbid—how many leaders, and in what order. Noble, your theory appears to be sound."

"Assume it's not. What other possible theories could there be?"

"That he's not planning to assassinate a world leader," she submitted somberly.

"Okay, make that theory number two."

"Another one," he pressed.

"He's not going after a head of state, but someone else," she concurred, starting to see where he was heading.

"That's theory number three. Another," he persisted.

"Noble! Okay, he's not going after a person at all, but he's going after something tangible."

"Max, you have just come up with three theories, other than mine, and they're all plausible."

"Aren't you forgetting that we've frozen his bank accounts, exposed his encampment, and have his recruits in custody? Whatever plan he had, you thwarted!" she underscored, driving home the point that the game was over.

"And, what if he's not working alone?" Noble cried out.

"All evidence points to the fact he is, but I get it. The only way to be sure is to check out all possible theories." Max succumbed. "I'll comb through the evidence, apply it to each theory, and look for any fallacies."

"Thank you," he responded with tempered frustration. "Also, I want you to get me a copy of the latest pentagon briefings with the status of the Middle East situation."

"The Middle East? Why?"

"Please, Max, just get it."

"Okay, but Noble, there's still one troubling aspect of this case. Simon's capture—it was much easier than I expected."

"Not at all. I believe Simon planned his escape with great precision. He just made a fatal error."

"Yeah, he completely underestimated you."

"No, he completely underestimated you."

Max was obviously confused. "I don't get it."

"I know how Simon thinks. He would assume, after almost killing you in the explosion, that I would insist on being the one to reenter the encampment. But, you persuaded me otherwise. I'm convinced his intent was to lure me into the site. That explains why he never changed the security access. It was for the sole purpose of trapping me inside— finally ending the cat and mouse game.

"Perhaps, but I would have sent in troops immediately to unseal the entrances."

There was a noticeable pause, but Max waited for Noble to respond.

"There's something I didn't tell you." He hesitated.

"Yes, keep going."

"While reviewing Simon's programming code in the command center I deciphered code that would have set off a series of explosions, blowing up all of the tunnels. He would have detonated them remotely after he escaped." He blurted out in a single breath.

"You son-of..."

"Wait. Max. By following my instructions, you disarmed his code and saved many lives. It was a close call, but here we are."

"That's not very comforting."

"Later, Max." Noble quickly shut down his xPhad, giving Max time to cool off.

31
THE VISITOR

The darkened room, with a row of lights dangling from above, was
the same room from which Noble had departed an hour earlier.
Curiously, Simon had just been returned to that room and was placed
in the same chair he had sat in before. The guard had just finished
securing his handcuffs to the rungs on the chair's armrests.

"Why am I back here?" Simon protested.

"You have a visitor."

Simon was puzzled as to why Noble would return so soon after their
first encounter. *He wants to torment me with another round of inane
questions.* "Not interested," he barked to the guard. *Doesn't he know
when to quit.*

"She's quite attractive. You might want to reconsider." The guard
flashed a wink.

Simon's expression swiftly changed, and he beamed. "By all means,
do send her in. Anything is an improvement over you."

"You have ten minutes," warned the guard as he closed the door
behind her.

She walked slowly across the room, sensing Simon was ogling her
from head to toe, as if he were mentally undressing her. Unperturbed,
she sat down in the chair across from him and stared at him intently,

letting the silence hang for a short time.

"Are they treating you well?" she inquired with her back to the video camera.

"They haven't tortured me physically—yet. But, if that's what you have in mind, I'm all yours." Simon reacted with a leering smile, also aware of the camera.

Maintaining her cool composure, she probed, "Has anyone interviewed you?"

"Director Bishop just left, after six hours of enjoyable repartee," he complained sarcastically.

"He was supposed to have waited until we arrived."

Simon noticed she seemed quite annoyed, and wisecracked, "Bad Noble."

"I'll deal with him. Have the guards been difficult?"

"The guards, they fit the usual mold. Mostly they just escort me to and fro from this hellhole to my other personal hellhole. I guess I should feel relieved that's all they do. As for my little session with Noble, he refused to let them remove the handcuffs when they graciously offered. Do you think you might have some sway?"

She denied his request with silence.

Simon watched as she lifted her large handbag off her right shoulder and leaned over to place it on the floor next to her leg. As she returned upright, Simon felt a hand brush his ankle from under the table.

Feeling a slight rush, Simon ignored the contact and continued with small talk, fully aware of the camera.

"I can't stay, but I'll be back in the morning with the others. We'll be monitoring the rest of the interrogation. You understand that we will be transferring you to Gitmo the day after tomorrow."

"Yes, I got it." A hint of a smile returned.

All of a sudden, she pulled back as she felt a leg rub against hers. She quickly sprang up from her chair. "I have to go," she said nervously, then yelled, "Guard!" She grabbed her handbag and headed for the door. Turning her head ever so slightly, she caught Simon's eye.

"Tomorrow," he mouthed.

32
ACING THE ENVOYS

Noble sorted through the organization charts and grids Max had forwarded to him, but he wasn't able to find any pattern shedding light on their unanswered questions. Most troubling, though, was the organization chart for FEMA with the red circle around the box for the administrator. Again, he was mystified by the absence of a connection. Exhausted and frustrated, he glanced at the clock on the nightstand: 11:39 p.m.

He grabbed his xPhad, opened the tablet, and dialed Max.

"I'm missing a vital piece of the puzzle, and Simon knows it. We have to think like a terrorist. What decision-making process is he using? What is his underlying psyche?" What is his overall goal—his motive?

"Noble, slow down, you're starting to rattle me."

"Set up your webcam."

Max moved aside the stack of manuals she was still rifling through for clues and opened her xPhad. Baffled by his questions, she eyed Noble on the tablet screen for a brief second. Then, on impulse, she suggested, "Why not reiterate that you are smarter than he is?"

Noble looked back at Max. Intuitively, he sensed the direction she was about to take. "You think I need to prove—to him—that I really am smarter? Yes, I believe it could be the coup de grace."

"Exactly! His ego won't be able to cope with it. He needs to be in control full-time. The only way for Simon to feed his ego is for him to convince himself that he's been outsmarting you all along. And, the only way he can is to leak some vague clues on what he's planned next in an effort to prove his superiority."

"Or, at least slip up and reveal one of the missing pieces. He has no idea of the information we already have on him," Noble added, buying into her logic. "Max, you're absolutely correct, but I won't be the one convincing him. You will—tomorrow. Besides, you're more deceptive than I am." He smiled faintly.

"Noble, are you clinically insane? I know nothing about this guy other than what you've told me and what I've read in his dossier. And, that he's a Scorpio or, rather, a scorpion in real life."

"If my recollection is accurate, many believe that people born under the sign of Scorpio possess extraordinary genius. And, while they have many positive traits, they are reserved and secretive. Some are even capable of unmistakable evil traits of character."

"Are you trying to unnerve me?"

"Just be wary. Simon prides himself on manipulating others and, he especially believes women are easy marks." Noble winked. "I know you, Max. No one can put anything over on you. Being bested by a female is more than he can bear."

For the first time in a while, a huge grin appeared on Noble's face.

Max took notice of his jocular demeanor, but sensed it had nothing to do with his last comment. "What are you thinking about?"

"Remember the allegory about the scorpion and the turtle? When I asked Simon what possessed him to carry out such an involved plot, requiring years of his life, he calmly answered, 'It's just my character.'" Noble paused, and then posed, "Perhaps, it's all about proving his superior intellect to the world. That obsession may be his downfall."

"Perhaps it's that simple. Maybe that's the answer to his motives."

"It still doesn't get us any closer to his end game," Noble groused, leaving his sense of humor behind.

"And, it doesn't make me feel any better about taking this guy on tomorrow. For the record, I still think you're out of your mind," Max protested.

As for her protestations, Noble suspected she was moments away from relenting.

"Okay, what's the storyline?" She leaned back and crossed her arms, readying herself. "This should be interesting."

Noble detected her tentativeness, and took a moment to pause.

Max knew he was conjuring up a doozy of a narrative.

"Here goes." Noble sprang into action. His renewed enthusiasm was obvious.

Max listened carefully as she took notes and watched the animation on her tablet.

"First, convince Simon that I was in Florence with Hamilton during the sting operation, and that it was my plan to lure him there. Tell him that while he was staking out Hamilton and Enzo, I had him under surveillance. In fact, tell him I stayed at the Hotel Galileo in room 1509, next to his room, and across from the Banca Nazionale. Assure him Professoressa Ducale was working with us. That she was the one who informed us that he would be entering the Vasari Corridor and where she was to leave the satchel of money."

"Noble, I don't think that will be enough to persuade Simon that you've outfoxed him."

"Hold on. You have to make him believe that I planned to let him escape in Florence. That I knew after having siphoned off most of his funds that he'd need to replenish his war chest. He knows I am more than capable of following the money trail. You must persuade him that I knew his ultimate plan would have to be completed while Baari was still in office—something he already confessed—and that is why, through our efforts, Baari was forced to resign. Convince Simon that I knew my actions would force him to escalate his timetable, causing him to make mistakes."

"Shall I cite the loss of the flash drive?"

"Exactly. He thinks I'm convinced he lost the drive intentionally to lure me into the encampment. You'll have to disabuse him of that notion, and that we have proof it was accidental."

Max still wasn't sure it would be convincing enough. She thought they needed to throw some other piece of evidence at him. "Should I let him know what I uncovered in the boxes?"

"Let's see how far you can run with the fictitious pieces of the story. Let's see if he takes the bait."

"Suppose I come up empty-handed and we don't know any more than we know now?" she asked with some skepticism.

"Then, we'll have to resort to luring him with words such as electrical power grids and FEMA to see if we have glommed onto a missing piece of the puzzle. These could be the more potent areas, and they just might induce a reaction."

"It sounds risky to me. What if Simon challenges me, especially with regard to the grids and the charts? We're not even sure what they mean."

"Don't allow him. Simon has always been blatant about his view that women are intellectually inferior. I'm relying on the fact that he'll let down his guard if he believes you're vulnerable. Trust me. He'll relent—if you convince him he trumped me." Tempering his over-confidence, Noble affirmed, "Max, you'll have to be more conniving than him. He'll have doubts about my actual role, but remind him of my one vulnerability, the one he'll never be able to exploit."

"What's that?"

"Integrity."

"Boy, does he have you pegged. By the way, where will you be during the questioning?"

"Watching from a box seat at the guard station nearby while it all plays out on the video. I'll move in if it's appropriate. We'll just have to play it by ear." Noble was confident Max was onboard. "You can do this!" he punctuated encouragingly.

"I'll give it my all. We'll see how the scorpion deals with this woman!" For the first time, Max appeared excited and up for the challenge.

Noble expected no less. "Now, I want to begin the second round of questioning with Simon at six a.m. sharp, before he has an opportunity to get his morning coffee. More important, before the president's envoys arrive to monitor our interview."

"I still don't get it. Why are they coming here?"

"Don't try. It's purely political."

"Who's Post sending?"

"All I know is that there are three senators from the Intelligence Committee."

Max rolled her eyes and then confirmed, "The Colonel won't be happy with me calling at midnight, but I'll ask him to arrange to have a helicopter transport me to the prison at five thirty. Will you alert the warden so he won't think the prison is under siege or, worse yet, that there is a prison break?"

"I'll make a midnight call as well and ask the warden to block off the south end of the parking lot. You can land there, and then meet me in front of the guard tower. Now, call the Colonel and then get some sleep. And, Max, thanks for your support. I knew I could count on you."

"Thanks, Noble. Goodnight."

"Goodnight, Max."

33
SLEIGHT OF HAND

The aroma emanating from the freshly brewed coffee caught up with Noble as he pulled aside the shower curtain. He dried off, made his way to the mini bar, and poured himself a cup of java. The shower was refreshing but, after a restless night, he needed a caffeine rush even more than usual. Sipping on his coffee, he glanced at the clock on the nightstand. It read 4:45 a.m. He instinctively reached for his xPhad and checked for messages, hoping Max had discovered something that would help them in their second round with Simon. There was none. Evidently, she had nothing new to report, or, perhaps, she was waiting to spring it on him when they reconvened. Noting the time once again, Noble hurriedly dressed and gulped the remainder of his coffee. He placed the charts and graphs he had printed into his briefcase. And, although he didn't fully understand their meaning, he had a sense they might become useful during the interview. He left the hotel and headed to his car.

The prison was only nine minutes from the Ramada Inn, a straight shot down Route 15. By his calculation, he should pull in just as Max's helicopter was setting down. He was now five minutes away. There was hardly any traffic at that time of the morning. He was enjoying the solitude but, while his eyes focused steadily on the road, his mind was busily compartmentalizing an abundance of false information Max would feed Simon. If Max should fail in her interrogation, unable to uncover any new leads, then he'd have to take another pass at Simon. He'd have to be even more convincing than during his first foray.

While he attempted to gather his thoughts, an eerie sound in the distance became a distraction. As he neared the prison, the sound became appreciably louder. Suddenly, he realized it was actually an alarm of some sort. When he turned onto Bitterbrush Lane, the sound became piercing. Immediately, he became concerned as he sped into the parking lot, veering his car into an empty space nearest the guard tower. The commanding alarm was clearly from the prison, and obliterated the whirling sound from the sky. Despite the noise, Noble noticed the helicopter had arrived precisely on time. He snatched his briefcase and headed for the heavily guarded gate where he met up with Max.

"What's happening?" he shouted to the guard over the earsplitting sound.

"A prisoner escaped, and we're in lockdown," he yelled back.

"Who escaped?" Max cried out with dread.

"I don't know his name. Just that he was in Supermax. What I do know is that he's one clever son-of-a-bitch," he hollered as he shook his head in disbelief. The alarm finally quieted while the guard was in mid-sentence, but he continued to shout, making his facial features seem distorted.

Noting the look on their faces, the guard apologized, "Sorry, Director Bishop, sorry, ma'am. The warden is expecting you. Here are your visitors' passes. This officer will take you to his office."

Noble grabbed the badges and handed one to Max as he hollered back, "Thanks." Then, they closely followed behind the heels of the officer and stepped into a golf cart for transit. It was a five-minute drive across the prison quad to the warden's office.

"It's not possible," Noble whispered to Max.

Max knew she would have little time before reaching the warden, so she spoke quickly. "Noble, after we spoke last night, I couldn't sleep. I reviewed the manuals and organization charts repeatedly. Your theory is proving correct. He is targeting the governments, but each plan appears to be in two phases."

Noble looked at her directly, urging her to continue.

"For instance, phase one was to place Baari in office, allowing him access to the treasury and hoards of cash. Phase two appears to have something to do with disrupting or controlling our energy supply. If he had completed the final phase of his plan, it appears Simon would have also tried to implement similar plots in Europe."

"Slow down, Max. Are you sure?"

"No, we need more time," she insisted, then added, "But it all fits." Max suggested that she and Noble go in together, and that he first lay out their theory. "If Simon takes the bait, I can always jump in with how you had his number-the-whole-time tactic."

"No, Max. We go as planned." Before Noble had a chance to elaborate, the golf cart came to an abrupt halt. The warden had been alerted, and was standing at attention in the doorway waiting to meet them. From the expression on the warden's face, Noble and Max surmised, instantly, that their worst fears had been realized.

"al-Fadl has escaped," the warden stated balefully.

"But he's somewhere in the prison, right?" Max implored.

The warden took a deep breath, reluctant to respond. "We just finished reviewing the video. He just casually strolled out of this damn place."

"Why the hell didn't you call me?"

"Sorry, Director. We've been rather busy the last few hours." Not meaning to seem surly, he added, "Don't worry. We'll nail him. I've put out an all-points bulletin, and I have the highway patrol setting up roadblocks on every road leading out of here. The state and local authorities are plastering his face everywhere—train stations, bus stations, airports, hotels, and motels. We might have wide-open spaces in Utah, but there aren't many passable roads throughout the state. There are few places for him to hide," he explained, with confidence.

"You don't know him! Trust me. He's gone." Noble raised his hand to silence the warden from further swagger as he placed an urgent call to Colonel Evans. Continuing to stare unswervingly at Warden Lowell, he announced, "Colonel, al-Fadl has escaped. Reassign the National Guard at Draper to assist the state police in the hunt. He must not be allowed to leave the state!" It was glaringly evident that Noble had directed that comment to the warden as well. "Colonel, you have my authority to transmit al-Fadl's photo to all cell phones in Utah and the bordering states. Message only that he is an escaped prisoner considered armed and dangerous. Set up a hotline number for anyone sighting him to call." It was clear from the Colonel's responses that Noble had his full support. "Thank you, Colonel. Let me know the moment he's spotted."

"Now, I want to see the video!" Noble demanded as he replaced his xPhad in his pocket.

The warden seemed perturbed, sensing rightly that Noble had usurped his authority. Choosing to stave off further accusations, he simply said, "Please," as he gestured Noble and Max to enter his conference room.

Noble looked up at the large monitor on the wall and stated evenly, "Show me what you have."

Max stayed out of the fray and fixated on the screen.

As the warden rewound the video, he explained curtly, "As you know, the prisoner was escorted back to his cell at 6:30 p.m., after your interrogation. At seven o'clock, he was served dinner and, at eight o'clock, it was lights out." The warden hit the *Pause* button.

Noble could plainly see Simon sitting on his bed with his back resting against the wall. He appeared to be picking at the food on the serving tray. The warden fast-forwarded to eight o'clock when Simon was then lying down on the top of his bedcovers. It was lights out, but a partial glow from the revolving search light on the guard tower penetrated the small window at the top of his cell.

"I've been through this tape and nothing else happened until four o'clock this morning," the warden pointed out. He then fast-forwarded the tape again until Noble could view Simon standing in front of a large steel door. Magically, the door swung open to his left, and he walked through. "The only way to open that door is with a retina scan. Only our guards can pass the security barrier using the scan."

"Then how is it possible Simon passed the barrier?" Max, no longer able to stand back, was incredulous.

"I was hoping you two would be able to answer that. There's more. Hold on."

They continued to watch the tape and noted that no one was seated at the guard station on the other side of the door.

"Why isn't there a guard on duty?" Noble's irritation had not waned.

The warden paused the tape and explained that the guards relieve each other after every eight-hour shift. "During the changeover, they meet in their nearby lounge to fill each other in on what's been happening. It's Supermax, and the prisoners aren't expected to go anywhere." As the words left the warden's mouth, his face began to flush in several shades of red.

Noble didn't find it necessary to antagonize further.

Max also worked extra hard to hold her tongue.

The warden evaded eye contact and hit the *Play* button. On the monitor, each of them watched the video as Simon walked through a series of gates and then walked directly out of the prison. He slithered by the guard tower and ducked behind several cars as the revolving search light headed in his direction.

Simon had simply vanished.

"Rewind the tape slowly!" Noble called out.

The warden readily complied.

"Stop right there! Zoom in on his left hand." Noble watched carefully as Simon's hand appeared larger and larger on the screen. "Can you get in any closer?"

As the warden adjusted the zoom, he heard Noble shout, "What in the hell!"

"What do you see?"

"It's partially hidden by his sleeve, but Simon is holding something in his left hand."

"What is it?" The warden shouted in return, still mystified.

Noble snapped, "An xPhad!"

Both the warden and Max turned around abruptly toward Noble.

"You might say it was a sleight of hand." Noble winced as he held up his own xPhad.

They were stunned as they turned to stare back at the screen.

"Continue to rewind slowly," Noble requested again.

The only view on the rest of the tape, other than Simon lying on top of his bedcovers, was Simon lying under his bedcovers apparently asleep. In a few of the frames, the revolving search light from the guard tower outside illuminated the room but, for the most part, the screen was black.

"Stop!" Noble shouted. "Look at the room. It's in total darkness, but there is a small beam of light emanating from under his blanket. Can you see it? Zoom in."

The only illumination in the tiny cell was from the tablet he was hiding under his bedcover.

"So, he was using the xPhad to program his escape right from his cell," Max bellowed.

"I personally saw him in that cell at six thirty. His food was delivered through the cuff hole at seven. And you are telling me he used a computer to walk out of his cell at precisely four o'clock this morning?" the warden questioned, completely bewildered.

Throwing it back at the warden, Noble elaborated. "Yes, that is exactly what I am saying. I suspect he used it to download a photo of his retina and then used it to replace a guard's retina photo in the prison's employee database."

"You're saying he hacked into the Utah State Penitentiary's computer system? Damned clever—a retinal switch!" The warden was beside himself, still not comprehending the extent of al-Fadl's capabilities.

"He's notorious for hacking into systems, all kinds of systems. What I want to know is how he got his hands on a computer. Who slipped him the xPhad?" Noble demanded in a pointed manner.

"I vouch for my men. They are personally selected by me to work in Supermax," the warden pushed back.

"Then how did it happen?" Max pressed.

At that point, an officer entered the conference room. "Excuse me warden, but this envelope was found at the guard's station in Supermax," the officer explained, realizing he had interrupted a heated discussion. Somewhat shaken, he stammered, "It's addressed to Director Bishop."

"Well, hand it to him!" The warden's directness only added to the officer's discomfort.

Noble reached for the envelope and, with trepidation, he opened it. He knew it was from Simon.

As he opened the flap, he could hear the warden quiz the officer, "Where, specifically, did you find the envelope?"

"Sir, it was in the visitor's logbook," he responded nervously.

"Bring the logbook to me now!" the warden commanded, and then asked, "Wait, whose shift did you take over?"

"It was Murphy's sir."

"Get him here too, both in my office immediately."

The warden refocused on Noble and noticed an uncomfortable look on his face, leading him to ask with concern, "Are you all right, Director?"

Noble looked toward the warden and attempted to seem nonplussed. "Let's wait for the logbook." He offered no further explanation and the warden didn't ask for one.

Max also knew from experience not to inquire further at that point.

During the next five minutes, as they waited together, Max reviewed the video for a second time, with the warden managing the remote control.

Noble stood off to the side, disregarding the video, as he studied the piece of paper in his hand. The creased lines from the folds were prominent against the aged yellowed background with one edge tattered. Noble shook his head in disbelief as he studied the blueprint of the Presidential Lair that Hank had stolen from the President's *Book of Secrets*. While it seemed to him that he had been staring at the blueprint for hours, it was only minutes. He glanced up when Officer Murphy appeared in the doorway of the warden's conference room with the visitor's logbook in hand.

"Sir, you requested this." He handed the book to the warden.

The warden opened the book to the sign-in sheet for the previous day. He spotted Noble's signature and, written next to his signature, was the sign-in time, 11:00 a.m., and the sign-out time, 6:30 p.m. Under Noble's signature was the name, Mohammed al-Fadl, Level 1, Cell 6. Abruptly, the warden glared in Murphy's direction and stated sternly, "You escorted the prisoner to the interrogation room at nine o'clock last night." As he raised his voice perceptibly, he continued, "That prisoner was not authorized to receive any visitors, other than Director Bishop. Did you not get my order?"

Noble's mind was multi-processing furiously.

Max's heart raced as she focused on the monitor and again watched Simon stroll out of the prison.

Officer Murphy was visibly shaken as the warden stood with his face placed in close proximity to the officer's.

"Sir, no one argues with a senator, especially a special envoy sent here on the president's orders," he explained. He knew his words seemed sarcastic and waited for the onslaught.

Without hesitation, the warden surprisingly toned down his rhetoric. "Did you at least conduct the appropriate search procedures?"

Still uncomfortable, he responded, "No, sir," as he held his head low.

"What!" the warden shrieked.

"Sir, a presidential envoy has an implied security clearance and…" he stammered, "the envoy was a woman."

As the warden glanced at the signature in the logbook next to 9:00 p.m., he heard Murphy say, "Sir, it was Senator Maryann Townsend."

ACKNOWLEDGEMENTS

Special thanks go to my inner circle of readers for agreeing to critique my novel. I'm eternally grateful to Alfredo Vedro, Ann Howells, David E., Maestro Debra Cheverino, Donna Post, and Ray Fernandez who diligently read and offered suggestions. They more than fulfilled their promise to provide honest feedback.

I offer my deep appreciation to my publisher, David Dunham, for his enormous support and the confidence he has shown in my abilities as a writer and storyteller.

Lastly, I can't thank enough all my family and friends, near and far and too numerous to list, who continually cheered me on throughout this journey. Their support was inspiring.

ABOUT THE AUTHOR

 Sally Fernandez' career background includes project management, business planning, and technology, with additional experience in technical and business writing. Her books of fiction are based on knowledge garnered from careers in banking, computer technology, and business consulting, while living in New York City, San Francisco, and Hong Kong.

Fernandez' foray into writing fiction began in 2007 when the 2008 presidential election cycle was in full swing. The overwhelming political spin by the media compelled her to question the frightening possibilities the political scene could generate. A confirmed political junkie, she took to the keyboard armed with unwinding events and discovered a new and exciting career. *Noble's Quest* is the sequel to her first widely read novel *Brotherhood Beyond the Yard*.

A world traveler, the author and her husband split time between their homes in the United States and Italy.